Dearest Sophie
I hope you
           journey

THE
LEGACY OF
CRYSTAL
ISLAND

Love
Colleen

About the Author

Colleen O'Flaherty-Hilder has been a Health and Wellness Practitioner for over 35 years. Her initial training in Mind Dynamics in 1981 prompted her interest, which became a passion, in how emotions affect physical health. After extensive research, trainings and personal experience she created Alchemical Transformation Programmes™, which embraces a confluence of modalities to facilitate profound change on the physical, mental, emotional and spiritual levels.

www.colleenoflaherty.co.uk

BOOK TWO: TRUTH AND COURAGE

THE LEGACY OF CRYSTAL ISLAND

COLLEEN O'FLAHERTY-HILDER

Copyright © 2019 Colleen O'Flaherty-Hilder

The moral right of the author has been asserted.

Apart from any fair dealing for the purposes of research or private study, or criticism or review, as permitted under the Copyright, Designs and Patents Act 1988, this publication may only be reproduced, stored or transmitted, in any form or by any means, with the prior permission in writing of the publishers, or in the case of reprographic reproduction in accordance with the terms of licences issued by the Copyright Licensing Agency. Enquiries concerning reproduction outside those terms should be sent to the publishers.

Matador
9 Priory Business Park,
Wistow Road, Kibworth Beauchamp,
Leicestershire, LE8 0RX
Tel: 0116 279 2299
Email: books@troubador.co.uk
Web: www.troubador.co.uk/matador
Twitter: @matadorbooks

ISBN 978 1838590 017

British Library Cataloguing in Publication Data.
A catalogue record for this book is available from the British Library.

Printed and bound by CPI Group (UK) Ltd, Croydon, CR0 4YY
Typeset in 11pt Minion Pro by Troubador Publishing Ltd, Leicester, UK

Matador is an imprint of Troubador Publishing Ltd

Contents

The Story So Far...   vii

ONE	Orla Comes Home	1
TWO	Choosing The First Pioneer	43
THREE	Choosing The Next Six	117
FOUR	Seven Become Fourteen	132
FIVE	The Gifts	224
SIX	The Responsibilities	240
SEVEN	Crystal Strategy	254
EIGHT	The Crystal Initiations	284
NINE	The Generals Of The West	302
TEN	The Next One Hundred	321
ELEVEN	The Chief Generals	324

THE STORY SO FAR...

Crystal Island appeared in the Atlantic Ocean shortly after the last ice age. The intelligence of the mineral-rich ocean created a Crystal Fortress around the island that protected it from the cumulative effects of man-made pollution and destruction that had occurred on the Earth over the centuries.

Shortly after the formation of Crystal Island, a species of supra beings arrived on Earth, the Crystalanders, the Guardians of Eternal Wisdom, who brought Gifts of Creation to the Earth. They genetically introduced Crystal Wisdom to twelve women of the island who became the Royal Family of Crystal Island, and at the end of the 22nd century, Queen Maeve and her consort, Patrick, are direct descendants of those first crystal-humans.

Princess Orla is their fourteen-year-old daughter and future Queen who must undertake a seven-year journey of initiation to the seven worlds of Crystaland to awaken the ancient Crystal Wisdom in her memory, equipping her with the necessary qualities to spearhead the healing of the planet

Her grandmother, Grace, as a royal Crystal Elder, accompanies Orla for the initial part of her journey with the Diamond Elders who give the young princess the first understanding of her destiny. She is also introduced to Unicorn who is to be her guide and mentor through all of the Crystal worlds.

After leaving the Diamond Elders, she embarks on her journey. Each world is defined by the specific coloured crystal that holds unique qualities of Crystal Wisdom: Violet and Turquoise – Sound; Green and Yellow – Sacred Geometry; Sapphire and Silver – language and numbers; Ruby and Iron – Courage; Coral – communication; Emerald and Copper – Health; Golden – Beauty.

In each world, she is given a piece of crystal jewellery that embodies the qualities of those worlds. She also experiences the original Crystaland Gifts given to the Earth: Energy; Health; Intelligence; Courage and Leadership; Song and Intuition; Words and Communication; and Support.

The Crystalanders eventually leave the planet in the capable hands of the crystal-human Elders. But, after thousands of years, man begins to lose his connection to Crystal Wisdom and his primitive side resurfaces which attracts Shadow, a dark force from the deepest part of the cosmos.

In the final part of her journey, Orla travels to the Turquoise Crystal world where she is shown the fear myths created by man under the influence of Shadow which has contributed to Earth's downfall.

Before leaving for her awakening, Orla is promised to her future consort, Finn, who has a direct lineage to the Ruby Crystal world.

CHAPTER ONE
ORLA COMES HOME

Orla woke suddenly from her dream to the sound of familiar voices. As she opened her eyes, she immediately realised that it was Finn talking and laughing with John under the window of her first-floor private chamber. Identifying the voices, she relaxed and smiled. As she unconsciously massaged her expanding abdomen, she took a moment to absorb every detail of her private sanctuary, relieved to be in this safe space and not still in the dream.

This room has given me so much comfort and wonderful memories, she thought. She slowly rose from her daybed and walked to the full-length window overlooking the green carpet of lawn stretching from the palace walls down to the river that swept through the island.

Orla rested her head on the window frame as she reflected on her dream, recalling those early days when considerable effort had gone into reversing the apocalyptic trajectory that Earth was pursuing governed by selfish and hapless leaders. The Diamond Elders had warned her of the challenges she would encounter, but nothing had prepared her for the intensity of hatred that man expressed towards his fellow man. Indeed, in the latter part of the 22nd century, hatred had become the default emotion expressed by humanity. Orla cringed as she remembered the images of savagery she had unveiled whilst accessing the ancestral memories of the Chief Generals, the leaders of the Federations. For Orla, this disturbing experience had confirmed, unequivocally, that those Generals would never be suitable leaders of a world based on Crystal Wisdom.

The new life inside her kicked, protesting at those dark memories, forcing her back to the present and the impressive view from her window; the sunny spring afternoon was playing host to a concert of birds singing their praise of the sun's rays caressing the branches of the trees, coaxing the new buds from the seclusion and comfort of winter. Orla looked down fondly at the two men below who were still chatting and laughing in a comfortable and easy manner. They were from very different worlds, but their friendship was based on a strong foundation of mutual respect and trust, developed over the years from the many challenges they had experienced together. Orla gave thanks, as she often did, for John and the other pioneers. Those first pioneers bravely joined forces with the royal house of Crystal Island to spearhead the restoration of the noble gifts that the Crystalanders had bestowed upon the planet thousands of years ago.

The luxury of time she now had, for the first time since her return to the island, allowed her to reflect on the years that had followed her initiation into Crystal Wisdom. She had been fourteen when she left the island – an innocent young girl with no notion of the future, and no concept of the terrors encountered by the world outside of her island – returning seven years later, a woman who had been exposed, albeit in a censored way, to the bleak reality of the state of the planet. There had been such a deep level of degeneration in the world that even now, at thirty eight, she found it difficult to comprehend how the whole notion of Crystal civilisation had turned a corner centuries before and disappeared down a rabbit hole of bitterness and hatred.

Conscious of the important role that her collection of crystal jewellery had played in helping her to navigate so many challenges, Orla walked over to the clear crystal case that protected it whilst it was inactive. She opened the lid and lightly touched each piece, conscious of their unique connection to each of the Crystal worlds. Her mind drifted again as she remembered her return to the island from Crystaland, her reunion with Finn and her subsequent exposure to the full extent of the planet's destruction.

Orla returned to her daybed, rearranged her numerous cushions, and eventually relaxed into a comfortable position, which was becoming more challenging as her body changed shape to accommodate the pregnancy. She allowed her mind to run loosely and randomly over those events and eventually settled on the memory of the warm welcome she received from her parents and Finn on her return from her Crystaland awakening.

*

After her reunion with her mother, Maeve, in the Secret Garden, Orla realised how much she had missed her parents over the seven years and hurried to the palace, eager to see her father, Patrick.

As she entered the palace gates, Orla saw her father, broke away from her mother, and ran straight into his arms. He hugged her, trying to sense every change in his precious daughter. Eventually he disentangled himself and held her slightly from him, searching her face, looking deeply into her eyes. Yes, he saw the maturity that Crystal Wisdom brought, but also identified what was missing. He knew the innocence that once gave him so much pleasure was now replaced with an authority he had not expected. This was not a victim of what she had witnessed, this was a champion of a very different kind. He was in awe of her unique power, encased in what had become a beautiful body. His daughter had matured, and the planes and curves of her face carried a beauty that made him both happy and a little nostalgic for the young girl who had left him seven years before. No longer a girl, Orla was a woman, a woman with an inner courage and subtle expression of regal presence, the like of which he had never witnessed. His wife and mother-in-law both projected a brand of regal bearing, but this was different; this was much stronger and, whilst she stood there in her simple travelling clothes, her hair tumbling down her back like any young woman of her age, he was both proud and a little overwhelmed. He thought his heart would explode as he hugged her again tightly, shedding a few silent tears of joy, confident that she had been sufficiently prepared to launch the next stage of transformation for his much-cherished planet.

The three held hands and stepped inside the palace. All the palace staff greeted Orla with excited fondness. There were no servants on Crystal Island as all islanders held positions of responsibility, took their roles seriously and were happy to be of service, contributing to the wellbeing of the community. The people who ran the day-to-day tasks of the palace were mainly men, as the business of cleaning, maintenance and cooking needed strength and stamina, and the island men undertook those duties with ease and grace. They all looked at her in the same way, with delight but also quizzically, because she radiated a quality unfamiliar to them. Yes, Orla had completed the initiation, as had all the previous princesses, but hers had been more formidable, moulding her for more responsibility.

Sensing that Orla needed to reintegrate herself into the island, Maeve led her to her chamber where a fragrant herbal bath had been prepared to harmonise her body and memory.

The young princess sank into the welcoming aromatic water, allowing her muscles to yield completely to its warmth. As her mind relaxed, she reflected over the details of her return to the Secret Garden. Initially, she had been overwhelmed by the explosion of colours, fragrances and noises that engulfed her senses. Her experience of Crystaland awakening had increased her awareness of everything in the material world, leaving her hyper sensitive to every nuance of nature. She had adapted quite rapidly, but knew she needed to be able to switch to that level of sensitivity whenever she worked with the leaders of the Federations. To help her, the Diamond Elders had instructed her to tune into her different items of crystal jewellery to activate their unique qualities of Crystal Wisdom before contacting any of the world's leaders.

She relaxed a little, somewhat worried that she might forget all she had learned on the different Crystal worlds, when her thoughts shifted to Finn. Her mother had told her that Finn would come to the palace that evening, but she was a little hesitant about seeing him again. Even though she had dreamt of him every time she slept on the Crystal worlds, she was deeply conscious and a little apprehensive that he too would have changed.

After her bath, she dried herself on the familiar soft, homespun towels and slipped on the new robe her mother had prepared for her. Orla lay on her bed, familiarising herself with every detail of her bedchamber, and drifted into a blissful slumber filled with dreams of her visit to the Emerald Crystal world and of being immersed in the healing Emerald vapour pool. She woke to her mother brushing her cheek, gently drawing her back to the material realm. Orla's eyes shot open, and for a moment she wondered where she was, part of her still in the memory of Crystaland. She squinted, struggling to see more clearly, but her mother's beautiful melodic voice drew her fully back into the room, as she turned to her, smiling, reassured that she really was home.

"Finn has arrived and is waiting for you with your father." Maeve smiled at her daughter, feeling slightly uncertain what would transpire between these two young people who had not seen each other for several years.

Orla dressed quickly in a new blue cotton summer dress that seemed to cling to her figure in a way that was also new. She studied herself in the mirror, the first time since returning, and realised she had changed considerably. Her skin and eyes were lighter, and interwoven in her dark tresses were a few strands of white hair. As she smoothed her hair, she noticed that the shadows of the fading sun outlined her cheekbones, making them appear more prominent than she remembered. Gone was the round face of adolescence, and in its place were delicate contours highlighting her fine bone structure and translucent skin that gave her an almost ethereal quality. Staring at the unfamiliar face before her, she wondered how Finn might have changed. With that lingering thought, she gathered herself up and swiftly made her way downstairs.

Orla entered the family's sitting room, which always smelled of the lavender and rosemary wax that preserved the ancient carved wooden-clad walls. Standing at the fireplace was Finn, talking to her father in a relaxed way with one of his sturdy legs slightly raised, resting on the metal fender. She paused briefly at the door, trying to capture every little detail about him, but she couldn't contain herself. She leaped towards him and, as he turned towards her, he caught her in his powerful arms. They hugged for what seemed like an eternity, then separated slightly and stared into each other's eyes. Orla's parents had discreetly left the room and the couple finally kissed each other for the first time, initially hesitant and then with an intensity that neither thought possible. They eventually untangled themselves from their embrace and studied each other closely.

She realised that he had become a physically powerful man – he was taller even than her father, with broad shoulders and the broadest grin set in a strong jaw. He gazed at her, a little mesmerised, unable to comprehend how beautiful she had become. When he had last seen her on the Ruby Crystal world she had changed slightly, but nothing could have prepared him for what he was seeing in her now. He was enchanted and completely lost for words.

The young couple alternated between hugging and chatting in an animated manner. Questions and answers tumbled from their mouths in a chaotic and unrelated fashion; they were not really asking questions that needed answers, instead just doing a dance of communication, which was part of the ritual of deep knowing that evolves after two people are joined in the Crystal Binding ceremony.

Orla's parents eventually came back into the room with a conspiratorial smile on each of their faces because they too had once been like this young couple and were thrilled that their daughter had found such a perfect partner. Maeve indicated for them to sit down at the large, beautifully carved wooden dining table and, after blessing the food, and the general exchange of pleasantries, she broached the pressing subject of the strategy for the future.

"Orla, whilst you have been away the degeneration of the planet has accelerated. For a number of years, we have been in touch with a group of people on the mainland who asked for our help. These people are from various walks of life and different levels of society but with a common objective. They have seen through the veneer of what passes for 'normal' that is projected onto the masses, and seen the ugly picture of the truth. Your father and I have been advising them in a simple language that they can understand, and we have supported them, but requested that they wait until the time is right before initiating change."

"Being unevolved humans, they wanted to start a revolution quickly, as revolution is embedded in their memories," Patrick said, "but I advised them to be clever and wait until they could be more effective. They also needed to understand that the normal way of revolution would not be appropriate this time: acting too soon would cause them to be branded traitors, punishable by death. They had volunteered to give their lives for this cause, but I reminded them that the concept of martyrdom was vilified decades before; martyrs were ridiculed and shunned. What is important though, is that there is a growing number of people who are questioning, and that is all that is needed to indicate that Crystal memory is stirring in a few. However, it is the leaders with whom we must engage first."

Orla recalled some of the images she had witnessed when she was shown the myths of leadership on the Crystal worlds and asked, "How have the leaders been acting?"

Maeve rolled her eyes, and Patrick responded: "It's as if they have lost any intelligence, even human intelligence, that they had and are acting just like predators."

"However, what I am concerned about is the plight of women," Maeve continued. "In the last several years all women have been pulled from any role of authority. To marginalise them, men decided that the natural cycle of female hormones rendered women unpredictable and unreliable, and therefore judged women to be unsuitable for leadership.

Orla dropped her cutlery in shock. "Yes, I had seen how women were treated over the span of Earth's history but thought, although it was difficult for women, some could at least hang on to some positions of authority."

Maeve sighed with impatience. "When the resources of the planet became increasingly compromised, men unconsciously grouped together, feeling under threat yet again by any authority expressed by women, and colluded to make it more difficult for them to be effective, so they put them into positions that were untenable for anyone. To guarantee their failure, men isolated women – withholding support they normally gave to their brotherhood – which left them wide open to criticism, abuse and attack. The warlords were starring in their own epic war movie once again.

"To add to this sorry story, at the same time the medical profession had labelled all the transition moments in a woman's natural hormonal life as conditions of ill-health and disease, unaware that these transitions contribute to a woman's ability to read the truth of situations and find creative solutions. The suppression of the magic of these transitions caused conflict in the minds and bodies of women, adding yet another burden to their roles of authority.

"And so, the younger women looked at the older women, who were gradually losing the strength to continue banging on the glass ceiling, and deduced that men were better equipped for this particular battlefield, which of course they were. The world of leadership was a battlefield and their solutions were based on the blueprint of war."

Orla remembered from her Crystaland journeys how the warrior leaders had evolved to become modern power leaders, but that evolutionary step had now been accelerating underneath the pressure of the planet's survival.

Patrick looked at Finn, prompting him to continue with this subject. Finn identified that Orla had lost a lot of that pure innocence of her youth from witnessing the dark episodes of Earth's history on the Crystal worlds. However, he knew he had to share with her more of his experiences on the Ruby Crystal world to equip her with the understanding of the full extent of the primal predatory behaviour that had seeped into every aspect of the Earth controlled by humans.

"Orla, before we can start, the Ruby Crystalanders instructed me to show you what I witnessed on their world." Finn knew by projecting this through his memory, it would soften the experience for her. Few men could have dealt with what he had witnessed, let alone a beautiful Crystal princess.

Maeve and Patrick looked at each other, and then at Orla, with affection and concern. Here she was at the start of her adult life with an enormous responsibility, which would at times bring her to the point of near exhaustion. They both knew that there would be little time for carefree fun for this royal couple.

"But," Maeve interjected, "the most important priority is the arrangements for the ceremony of Crystal Union."

"What actually is involved?" Orla asked.

"There are three parts. The first is the Preparation, which takes place in the Crystal circle. The second part will take place on the Emerald Crystal world. The final part is the actual ceremony of Crystal Union that will also take place in the Crystal circle. But the most important thing is to conduct the Preparation, which will begin tomorrow at the new moon. You will need to go through several levels of connection to establish the degree of intimacy necessary to be able to access Crystal Wisdom before entering into physical union."

Orla had pondered on the physical union, which she understood was an important aspect of Crystal Union, knowing it served two very important purposes. The first was to conceive a child, and the second was to anchor all aspects of Crystal Wisdom into every facet of the environment.

Orla began to tire just listening to the conversation about the ceremonies and asked to be excused.

"Before you retire, I will take you to your new private chambers that you both will share after the Ceremony." Maeve led them to a suite of rooms in the east wing of the palace. The set of rooms was lovely, light and comfortable, comprising two bedrooms with connecting doors, a sitting room and their own crystal-viewing chamber.

Orla and Finn walked around the rooms inspecting the detail. Orla noticed that both bedrooms had very large beds, as was normal for the royal family. Sleep was an important part of the crystal-human regeneration, so separate and comfortable sleeping quarters were imperative, particularly for the female line.

The young couple were delighted with their future accommodation, and Orla contentedly returned to her single chamber, prepared for bed quickly and sank into a deep sleep.

The following morning, Maeve met the couple and took them to the Crystal circle. It had been a long time since Orla had been there and she was keen to see whether her memory was accurate. As they came closer to the circle, she marvelled at the size and majesty of the crystal pillars. As she followed Maeve through the entrance, she was aware of a change in her response to the circle. Every cell in her body was vibrating, producing subtle tones that bounced through her body as she closed her eyes, embracing the many wonderful sensations she was experiencing.

Maeve instructed the couple to stand in the centre of the circle on the crystal six-pointed star engraved in the ground. The three closed their eyes and Maeve began to intone a melody that activated the copper, gold and silver geometric shapes engraved into each crystal pillar, prompting them to glow and pulse.

Placed in front of the six-pointed star was a crystal seat that had been crafted to allow two people to sit opposite each other, with a connecting crystal base.

Maeve stopped singing and directed them to be seated. The couple looked at each other but had no physical contact. There were places for their feet and hands carved in the base and the arm rests. In the centre of each seat there was a dimple, creating a space between their bodies and its base. Suspended under both seats was a large crystal orb. Maeve stood over them and began to sing in the ancient language of their people: strong lilting tones that activated the geometric shapes in the crystal pillars again. As the shapes were activated, they emitted rays of light that radiated down the length of each pillar, connecting with the floor, spreading the brilliant rays across its surface, encircling the base of the seat. Maeve focused her attention over the couple, anointing their foreheads with sacred oil that immediately shifted them from their conscious mind into their Crystal memory.

Maeve placed her hands over their heads. Immediately Orla's eyes shot open as she saw what appeared to be a flash of lightning above her mother's head. The brilliant light passed through Maeve's hands, into their heads, moving quickly through their bodies, hitting the base of their spines, at which point it spiralled in a clockwise motion, activating the crystal orb under the seat. The spiral movement prompted a pulsing in the base of their spines, which travelled down each leg, where it joined with two crystal orbs that magically appeared glowing underneath each foot. Once those orbs were activated, the energy travelled back up their legs. Orla looked over at Finn, who was staring at his arms. She felt the pulsing travel from the top of her spine, stopping at her shoulders, where two crystal orbs were activated, then pass down her arms, connecting with two orbs under her hands. She turned her palms up and the orbs followed the movement of her hands. Her attention was drawn to the base of her spine by an increased intensity of pulsing, whereupon it travelled up her spine, from her hands to the shoulders and finally through her crown, back into Maeve's hands. Quietness fell upon the circle. The young couple both sensed that they had been awakened to something incredible, but not quite comprehending what it was.

"As I told you before, you will need to practise this several times to allow your body to truly resonate with this powerful Crystal energy, to prepare you for when your energies are joined in Crystal Union. You are both very powerful individuals, each one with amazing, specific crystal gifts and, when combined, that power must be handled correctly, otherwise the fibre of your human side will be damaged or corrupted. You will now need to go back to the Emerald Crystal world for further initiation. Today we have activated the human side of Crystal Union but, as members of the royal family, you must also activate your Crystal memory,

*

Orla and Finn walked back to the palace in silence, strangely not holding hands but feeling closer than before. They both turned at the same time and looked at each other, trying to determine what the difference was between them, and in fact it was a difference, it was a closeness that went beyond words. Whilst they had an emotional connection since the Binding ceremony, this was something more complex and more profound – the creation of a completely new experience. No two people on the planet had ever had this experience before, not even the previous royal family members. The initiation that both Orla and Finn had received equipped them with the necessary qualities to confront the many shades of darkness that were shrouding the world in its final death throes.

As they neared the palace, Orla asked Finn about his experience on Ruby Crystal world. He stopped and hesitated; he knew this question was coming and he didn't really want to be the person who gave the answers. Orla looked at him enquiringly.

"My experience was twofold. Like you, I was exposed to the path of destruction that the power leaders had created. However, I also have been exposed to the deep depravities of the actions of men over the centuries." It had in fact left him with a sense of revulsion to the point where he would have liked to disassociate himself from human males, but he could not deny his gender.

The Ruby beings had helped him to understand the flaws in man as well as giving instructions on how a balanced crystal-human male should conduct himself. But crucially, he had to go through tests to ensure that every vestige of primitive male programming that carried the misuse of male strength was removed from his memory. And it was indeed that initiation that became his greatest challenge. Finn had not just witnessed poor leadership, which he understood, but he had also seen the subjugation of women, which had brought up issues in him that he did not like. The Ruby beings emphatically assured him that he would never act in such a debased way after he had completed his initiation. Every vestige of domination programming would have been removed.

Whilst Finn was prepared to allow Orla to access part of his initiation, he would wait until after their physical union before he introduced her to what now passed for intimate relationships between men and women in the world. He shook his head, breathing deeply in an attempt to expel that unpleasant thought.

They walked into their new apartment and went to their viewing chamber. This was the place where they would spend a lot of their time in the early days, identifying individuals who could initiate Earth's transformation process.

For Finn to share with Orla any negative scenes he had witnessed, their viewing chamber had to be protected to safeguard the integrity and purity of the memory of that space. They sat down next to each other and Finn retrieved from a pouch around his neck a large ruby, probably about twenty carats, beautifully cut, its diameter across the crown matching the depth of the stone. Orla put on her ruby and iron necklace and felt the familiar flow of strength that ran through her veins every time she placed it around her neck. Satisfied that Orla was secure with her necklace, Finn held his crystal in his right hand and closed his eyes, focusing on the special connection he had with the Ruby Crystal world. Within seconds the ruby came alive, releasing a deep glow. Finn placed the stone on an iron plinth, which rested on a round table in the centre of the room. Simultaneously Orla's rubies began to glow around her neck, and she followed the connecting red beam from each of her stones to the larger stone on the iron plinth.

When the room was safely under the protection of the ruby ray, Finn communicated directly to the Ruby Crystal world. A hologram appeared above the plinth, initially just a large red glow followed by shapes, and then the familiar terrain of the Ruby Crystal world appeared. Finn was obviously selective about what he showed her, but firstly he wanted her to understand his ability to control his physical strength and not be controlled by his emotional responses. He wanted her to be confident that he could protect her in any situation, no matter how challenging, using wisdom rather than brute strength.

Orla watched the Ruby Crystalanders take Finn to a similar planet to Earth in a different solar system, which was covered in what appeared to be thick weeds. This was a planet that had been put into dormancy and was in its early stages of regeneration. It still had life, but that life seemed only to produce thick vines that grew horizontally across the open planes. Finn had judged the vines to be weeds because they were coarse, without buds or berries, and their roots only connected to the first thin layer of soil. What he later learned was that the soil of this planet was depleted, but the survival instinct of the plants was so strong that the plants began to grow their roots above ground to form thick plaits to protect the papery soil underneath from further erosion.

Finn was with a group of ruby apprentices who had been taken to fields covered in the strange plants. Their first instruction was the simple request to clear a small section of the field each day, to burn the plants and then collect the ashes into earthenware vats.

"What is the objective of doing this, and what is the purpose of the ashes?" he asked his crystal mentors.

"All will be revealed once you have completed the task," came the obscure response.

On the first day the apprentices began clearing their allocated section of field with primitive scythes. Finn embarked on his section, swinging his scythe with gusto, but he didn't seem to achieve very much at all. He looked at his peers and saw them being more successful, seeming to have a skill that he lacked. This brought up in him a reaction that he could not identify, which was beyond indignation, and a surge of energy shot through his muscles that he also found hard to identify. He began swiping at the roots, but they were so deeply matted that it took all his energy to pull up one weed. The scythe was not working. He needed a different implement. He wasn't given one, and in desperation and frustration used his hands. He was beginning to feel frustrated and angry, aware of an increasing surge of energy straining through every capillary in every muscle. He continued to use his raw strength, pulling and tugging, but by the end of the day his hands were in tatters. He looked at them with dismay, perplexed at his challenge.

What am I to do? The Crystalanders had told him this was one of his initiation tests and he had to find a solution. Yes, he had grown tall and strong under their tutelage, but he didn't really understand what he should be doing or why.

His mentors looked at him, waiting for him to surrender; they would not intervene. So he went back to his small dwelling that night, where he bathed his hands, had some welcome refreshments and fell into an exhausted sleep. He dreamt of being back on the Ruby Crystal world and scanned the crystal beings, noting how they appeared to move obstacles with their minds and not rely on physical strength. The next day, fully refreshed, he went out to the field with great enthusiasm and started again, but this time he remembered his teachings; he had been taught to produce the male hormone in his body and direct it to certain muscles to make them stronger, and not allow it to be dissipated by anger. He stood in front of the field, focusing on the large muscle groups in his body, and initially experienced a rush of heat push through his veins, but he controlled the energy with his breath, allowing only a specific amount to be directed to his muscles.

His dream the previous night had reminded him of the full meaning of the word 'power'. On the Ruby Crystal world, the priority of the training was to enable the apprentices to harness the male energy in all its shades of power and use it in service of the planet. This was no mean feat. Every male carried the genetic memory of the human power formula: dominate or be dominated; when confronted push forward; when challenged use force to overpower. This formula not only fuelled physical confrontation, but it also found its way into the negotiating process between leaders in any situation where there was a challenge to leadership, however subtle. The addiction to this form of power increased when leaders realised that they could manipulate people and events by weaving fragments of fear into the tapestry of negotiation, guaranteeing no real challenge.

Finn's body began again to produce the male hormone responsible for power and strength, but this time he controlled its action by directing the strong pumping sensation to his hands, his arms, down his back and into his legs. This prompted a sense of euphoria to flood his body and he began to attack those weeds with his scythe, swinging the tool low and firm, skimming the surface of the soil and cutting them right at the point at which the plants connected to the soil. He cut a swathe through the field, powered by chemicals that had triggered a cascade of neurotransmitters, urging him to power through without stopping. He was like a warrior, attacking those weeds as if his very life depended on it.

The Crystalanders looked on and saw that the small vestige of human male conditioning that was present in Finn was coming to the surface again; competition coupled with the survival programme had kicked in; he was firing on all his human cylinders to the power of ten generated by his immense physical strength. He cleared the space, gathered the plants and, as instructed, burnt them down to ash and stored them in the vats provided. He finally stopped and surveyed his flattened field. He was triumphant and looked down, admiring his strong muscles, which were glistening from perspiration, and watched the blood pump through his veins, prominently displayed over each muscle. He had never felt this powerful before, and he liked it. This feeling echoed through his memory and triggered a reaction in him that felt very familiar. Just at the point of his self-satisfaction, two large flying insects landed on his arm. He swatted at them impatiently and missed; they landed again and he missed again; they flew around his head, taunting him all the while. He was furious. But then he paused, realising that he was becoming angry over two insects, which was a ridiculous response.

Whilst he was still immersed in questioning his self-satisfaction, a powerful, large white lion padded quietly into the top of the field, stopped and glared at Finn. He puffed out his chest, raised his head and then charged directly at Finn. Finn, in his heightened state of physicality, stood up and faced the lion square on without an ounce of fear and raised his two fists ready for combat, but immediately halted, and realised that he had been taught another way of deflecting danger. He immediately scanned his memory and found the tool that he needed, but first he had to reduce the hormone that was coursing ferociously throughout his body, preventing him from accessing his crystal communication skills. He breathed deeply, which was not easy as the lion was still charging towards him, but Finn didn't waiver. He calmed his mind, found the tone that he needed and emitted a sound from his mouth, silent to the human ear, creating an energy force around him that stopped white lion in his tracks. White lion observed, listened, changed his demeanour, and thought, *Here is not one of those primitive humans who had destroyed the planet with their stupidity; here is a young human who has understanding.* White lion walked slowly over to Finn, who stood in awe of this mighty animal towering over him with the ability to kill him with one swipe of his snowy paw.

The lion announced, "You have today learnt one of the first lessons of courage."

Yes, he thought, *I have learnt how quickly the hormone that has the ability to give male humans immense strength to protect nature quickly turns to rage and destruction when faced with competition or threat.*

"You have demonstrated that you can access that ability to turn the primitive response of rage into courage by learning to speak the language of your aggressor," said the lion as he turned, slowly exiting the field.

Finn reflected on what had just transpired, acknowledging that, initially, he had failed to observe some basic crystal rules. When his mentors had told him to clear the land he had asked like a child, 'Why?' He now knew he had the knowledge to understand the reasoning behind their instructions, and he began looking at the landscape differently. Yes, it appeared there were thick weeds everywhere, but this must have been a vital planet at some time in its history, and because there was still organic life in the plants, Crystal Wisdom must be in there somewhere. So, instead of picking up his scythe, he walked into the centre of another field and sat down amongst the knotted plants.

He looked deeply into their thick criss-cross formation and silently asked the question, *Is the soil active, and if not, what does it need to make it active again*?

He touched the plants, feeling their strength run through his fingers, and instantly knew he had misjudged them to be weeds. He spoke softly, asking them what they would like him to do. He patiently sat and waited for an answer. Eventually, to Finn's surprise, a plant spirit appeared. He had not expected a plant spirit to still be on a dormant planet.

"What are you doing sitting in the field?" demanded the indignant plant spirit.

"I want to know what I must do to help this field," Finn replied.

"Leave it alone!"

"But the Ruby Crystalanders told me to clear the field."

"Do you do everything that you are told without question?"

Finn reflected on the folly of his earlier endeavours.

"So the boy has now become the man," the plant spirit observed, and continued: "This planet was once like your planet, and did not listen to Crystal Wisdom, so it died. Before leaving the planet completely the spirits sewed seeds of these plants, knowing that the memory in the soil would configure the growth of the plant to protect it from being used before it is ready."

Finn was humbled by his naive judgement of the weeds based on their appearance. He had thought they were an accident of nature, but realised that there were no accidents in nature. The only accidents that occurred were man-made. He touched the plants with a new respect and thanked them for doing such a perfect job. "Is this land ready to be fully regenerated?"

"Not yet, the soil is still lacking the basic catalysts to hold it together, it is still resting."

"Why did the Crystalanders ask me to clear the land and burn what I removed?"

"The Ruby beings were trying to help you detect when your primitive side became dominant with your increased physical strength; and also for you to learn to defer to Crystal Wisdom for answers. You needed to learn that power is not about domination. You initially attacked the soil as if it were an enemy you needed to subdue."

Finn sat quietly, considered this, and then another question popped into his mind: "So why do the ashes have to be kept in vats?"

"When the soil is fully recovered, the protective plants will be burnt, reducing the entire landscape to ash. The ash is concentrated minerals and the intense heat from the fires will instigate rain that will drive the minerals deeper into the soil, providing the important catalysts for regeneration, thereby completing the alchemical process."

"I am a little concerned that I have affected the delicate balance of this planet's recovery by burning those plants too soon."

"The Ruby beings knew what you would do, so they made sure that nothing was wasted. The ash in the containers will always be useful. The most important thing is that you have learnt a very valuable lesson. Take this experience with you back to your planet and try to teach those silly people on your planet this very important lesson."

Finn thanked the plant spirit, who disappeared as fast as he had appeared.

He realised that his warrior strength had the potential to override his crystal intelligence; it was a primal survival response to charge into a threatening situation with great energy, because that energy was available; and the more strength one had, the more this would likely happen.

Orla reflected on the actions of the beautiful lion, in awe of its whiteness and size, but more importantly she was reassured that Finn had harnessed his immense physical strength and learnt to channel it correctly by deferring to Crystal Wisdom. Orla smiled warmly at Finn as she searched for his hand.

The view changed and images appeared, reflecting the evolution of man's immense strength, designed solely for service to the planet. But, after the Crystalanders left Earth, man had reverted to using his strength to dominate the weak, which was, of course, a pattern of behaviour conceived by their original creators. Orla was amazed at man's ability to push himself to fight fearlessly in battle, for hours and days on end, using immense physical power to overthrow his enemies. But once that power was released, it could not be controlled, unleashing the primal programming of raw aggression, which, if unabated by Crystal Wisdom, led them to fight stronger and harder, moving from one battle to the next without a backward glance, destroying everything in their wake.

The scenes progressed through history and, as man developed industrially and technically, nothing much changed, their actions just became more sophisticated. The generals of armies fought according to a very predictable formula – invade, overthrow, suppress and move on to the next area to dominate. The wonderful protective qualities of physical power designed to be used to support the planet had been hijacked and manipulated by the power leaders.

After a few moments the hologram cleared, and another new scene appeared which was quite hard for Orla to understand. She saw Finn in all his physical glory, but he was surrounded by Shadow. Orla was once again reminded of this dark threat that pervaded humankind. She had been innocent of Shadow until her Crystal awakening. Shadow had appeared on Earth thousands of years after the Crystalanders had left the planet in the hands of the Crystal Elders. Attracted to fear and doubt, over the centuries Shadow had gradually infiltrated every level of society, particularly leadership, implanting their brand of hatred into all of their hosts.

Shadow had been attracted to Finn's strength but was confused by his lack of fear, so its instinctive reaction was to destroy strength that it couldn't control. Initially, Finn couldn't see them, he was just aware of an uncomfortable sensation of tension and dread around him. The Crystalanders communicated with his Crystal memory, warning that his human side was under attack, and instructed him to use his crystal intelligence to deflect that attack; but he was not to use his physical strength under any circumstances as this would attract Shadow closer to him.

The first task was to open his inner vision to identify what was threatening him, but because he had no doubt or fear, he could not identify the darkness. He increased his Crystal focus until he eventually identified the black jagged tentacles that Shadow used to engage and imprison humans. As soon as he detected those tentacles a feeling was triggered from deep within, which he immediately identified as anger, the very emotion he knew he had to transmute. Unlike his experience with White Lion, this was not an obvious threat, but a dark and insidious creeping danger that triggered the last vestige of his human programming to appear. The anger rose so strongly that he was nearly overwhelmed by its power, but he was able to control it, observing his reactions rather than responding to them. His initial reaction was to use his strength to repel them, which he quickly discounted, and in that moment of discernment he accessed his full crystal intelligence and knew what to do.

He took from his inner chest pocket the ruby crystal that had been given to him at the beginning of his experiences on the Ruby Crystal world. Gently taking it from its pouch, he looked deep into its core and, resonating with the purity of his faith, it began to emit a warm glow. Immediately that glow converted into a strong ruby ray which surrounded him, creating a safe cocoon of ruby crystal. Finn continued to feel the direct connection with the crystal, and while he was enjoying the sensation of being bathed in its wonderful glow, he opened his mouth and produced a sound. He knew he had made the final connection to the greatest weapon of all, the sound of courage. He vibrated the sound through his body, which released an energy that Shadow had not witnessed on Earth for thousands of years – pure faith, without any shades of doubt. The message engraved in the sound rendered the vibration of that particular space inhospitable to Shadow, and unable to survive within that pure vibration, it began to retreat. With Shadow's retreat, Finn's confidence increased, and he connected deeper to the sound stored in the Crystal memory in the cells of his adrenal glands. There was no anger, nor rage, just sound which changed the environment, rendering Shadow temporarily impotent. Shadow retreated slightly but was not happy and gathered more forces to increase the attack. The ugly tentacles multiplied. Finn, unfazed by the further onslaught, produced more sound, which finally sent Shadow screeching into further retreat. He had accessed a powerful formula to keep these forces at bay, which took no physical energy, only pure intention.

Orla observed the scene and naively reflected that Shadow had initially not disappeared completely; on the contrary, it had increased its force. She began to get the first inkling of what it would take to remove these entities from the planet completely, knowing that it would not be a simple job of sending Finn and his helpers out to confront Shadow. Shadow was now within all sectors of leadership in the Earth's Federations, and so deeply entrenched in all levels of consciousness that it would be a tough job to unravel humanity from Shadow's vice-like grip of hatred. Finn looked at her, squeezed her hand and reassured her that they were both more than equipped for the job ahead. Comforted by his certainty, she gratefully returned his squeeze. She knew why she was dependent on Finn – there was no possibility that she could confront Shadow face on. She was a female and did not have the physical attributes to thwart such darkness; her gifts and talents lay in a very different area.

Orla was silent as she reflected on the images she had just seen, entranced and intrigued by the sound of courage. She looked at Finn with fresh eyes, now fully aware of the physical and emotional control that her soul friend possessed.

The couple were tired and left the viewing chamber, returning to their separate chambers to prepare for their next level of initiation.

The following day Maeve came into the breakfast room and announced, "You will be going back to Crystaland tomorrow, specifically to the Emerald Crystal world. This is an important level of your initiation when you will experience the depth and meaning of true intimacy." Maeve gave the instructions quite sternly as this step was critical to their transformation. She knew, though, that when they returned they would have changed yet again, which caused her to smile inwardly.

*

The following day Finn and Orla set off to the Secret Garden and passed through the wonderful scented floral beds on their way, preparing their minds for the journey, as was the tradition. Maeve went with them to the oak tree and kissed her daughter on the cheek as she said goodbye, knowing that when she came back this time, she would have a very different understanding of intimacy. She also knew that Grace, her mother, would meet Orla on the other side, which gave her comfort. She kissed Finn on his cheek and whispered words to him, which he knew was a mother's concern for her child to be initiated into the deeply subtle world of intimacy with tenderness and protection.

They entered the travelling vessel, Orla activated the code, and the vessel began its journey. They were both relaxed from the aromas of the garden and sat silently and patiently waiting for the vessel to land. They stood in anticipation of the change of brightness as the door slid open and they were confronted with the dazzling brilliance of the diamond crystal. They blinked and adjusted their eyes quickly as they stepped onto the crystal path. There on the path, waiting, were Grace and Unicorn. Grace hugged them both. Orla was excited to see her grandmother, who she had left at the beginning of her Crystal awakening, which to the young princess felt like many moons ago. Orla quickly noticed that Grace seemed to have changed; yes, she still had the same colouring, but she had lost any signs of ageing – her skin was smooth, her eyes bright and she stood with excellent posture. Orla was delighted to see that her grandmother was so well, and with that thought lingering, Unicorn came trotting over and sidled up next to her. She hugged him tightly and was delighted to be reunited with her equine friend.

They all knew what was to happen and began walking on the path, which eventually changed colour from the diamond crystal to the palest jade crystal flecked with copper, until it developed further into the deepest emerald crystal that looked almost black. Orla was amazed at this intensity of colour. When she had first come to the Emerald Crystal world, the emerald was clear, pure green, but now there was a depth in the colour and vibration that was not present before. As she walked on the crystal, she felt the vibration pass through her body, pulsing to a deep rhythm, rather than the familiar tingling she had previously experienced. Equally, Finn, who had never spent any time in the Emerald Crystal world, felt the energy of the crystal pulse through him in a steady rhythmical pattern starting from his feet, passing up his legs, through his trunk, over his head and then down the front of his body. They both looked at each other knowing they were experiencing the same feelings. As they walked further along the path the colour increased in depth and the vibration became stronger. At one point Orla had to stop because she thought she would be flipped over from the strong sensations surging through her legs. Finn instinctively took her hand and steadied her, and she realigned her balance so that she could absorb the strength of the crystal into her body.

They arrived at the Emerald Crystal Hall, and the crystal beings approached the group. These were not the jade and copper beings from before, these were a deep emerald-black with copper bands around their foreheads, necks and wrists. They wore cloaks of deep emerald crystal that swished like silk as they moved towards them, beaming their greeting to the group, and led them to the Emerald healing chamber.

Grace sat on a crystal stool as witness to their initiation, with Unicorn laying alongside her. The beings placed the couple facing each other on two emerald crystal thrones with a small circular indentation in the seat.

"You must position yourselves so that your back is touching the crystal chair from the base of your spine up to the crown of your head," instructed the beings. "Focus on breathing just through your nostrils, alternating the breath from one side to the other using your thumb to close one nostril."

The beings put their hands just above the couple's heads. Orla and Finn closed their eyes, experiencing a sense of warmth diffuse through their bodies as a series of mystical shapes were traced over their heads. The couple felt as if their entire heads were being opened and exposed, but almost immediately that opening was filled with a deep emerald crystal shower that entered the top of their heads and went in a straight line through their bodies, stopping just underneath their sitting bones, resting for a while in their pelvic area before returning to their heads.

With every breath the crystal shower ascended their body and then cascaded down, activating a powerful electrical sensation that neither of them had experienced before. Each time it travelled down the body it carried a stronger sensation, hitting the pelvic area, expanding, and then the cycle repeated. After several cycles, the sensation passed down their legs into the ground, connecting with a golden crystal orb of light. The couple were instructed to open their hands, into which orbs of golden light settled gently. By now the sensations were becoming so strong in both of them that they felt they couldn't contain it for much longer, but they were instructed to control that feeling with their breathing. The beings touched the front of their foreheads, which activated yet another orb of light that hovered just in front of their faces, followed by another orb at the point of their solar plexus. All the orbs were in alignment, from their forehead down to their feet, reconnecting with the golden orb. They gazed at each other, sensing a feeling that went beyond Earthly emotions. The Emerald beings put their hands over the couple's heads again, simultaneously activating all the orbs. The couple automatically brought their hands to the centre, merging the orbs in their hands, which prompted all spheres of light to move forward into the small space that separated the couple, hesitating for a split second before merging together. Immediately a fountain of Emerald crystal spilled from the orbs that emitted a specific tone, creating a melody of both colour and sound that embraced the couple.

Grace looked on with joy – she had experienced this sensation many times and knew how it filled her with regeneration and connection, not just with her beloved partner but also with Crystal Wisdom. They were both reaching a pinnacle of sensation, but Orla was having difficulty keeping conscious, such was the power of the crystal and the sound that was reverberating in every cell of her body. She felt Finn's energy steady her and was able to continue breathing rhythmically. At the apex of that feeling the crystal cascade separated and went inward, penetrating their individual bodies, passing through their spines, shooting through their heads where it merged again and ascended higher and higher, carrying the memory of that extreme moment of their bliss out into the universe where tiny spirit beings of emerald captured the crystal particles and carried them to the four corners of the universe.

This magical process continued with every breath the couple took. There seemed to be no end to this feeling and neither wanted the blissful sensation to stop. Eventually the pulsing ceased, the orbs retracted, and the cascade of crystal subsided. Their bodies became quiet but they were still aware of the aftermath of the energy flowing through their bodies. A feeling of calm washed over them as they gazed into each other's eyes with deep love and connection, knowing that they had both experienced the most sacred of crystal experiences that the universe could offer. And they, in turn, had reciprocated that depth of feeling by sharing it with the universe.

Grace continued with their education. "This is a ritual that must be practised regularly as it is vitally important that the Earth's atmosphere is regularly recharged with Crystal Wisdom. On this occasion you have only experienced the ritual, but it is normal to have an intention that can be amplified into the universe.

"The first human-crystalanders were taught this ritual, but over the millennia, after Crystal Wisdom was lost to mankind, it became distorted and manipulated. People who described themselves as magicians stole this sacred rite and used it for their own material gain and power. They reduced the ritual to its most basic level." Orla looked, puzzled, at her grandmother. Finn knew what she was about to say and cast his gaze down, a little shy of how Orla would respond. Grace did not go into detail as she knew Orla was not ready yet to understand that level of depravity.

"It can be used for the regeneration of individuals and also for the planet, but it is also to be used for the conception of a child." Orla became a little embarrassed – she knew the process for conceiving human babies and was a little intrigued, but also apprehensive.

"As a human you will want to be physically intimate; each act of Crystal intimacy must be preceded by this ritual. You can set the intention of whether that coupling will result in a baby, or whether it is to empower a specific request for the universe." Orla was still looking baffled, but Finn understood what Grace was describing.

During his Ruby initiation he had seen how "men and their magic", as he described it, had distorted the most sacred creative process that a human could exercise and reduced it to something that was more base than could be described. The intense energy produced by a couple during this ritual was the most powerful to activate an intention. Initially this practice was only undertaken by Elders and their partners, who had the correct purity of memory, but after the Crystalanders left, man had eventually learnt of the power of this ritual and decided to harness it for his own selfish needs rather than those of the planet. Man had seized the opportunity to use this ritual to debase Crystal intimacy, and indeed, at one sorry point in history, certain women were identified as strong receptors of this sacred energy and were used solely for its dark side.

The correct use of Crystal intimacy was a major part of Finn's initiation because the energy that was channeled by male humans was very powerful. It was the energy required to draw in all of creation's knowledge of perfection to merge and enhance the beauty of the Earth held in the ovaries of women.

To impress on Finn the correct use of Crystal Union, his mentors had shown him many examples throughout history of its misuse, and when he thought he couldn't deal with any more depravity, his mentors introduced another layer to him. The 20th century had spawned an industry that had mushroomed out of all proportion. It was an industry based on male dominated copulation. Women were regarded as vessels of pleasure for men to use in any way they pleased. This formula became more widely accessible through the plethora of online material and eventually it became the standard to which young men and women aspired – the opposite to intimacy and contrary to the laws of Crystal Union, but the perfect ground upon which Shadow could flourish. The more men and women followed this path, the more they closed down their connection to Crystal Wisdom. The unconscious intentions radiated out to the universe from their primitive coupling unwittingly reinforced the success of Shadow. The entertainment media had sold them yet another myth, but deep down women began to recognise that this was not the truth. But their questioning was judged an emotional reaction, so it was not validated. With no authority, women did what they had done for centuries; they closed down and tried to ignore the truth.

Fortunately for the planet, women still channeled creative wisdom, even though it was small, but it was limited to when they conceived a baby and it was at these times that women started to question the pressures that they were under to perform for men. After a woman had a baby, her requirement for physical intimacy shifted onto a different level. She was seeking more, she was seeking that universal intimacy that is the birthright of all men and women. She didn't know that, as she had never experienced it, but she just knew something was missing.

Finn's attention was drawn back to the beauty of Orla and he saw yet another level of transformation had taken place from the Emerald crystal which had increased his attraction to her ten-fold. They linked arms as Unicorn led them back along the path. As the path reverted to the diamond crystal, Grace bade them farewell, knowing that Orla would need to contact her crystal mentors many times in the next few years.

They arrived at the travelling vessel and Orla reluctantly bade farewell to her beloved Unicorn. The couple sat down in silence as the door closed. Finn was considering the enormity of all the information that Orla was processing. She had undergone this wonderful physical and emotional explosion of experiences, and then discovered that this would be the precursor to their physical union, of which she was a little in awe. He understood this and gently held her hand in a gesture of love and reassurance.

When they returned to the palace, Maeve saw the change in her daughter and gave Finn a conspiratorial look. Of course, Maeve understood what had transpired, she had undergone this herself, but this was her daughter and although she was maturing she would always be her child, and with that came all the protective nurturing instincts of a mother.

Orla felt weary and a little strange and, addressing Finn and her mother, said, "I think I will go to my personal chamber so that I can assimilate what has transpired on the Emerald Crystal world." Her mind was going through the usual pattern of juggling several concepts at the same time until they found a familiar place, settled and gave her insight. The experience on the Emerald Crystal world was beyond words. She knew that the whole encounter had given her a much deeper connection to Finn. *Could it be any deeper?* she thought.

But, equally, it had given her a feeling of strength and security.

She lay down on her daybed and closed her eyes, drifting off to sleep. Her dreams were filled with various shades of emerald crystal in various shapes, forming a kaleidoscope of colourful images.

When she awoke, she felt strangely refreshed for the early evening and wondered what Finn was doing. She jumped off the bed, slipped on her shoes and set off to find him. She found him deep in conversation with her parents in the small sitting room where they held small gatherings. Her parents smiled at her entrance and beckoned her to sit next to Finn. They were discussing the latest disaster newsflash from the mainland.

"There has been a massive storm accompanied by torrential rain that has continued for weeks," Patrick explained. "The land did need the rain as it hasn't rained for several years, but it was so heavy, it battered the parched soil, running in rivers before it could soak into the land, gathering momentum on its journey and destroying everything in its wake."

"Which area is most affected?" Orla asked

"The worst area is the south east coast of the Federation of the West, not unknown for its monsoons in the last few decades, but this one has been really bad. This time the whole of the south eastern seaboard has been submerged under water. It was as if the sea wanted to bring the coastline under its protection, preventing any further damage. Unfortunately it is a place where many homeless and stateless people have set up camps, so it was heavily populated, with very few resources. In one fell swoop the population of a state has been decimated."

Orla was horrified. Patrick knew that there was a recurring pattern with these storms in this part of the world, but nothing was done to protect the ordinary people, nor were the leaders acknowledging why the weather patterns had become so extreme. The people who had money and power had moved inland onto higher ground under the protection of the domes. The offices of power were housed within domed communities where the infrastructure was completely artificially controlled. Compared with the life of the people outside, the dome-dwellers appeared to lead an idyllic life. And when the violent storms came, it was the areas where most of the people were living outside of the domes – barely surviving in fragile, makeshift dwellings – that were always badly affected.

Their gaze finally fell on Orla, and she looked at them, realising that the time had come for her and Finn to start their work. The fact that different areas of land were suddenly being lost meant that the competition between the water and landmasses was proving to be disastrous, one of the many indications that the planet had started reacting in a punitive way to mankind's disrespect.

"We need to decide on a date for the Crystal Union," Maeve urged. "After the ceremony you will be a much stronger unit, which is necessary for your future work, and I suggest this Friday, in three days, is a good choice." Orla and Finn nodded their approval and Maeve set off to prepare for the ceremony.

*

On the Friday morning Orla had breakfast in her room, as was the custom. Her mother came in with her white and gold embroidered robe that all princesses wore at their Crystal Union. She dressed slowly, wondering what Finn was thinking, and felt herself tingle with excitement.

The ceremony of Crystal Union took place, like all sacred ceremonies, under the protection of the circle of crystals. Orla and her parents made their way to the ancient circle and met Finn and his parents. Finn was wearing the traditional white and gold ceremonial robes of a royal consort. They entered the circle and Maeve indicated for the couple to stand on the crystal six-pointed star.

"This ceremony of Crystal Union is part of our heritage and a gift from Crystaland. Those who receive this gift can never break its sacred vow. This is a union for life."

"Do you, Orla, accept the gift of Crystal Union with Finn?"

"Yes," Orla replied, smiling at Finn.

"Do you, Finn, accept the gift of Crystal Union with Orla?"

"Yes," he replied, returning Orla's smile.

"Do you both agree to singularly serve the planet for your whole life, placing the needs of the planet above all personal or family needs?"

"We do," they both replied solemnly.

"I ask the witnesses present to confirm that they are all initiates of the Crystal Union."

Patrick and Finn's parents replied, "We are."

If there had been one person not initiated into that level, then the ceremony would have been invalid. This was yet another level of protection designed to safeguard Crystal Wisdom.

Finally, Maeve anointed the foreheads of the couple with a pungent oil and gave them each a small bottle of the oil blend to take to their chambers. She then gave Orla a second bottle of oils which would not be required for several years.

As a symbol of their union, Maeve gave them each a rose diamond pendant held on the finest of gold chains that they were to wear for the rest of their lives.

After the ceremony they went back to the palace gardens where there was a table laid with special crystal goblets filled with celebratory wine. The wine had been produced from the island's rich vines, to which had been added minute amounts of copper, gold and silver and special crystals from Crystaland to ensure the memory of that day remained embedded in the memory of every cell of their bodies.

Maeve reflected on the way the ritual of Crystal Union had been manipulated by man in the last few centuries to mean something very different. When Crystal Wisdom had been lost, Union between couples had been relegated to be just a transaction. Men needed housekeepers and providers of physical comfort – a euphemism for unpaid slavery – and women needed financial and physical protection. Ordinary people linked together in marriage out of necessity, not love, and the wealthier echelons used marriage to strengthen power and wealth.

Before the domes, a whole new way of exploiting the act of Union financially had evolved around what had become known as the wedding industry. The concept of Crystal Union was lost in a sea of sequins, froth and lace, champagne and cake, the cost of which could have fed a community for a year, or secured the financial future of the newly-weds. But for the sake of one day's excessive celebrations, they sacrificed financial security.

Where had it all gone wrong? Maeve wondered. She shook her head in disbelief but understood that these poor young people had no real potential for experiencing wonder in their lives. Their lives were pretty much mapped out for them: working hard, battling to survive by following the strict dogma of their leaders which ensured that just a handful of people had real power. So, the idea of just one day of their lives being like a fairy tale was enticing. Yes, Maeve could understand why this had occurred. Everyone was in fact special, unique, and had something about them to honour, respect and cherish, but Shadow had ironed that out of their memory, so they felt generally unworthy, rendering them more vulnerable to fear. Maeve recognised that deep within mankind they sensed that life could be like a fairy tale and they traded all their financial security for that one day of connection to something that echoed the magic that is creation.

When the ceremony and celebrations were over, Orla and Finn went to their new chambers, which had been prepared with herbs and flowers that filled the room with an intoxicating fragrance. Orla went to her bathroom and prepared herself with the first bottle of essential oils that had been given to her during the ceremony. She had been given two blends: one was to empower the intentions for the Crystal Union, the second was to be used to conceive a child. For now they would need all their energies for their new responsibilities, and the idea of a child was definitely put on hold. She inhaled the oils and allowed them to merge into her mind, connecting with her Crystal memory, imparting an immediate calming effect. So much had happened since returning from her Crystaland awakening that she was feeling slightly giddy.

Finn had gone into his bathroom and also used the blend of oils which connected with his Crystal memory, activating the energy required for the physical union but leaving the procreative energy dormant.

Finn walked into Orla's side of the chambers and, taking her hand, led her to their special seat at the foot of her bed, and facing each other they went through the process of energetically connecting. They had been told on the Emerald Crystal world that this occasion would be very special and their one intention should be to unite together on every level in every cell of their bodies so that they exchanged and integrated their individual memories and gifts.

As they went through the process of circulating the orbs, Orla felt herself change and her body begin to vibrate. They held each other's hands and felt the subtle vibration go through their bodies, both controlling it so that it didn't dissipate too quickly. Once all the energy points were connected, Finn gently guided Orla to the bed, settling her gently down. He lay beside her, and they turned on their sides, looking into each other's eyes, both experiencing an overwhelming sense of connection and deep love. Orla was happy for him to take the lead; she trusted him implicitly. When they both felt the time was right, Finn instinctively knew when to go to the next level and gently made the physical connection with Orla where they became one, both of them aware that they had to contain the desire to release their energy too quickly.

They reconnected at the base energy point and initiated the Emerald crystal fountain, which turned into a focused ray; they then raised the level of the ray, which had become united in their bodies through the energy points. Eventually it ascended and burst through both their crowns and travelled rapidly to beyond the Earth's atmosphere, eventually connecting to the various planets of the solar system where there was an interchange of information between the couple and the individual planets. After that, the ray travelled further, and eventually connected with the Crystal worlds, where it paused, and then finally arrived at the Source of all Creation. The couple were transfixed in that moment of connecting to the Source. This was an experience that took them completely from their bodies to a space in time where they merged with the universe and expanded their consciousness to view and embrace all the qualities and gifts offered by the Source.

They continued in that state of universal connection for what appeared to be an eternity and then the Emerald ray re-engaged with them to begin its descent to Earth, revisiting the memory of the planets on its way, eventually bringing the couple consciously back into the material world, settling in each of their energy centres.

When there was a complete connection of giving and receiving, it was as if creation said "Ok, that is enough for now," and the energy centres closed down leaving a feeling of tranquility in every cell of their bodies. When they eventually became more lucid with their thoughts, they shared their feelings.

"I have never experienced, or expected to experience, feelings so profound, but I feel unable to verbalise or do it justice by using words," Orla confessed.

"The Source of all Creation is beyond the physical material worlds and it is impossible to downgrade that experience by giving it a three-dimensional description. By connecting on that level, we directly access Creation's deep and unique wisdom for which the initiations on the Crystal worlds were just the stepping stones," Finn explained.

Orla sensed that she had taken on some of Finn's strength when there had been a merging of their physical cellular memory, which had bathed her cells with a protective wash of Ruby Crystal Wisdom. Equally, Finn had received an injection of the Sapphire Crystal Wisdom from Orla. The Ruby and Sapphire crystals had integrated, forming a solid matrix of Crystal Wisdom in their memories. They drifted into a deep sleep, sharing the same dreams, the same experiences, confirmation that their deep and undivided connection was sealed for eternity.

The following morning, they both awoke and embraced each other with pure love. Orla could not believe how lucky she was and silently expressed deep gratitude for having Finn as her lifetime partner. Finn was delighted with his beautiful partner, his heart bursting with love and protection. They were one and at peace, for which they would both be eternally grateful. They knew that they were exceedingly privileged for a very specific reason and function, and with that they realised that time was pressing and they needed to move forward with their project.

They went to the breakfast room and sat down to eat heartily in silence.

Orla broke the silence. "Do all couples experience this?"

Finn, putting down his cutlery, carefully replied, "Only initiates of Crystal Island hold that privilege. It was a privilege available to all humans, but they had really lost their way and the process of Crystal intimacy had been lost in a sea of domination."

"Can you explain more?" Orla asked.

Finn was reluctant as he felt that she should not have the beauty of their first physical experience sullied with the story of man's primitive behaviour. However, he knew that she needed to understand what they were up against, particularly as it related to the future role of women.

"When we have finished breakfast we can go to the viewing room and you will understand more." He hadn't really wanted to expose her to this information just yet, but she was pressing for more information and time was short. They needed to start their work as soon as possible, but he would once again censor what she saw.

After their breakfast, they went to the viewing room. Finn engaged with his ruby which connected him to his experiences gained on the Ruby Crystal world. The hologram appeared above the iron plinth and Orla began her induction into the "coupling" history of mankind.

Orla saw that primitive man had a strong urge programmed within him to procreate – a survival instinct

– and men had responded to women accordingly in a bestial way. They had learnt this from the animal kingdom, which had shared their world before the Crystalanders arrived. Their physical urges superseded conscious thoughts of restraint; they were purely reacting to an instinct activated when around fertile women. Thankfully, the Crystalanders changed that; man was taught first to acknowledge and respect the beauty within himself, and then take that respect into his relationship with the beauty of Crystal Wisdom that was reflected in everything in his world, which of course included women. They were introduced to Crystal Union, and men and women had enjoyed intimate fulfilling relationships that not only regenerated them physically and emotionally, but also increased the purity of creation in their environment.

As time passed and mankind turned his back on Crystal Wisdom, those primitive, procreative urges became more and more dominant. Eventually, conflict surfaced within man when he was around women. He was confused that he could not contain those primitive responses, and cleverly laid the blame securely at the feet of women. Women were at the root of their responses so therefore were seen as manipulators whose sexual unruliness, as it was perceived, needed to be contained, controlled and closed down. This concept gathered momentum over the centuries, becoming exaggerated and distorted until eventually women were blamed for all of man's mistakes. Shadow had orchestrated this whole scenario to downgrade the importance of women by introducing fear of her natural qualities. This particular judgment was reinforced by most religions at some point in history and led to the sin of the world being placed securely on the shoulders of women.

"I am not understanding what is happening. The experience we had together is completely different from this picture," Orla said.

"I know, and that is the tragedy. Intimacy disappeared and was replaced with transactional relationships. Men were responding to their primal urges, and took their pleasure as and when they wished. Equally women were desperate not to allow their spontaneous urges to come to the surface in case more guilt was loaded upon them. Unfortunately this happened for more than 2000 years, and although in the latter part of the 20th century this attitude began to change in many cultures, that programming still haunted women on a very deep level, overlaying many shades of guilt into their memory, influencing their thoughts and actions in the 22nd century."

Orla realised that she was very new to the level of intimacy that she had shared with Finn and could not comprehend what it would be like to be submissive. She shook her head, and Finn looked at his innocent bride knowing that this was just the beginning. She would uncover Shadow's dark influence on relationships between men and women soon enough.

CHAPTER TWO
CHOOSING THE FIRST PIONEER

Patrick and Maeve joined the couple, comforted to see that their daughter and son-in-law were so happy, silently reflecting on their own first physical union many years before.

Patrick brought them all out of the reverie. "We must now focus on the plans for the future. The first objective is to infiltrate the leaders and choose a group who have some tiny piece of Crystal memory still accessible."

"How many do we need to engage?" asked Finn

Patrick smiled. "We initially only need to target seven."

"How do we choose them?" Orla asked, eager to move ahead. She had realised very quickly that Shadow had made such a dent into the minds of man over the centuries that they needed to work quickly but thoroughly if they were to transform the planet.

Patrick continued. "Finn and I have been monitoring the different Federations and I have been in dialogue with sympathetic factions in the Federations to determine which one would be more responsive. I believe that we should start with the largest Federation, which is also geographically closest to the Island, the Federation of the West. It had once birthed great pioneers but had crumbled into disparate states, losing its cohesion as their philosophies had become confused and polarised. But, the basic tenets of the original formation of that Federation resonated on a very small level with Crystal Wisdom. Once we identify the individuals, Orla, you are the only person who can access their memory to verify if they are good candidates."

Finn knew that, initially, this exercise would take a great deal of concentrated focus for Orla, and he also knew that the process of identifying Crystal memory meant that she would have to wade through a lot of ugly information.

"We have eliminated the Generals already as their Crystal memory has been deeply buried for many generations, allowing them to step fully into the Shadow's archetype of power, releasing the savage warrior within. So we suggest that you target their aides, their second-in-command." As Patrick finished speaking he looked at his daughter, who was about to take on the biggest challenge in the history of the planet, and he was concerned. He knew Finn was an excellent foil and complement to her, but still this was his princess and he yearned to protect her from such awful experiences. He inhaled deeply, remembering his position and responsibilities. Duty was the most important quality of the royal family and each one of them was duty-bound to dedicate their life to the healing of the planet.

Orla and Finn went to their viewing chamber and selected the crystal jewels necessary for accessing the memory of Earth's leaders. They began the ritual of joining their energy centres. Orla put on her sapphire ring and Finn held his ruby tightly in his hand. They sat on their conjoining seats and Orla closed her eyes, inhaling the molecules from the essential oils that opened her mind to accessing a deeper level of memory that remained protected. Finn closed his eyes as the essences wafted over his head, opening and merging their energy centres. Finn stroked the palm of his hand gently over the ruby, activating its ray, and directed the ray to completely embrace Orla with a field of ruby to protect her from interferences from Shadow and the negative memories stored in the many levels of man that she would need to penetrate in her search for their Crystal memory. Fortunately, Finn would see everything that she was viewing so that he could intercept any situation that was too harsh before it overpowered her.

Before selecting an individual, Orla's first task was to learn about the structure of leadership that had evolved over the years. Finn opened up a viewing portal in his mind so that Orla could see the truth of the world as it stood at the end of the 22nd century. Her eager gaze went to the Federations and their governing principals – the Generals, as they were called – a few men in each country controlling every aspect of life for the masses. As she looked closer she saw the familiar tentacles of Shadow sinking into their spines. She scanned closer, trying to see if their spirit guides were close to them, but they were nowhere to be seen; they had retreated far into the distance as the language of the spirit guides and that of Shadow were incongruent. It was evident that these Generals had no connection with or understanding of the needs of the planet; they were focusing on their own selfish needs, which were numerous.

She travelled further outside their offices of power to access their private dwellings and couldn't quite believe what she was seeing. This country, which at one point in its history had been self-sufficient with abundant, rich soil together with a balanced climate, could have supported the food requirement for many countries, but all that remained were dustbowls and shanty dwellings clustered together in vulnerable communities dotted over the depleted landscape. And then Orla came upon the domes.

Finn glanced over at Orla and saw that she was confused. "Unfortunately the few resources that were left could not be made available to everyone, so they had to contain their communities and only allow people inside who were useful or who served the useful. The domes protected the inmates from the pollution from outside and also protected them from the diminishing population left outside who were becoming increasingly dangerous and harder to control."

Orla saw a landscape blighted by disease, pollution and poverty everywhere except for the domes that sat like oases dotted across the country.

"How do the domes keep the rest of the people out?"

"The domes are equipped with the latest electronic devices which repel anyone who gets too close. The inhabitants of the domes are microchipped, allowing them to enter and leave," Finn explained.

"Microchipped?" questioned Orla.

"Yes, a microchip is inserted under the skin at the base of the neck."

Orla shuddered with the thoughts of invasive surgery just to keep people out of the domes. What Finn hadn't told her was that in the early days, the inhabitants had freer access to travel between the domes, but hijacking had taken place where people had been killed for their microchips. This had instigated the building of tunnels between the domes with high-security access points.

As Orla penetrated the domes further, she saw that, on the lower levels, the men of science had created all the technology to produce food; plants were grown by technology and chemicals, but were depleted in nutrition. No animals were reared for food; plants were genetically modified and protein was produced by very dubious chemical combinations. Calories yes, but no nutrition. To her dismay she also saw that even deeper in the recesses of the domes the men of science were creating a very lethal weapon, one that had not been produced before.

"Why are they doing this?" Orla asked. "I thought the union of Federations were in agreement on survival and there had been a peace treaty signed so that they could join forces and collaborate to find solutions."

"Ah! But the fear trigger still functioned in the minds of the leaders! The leaders responsible for defence still had war programming, and a peace treaty would not reverse that. The anticipation of invasion by an enemy was deeply engraved in their memories – the cycle of war throughout history had left its mark and they could not break the habit of manufacturing 'secret' weapons as an answer to their ingrained paranoia."

As Orla scanned more closely, she could see that they were experimenting with chemicals to develop superviruses as weapons. She sighed with disappointment, and then saw something else which was much more intriguing. On a much lower level – a level that only the highest level of security could access – was an installation that seemed to be manufacturing many parts of a vessel.

"Finn, could you give me more protection to go in deeper?"

Finn increased the ruby ray, allowing her to go into the main centre of that level where groups of scientists were working intently on their communication screens. As Finn accessed Orla's view of the screen, within a few moments he had deciphered the complicated coding. Not quite believing what he was seeing, he double checked the coding. He was not mistaken.

"Orla, they are working on a blueprint for the next phase of the Earth, but it is not going to take place on the Earth."

"Typical," Orla said, realising what they were doing, "rather than trying to re-establish the Earth's natural resources, the leaders had been seduced by scientists to believe that they could find another planet similar to Earth and replicate their science to establish a new community for humanity. Science has created yet another quick-fix illusion for a solution so tantalising that it hooked the leaders completely."

Orla and Finn looked at each other in quiet disbelief. They both knew that twenty years before, two new planets had been identified at the furthest point of Earth's solar system. It had been publicly established that they, like the other planets in the solar system, could not sustain life, and the general masses switched off from further enquiry. But the Generals continued with their secret investigations, believing that these planets could allow access to other solar systems. Research stations were established on these two planets from where space probes were launched seeking a cosmic destination that could sustain life. Of course, this took time, but science had been working overtime to develop this project as Earth's resources were diminishing fast. Orla and Finn also identified a complementary plan to mount a large fleet of space vehicles, which would take selected groups of people to the next destination. The vehicles were controlled by AI, and life would be cryogenically preserved, as it was expected that the journey would otherwise outlast most of the travellers' natural lifetimes.

The couple knew this was a hopeless project. Yes, there was another solar system close to Earth which held the promise of new life, but that solar system had already been visited by Crystalanders, and had undergone the necessary transformation, successfully embodying Crystal Wisdom. Their superior level of evolution rendered them invisible to the relatively primitive methods of man's science. The only solar systems that Earth could identify with would be those with parallel levels of degeneration.

Orla's focus went back to the selection process, and with the help of Finn's rapier-sharp mind and his ruby ray, went inside the largest dome and focused on the House of Laws. In this dome the leaders of the Federation resided. It appeared that there were several domes in this Federation, each dome controlling different aspects of society. Orla observed the men in positions of authority but couldn't find any women occupying these roles. They were all men, and as far as she could see, all with the tentacles of the Shadow deeply embedded in their tissues.

"Where are the women?"

"Orla, as your mother told you, you won't find any here. Women are not in any positions of authority, we have to just work with the men at this stage."

"Ridiculous!" Orla snapped.

She eventually identified a relatively young man. He was in his early 40s and looked unscathed by the blight of disease, evidence of which was on the faces and bodies of the other leaders. She wondered about this and looked closer and saw that his Crystal Guardian and spirit guide were very far from him but, encouragingly, were still visible. As she looked more closely at the guardians, she was able to determine the qualities that this man had been given at birth and that he was still engaged to that guardian by one connection in the lower back.

"This is very rare, to find someone with this connection," Finn interjected.

The man's connection often caused a niggling pain in his lower back because it was out of rhythm with the Shadow connections controlling the rest of his spine. But, apart from that, he was amazingly unscathed by the 22nd century. He had a jaundiced, unhealthy look about his skin, but apart from his sallow appearance he was a relatively healthy specimen, an indication that the Crystal memory was still in there somewhere. His name was John.

In addition to spirit guides, the Crystalanders had introduced to man Crystal Guardians, who guided an individual throughout their life, each one having a specific quality. One quality was always more prominent, and John's prominent quality was in fact a combination and interdependence of two which was ruled by one guardian – loyalty and incorruptibility. Finn was intrigued, as these qualities came mainly from Ruby Crystaland, but he could see this man was not accessing this particular guardian at all. John's understanding of these qualities came from the house of man-made laws, which was in fact the opposite to Crystal Wisdom. Laws were made from the mathematics of words and not from the intelligence of wisdom. It was a very one-sided and incredibly limited view of the world but, and here was the big 'but', it could be manipulated to suit the needs of the power leaders of the day.

Finn and Orla looked on this poor man who led most of his life in a state of unconsciousness because he was a product of many generations of programming that did not question authority. He accepted instructions automatically, even though some days he did think that they did not make sense, but when he began to question, the Shadow in him penetrated deeper, prompting fear, and so he backed off. He was also happy in the knowledge that everyone was doing the same thing, and hid behind the smoke screen of safety created by the common practice of the majority.

I wonder how these people will ever get back to accessing Crystal Wisdom?

Finn read Orla's thoughts and responded, "Once we have transformed a few then the transformation of others will happen quite quickly." Orla still looked unconvinced. She was looking at specimens of mankind that bore absolutely no marks of the natural world, of creation, and definitely no signs of Crystal Wisdom.

"By accessing the water supply of the domes, we can introduce the important catalysts that will start to change their memory, preparing them for change. This is the safest thing to do. It works on the cells of the physical body and Shadow isn't interested in the physical body. Shadow's focus is purely on the emotions of fear and anger and the concomitant hatred."

Orla nodded, understanding Finn's explanation but still finding it difficult to match what he was saying with the horrible pictures she was witnessing of Shadow.

"I don't think I will ever comprehend the way in which Shadow penetrates its hosts and holds them in a state of captivity for the rest of their lives."

Finn had already shown her how Shadow lurked around an individual, waiting for doubt to appear, usually around puberty. With that first inkling of doubt, Shadow sunk its black tentacles into the spine of its host, attaching itself one by one to each vertebrae, injecting fear into that individual. The more fear that individual experienced, the more he responded with anger and hatred, nourishing and perpetuating Shadow. As the cycle of doubt, fear, anger and hatred increased, the more Shadow was able to entirely encase its host in a web of the darkest hatred and bigotry.

Orla brought her attention back to John and asked Finn to help her to access John's memory.

"Orla, before you enter his memory you must remember why Shadow had been attracted to Earth. It will help you understand the dark side of John's memory."

Orla recalled that Shadow had been attracted by doubt in man after the Crystalanders had left Earth; that was the beginning, the doubt. Shadow knew that doubt was the precursor to suspicion and fear, and fear developed to anger and hatred, the putrid quality that coursed through Shadow, propelling it around the cosmos, gathering momentum. Its objective was universal domination, which had been its goal for so long that it did not know why, but it had a deep primal urge to survive through domination.

Finn gathered Orla's focus and supported it to allow her to penetrate John's dominant fear memory. Unfortunately, in order to access his potential, she had to wade through those fears and see what this poor human had experienced in his life, and more importantly, the fears held in his genetic memory.

His family had originally come from what was known as Europe, several centuries before, as economic refugees. Their poverty was indescribable: she saw them in rags, in freezing temperatures, outcasts in society. Their political and religious beliefs had made them outcasts, persecuted and enslaved. Their lives were so bitterly painful that they had had no alternative but to escape and leave the country of their birth by walking to a new country. Excluded by the same persecutions, they moved to the next country, but those persecutions followed them generation after generation. Time passed and they eventually had walked so far, they were confronted with the sea. There was nowhere else to walk so, with other economic and political refugees, they got on one of the many boats to travel to a newly discovered continent. Many refugees had gone to that country because it offered the promise of a fresh start without the prejudices of Europe.

John's ancestors had made successes of their lives in this new land but they retained the memory of persecution and privation of previous generations. Fear of poverty and exclusion was seared deeply into their memories, forcing them to be selfish and blinkered. And because each generation strove for more social acceptance, their inherited fear of judgement and persecution stopped them from questioning deeply, eventually forcing the Crystal memory to recede into obscurity.

Fortunately, John's Crystal memory was still accessible because his ancestors were some of the few who had tried to abide by crystal laws. But this had been the quality that had led to their being branded outcasts and different, and therefore judged as dangerous, which invariably led to punishment.

Orla was intrigued by this man's history and looked at him more closely. He was not one of the Generals of his Federation, but he was close enough to them and, more importantly, had all the makings of a just and strong leader.

"Finn, I need more protection to go deeper into his tribal fear memories. I am not seeing anything related to his aspiration to leadership in there – the walls are too thick for me to break through."

Orla had been informed on Crystaland that not only did the humans have their own memory and that of their genetic line, they also carried the memories of their tribes. Crystaland viewed the different communities of the Earth as tribes, as they each carried different cultural practices, some of them quite different, which they found interesting. They also carried the imprint of all the places that they had visited, so within their memories there was an homogenous blend of information like layers of an onion. The first layer was their personal memory, the second their genetic memory, the third was their tribal memory, followed by the memory of their Federation, and then that of the whole planet. Underneath all of this was the Crystal memory. But, if each of the layers was weighed down by fear, Crystal memory receded further and further into oblivion.

Finn battered down the walls that were protecting John's tribal memory with the ruby ray and as Orla entered, she could see why the walls were so strong. She saw that he had a strong imprint of the history of politicians and leaders of communities in his Federation who had dared to stand for equality, to end the incessant wars, to fight for true democracy, and with dismay she saw how they had been, one way or another, silenced. Orla was acquiring a deeper understanding of John. Within him was a fear mantra that played over and over again, unconsciously, in his memory: "If you stand up for what is right, for that which will benefit the planet, then you will be punished; that punishment is death and your family disgraced."

The couple followed John's daily movements; leaving for work and returning to his home at the end of a grey day. He had a lovely wife, Sheila, a homemaker who adored her two children, but Orla could see she was just a shadow of her potential. Orla knew that she could not focus on Sheila's development at this stage, but recognised that she was genetically a good match for John, added to which, with the birth of her two children, she had opened a small doorway to Crystal Wisdom. The emotion of love – even though it was a human version of love that Sheila felt towards her children and her husband – was the most important thing in her life. Admittedly it was quite insular, with her entire focus on her family, but the essence of love and sharing was definitely intact.

"It's interesting how mankind has misunderstood the word 'love', isn't it, Finn?"

Finn nodded in agreement and added: "The problem is, with the standardisation and downgrading of languages over the centuries, the word 'love' now embraces all aspects of intimacy, whereas ancient languages, a legacy of Crystaland, had several words to describe the different levels of relationships between people. Unfortunately, those ancient texts were eventually translated into simplified language and the complexity of the word 'love' lost. Major religions had translated the singular meaning of love to 'love everyone equally', which humans found very confusing. Their concept of love was put into limited categories: the love they have for children or parents, or the physical love they have with a partner. They could not comprehend translating that degree of intimacy to strangers in the street."

"How simple but how clever," Orla commented. "If you are telling people to be a good person, you must love everyone unconditionally with no qualification as to the levels of love, it pitches the bar too high for nearly everyone to achieve, leading them to believe that they are failures. These people need to understand that 'love' has many shades, and many meanings and interpretations."

When Orla was satisfied with John's pedigree, she turned her attention to the Generals to see what she would be up against with these power leaders. She scanned the leaders in the dome and noticed that the Chief General had quite an ugly personality, but more interestingly, noticed that he had an extra Shadow attachment to the first vertebrae of his neck.

She couldn't quite understand what this connection was: on the surface the attachment looked like a fine silver thread, unlike the normal thick jagged black attachments of Shadow. She asked Finn to help her determine where this came from. He knew but she needed to make this discovery herself, so he increased the ruby ray around her. She followed the fine silver thread and noticed that there were more; each one was attached to the Chief General of each Federation. She followed the path of the silver threads, which went across the seas, eventually congregating in one central place – a dome. This dome was different from the others that she had seen dotted over the landscapes. It was high in the mountains – far away from the main pollution – and was relatively smaller than the other domes, but it had a super strong energy shield that she needed to penetrate.

"Finn, I need help going through the energy shield of the dome."

He immediately increased the intensity of the ruby ray, which opened up a portal for Orla to enter the dome. As she went through the dome's outer skin, she could see that this place reflected all that was regarded as luxurious in the hyper materialistic modern world. All of Earth's precious metals and jewels were displayed in various forms. The people here were also different: there was an arrogance that she had not seen before, an arrogance that was not born of fear, but of certainty. Orla had finally discovered the true puppets of the Chief Generals, the small group of men who controlled the whole planet.

"But who or what is controlling them?" Orla wondered. "This level of selfishness and arrogance could only come from Shadow."

Finn urged her to look more closely, and found it interesting that Orla always took a little while to identify Shadow. Such was her purity of wisdom that it was not easy for her to identify this menacing presence. She eventually identified the largest collection of Shadow she had seen in one place. The tentacles were thicker, the shapes more ugly; here was the true controller of the planet. This small group of men called themselves the Elite, the direct puppets of Shadow, who were given trinkets and sparkly rewards in return for the planet – they had been bought very cheaply. The future of this beautiful planet was in the hands of a small group of corruption. They had no compassion or empathy; they were callous predators whose sole objective was to ensure that fear dominated every Federation of the world, each one having a direct connection to the Chief Generals of the Federation feeding them daily servings of fear-based manipulation and blackmail. Whenever there was any hesitation or questioning from the Chiefs, the Elite would transmit messages of pain and poverty into their memories, bringing to the fore their primitive fears, forcing them to be selfish and insular. Fear had corrupted their actions. If they did ever stray into the realms of thinking of the health of the planet, Shadow would bring forth so much fear that the Chiefs felt physical pain, followed by emotional chaos, believing that disaster would follow if they deviated from the path of fear. They were clinging to life with their fingertips, and whilst they thought they were leaders making important decisions, finding creative solutions to the endless problems of Earth, they weren't. In fact, they were just puppets of the Elite, with Shadow in the role of chief puppeteer.

To access the memories of the Elite, Orla had to go via the Generals. Finn ensured that the ruby ray and the sound of courage enfolded her on every level as she entered the dark caverns of the Chiefs' collective memory, and had to blink and swallow as she waded through the quagmire of repulsive images. Eventually she accessed a part of their memories which dealt with historical fact and not emotion.

This group were a handful of men who had been successfully recruited by Shadow to act as custodians of hatred. They had been engaged many centuries before and their bloodline secured that position. Shadow had recruited the original Elite from power leaders with unusually high levels of fear and anger, and with each generation they had become more and more greedy and bigoted. Their pay off from Shadow was access to, and manipulation of, immense wealth, and with that wealth came power. These families had acquired immense wealth and created formidable dynasties, including some of the old royal families of Europe.

The veil of enchantment that shrouded royalty's every move was torn down completely in the 21st century when the population realised that royalty was not deity; they were ordinary human beings, no different from anyone else. The spell had been broken and genuflection ceased. The final nail in the royal coffin came when royalty began to empathise with the wellbeing of ordinary people, and the health of the planet. The Elite were disgusted, and when resources began to diminish in the 21st century, the Elite initiated a major culling exercise and cut royalty adrift

With the Crystalanders gone, religion not relevant, and royalty downgraded, the Elite saw a wonderful opportunity to manipulate mankind even more. The desire for deity had not gone away, nor had their aspiration to be special – a strong motif in the memory of humans – and through the ever-increasing power of the media, the public were manipulated to shift their gaze from the redundant forms of deity onto celebrities and politicians to fill the gaping void. Without Crystal Wisdom to guide the new 'deity', they become susceptible to influence from the Elite and eventually became role models for the perpetuation of materialism. And when society had finally realised that these people were just ordinary, no different from anyone else, sharing the same flaws and impediments, material man found himself in a place of abandonment with no hope or aspiration, lost without true wisdom, a prime opportunity for Shadow to strengthen its grip.

The Elite eventually took control of the market forces. Playing with the fear of poverty, they manipulated trading so that there were cycles of boom and bust, causing regular waves of fear to be implanted into each generation, which led to more acquisitive and selfish behaviour in an attempt to guarantee financial security.

"This is all very primitive, Finn," Orla commented. "Didn't people realise that the cycles of boom and bust in different sectors of the community, which had in fact seemed to be happening for the whole of the millennia in different shades and forms, could only be the result of manipulation? It's as if people thought that these trends happened mysteriously." Orla shook her head in disbelief.

But the most hateful of fears that the Elite introduced was the primal territorial fear of that which is different. This fear spread like a disease across the landscape and embraced many characteristics: skin colour, religion, physical and emotional disfigurements, sexual persuasion and many, many minor details, ensuring that people stayed in the safety of their different groups, splitting and splintering the population, guaranteeing that mankind never became too powerful to form one main group against the Elite.

This tribal suspicion became more prevalent when large numbers of people formed communities, which happened with industrialisation. The more the population became institutionalised by the concrete cities, the more they lost the ability to use their Crystal intuition. And the major group to be targeted with suspicion was women.

These differences amongst people were the main triggers for most of the wars over the centuries. But when people are preoccupied with differences, they are not asking questions of authority and, as a bonus, the by-product of war is the manufacture of weapons, which made vast profits for the Elite. A win-win situation for them.

Their main fear-based desire was to control the outcome of the future. Those with the most wealth, the Elite, had originally come from the abject fear of poverty, and over thousands of years they developed a formula for making and retaining money. So whilst the majority of the population were just financially surviving, the Elite were amassing more and more wealth. In the world of Shadow and the Elite, money and power are interchangeable. The families of the Elite never made themselves known publicly; in fact, only one of them made contact with the Chief General of all the Federations. The Chief General visited the inner circle under the seductive cloak of secrecy, which pandered to his desire to be special. He felt he was at the pinnacle of power and was given to believe that he too would one day hold a position within the Elite. But the Chiefs were being cleverly manipulated – no one was ever recruited into that inner circle. The position within the Elite was hereditary to ensure that Shadow was securely in control of the planet for eternity – or so they thought.

Orla and Finn agreed that this had been a very simple but clever plan by Shadow. Instead of allowing those of privilege to find ways of helping the planet, they used all their abilities to fuel their own hedonistic lifestyles, to which, ironically, the average person also aspired. The impediment of man was that he needed to find validation from the material world rather than through his connection to the Crystal world of wisdom.

Orla took a deep intake of breath and began to see what she was up against. Not only did she have Shadow to deal with, she also had the added annoyance of the second-level interference from the Elite. But she was not deterred.

Her attention went back to John and his suitability for the role. She shared with Finn some interesting information she had discovered that helped them both understand what the challenges would be when it came to engaging further candidates.

Orla had realised that John's very tenuous attachment to his Crystal Guardian had contributed to his natural intelligence. Even by human standards, man had a very limited way of measuring intelligence, which could only ever identify ten per cent of their potential. Within that restricted range, John was in the top two per cent. He went to school earlier than his peers but when he got there he was disappointed and bored. Whilst the other boys were grappling with the very first level of reading, he could already read fluently. More importantly, unlike a lot of children of his generation, his grandparents were still alive and he had spent a lot of time with them before starting school. His grandfather, aware of the boy's unusually high intelligence, encouraged him to read the old books that he had secretly kept, depicting fantasy and possibility, even though books had been replaced decades before by texts only available via computer screens.

Once he began school, his teachers also became aware of his ability and allowed this bright little boy to choose his own texts. He wasn't impressed with what they offered in the ordinary e-library, the content of which was changed regularly in line with the politics of the day. Fortunately, one teacher identified something special in this boy that she couldn't quite understand but, going against all her training and dome indoctrination, took him to a room with a collection of old books that, for some inexplicable reason, had been archived rather than destroyed before being altered and uploaded onto the e-libraries. These were the old fairy stories that had peppered the legends of civilisations for centuries, beginning as oral traditions and then, as man acquired the ability to write, these morality tales were committed to paper. The oral tradition was one of the gifts from the Crystalanders and those powerful stories were eventually transcribed into text by the Elders. But, by the time the legends had been changed over the centuries to adapt to the changing cultures, they had been distorted and manipulated to objectify women and praise the hero who almost always was a warrior. However, the boy connected with tapestries of imagination woven into those stories, which awakened and nurtured his own creative thoughts.

Whenever his teacher allowed him into this special room, he would read voraciously. He was a fast reader and could consume a whole book in a very short period of time. He was never allowed to remove the books, so he stored the graphic images that he translated from the words into his memory, and during those endless boring lessons that he had to sit through, he would lose himself in his imaginal mind. He created an alternative reality for himself into which he escaped whenever he was bored. But he spent so much time in this special world that he began falling behind in his school work, to the consternation of his teachers and parents. They decided that he be taken from that school and put into a strict disciplinary school where there were definitely no books, just teachers and computers, and within a few years his private creative world had receded, but did not completely disappear. Orla could see that part of his mind was just sitting quietly, like a very obedient child, waiting to be called upon again. This was the access she needed to bring forward Crystal Wisdom.

When Orla looked at his later school years, she felt sad. This was a special boy, but his unique identity had been suppressed under the near military rule of his school. This was the school from where the leaders and their aides were chosen to rule every sector of society; but in fact their form of leadership was contingent upon their following Shadow, so their concept of leadership was deeply flawed. To add to the military flavour of this education, they segregated the genders so that they grew up having little communication skills with the opposite sex. The girls were prepared for housewifery and the men were prepared to be Shadow marionettes. A distinct two-tier system. Orla really did wonder at the natural intelligence of these people and realised the damage and the long-term consequences that can arise from the rewriting of history to support the aspirations of selfish leaders.

When Orla was on the Crystal worlds, she had been shown that in the early part of the 20th century, women had woken up to the idea that they possessed intelligence and they had more to offer than just a willing womb and bread-making hands. So, they rebelled, and it took almost a whole century for women to come out of the veiled corners of society and begin to take roles of importance and authority. But, unfortunately, they never got to the point of true equality, which made it easy to bring them back 'under the thumb' of the suppression of patriarchy within a few short generations.

Leaders decided that women were just a problem in the work place and should therefore be programmed, once more, to be supporters of men. So the gradual downgrading of women in industry began with their many and various psychometric assessments. They were gradually encouraged to believe that they did not have leadership qualities, but were more suited to supporting roles. Lauded for their ability to communicate with difficult people, they were directed to work in the emotionally strained world of middle management, rather than rising to the lofty towers of command. Their unique creative skills became hidden and overwhelmed by the constant strain of managing so many conflicting and changing policies meted out by failing leadership.

Eventually, the facts reflecting the achievements of strong women in history were reworked and another brand of history was written that focused on the importance of women being at home to support the men in their lives. Orla was amazed at how quickly the cycle of evolution had regressed, and how cleverly but craftily the leaders in charge of communication had reshaped history, rewriting women out of the boardrooms, placing them back in the kitchen. During the latter part of the 20th century, programmes of assessment and development were introduced to determine and develop the potential of leaders. But women did not respond as well as men to these programmes. The essence of the new wave of leadership was still based on the blueprint of war, which of course was incongruent to women, who were still connected at some level to Crystal Wisdom.

The most important role for mankind was to access Crystal Wisdom and communicate that wisdom across the planet. These power leaders had the opposite idea. The planet could be an abundant reflection of Crystal Wisdom, but the general belief of humankind had degenerated into a fear-based paucity mentality. Earth was more than capable of supporting and nurturing everyone, but it was impossible where there was an imbalance in priorities, where personal desires were placed above the needs of the planet.

Every generation repeated the same mistakes because people had lost the ability to enquire thoroughly and deeply. Opportunities were missed, lessons were not learnt and the bigger picture became lost in an ocean of fear.

Orla's attention went back to John, and she considered her next step. She knew that she had to contact him at a level far beyond his conscious mind, which meant accessing his dream world. That night, when he eventually fell asleep after taking his regular sleeping medication, she waited for his breathing to become deeper and more rhythmical. She then asked Finn to increase the intensity of the ruby ray, allowing her to move through the fog of his sleeping medication to access the part of his mind that was not controlled by Shadow.

"That was difficult! I had to navigate such dark stories before I got to his dream memories, and some weren't real, they were created by horrible entertainment that he had viewed. They really should have much stricter censorship on their media!" Orla exclaimed angrily.

When she eventually accessed his dream centre, she first streamed in a melody that matched his gifts, which would connect with him on a deeper level and lay the foundation of trust. This was the key to unlocking fear. She then projected herself into that space and introduced herself.

"I am going to take you on a journey, come with me and hold my hand." In his dream state he followed Orla obediently. She led him by the hand out of the dome and into the badlands, as they were called, where people lived in shanty towns. The shells of old vehicles or crates or whatever else offered a small vestige of personal space against the constant threat of danger and privation of the basic human needs. In his dream, John was disgusted at the appalling scenes of suffering and turned his head, trying to avoid the emotional reaction that was beginning to seep through to his unconscious. But before he could shut down completely, Orla superimposed the faces of his children and his wife onto the faces of the people in those dwellings. He was shocked and horrified and covered his eyes, trying to stop the images, but Orla was relentless. She urged him to go closer, and when he could almost touch them, he couldn't turn away. He tried to reach out and help them, but this was a dream and he couldn't. This only made him try harder, but he still couldn't reach them. He watched helpless at their life filled with suffering, but was unable to lift a finger to help. Orla led him from that ugly scene to yet another.

In the 22nd century the elderly were taken to a place where they waited for death. Not calm, relaxed places of comfort and repose, just a grouping station where old people in the various stages of disease and dying were corralled like animals, their needs unaddressed, as any intervention would have prolonged their lives. No one was interested in 'useless' humans and wouldn't waste resources on them. These old people were not from the badlands outside of the domes – those people didn't make it to old age – nor were they people who had held positions of authority. They were the people who serviced the needs of the dome-dwellers. Although they were not exposed to the full menu of pollution outside of the domes, their diet was of the poorest quality and they were exposed to dangerous chemicals on a daily basis. Little more than slaves, they had been sold on the concept that it was better to be in the domes, no matter how lowly the position, than to be outside. Unfortunately, their children, who held similar positions, didn't have the energy or resources to help, and so the elderly were grouped together until certain death took them, which of course didn't take long.

Orla watched John's reaction, and again distaste was written across his face.

How does he not see that these are human beings entitled to being treated with dignity? But what did dignity mean in the 22nd century? Orla reflected.

To make a stronger impact, she superimposed the face of his elderly mother onto one of the faces of the suffering aged. His mother was still alive and he was deeply attached to her. When he saw what looked like his mother living in shocking conditions, with very little food and in great pain as every joint in her body was swollen and deformed, he clasped his hand over his mouth to stifle the scream that was rising in his throat. The stinking mass that was now his mother filled him with revulsion, but when he recovered from the initial shock, he wanted to take her out of that desperate place to her lovely home where she lived – he couldn't understand how she could have got to this awful condition. Confusion raced through his dream state: reason, followed by anxiety, forced him out of his dream in a cold sweat – his heart thumping in his chest. He sat up, looked around urgently, scouring the room to identify the familiarity of his surroundings. He looked down at his wife and gently touched her face, just to make sure that she was safe. Grateful that he was definitely awake, John sank back into his pillows, breathed deeply and took stock of the dream. He was both fearful and disgusted by what he saw but decided to ignore it and just try to go back to sleep. *I really have to watch what I eat before going to bed.* And with that simple explanation, he took more of his sleeping medication and drifted back into his normal chemically induced state of bland sleep.

Orla knew that she had to be careful not to overdo the fear as this could prompt him to shut down completely. Equally, if she went too deeply too fast, Shadow would become suspicious. Shadow controlled the fear dial in each person, and if their natural responses peaked or troughed, its attention was alerted. Orla waited a few days and repeated the process. She went into his dream state, introduced herself again and took him on the same journey. He woke again in the same panic and began to wonder why he was having the same dream, but this time he remembered the beautiful young woman who had come to him in the dream with a reassuring face and confident demeanour.

A few days went by and Orla repeated the dream, but this time she addressed him differently. She used a different sound, unlike the original melody. This was a sound with which he could identify easily, and when he awoke he wasn't in a panic, just intrigued. Orla continued with this process five times over two weeks, and each time John woke his curiosity intensified. The pictures of his family appeared not to concern him as he became increasingly connected to Orla's sound, which was stimulating his tiny Crystal memory. The whole process was making him inquisitive, and each time he awoke from the dream he tried to recall the melody. On the last night, Orla projected into his dream a scene from Crystal Island, where he saw his family enjoying its open unpolluted countryside with its abundance of lush plant life, food, comfortable dwellings and joyful people. He loved this dream and wanted to stay there forever. He woke up in the dream's afterglow relishing an unfamiliar sense of comfort and calm, reflecting on how healthy and happy his children had looked.

When he pulled himself completely from the dream state and realised he was back in the world of the domes, he reflected on the reality of his own children. They looked nothing like the island children; they were not as robust, nor were they spontaneous. On the island the children played games that were loud and noisy, they ran freely, helped with the farming and enjoyed a healthy diet. John was quiet, his mind trying to make sense of what he had witnessed on the island compared with the reality of life under the domes.

Later that day he began humming what he thought was a random tune. When he came home from work, he was still humming the same tune unconsciously, and his wife asked him what it was he kept repeating as it was nothing with which she was familiar. She secretly wondered if the pressure of his job was becoming too much for him, as the role had been difficult from day one – he had inherited a multiplicity of problems with no apparent solutions.

His family had all been involved in politics and decision-making in some form or another, dating back to before the formation of the Federations. They had tried to bring equity to the population and embrace all members of the community but that was all in the past, in the present century, all that had been forgotten. There seemed to be so many natural catastrophes to address which had occurred after the many man-made catastrophes. His grandfather had tried to bring the focus back to a more humanitarian objective, but a new order had evolved, and his father finally accepted that for his family's survival, he had to go with the tide of change. He knew that he could be of more benefit by appearing to be part of the new order, rather than a dissonant voice on the outside. And he knew what that meant – he had seen so many of his colleagues disappear from public life slowly, followed by their families, never to be seen again. John's father finally conceded that the world he and his family inhabited was a dangerous place and that democracy was truly dead. He was in survival mode and he taught his son to be the same. John had attended a university known for grooming men for responsible positions, but all the history texts had been gradually altered, reframing the decisions, mistakes and catastrophes of previous political policies. All the texts had been doctored to reflect that the order of the domes was successful and therefore didn't require challenge. The general population was not being fed the truth about the past or the present, so the future was destined to be an illusion based on fear.

Diseases had grown into epidemics and the pharmaceutical industry had failed in its efforts to upgrade their armoury of chemicals. They had exhausted their repertoire of pharmaceuticals and were faced with frightening consequences of drug-resistant diseases and dangerous side effects of chemicals. However, this was the very excuse that the Elite needed to be able to exclude diseased people from the society of the domes without too much opposition.

And so the domes were created. The concept sold to the population was that people who were not infected with the many diseases lived in the domes so that they would ensure the survival of the species. When the pharmaceutical industry found the answer to the incurable diseases, then everyone would be allowed to live in the pollution-free domes. Most people believed this fairy story, clinging onto anything that whispered a means of survival. But this was not the whole truth. The domes were for those people who served the new order unquestioningly. People who had no original thought, no Crystal Wisdom and never challenged instructions from their superiors. Although on the surface it appeared that the leaders were in control and in authority, they were in fact just puppets of Shadow. Shadow controlled the Elite, the Elite controlled the Chief Generals, who in turn controlled the leaders of politics and industry – a very simple formula of controlled hierarchy. The education experience of the dome dwellers had fashioned them into being empty vessels with no understanding of their true creative process. Yes, they had all been instructed on how to implement a 'creative process', as was described in the curriculums of many business schools, but this was a juvenile version to limit the degree by which the individual could really access his personal and unique creativity. With all links to Crystal Wisdom severed, creativity was non-existent. Shadow had its tentacles well and truly secured in the memories of all the people in power, which precluded access to creative solutions. Consequently, the same mistakes were repeated over and over again.

John was one of the very few people in authority who understood the rationale behind the creation of the domes. The majority of people knew that life outside was harsh, dangerous and hazardous, but when the domes had been created there had been a near mutiny. The building of them had been carried out secretly, and governments in each Federation had determined who would go to the domes and who would remain outside. This was just another act of genocide, a part of man's memory that surfaced whenever his territory was under threat. The real plan was that those who lived outside the domes would eventually die, as everything had become polluted with poisons. The military had of course been involved, and each dome had installed an electric field around its perimeter to keep out the undesirables. Military crews would go out on sweeps periodically and exterminate people who came too close to the perimeter. Eventually, people gave up attempting to break into the domes and tried to establish makeshift lives in pockets of communities dotted across the blistering landscape.

From the outside, the surface of the domes was grey and matt, but from the inside it was completely different. They provided a bizarrely idyllic tableau of paradise. The sky was blue with fluffy clouds, hovering over a landscape of grass and plants that were definitely not real but were pretty good imitations. People had quickly adapted to this way of life and just as quickly forgot what it was like before the domes. In addition to the domes that housed the law makers, there were other categories of domes: the manufacturing domes that provided all the people and equipment to manufacture whatever was possible with depleted resources; medical domes that were dedicated to finding antidotes to ageing and disease, where scientists performed unspeakable tests on the old, deformed or just plain different in their quest to find solutions to their chemical impasse; and domes for the development of science and technology. Tunnels had two functions: they connected the domes, which meant the dome-dwellers didn't have to leave the dome world their entire lives, and their other function was to add an extra layer of security to keep out undesirables. There were smaller domes attached to the larger ones where the staff were kept. The staff were the people who kept the life of the domes ticking over; they did the menial work and were bred specifically for this purpose. The children of these workers went to different schools and learnt not to aspire to anything higher, conditioned to believe that they were lucky just to be in the domes, their future sealed for themselves and their descendants.

The long-term plan was to save a select proportion of the world's population. Scientists and economists had put their heads together to determine the size of the population Earth could support before a new planet was found. They understood that there was a limited amount of time before all resources ran out completely and they also knew that life under the domes was not healthy. And, erroneously, they had presumed that those people outside of the domes would die. A lot did, particularly the children and the old, but a hardy number adapted, mutated and survived. They had harnessed everything from their primal survival memory and were clinging onto life desperately. Shadow of course welcomed this and attached itself to these survivors. Shadow was attracted to fear and anger and was not fussy where it came from. In fact, in recent years, there was more fear and anger outside of the domes than inside, so Shadow rejoiced in the polarity that fear had created.

One of the many constant challenges the badlands survivors had was their health, which was very different from their dome-dwelling counterparts, who had been quarantined from the majority of infectious diseases and the toxic environment. The people outside of the domes had been exposed for many generations to the toxic environment that polluted their air, water and food, and their immune systems had become exhausted from the constant onslaught in the world that they had the misfortune to inhabit. Surprisingly their fertility was still strong enough to conceive, but their offspring, if they survived the pregnancy, bore the marks of those pollutants. It was a common sight to see children malformed, and often mothers didn't progress to full term with pregnancies, delivering underdeveloped stillborn foetuses. So, whilst the population had been severely depleted, as was the intention, there were still sufficient survivors to cause the dome-dwellers concern. Such was their survival instinct that they attempted, any way they could, to access the valuable resources held within the domes. When the tunnels had been created, they became increasingly resourceful in their attempts to break through the security, and the military had to take harsh measures to protect the tunnels. But this did not stop the survivors; it was almost written in their DNA – every generation was born with the burning desire to break through the walls of the domes to access what they perceived as the means to survive.

The landscape outside of the domes was shocking, and John was anaesthetised to its horrors, but after seeing Crystal Island in his dreams he couldn't help but make comparisons. The land where he lived was barren and the soil was dust. The waterways had all but dried up because the rain had stopped coming in useful cycles, oscillating between absolutely nothing for months or even years on end, and then the drought was briefly punctuated by such a violent deluge of rains and storms that it battered the already flattened soil without being absorbed, running off the land into the rivers that flowed into the seas. People outside of the domes were reduced to getting water from the few remaining boreholes that were still active. The dome-dwellers had created their own reservoirs, which captured as much of the rain as possible, limiting its availability to the badlands. There was just enough for the remaining people to survive if they managed their rationing. Before the domes were created, water was metered and charged at a high rate depending on its quality, making it impossible for the people in the lower levels of society to obtain as much as they really needed. But this had prepared them for life in the open planes and their bodies had adapted.

John was yet to discover that these very people who had been excluded from society and regarded as the lowest of the low were in fact stronger than the dome-dwellers (which would be important when it came to populating the world with genetically strong people), but that was definitely for the future.

The following night Orla entered his dream again, instructing him to contact her on Crystal Island and giving him the co-ordinates for the protected communication channel. He woke up the next morning puzzled, but he was unusually late for work and promptly put the dream out of his mind, getting ready for the day ahead that was packed full of pointless meetings. He stopped in his tracks: he actually had thought of the word "pointless" – *Where did that come from?* During the day, he was distracted by Orla's melody playing in his head over and over. He could not focus as he normally did at his meetings, and at one point his aide had asked if he was ill.

Later that evening, whilst sitting quietly in his study, he thought about the dreams, and considered his changing attitude. Suddenly he realised that he had been given communication co-ordinates. He had to find out what was going on and was too impatient to wait for morning. He stopped to hear if there was any sound in the house – it was quiet, his children and wife having gone to bed hours before. He got up and quickly walked across the room to lock the door, instinctively understanding the need for secrecy. He sat at his desk and clicked open his communications portal. As a senior Federation official he had the latest technology, which offered the highest level of security. The portal's screen looked like a large rectangular transparent glass screen – almost like a window pane perched on a desk. When the centre of the screen was touched a selection of icons appeared. Each icon was the main connection to the different Federations and within each of those icons, all the departments were accessed according to the user's level of security. As he looked at the screen the melody began to play in his memory, prompting the co-ordinates into his conscious mind. He keyed in the numbers in a state of disbelief, as he didn't quite understand how he was remembering this information.

Very quickly a new window appeared on the screen advising him that he had landed on Crystal Island. *Hmm*, he thought, *well, there is a place called Crystal Island, after all.* He was intrigued. Within a few seconds the screen opened up and Finn's face appeared. John was momentarily thrown off guard by Finn's physical presence. He could only see his head and shoulders, but that was enough to tell him that this man had immense strength and vitality. Finn quickly introduced himself and prepared the communication space for his wife. Orla came to the screen and John stared at her, momentarily disarmed by her beauty. In his dream she had appeared as a beautiful woman, but seeing her on the screen, he identified that she possessed more qualities that were too difficult for him to define. She greeted him warmly and explained that he had been chosen to help with a planetary problem.

He stared at her and asked sarcastically, "Which one are you referring to: the lack of precious metals, the lack of fossil fuels, the poor food supply or the ever-increasing incidences of disease?"

She responded. "It is the main one, which has caused all these problems."

He looked baffled.

"John, I have to tell you a story about the planet that is quite different from your understanding, and I will have to start at the beginning, so I ask you to be patient."

John nodded, indicating that he was listening.

"Far back in your family's history, many generations ago, your ancestors escaped persecution and came to the country that is now your Federation."

John was amazed at her knowledge, as his own information about his ancestors was a little sketchy. Researching one's family's origins was positively frowned on and the archives that once existed to facilitate this had been secreted in a place where only the Chief Generals could access via permission from the Elite.

"Your ancestors' lives were incredibly stressful, which has impacted on the genetic memory that you inherited, tainting your view of the world."

She paused, allowing him to digest this information, and he indicated for her to continue.

"The planet has the capabilities to regenerate itself, but man has taken that possibility out of the equation through fear." John looked bemused at the word 'fear', as he had never regarded himself as particularly fearful. Orla realised that she would have to show him what fear looked like in its many shades and guises.

"John, if you look at the screen, we are going to show you a summary of mankind's legacy to the planet." John watched intently as he was shown what the planet had looked like before man had begun to doubt and attract Shadow. He was shocked at the beauty of creation at work, with the full cooperation of man. He felt confused, his mind grappling with a new concept, and was experiencing a great deal of resistance. He wanted more information, so Orla showed him the story of man's rejection of the wisdom of creation and how the planet had fallen into a cycle of domination and destruction.

"Man has a predatory streak inherited from his original creators that was almost eradicated when the Crystalanders came to help the planet."

"The who?" John asked, baffled.

"The Crystalanders," Orla continued, "gave Earth many gifts which transformed the life of humans into the bountiful scenes that you see on the screen. But, unfortunately, man's primal predatory nature resurfaced after the Crystalanders left, is still present thousands of years later and the reason why the planet is in the dire condition it is today."

John sat back in his chair with his mouth slightly open in a half-formed question. For the first time he had seen the before and after pictures of Earth. He couldn't quite believe how wonderful it had looked, and had definitely decided he would rather have the 'before' version.

"Who else has been shown this?" John asked.

"You are the first person we have selected because you still have some of the very precious Crystal memory accessible in your genetic memory."

Confusion was etched across his face. Orla had purposely only given him a very brief description of Earth's history as he would need to absorb this information gradually. She could see that he was questioning his understanding and also her authenticity. She was offering him what appeared to be a magical and idyllic lifestyle and therefore too perfect to be believed. Such was his conditioning that the concepts of perfection, beauty and balance were very difficult to comprehend.

"What do you mean, my genetic memory?"

"It has been a long time since your scientists acknowledged that each generation passes on memory to the next generation and that has been the case since the beginning of time." Orla paused, waiting for his reaction.

"But, if that is the case, and I am still not believing one hundred per cent that it is, why did we stop acknowledging this? There must have been a very good reason."

"There is a good reason, John. The beauty and bounty of Crystal Island was in everyone's genetic memory at some point so that it continued without interruption, giving mankind the wisdom he needed to make the correct decisions for the planet. That memory was against the wishes of the leaders at the time as it challenged their concept of leadership."

Sensing his accelerating confusion, she paused again, allowing him time to digest the information. "John, this is just the beginning, you will need to get the full story gradually as it is too complex to understand in one sitting."

She could see that his memory was trying to sift through the images of many generations to find something that matched what she was telling him. Orla reflected on the human survival memory and thought how limiting its function was, but for the creators of this fear-based species it was perfect. The challenge would always be that the survival memory searched for that which was familiar in its information banks to determine whether a situation was safe. It would therefore always be difficult to accept new concepts and new experiences, as the creeping progression of fear over the centuries had branded 'new' as holding the potential for danger. This was also how Shadow triumphed. Man's memory had been manufactured to incorporate many fear-myths – except one, Shadow itself. Shadow had been omitted from their programming so that it remained invisible to man. Only those who had been initiated into Crystal Wisdom could see this dark menace that controlled humans, their memories unhindered by fear and therefore open to all the experiences of the material and immaterial world in all universes.

John had a multitude of questions, which Orla anticipated, and she reassured him that these would all be answered if he agreed to come to Crystal Island for a few days.

"Where is Crystal Island? Why haven't I come across this island before?" John asked.

"I assure you it exists, but it is protected by a special crystal energy field to protect it from your technology." Orla tried to reassure him, but she could see he was beginning to withdraw mentally from language about crystal energy fields. Orla reached into his mind before he disappeared completely and sang the melody, which caught his attention again, allowing her to claw back his focus.

She could tell his concentration was flagging so she decided to draw the session to a close. He was intrigued and wanted to ask more questions, but she knew it was futile trying to explain the qualities of Crystal Island – he had to experience it to fully understand.

"To enter the energy field of Crystal Island is a challenge for most humans and you are genetically relatively fit, but I will send you some natural remedies to help your body adapt to the change of atmosphere."

Orla scanned his body and could see he was deficient in the catalysts that enable the cells to function correctly, so not only were the systems of his body not firing on all cylinders, his brain was working at only five per cent of capacity. She was horrified to see that the majority of his brain cells were just shut down. "*What a waste,*" she shared with Finn. She quickly identified that he was taking chemicals to help him sleep, which made his brain chemistry completely unbalanced during the day. The heavy medication made his thought process foggy, which had a detrimental affect on his decision-making ability – an epidemic of the modern workplace. This chemical manipulation did not only affect John's generation, it had been happening for numerous generations before him.

Orla knew that he needed the remedies that her mother made, which were enhanced by the powers of crystal technology to increase the value of their therapeutic qualities.

"How on Earth will you get the remedy to me?" John asked incredulously.

"Do not worry, John. Finn has access to the domes, invisible to everyone, and he will deliver the remedy to you. It will be in the same bottle as your sleeping medication, so your wife won't be suspicious. You will need to take the remedy each night."

John was surprised that she knew that he was taking medication and exactly what it was. He faltered slightly, questioning his reasoning. He was being told what to do by a complete stranger who looked like a character from one of the old legends his grandfather had told him about, and her husband looked like a super human with hair colour not seen on the Earth for decades. He shook his head, but deep in his memory he connected with this woman and what she was saying. She asked him to trust her and reassured him that no harm would come to him or his family. He agreed, with more than a little scepticism.

The day came when he was to travel to the island. When Orla contacted him to confirm the arrangements, he enquired, somewhat innocently, if he needed any travel documents or ID. She reassured him that it would not be necessary. By now he was beginning to accept the bizarre as normal, which caused him to smile to himself. His mind had been playing the normal fear-based tricks, filling his imagination with thoughts of being kidnapped and held hostage, but he pushed those thoughts out of his mind, his curiosity more pressing than fear.

Orla and Finn walked to the Secret Garden together, and when they got to the oak tree, Orla hugged Finn, wishing him a good and safe journey. She was not able to go to the mainland easily because the pollution was too detrimental to her delicate hormonal balance. Finn on the other hand was strong and could repel the many levels of toxicity, both chemically and emotionally, that were present on the rest of the planet at that time. Finn entered the travelling vessel and programmed the destination, grateful that this vessel could transverse any realm of the universe with ease.

Orla had instructed John to go to a specific area that was in a secluded part of his dome where Finn would meet him and bring him to Crystal Island. In his mind he was expecting to be driven to a helicopter pad or to one of the many airborne vehicles for short journeys that were now common for travelling to different states or Federations. The roads between the domes were far too dangerous to travel, populated with roaming gangs of desperate people looking for a means to survive.

John went to the meeting place that was behind a large fake oak tree and waited for the noise of a vehicle. Instantly Finn appeared next to him, which made him jump back, startled. He hurriedly scanned the area, trying to make sense of Finn's sudden appearance as well as the enormity of his actual physical appearance. He had never seen anyone so big in his life. He wasn't just tall, he was broad and muscular and exuded an amazing strength, which was both alarming and compelling.

"This is just the beginning of many unimaginable experiences, John," Finn reassured him, leading him to the travelling vessel which was invisible to the human eye. Finn took John by the arm and guided him through what looked like an opening in an empty space. Inside the vessel, John's eyes were popping as he looked around, his breathing quickening with the sudden realisation that he had absolutely no understanding of where he was, where he was going or who this immense creature really was. Finn reassured him, gesturing for him to sit down. John stroked the smooth crystal surface of the seat and the walls and shook his head in disbelief. Finn programmed in the Crystal Island destination and sat back and observed his charge. Physically, he was a smallish man. He could see that there was potential for growth, but something had prevented his development, both physically and emotionally. He sighed and wondered how this experiment would work. Orla had a huge job on her hands, and he felt a surge of protection for his beautiful bride to whom he was completely and utterly devoted.

The vessel came to a quiet sharp descent and the doors opened. Finn led John out of the vessel, through the tree and into the garden. John stopped just outside of the entrance of the tree, looking behind him, then in front, and then stood still, amazed by what he was seeing. He began to experience a little discomfort as his eyes were not used to the bright natural sunlight or the noises of nature, as he took in the images of the lush garden, the sounds of the singing birds, the aromas of the plants and the many beautiful products of natural life that were merging together causing chaos amongst his senses. He looked down at the floor and was amazed at the green springy carpet of grass that was under his feet. Finn smiled at this man who was in awe and speechless, experiencing the wonders of nature for the very first time. Orla come towards them, and as she came closer, John stared at her with his mouth open. He had never seen anything quite so beautiful: a young woman, brimming with natural beauty. He was mesmerised by her as she walked towards him, smiling as he identified her immediately as the woman from his dreams. But those dreams had not prepared him for the reality of Orla.

She greeted him warmly, and when she spoke, he connected on a very deep level with the resonance of her voice, which relaxed the tension he was holding in his body.

"Let us walk slowly through the garden just to help you adjust to our environment," Orla suggested.

He felt as if he was in a trance and gladly followed the two magical people, his mind totally blank, overwhelmed by the experience of his surroundings. All his senses were being shocked into awakening and it was a little uncomfortable. One of the first things that he noticed was the sharpness of the colours of everything, from the beautiful blooms of the abundant rose bushes to the lush green leaves of the many trees. There was a clarity about this place that he had never before experienced.

Orla guided John to the well and offered him some water. He drank thirstily and then stopped, slowly savouring every drop in his mouth. Each drop of the water held an explosion of subtle sweetness which he immediately compared with the harsh water that came from the dome's reservoirs.

He placed the cup down and asked Orla if he could rest a while. The water was beginning to take effect on his body and he was succumbing to the heady scents of the floral banquet that accompanied him throughout the garden. He sat on the thick grass and ran his fingers through the rich spiky tufts and stroked each blade, trying to comprehend what he was seeing. Real grass was a thing of the past in his world. Yes, under the dome they had grass, but it was manufactured and only brought in for decoration. This grass, which sprung from such moist healthy soil, gave him an unusual feeling of comfort. Orla looked down on the confused man and knew that his experiences in the garden were beginning to open up the closed cavities of his memory. The heavy doors that had been closed to his Crystal Wisdom for so long were beginning to creak open, allowing him to access the images of nature handed down by his ancestors.

Orla quickly sensed that timing was now crucial. Shadow would soon notice that John was beginning to question. This was where Finn's strength was particularly required. Orla asked John to stand up so that Finn could adjust his energy centres. John didn't question. He was in a daze going through the motions of consciousness, but only as an observer. He had once taken a drug when he was younger with some friends and it had given him the same feeling, a lovely sensation of warmth and a sense that all is well with the world, but everything was in slow motion.

Finn was much taller than John and looked down onto the crown of the older man's head. His thin hair was sparse and his pale unhealthy skin peaked through the poor quality hair. Finn reflected on this as he knew the quality of hair was an indication of health. Here was a man who should have been at his physical peak – he was 45 but looked much older. His posture was bowed, not just because he lacked the physical strength to support his body, but Shadow inhabited his spine and caused it to curve.

With her ability to scan the interior of man's physical body as well as his mind, Orla looked through the tissues of John and saw the fine black tentacles wrapped around his vertebrae. She indicated to Finn that not all the vertebrae were attached, which was a blessing. Finn focused on the vertebrae at the base of his skull which were free, and placed his fingers on his neck. As soon as he did this the tissue surrounding the bones relaxed and Finn projected a laser-like ruby crystal ray into the junctions between each bone. Finn saw the crystal colours gradually begin to reappear in the bones: magenta, violet and blue, which cascaded down his spine, replicating that tricolour sequence into every cell of the vertebrae. This acted as a protective wall, and Shadow's tentacles, unused to the vibration from the colours, shrank away and gradually released their hold over the other vertebrae. Orla and Finn knew that the disconnection would not be permanent but would give them sufficient time to open John's eyes, and more importantly to access his Crystal Wisdom.

John was the first initiate, so his immersion into Crystal Wisdom would have to be conducted more slowly to avoid attracting the attention of Shadow. Once alerted by the shift in energy, Shadow would react defensively, which would make it difficult to access John's memory. When it came to initiating others, John's awakening would pave the way for them to open to it more easily.

With this first stage of initiation nearly over, the three walked through the gardens slowly, allowing John to absorb as much information as he could, even though he was not conscious of all that he was experiencing. His many observations included the confidence and ease with which the gardeners carried out the work with the plants. He was puzzled by their gentleness and respect for the plants. What he couldn't see yet, of course, was the plant spirits dancing around each plant communicating with the gardeners. Orla smiled inwardly, knowing that this was something for him to understand much later.

They walked to the palace, meeting people who greeted the young couple with great respect and happiness, and the royal coupled reciprocated that respect.

"Everyone seems to be in a very good mood. Is this perhaps a holiday?" John asked. Although under the domes most people did not get holidays, men in John's position were given several days a year to 'regroup' with their families and not go into work.

Orla's eyebrows shot up in surprise. "There are no holidays on the island, John, people's responsibilities are woven into their daily lives in a very comfortable and relaxed way. No one has a responsibility for which they are not naturally gifted and therefore they are passionate about their roles. If someone needs to take a rest, they rest."

John sighed in disbelief and wondered what drugs these people were taking. But he continued walking and observing, trying to be as open-minded as possible. One thing he couldn't argue with was the degree of good health reflected in all of the islanders.

They arrived at the palace and John stopped as he walked over the threshold of the front door. In the distance he could hear music and he stopped to listen. Orla indicated for him to move further into the room, where he saw Maeve playing her harp. He closed his eyes and allowed the music that was coming from this ancient instrument to enter his chest; he felt it deep in his solar plexus, allowing him to relax more of the tension that was still gripping his muscles. This was unfamiliar music, but it was resonating with the deep recesses of his memory, and the Crystal Wisdom hidden in that quiet place began to awaken and twinkle in the darkness. John stood transfixed, and when Maeve stopped playing, she turned to him and greeted him warmly. Again, he was shocked by her appearance He knew that she was Orla's mother, she was just like her, not just physically, but it was her radiance that beguiled him. It was as if he was hypnotised by her, and he didn't know why. Maeve smiled: she knew what was happening to him. The attraction he felt was genetic; she embraced all that it was to be a crystal-human, and his memory connected with the beauty and wonder that it conferred. She spoke, breaking the spell, and invited him to join them for a meal.

Maeve led the way to the dining room, and John observed his surroundings, noting with curiosity that everything in the building appeared to be made from natural products. When they had walked towards the palace, he had not seen the building until they were quite close, as it blended seamlessly with the environment. The walls were made of a special stone speckled with crystal that glistened in the sunshine, and inside the floors and walls were clad in beautiful wood and stone.

The dining room was large with a high ceiling, and the sunlight diffused through multicoloured glass windows. The table was laid with beautiful, fresh flowers, crisp linen and, most importantly, fresh food. *What a novelty, fresh vegetables that look like they are fresh*, John reflected. Orla suggested to John to drink plenty of water with his meal as his body needed to adjust to a completely different set of nutrients. John silently compared the vibrant food in front of him with his normal bland, processed meals that had very little taste or nutrition.

Maeve blessed the food and all the diners and invited them to eat. John began to sample the dish and was totally distracted by the riot of tastes that was erupting in his mouth. He was so distracted that he did not notice Patrick entering the room. As Patrick walked closer to the table, John stopped chewing his food and stared at this mountain of a man who bore a slight resemblance to Finn in his stature and colouring, with a confident bearing as was befitting a man of his position.

"John, this is my father, Patrick," Orla said, smiling.

John stood up and offered his hand to Patrick, who grasped the younger man's hand warmly with both his bear-like hands. John felt a shot of heat go up his right arm and almost pulled his hand away in shock. Patrick smiled, indicating for John to sit down, and joined them at the table.

"So, John, what do you think of Crystal Island so far?" Patrick asked.

John was thoughtful and did not really know how to respond to such an open question. Patrick repeated the question and the younger man looked slightly embarrassed at his confusion. Patrick had asked him what he had thought of Crystal Island, bearing in mind everyone in the domes had repeatedly said that such a place could not exist and was just a legend.

John shook his head. "I just don't understand how this island could be so beautiful while the rest of the world is in such a terrible state of degeneration. But having experienced the bounty of this island in just these few hours, it has given me hope." Inwardly John knew it would be an almost impossibly long and hard task to try to take all the qualities of Crystal Island and introduce them to the rest of the world. Given the enormity of the challenge, he was both intrigued and flattered by the fact that he had been chosen, but was a little baffled because he thought it would have been easier to aim for the Chief General. The royal family exchanged knowing glances.

Orla, reading his thoughts, responded, "You have been chosen because we identified in you the ability to reconnect with our principles. The future of the planet will be dependent on a leadership based on a specific type of wisdom, not on power. The current leaders of the Federations lack wisdom. Their brand of leadership focuses on power rather than wisdom." She was very careful not to use language that may cause him to question and resist, so reference to Crystal Wisdom was limited.

"What do you mean exactly by power?" John asked, slightly confused.

Orla could see that he was battling to keep on top of all this information and advised, "Tomorrow we will explain everything, but now you need to rest and sleep so that you can assimilate all that has passed today and be fresh for the day ahead."

Finn led the exhausted man to the guest bedchamber and wished him a good night, closing the door quietly behind him. John glanced around the room and walked over to the long window which overlooked the palace gardens. The late summer sun was just going down, and the fading golden light appeared to be touching the leaves of the trees in a gesture of farewell as it disappeared over the horizon, bathing the landscape in a deep orange glow. He gazed out of the window, intoxicated by the colours of nature that were prompting strong emotions within him that were both disturbing and enticing.

In his bathroom was a large bath, and before Finn had left the chamber, he had suggested John take a bath with the mixture of flower essences and salts from the sea. John had politely declined as he was a shower man and was concerned about the shortage of water. Finn reassured him that there was no shortage of water on the island and impressed on him firmly that bathing was going to happen.

Reluctantly, John filled the bath and added the ingredients as instructed and immersed himself slowly in the warm water. He leaned back on the cushioned headrest and inhaled the mixture of herbal essences and salts, which seemed to draw all the tension from every part of his body and dissolve them in the water. He gradually dozed off and his dreams were filled with the beautiful colours of this new and magical environment. As the water became cooler, he roused himself and, getting out of the bath, felt an overwhelming desire to sink into the comfortable bed waiting for him. He dried himself and fell into the bed, luxuriating in its comfort. Within minutes he fell into a deep sleep. That night he dreamt of Maeve playing her harp, singing in a language that he didn't understand, but it seemed to communicate to him on an unconscious level that gave him great comfort.

The following morning he woke at first light, feeling a little heady as if he had been drinking alcohol. His sleep had been so deep, which surprised him; for the last twenty years he had only been able to sleep with the help of barbiturates.

By his bed was a glass of water, which he drank thirstily, which had the immediate effect of making him more alert and fresh. He got out of bed and went straight to the window to see if the landscape was still the same. It wasn't, it was even more beautiful. The early morning light had brought a sharpness to the landscape that revealed an increased intensity of the colours. He looked at the bush that was growing up the side of the palace next to his window and saw the droplets of dew on each cupped leaf. He could not believe what he was seeing: as far as the eye could see were blue skies, green healthy grass and lush vegetation. His thoughts immediately went to his wife and children and he wished they could be here to share this experience with him.

He finished getting ready and made his way down to breakfast where Orla and Finn were waiting for him. They ate in silence as they knew John had no words; he was just experiencing life on Crystal Island. He was reflective as he ate his breakfast of wonderful bread and creamy cheese, and, as he munched into his food, tears suddenly began to roll down his face. He was startled at his reaction; his food stuck in his throat as he tried to stifle this obvious outpouring of emotion. Orla touched his hand gently and reassured him that it was a natural reaction. His senses were overwhelmed at the perfection of his environment, which gave him so much pleasure that he began to grieve for that which he had missed his whole life.

He eventually steadied himself and, deeply embarrassed, apologised for his lack of composure. Orla and Finn reassured him again that this really was normal, knowing that he would face further emotional turmoil in the next few days.

Realising that they had a very short period of time to conduct John's initial reprogramming, they had assured him that he would only need to come to the island for three days. This way his family would think he was on one of the many political trips he had to make as part of his job. He told his immediate staff members that he was undertaking some research for a new project, which they totally accepted. He was a loyal and hard worker who had never wasted time at work, so no one was suspicious or questioning.

They took him to the common viewing room and directed him to sit in front of the screen. They didn't have time to take him to all the different experiences on the island, but they knew they had to show him the possibilities that Crystal Wisdom offered. He settled into the chair, and Finn began projecting images onto the screen of healthy children playing in the woodlands and fields, their pets accompanying them, animals and children sharing equal authority and respect. John noticed how joyful and spontaneous the children were and struggled to identify with that experience. He thought maybe the holidays that he had shared with his family when he was young were similar, but the landscape he experienced on holiday could not match what he was seeing on the screen. The scene changed and more images of the landscape appeared: beautiful lush green grass and healthy trees laden with fruit. His eyes darted from one image to another, hungry for more of the beauty that he was witnessing for the very first time. The screen eventually became blank and Orla asked John if he could remember a time when the Earth was like this. He shook his head sadly.

And so the concept of nature's abundance began to be seeded in John's memory. This began to release some of the many blocks in his mind and he became more comfortable with what he was witnessing. As he relaxed, his concentration veered from the screen to Orla and Finn, as he was intrigued by their relationship. Yes, he and his wife loved each other, but he began to reflect on what he thought was 'love'. His wife was attractive, kind and ran his home beautifully, but he would not have thought of asking her advice about his work at the House of Laws. It was generally accepted that the men made the decisions that controlled the communities, and the women looked after their husbands and families. *A very good transaction*, he thought. But this concept of relationship, which had been in practice for generations, and was now deeply embedded in the memory of humans, was being challenged by the relationship he observed between the royal couple.

He could see that they were both extremely physically attractive and charismatic, but there was an equality between them that he didn't realise could exist between men and women. They both contributed to his process equally, neither one having authority or importance over the other, and he was amazed that Finn consulted with Orla on absolutely everything.

He wondered how this would work in his office. It was generally agreed that women were the supporting act, this is what they did best; and if women had roles of responsibility or leadership, who would be looking after the homes? History, he reassured himself, had shown that when women were in leadership roles they became tired, ill and confused, which had contributed to their being blamed for the falling birth rate. Stress experienced by women in the workplace had been identified as the culprit for their failing physiology and their resultant sterility. Reading his thoughts, Orla gave a wry smile – she was very much aware that the excuse for the failing birth rate had been manufactured in an attempt to give more weight to the argument against female leadership. So it was decreed that women would be better served by staying at home: this was their place, the supporters of the decision makers. The truth, which of course was not common knowledge, was that the environment had become hostile to the balanced production of both male and female reproductive hormones, and the subtle balance required for conception and pregnancy.

Orla was not surprised by John's conditioning. In the 20th century there had been a window of opportunity for gender-balanced responsibility. But, without role models to demonstrate the integration of female gifts into the male world, women mimicked men. Women became confused by the conflicting drives of their natural gifts, trying to compete with the constraints of the male power games of leadership.

Confusion, conflict and chaos hovered over male and female roles and had prompted a lot of hasty legislation related to gender. The Elite gradually infiltrated the minds of the Chief Generals, their first hosts, and sowed the seed of doubt about women, causing mistrust and suspicion, eventually relegating women to the fringes of industry.

Finn drew Orla's attention back to their protégé. She now had to access his memory and take him to a point where he was reminded of what he, and indeed humans, had once been. At this juncture he was still not ready to understand about the Crystalanders, as his comprehension was quite primitive and therefore limited. Orla's role was to ensure that he trusted them both enough to allow them to access his secret memories, where all his fears, shame and guilt resided.

At the end of the short session Finn took John back to his room to rest. He lay down on the bed and stared at the ceiling, reflecting on the different images he had witnessed. *How can this island be so beautiful? How can the inhabitants of the island look so healthy and joyful?* These images made him question the policies discussed and agreed upon in the House of Laws, which were based on the belief that the planet was hurtling towards a complete breakdown in society and there was nothing that could be done other than find a new planet to inhabit. Every ounce of resource was focused on finding a new planet that would sustain life, and the importance of selecting the necessary people to build the new world.

John had heard about Crystal Island years ago from his grandfather, and when he questioned its existence in later years had been told it was a mythical place, a thing of fairy stories and magic. He had been told the planet was never like that nor could it ever be – the island was a place of mythical perfection that nearly all cultures had woven into their verbal history. The concept of the island had been discounted by the men of science because they couldn't penetrate its protective forces. If they could not identify anything in the universe, then it didn't exist.

Finn and Orla went to their private viewing room to discuss what they had both discovered about their first candidate.

They had been able to access John's memory and discovered the detail of the hierarchy of his particular role. One of his main roles as second-in-command to the Chief General was being responsible for co-ordinating all of the departments but one of his biggest challenges was liaising with his counterparts in other Federations on the subject of providing sufficient energy for the dome-population. The job of finding sources of energy was a thankless task as all fossil fuels had been depleted a century before and no one had invested sufficient resources into establishing natural sustainable alternatives. The only form left was highly volatile and could only be used under very controlled conditions, which limited its use to a relative few – one of the reasons for the creation of the domes. The royal couple closed their eyes and concentrated so that they could jointly view the information. They saw that over the decades, indeed centuries, there had been an impediment of truth put into man that made him think that he was more powerful than nature. The couple frowned. Whenever they had to access the history of the planet they were confronted with the same cycle of events and its consequences: the Crystalanders had rescued man from the jaws of misery and bestowed wonderful gifts on the planet, but when Earth's inhabitants were left to their own devices they tumbled back into playing at 'deities and servants'. With that impediment came the inevitable separation within communities, which eventually extended further afield; separation triggered fear and fear attracted Shadow. Shadow translated that fear into hate in its hosts, and so the cycle of degeneration began and Crystal Wisdom receded.

"We need to begin thinking about the next people to initiate," Finn prompted.

Orla looked into John's memory and saw that he had six peers in the House of Laws who were responsible for the various divisions of society: finance, health, education, environment, security and energy. These were the key players who had to be persuaded to look at the world in a different way. Whilst these individuals were granted responsible positions because of their education and background, they were incapable of formulating creative solutions to the ever-increasing list of challenges the world was facing. It was impossible to use the part of their minds naturally designated for creative solutions because of the infiltration of fear from Shadow. The truth of creation is incongruent in the domain of Shadow.

Orla's natural instincts were to shake them roughly to induce a reality check and make them take responsibility for the world they had created, but it was useless. To them this was normal – suffering and challenge was part of the daily life of mankind, the default programming of Shadow.

*

John stood looking out of his bedroom window at the beauty in front of him and wondered what would happen next. He was a little apprehensive as, little by little, everything that he believed in was dissolving; his whole life was being brought into question, which was unsettling to say the least.

Finn knocked on John's door and entered the chamber, pausing for a while, observing John's confused demeanour.

"We need to go to the viewing chamber, John, as there is a lot to fit in to the time you are here. But the more you experience, the more you will feel comfortable with the many changes that are taking place within you," Finn urged, sensing John's natural inclination to delay the next stage.

They arrived at the viewing room to Orla spraying essences around the room in preparation. She smiled at John, trying to reassure him, as she could see the confusion in his mind distracting him, and invited him to sit in the viewing chair. Orla sprayed more essences specifically over his head, which relaxed him immediately. He wondered what these essences were as he had never experienced such a rapid feeling of elevation and relaxation. Only his sleeping medication worked that fast, but one of the unpleasant side effects of the medication was that, just at the moment before he went to sleep, he experienced an unpleasant feeling of confusion as his mind battled against the powerful chemicals working against the natural rhythms of his brain.

As he relaxed, Orla began speaking in her beautiful melodic style that had its own unique musicality.

"Close your eyes, John, and breathe deeply." Orla placed her hand on his solar plexus and regulated his breath, which was rhythmical and shallow. He was completely under her spell as she continued, "I want you to call upon your female genetic line, your ancestors." He followed her words and in his imaginal mind a queue of women appeared, going back as far as his inner eye could see. Orla asked him to visualise walking past these women and to observe their appearance, their body language, anything significant.

John was quite impressed at such a long line of ancestors. He had not realised there were so many. Dome society was not encouraged to remember anything of their relatives more than three generations back and they were forbidden to talk about times before this. That rule had been in place for so long that people just accepted that they were the product of just the last three generations, which, when he thought about it, was ridiculous. *Why do people accept these false truths?* he wondered, and then stopped, surprised by his question. *Where did that come from?*

His mother was still alive, only just, so the first woman to greet him was his grandmother. She was more bowed than he remembered with rounded shoulders and a very sad face. As he walked past her she lowered her eyes. He then met his great-grandmother, who was even more bowed and miserable and so it continued all the way along the line, the women becoming more and more bent and crooked and desperately sad. Orla urged him to go on as he was finding this whole experience unpleasant. *Why is she forcing me to go through such pain?* He reluctantly continued and found women who were poorly clothed, quite young but made old by hard work and childbearing, brought to their deathbed early. This was beyond miserable, but Orla forced him to continue.

"Please continue as you will eventually come upon a woman who is without fear." Almost immediately a statuesque women appeared who looked not dissimilar to Orla. She stood proud and tall with a smile that was filled with joy. Every part of her glowed with health, but John wondered what had happened to prevent this woman from passing on her health and happiness to her descendants.

"The line of women represent your memory handed down by your female ancestors. One of your ancestors carried the Crystaland memory and therefore embodied Crystal Wisdom. This was the critical reason why you were chosen by us to be the first pioneer," explained Orla.

John was perplexed and distracted by all this talk of Crystalanders, wisdom, pioneers, and asked impatiently, "But what does all this mean?"

Orla urged him not to question but just to experience what it was like to be in the presence of this woman in his memory. He relaxed again, focusing on this amazing woman, and he couldn't deny that he much preferred meeting with her than his other ancestors. The woman walked from the back of the long queue of ancestors and came to the front where he could see her in greater detail; she shone like a bright star, brimming with enthusiasm for life and beauty. Orla asked him to take a deep breath and then instructed him to open his eyes. She and Finn knew that John couldn't stay too long in the presence of Crystal Wisdom, otherwise Shadow would notice a distinct shift in his emotions and increase the level of fear in him.

He opened his eyes and blinked. He was confused and didn't know where to start with his questions, but blurted out randomly, "OK, what is the significance of all the crystal?"

Orla realised that he needed a lot of reassurance, as he was absorbing information on so many levels, which was tumbling around his conscious mind.

"There is a lot for you to learn about the checkered history of Earth, which is not the same as that which is being taught from the history texts in the schools. History has been changed, overwritten and doctored so many times that it bears no resemblance to the truth. On the last day of your visit we will give you a full explanation and you can decide for yourself what is the truth."

The small group went to the dining room and ate in silence. Maeve and Patrick knew that John needed to be on his own with Orla and Finn to increase his trust in them and feel secure. Once again John was amazed at the wonderful taste of such simple foods as vegetables and fruit. He hardly spoke, focusing all his attention on his food and on the delicately tasting water that accompanied every meal. After he finished eating he asked to be excused as he needed to be by himself. This was quite normal as small talk seemed to be inappropriate and John needed to get a lot of rest.

That night he dreamt of his ancestors, not the strong crystal woman, but all those bowed and bent mothers of each generation who had such miserable lives. He watched as they toiled, every day being told what to do, having no choice as to how many children they bore or when – men controlled every aspect of their lives.

When John woke the next morning, he took some time to make sense of his dream, but found it difficult to understand how his female ancestors had coped with such harsh lives. *Is this how my wife feels*? he wondered. She always appeared to be pleasant, but what was really going on underneath the surface? He had also been more disturbed by one of his ancestors who looked very different, so he deduced that she must have come from a very different country. She had refused to be submissive and had died fighting for her daughters not to be traded in marriage, but as a result of that display of courage her eyes and tongue were removed. She had been branded hysterical, was placed in a convent without the ability to speak or see, and her daughters traded in marriage in far-off lands. John admired the strength of the woman and was quietly pleased that he carried this memory, but equally was horrified at the way she and her daughters had been treated. He realised why the female descendants of this woman had learnt to be bowed and cowed. They daren't put their head above the parapet for fear of punishment.

He had his breakfast in his room, as Orla had realised he needed to spend some time on his own in quiet reflction before the next session, which would be particularly hard for him to confront. Finn brought him to the viewing room; there was no need for pleasantries or inane conversation. Orla and Finn knew exactly what he was experiencing. Once again Orla sprayed essences over his head, which he realised were not as sweet and soft as yesterday's – these were sharp and stimulating.

As before, Orla instructed him to relax and regulated his breathing by placing her hands on his solar plexus. She began speaking in her 'special voice', as he later referred to it, and he responded immediately. This time she instructed him to invite his male line of ancestors to appear. He saw the line of men appear and enthusiastically scanned it, observing first his grandfather – his father, like his mother, was still alive – great-grandfather and so on. The first thing he noticed was the ages they were when they died. His grandfather had been 75 when he died, which was a great age for dome-dwellers, but John noticed that he looked a lot older. Looking at his great-grandfather he could see he was quite young when he died, but also looked much older than his years. This continued for a few generations and then it changed; the men were older when they died. One thing was very clear though: all of them were angry and none of them were happy. He eventually came upon a man who stood more upright and looked a little stronger than the others. Finn asked him to look more closely at this man's environment. John saw what Finn and Orla had seen when they had looked into his memory. This was the man who stood up to injustice and decided to uproot his family and move continents in the hope of finding a new community which was more accepting and forgiving for future generations. John could see that the toil and strain that this caused him had resulted in his early death.

"John, this pioneering spirit is within you," Finn announced.

John stopped and reflected at the courage that it must have taken to walk away from all that was familiar into a totally unknown world. John resumed walking past the men, and the further he went, the more primitive and angrier the men looked. Some of them were quite ferocious, some of them had been decapitated or wounded in the many wars that must have gone on – each generation of male bore a wound gained from a battle. When he looked at them collectively, he realised that their battle scars were indicative of their main function in life – they were fodder for war, some of them extremely young men, cut down in their prime. Finn urged John to continue and asked him to find a man without fear. John thought this strange as these men must have been fearless if they were all going into battle.

"They didn't carry the fear that you would have associated with war; their greater fear was the awful repercussions if they disobeyed their commanders. Equally, men had been manipulated to be defined by their honour and valour in war situations, and courage was overwritten by rage for so many generations that it was an integral and important part of who they were," Finn explained.

John was perplexed but still continued down the line seeking that one man who feared absolutely nothing and embraced everything equally. His search seemed to be endless. Eventually a tall statuesque man appeared, beautiful in all ways, who shone with truth and integrity. John admired this man, and was inwardly delighted to have him in his genetic memory, but he also recognised the resemblance between this man and Finn. He enjoyed the feeling of deep strength he gained from this ancestor; it was a new sensation and he wanted to experience more.

The ancestor came to the head of the male line, and with that, the female line became more apparent with the fearless female at the head of the line. The male and female turned to each other, reached out and held hands, and in that moment John experienced a feeling similar to a surge of electricity passing through his body.

"The feeling you are experiencing, that you are finding so rewarding but unfamiliar, is courage. Not the courage that is prompted by rage; that is just mindless and a primitive response. Courage based on Crystal Wisdom is expressed when men and women stand side by side with nature, protecting the planet at all costs." Finn finished speaking and allowed John to fully embrace this new sensation before continuing.

Finn invited John to sit up and gave him a drink of water to help him assimilate all that he was experiencing. John had many questions this time. He could not believe he had had so many ancestors, nearly all of whom had been involved in mortal combat in wars. He was also grappling to understand what was making his female ancestors so bowed and cowed.

Orla and Finn knew that they needed to bring this whole story together and reassured him that tomorrow, on his last day, he would get the complete picture, the truth about the planet and himself. Orla knew, as with her awakening, the information would have to be given gradually in layers, and as each one was removed a new layer surfaced for examination.

"John needs to experience the Crystal Fortress, this will strengthen his Crystal knowledge," Finn suggested silently to Orla, knowing that his immersion in the beautiful waters near the palace that constantly bathed their coastline would enter the cells of his body and give a much-needed blast of catalysts, required to remove the many levels of blockages in his cells.

After changing into swimwear, John and Finn walked to the beach. John stared at the fine, clean sand devoid of any particles of oil and chemicals, which were commonplace on the coastline of his Federation. Finn invited him into the water to swim and John obeyed without question, anxious to experience the aquamarine clarity of the sea. The sea's abundant minerals provided a buoyancy that allowed him to completely surrender to the liberating sensations of freedom and expansion. He floated on his back and looked up at the sky, amazed yet again by the clarity of absolutely everything on the island.

"John, look out towards the horizon," Finn instructed.

Initially he just saw an expanse of sea and sky and gave Finn a puzzled look.

"Keep looking."

As he concentrated on the horizon he saw what looked like reflections of coloured light on the water. He blinked, thinking his eyes were playing tricks on him. Finn urged him to look more closely, knowing that John had developed sufficient awareness to be able to detect the Crystal Fortress. John traced the paths of coloured light around the horizon and saw that the lights were coming from huge crystal pillars that appeared to be growing from the sea and encircling the horizon. He stared in disbelief and almost lost his balance in the water.

"These crystals keep the quality of the minerals in the sea at a high level as well as providing an energy field that protects the natural integrity of the island and its inhabitants. This protective energy field has kept us invisible to the rest of the world and also protected us from the pollution," Finn explained.

John wondered if he had accidentally walked onto the set of an old film. He had heard stories of fantasy films popularised in the 20th century that had been colourful and fanciful, but had been deemed by the Federation of Generals as a dishonest representation of life, giving the misconception that the world was a magical, beautiful place.

He did wonder whether the combination of the food, water and the herb and flower essences was playing tricks on his mind, but there was no doubt – the seawater that was supporting him so well was very real. The two men swam back to the beach in silence. John was surprised by the number and diversity of the fish in the clear sea as well as the unusual pattern of their swimming formation. They did not travel in straight lines or in clusters but in lyrical patterns like synchronised swimmers responding to music.

"What causes the fish to swim in such beautiful patterns?" was John's first question. Finn looked at him, noticing that his eyes were beginning to change from the dull lifeless mud colour to a sparkling bright brown, and explained. "The fish are responding to the rhythm of the Earth; the Earth has its own unique melody." John's eyebrows began to shoot up as he thought about the concept of the planet having its own melody. *What a daft idea,* was his initial silent reaction, but there was a part of him that was intrigued because he knew how he had responded to Orla and Maeve's melodies.

They arrived back at the shore, and as they made their way to the palace, John was aware that there was a feeling running through his body that he had not felt for a very long time, if ever. It was a feeling of relaxation. His taut muscles were beginning to unravel at the deepest level and the circulation of his blood began to flow more freely, awakening muscle tissue that had been in spasm or had not worked properly for decades. The familiar feeling of tightness across his shoulders was easing and his hips were able to move freely with the movement of his legs. Finn observed the older man's relaxed gait and nodded in silent approval. As his blood moved more freely, it would allow the Crystal memory stored in the blood cells to circulate throughout his body, flooding his brain and spinal cord, and activating more memory.

The journey back to the palace detoured through the Secret Garden, and on entering the garden John stood still, once more amazed at the wealth of healthy, vibrant and lush plants, as if he was seeing the terrain for the very first time but with clearer vision. He knelt down and thrust his fingers in the rich, moist Earth, lifting a clump to his nose to inhale the sweet earthy aroma of healthy soil. He closed his eyes and breathed in deeply. As he did, he was aware of the sun on his face and the slight cooling breeze which lightly ruffled the leaves on the trees. He stood up and was distracted by a buzzing noise around his head, and instinctively flapped his hands. Finn held his hands back and instructed him to relax and observe what was happening before reacting.

Hesitating, John took a breath and allowed the large insect to buzz busily around his head. He looked closer and saw that this was a chubby, furry insect that he remembered from the secret books of his childhood. Yes, it was a bee and the bee was trying to make contact with him. As John relaxed the bee flew right in front of him and hovered, looking into his eyes. John was slightly concerned because he remembered that these insects could sting, but he was too mesmerised to do anything. The bee eventually turned and flew across the garden to a collection of hives into which bees busily deposited the valuable pollen which coated their bodies.

John was quite distracted now and went over to the hives, totally without fear as he was intrigued to discover more. As he drew closer he saw one of the gardeners removing some of the honey. He had no protective clothing on whatsoever and was gracefully working with the bees that allowed him into their space to take some of their precious honey. Finn studied John's interest in the honeymaking process, knowing that, as yet, John would not be able to understand the subtle exchanges that transpired between the gardeners and the bees. The gardeners always asked permission of the bees before taking their honey and only ever took what was offered and no more. As always, the gardener received the honey with gratitude and humility.

"This particular honey is highly prized as it contains the highest amounts of antibacterial properties ever to have been achieved on the Earth," Finn added.

The gardener offered John a taste of the honey, indicating that first he should smell the aroma. John was amazed by its multi-levels of fragrance. Yes, it was sweet, but not sickly sweet like the sweetening gels that were on offer in the domes, manufactured from chemicals. This was a heady sweetness with strong overtones of herb and floral aromas. Under the domes, there were decorative plants in the House of Laws which emitted fragrances, but they didn't come anywhere near to the rich aroma of the island's plants. He slowly licked the honey ladle proffered by the gardener and closed his eyes as if he was experiencing taste for the very first time. In fact he was; he had never tasted produce that was this close to nature in his life and it was a whole new and overwhelmingly wonderful experience, connecting and activating the pleasure part of his mind. Not wanting the experience to end, he held the honey in his mouth for as long as possible, allowing it to liquify in his mouth and dissolve slowly. He eventually opened his eyes when he had swallowed every last molecule and beamed with pleasure.

Orla had been waiting for their return in the Secret Garden and she giggled playfully. "John, I want you to begin to reflect on the wonders of nature. What you have seen on Crystal Island is a mere snapshot in time of what the whole planet can achieve with the correct leadership. Think what the Federations would look like if they allowed nature to dictate what happened, and if man was willing to awaken to and follow Crystal Wisdom, to be a willing assistant to nature."

John couldn't really absorb all this information. This island had been a total assault on his senses and also his emotional programming. Everything he had ever been taught was being challenged, and he felt a familiar feeling begin to rise inside his chest. He was angry. *Why had they done this to him*? He was quite happy in his ignorance living life day to day, and now these two meddlers had given him a completely different understanding of the world around him, and he was furious. *What do they want of me?* He clenched his fists and breathed deeply.

Finn went over to him, placing his strong hand in the centre of John's back, and the confused man immediately experienced a surge of reassurance rush through his body.

"Yes, the world that you inhabit is comfortable enough for you. You function at a reasonable level and your family has an adequate lifestyle as is befitting of a privileged dome-dweller. But is this really good enough? Do you really want your life as it is to be the legacy for your children, or do you want them to enjoy life as you have witnessed on Crystal Island?" Orla challenged.

Something inside him was wanting to say "yes" to the Crystal Island experience, but a far deeper feeling was surging through him. Orla could see the survival memory was kicking in.

Orla reminded him. "In your family's genetic memory there is the imprint of a man who wanted a better life for his children. He could have stayed in his country of origin and survived in a fashion, being regarded as a second-class citizen. But he didn't, he chose to take a leap into the dark, leaving behind everything that represented home and security, no matter how uncomfortable it might be, and seek a better life for the next generation. Your family were pioneers and deep down you are a pioneer too. Whilst it is uncomfortable for you at the moment, your children will have the opportunity of contributing to a healthier and happy planet."

John listened and, using his logical mind, was able to calm down and quieten the discomfort in his emotions, which was urging him to run in the opposite direction of all this information.

The idea of being a pioneer held a surprising attraction. The stories of pioneers had been suppressed in the history texts decades before – they gave people aspirations that were not conducive to the control of the masses, so they were removed. However, some of the stories told to him by his grandfather, a great storyteller, were of people who had been like superheroes, but John had thought that these were just fanciful stories of an old man. Little did he know that his grandfather had been telling him stories that had been handed down from father to son, from generation to generation. Stories such as these were forbidden in the texts that were taught from the information portals in the schools and colleges. The portals were merely blank screens where information appeared that could be doctored and formatted to suit the needs of the power leaders. His ancestors who had seen the decline in the world, particularly the suppression of information, had reverted to the ancient oral tradition of handing down stories of mankind through legend and fantasy to ensure that they were not lost. John thought of those stories, which his grandfather had told him in secret: *How magical and far-fetched,* he had thought at the time, and of course to a child they were highly entertaining, but now he was seeing proof of the reality of those legends.

He became silent again, and Orla could see he was processing a multi-dimensional raft of information that was rushing through his mind, questioning as he tried to put it all into some sort of understanding, but she was aware that for the time being he needed to have this level of doubt to keep Shadow engaged.

Finn suggested to John that they return to the dome as John needed to get back to his job before he was missed. John could not afford to spend extended periods of time from his position as it would raise suspicion, but having experienced the island he would now be able to communicate with the royal couple at any time via the special channel on his comms portal, which could not be accessed by man-made technology.

They made their way to the oak tree, and just before they entered the vessel, John turned to say goodbye to Orla and took a moment to absorb her wonderful appearance, wanting to commit it to memory and take it with him. This prompted him to think about his wife again. They had been married for fifteen years and she was devoted to him. However, he now saw that she, like most women of her circle, was lacklustre: it wasn't so much the dull eyes, thin hair and slight tinge of yellowing of the skin – they all had that – it was her whole disposition. She had no real enthusiasm for life. She was dutiful but not passionate. Even within their intimate life, she never refused him; he knew there was something missing but theirs was not an uncommon relationship. He cast his memory back over the conversations that he had had about girlfriends and marriage with his friends at school and later at diplomacy college. There was an inevitability about it all, with an unspoken understanding that if a man wanted to have a physical relationship with a girl she would submit. It was her duty after all. This worked well when he was a young man with hormones surging through his veins urging him to copulate at every opportunity, but as he got older, met his wife and married, he felt there was something missing between them, but he had no idea what that was. All these thoughts were tumbling around, and suddenly a major thought pierced through the chatter – if he changed, what would happen to her?

Orla, immediately intercepting his thoughts, replied, "You have been chosen because your wife is a matching candidate."

Orla had already scanned Sheila's memory and seen that her female genetic line contained pioneering women, fearless in the face of authority, which had often led to their punishment. In later generations, they had married men who supported their independence, and until the beginning of the 21st century they had been key players in the elevation of woman, but that was all before nature had withdrawn the crystal gifts from planet Earth as patriarchy made a revival in the face of Armageddon.

"You and your wife share similar genetic programming. When the time is right, she will be awakened to her Crystal memory, but unfortunately, the awakening for women will be more painful," Orla explained.

"Why more painful?" John enquired.

"The plight of women throughout history has been a constant cycle of suppression: suppression of intellect, suppression of morals, suppression of expression, but most importantly it was the suppression of creativity and all that it embraces. When a woman accesses her female creativity she accesses Crystal Wisdom, which can provide creative solutions to the many challenges that nature presents to mankind."

John, a little miffed, asked, "So what is the role of men?"

Orla, sensing his ego was a little dented, explained. "Women are better equipped to find creative solutions because of the delicate design of their hormonal network. This gives them direct and unique access to Crystal Wisdom because of their ability to create and nurture life. Without the conditioning of fear, a female should be able to look at any aspect of nature and identify where it needs help and what is the best form of that assistance. A woman is naturally programmed to intuit what is best for the planet. The planet is treated like one of her children. It is the role of men to work closely with women, formulating strategies so that the most effective route is taken to apply the necessary solutions. It is a matter of balance and a sharing of responsibilities. If a woman had to use her energy to intuit the needs of the planet as well as work out the detail of strategies, her intuition would not be so strong and she would not have sufficient energy to do the two jobs. Males and females are a powerful force if their abilities, their natural gifts and talents, can be harnessed and integrated."

John was finding this information all a little vexing. *Everyone knows that men make the best decisions and execute those decisions accurately.*

Orla realised that he really had no idea of how the planet had arrived at this point of chaos.

"John, you are right, for the last century men have been making all the decisions, but look at the condition of the planet as a result of that practice. Can you honestly look at Crystal Island, which is based on equality of the masculine and feminine gifts and talents and all the bounties that it offers, and not agree that we have a point?"

John had no argument to Orla's impeccable reasoning. He had witnessed the equality between men and women that resulted in the bountiful balanced lifestyle of the island.

To reinforce her point, Orla asked, "Think of the decision-making process that happens in the House of Laws."

His mind scanned the endless meetings that took place where the delegates would often discuss the same problem over and over again, unable to arrive at a new solution. In desperation they reverted to an old formula dressed in a different package. This was regarded as normal. For someone to suggest a solution to a problem the moment it occurred never happened. John's increasing clarity of thought and the effects of all that he had experienced on the island was allowing him to see through the familiar and identify the flaws.

Orla and Finn shared a thought as they watched John grapple with this concept. Yes, he had been shown the different qualities of men and women, but what he wouldn't be able to cope with, just yet, was the understanding that men and women had access to both feminine and masculine qualities but the expression of those qualities was different in each gender.

Finn and Orla, conscious of the time, prepared John for his journey back to life in the dome. Orla instructed John that when he was back, she would contact him via the comms portal and inform him of the next steps. She hugged him warmly before he left, which took him completely by surprise, as he turned, following Finn through the opening in the oak tree.

Finn and John entered the travelling vessel and sat down. Whilst Finn was punching in the codes, John shut his eyes and rested his head back on the cool, smooth wall of the vessel. He was trying to make sense of everything he had experienced.

Sensing John's apprehension, Finn said, "Over the coming weeks you will have a better grasp on what is happening to you, and with more information you will be able to help others."

John pondered on this interesting thought, his mind scanning his immediate colleagues, and could not think how any of them would be suitable.

Reading his thoughts, Finn said, "Orla will only choose people suitable for transformation, people like you, so it will not be so difficult."

What he hadn't been told, of course, was how Shadow would respond. But that was for another time; the first step was to help him understand that the way of life under the domes was not healthy for him, his family or the planet, but he had now been given a choice. Emotionally he was confused, but physically he felt better than he had felt for years. Finn observed the physical changes in him; they were subtle but they were changes, and he wondered if those changes would be noticeable to the people close to him.

They landed with the usually slight feeling of a sharp descent, and the door opened. Finn did not get out as they had landed in a place which was a little too public. The door opened silently and John walked through the door of the vessel into the world that was once very familiar to him, but now he was seeing the cracks and flaws in that world. He was not pleased to be back. Where were the colours, where were the trees and where were the happy people? The people he was seeing were not unhappy, they just looked bland, no expression on their faces, people going through the motions with no real understanding of what they were doing or why.

He made his way back to his house and hesitated before going through the front door. He took a moment to turn around and look at the view of the affluent street that was inhabited by the people who worked in the House of Laws. His thoughts briefly turned to the business of his day job, but his mind just couldn't cope with all the differences and comparisons. He shook his head, took in a deep breath, exhaled and went through the front door. His wife was in the kitchen, the usual place for her. She spent hours in this one room focused on making meals for the family. She was immaculately dressed, and his eyes swept over her as if he was examining her for the very first time. He noticed her thin body, her skin tinged with yellow. Her hair that had once been beautiful was a little thin, and she kept it in a short style to give the illusion that it was thicker and healthier. He felt pity for her. His mind skipped back to Crystal Island and he recalled the health and vigour of not just Orla, who was young, but also her mother, whose skin was fresh and beaming with health. Maeve's hair, although heavily interlaced with white strands, was thick, long and glossy. *When did women begin to look old before their time?* he thought. Sheila looked up from the work surface and smiled her usual neutral smile and stopped. She thought that the light was playing tricks and was about to ask him the normal perfunctory questions befitting a husband back from a few days' work away, but she hesitated. This was not the man who left three days ago. He saw her hesitation and was hoping that she would not enquire too much.

Sheila thought that she must be imagining things and dismissed any further thoughts of that nature as she had no confidence in her intuition, and just asked if he'd had a productive time. He said he had, and cleverly changed his posture and demeanour to project a tired and jaded business man, as was the norm. She was fooled for a while, but when she was preparing his meal, she kept wondering what was different about his eyes and his skin.

Before he left the island, Maeve had given him some envelopes with powders of plant extracts and advised him to take them every day for a month to help remove toxins from his body. His liver and kidneys were not functioning well, and she knew without help, his body would not cope with the changes that were taking place. She had been aware of the challenges of bringing someone from the mainland of the 22nd century to the island as their bodies carried crippling pollution that had been afflicting humans for a few centuries, evidenced by the feeble bodies that now walked the Earth.

He sat down to the food that she had prepared at the dining table. Being a dutiful wife, she had asked her mother to have the children on John's first night back. This was one of the many customs that she had been taught by her mother to demonstrate to her husband and society that she was a caring wife. One of the duties of the 22nd-century wife was to put her husband's needs before herself and those of their children. Their husbands had very important jobs, and to carry out those roles it appeared they needed mothering from the cradle to the coffin.

John looked at the food and realised his wife had put a lot of effort into the meal, but compared with the food on Crystal Island, this was beyond bland. He knew the raw ingredients were depleted and all their food was chemical-based and manufactured. The food science laboratories had become adept at creating functional foods that had more to do with "functional" than food. He toyed with his meal, and his wife, looking concerned, asked, "Would you prefer something else?"

He shook his head, trying to smile, and said that he was tired and would just have a shower and an early night. She looked puzzled, as they had a well-practised routine when he came back from a trip. They would have a meal, share a glass of alcohol together and retire to the marital bed for what passed for intimacy. She became suspicious that the trip had not been business at all but that another woman might have been involved. That thought must have reflected in her face because, surprisingly for him, he read it immediately and reassured her that he was just tired. His trip had been very long and intense and he just needed to sleep. She accepted his explanation and busied herself cleaning up after dinner.

He went to their bathroom and stood under the tepid shower. They were some of the privileged who had access to free-flowing water but the temperature was not predictable. A filtration system had been devised to recycle every single drop of water produced by man and industry, but that took a lot of energy, so only a few shared this benefit. He stood under the shower and lathered himself rigorously. He had only been back for a short while, but he still felt as if his body had been contaminated and he was feeling a little sick. The shower was timed so he knew he had to be quick. He finished his shower and remembered the powders Maeve had given him. He poured them straight into his mouth, and swilled them down with some water. He began to feel more calm and felt his body gradually drain away the toxins, which led him back to the bathroom to empty his bladder for what seemed to be an eternity. The colour of his urine was darker than usual, but he had seen this before. The first day on the island had prompted a similar outpouring from his bladder, and he knew it was his body trying to remove poisons. He went over to the bed and, sinking into it, was quickly engulfed in sleep. He remembered his wife coming to bed; she had put her arm over his body in a gesture of intimacy, which he chose to ignore. His sleep was full of dreams, not nightmares but memories of Crystal Island: the people, the plants, the food and the landscape, beautiful sunsets and birds that actually sang.

When he awoke the next morning, his wife was already awake and was looking at him with a concerned expression. *He is not the same. It's as if he is somewhere else,* she thought, trying to detect what was going on with him. She again tried to initiate intimacy, but he declined, jumping out of bed, disappearing into the safety of his study. She went to the kitchen, made him some coffee and brought it to him. He knew he needed to make contact with the island, he couldn't wait for Orla to contact him, and he had to do it before the children came back from his in-laws. He asked his wife for some privacy to make a confidential conference call. He smiled, reassuring her that once that call was over, he would spend the whole day with her and the children. She was comforted by this gesture and shut the door quietly behind her as she left.

John entered the co-ordinates of the island and immediately contacted Finn. He told Finn how he was feeling and expressed his concern that his wife had noticed a change in him, and was worried that other people would also notice sooner than was expected. Finn assured him that Orla was making the final selection, but she had to make sure that the men she chose had the right genetic programming that also matched their wives'.

Finn reminded him to take the powders regularly. It would help him retain his sharpness around others. Finn had discussed with John that when he returned to the dome he would have to act in his old way. At the time John had no idea what that would be like, but now that he had returned, he knew what was different. He had a spark about him, an awareness, that he didn't have before.

The children came home and walked through the door to greet their father. He beamed at them and gave them a big hug. They looked at each other, surprised – their father never beamed at them nor did he spontaneously hug them. Sheila looked at him again with a puzzled look on her face. He realised he would have to be more careful, and stood up, trying to regain his composure so that his children weren't confused. How could he tell them that he had seen a place that was alive, beautiful and flourishing, and in this place children were happy, lively and spontaneous? He wanted this for his children. *Let's be honest,* he thought, *I want it for myself.*

He spent the day in between two states: his old way of being distracted by work and the new way of wanting to engage with his family. So he made a point of being quiet when he was around them, but nonetheless spending more time with them than was normal. He wanted to observe his children and also his wife and the life that she had carved out for herself. He had been totally shocked by the authority that the women had on Crystal Island and the way in which they combined that authority with active motherhood. He had thought that the two were mutually exclusive. Orla had explained that raising children required the input of both parents, and the role of parenting should be shared equally. It was the duty of parents to do the very best for their children. Their teachers were part of that development but not the main influence. John wondered how this worked. Under the domes the children spent most of the day at school. There were a few holidays, but not many, so most of the time they were in school. He thought back to his school days again with sadness. He had hated school. He had hated the boredom and imprisonment that he felt going to the same place with other children, where so much fear dripped down the walls it was tangible. Punishment in schools was the excuse they needed to control the extended family. For, if a child did not conform, the parents and the whole family were excluded from the dome. This left the child with a great sense of responsibility, and therefore each child tried their hardest at school because no one wanted to live outside in the badlands.

CHAPTER THREE
CHOOSING THE NEXT SIX

Orla joined Finn in the viewing room and asked him how John had appeared when he had spoken with him. Finn conveyed what they both expected: John was awakening to a difference in himself and beginning to make comparisons.

"I think the scales are falling from his eyes," Finn concluded.

"I have finally identified the next six people," Orla announced. "While you were away, father and I managed to scrutinise their backgrounds and identified that they still have access to their Crystal Guardians. They were waiting in the background, waiting with their crystal gifts held securely away from Shadow. Thankfully, they all had pioneers in their genetic memory, each one with an ancestor who had lost his life in defense of the truth at some stage in their family's history."

Orla and Finn contacted John on his comms portal. He was always amazed that they knew just when he would be available. Orla began.

"We have made a decision on the next six. You already know them as they are on your level of seniority."

Finn read over the list of names. John knew each person and accepted them without question as he was rapidly trusting the integrity and intelligence of this couple.

"We will contact them and bring them to the island. Before they arrive, you will have to keep an eye on them discreetly and intercept should they look as if they will betray the secrecy of their dreams."

That night Orla and Finn began the same process that they used to contact John, but this time Orla went to all six men simultaneously. And so the story unfolded…

They had responded in exactly the same way as John, first just brushing it off as a bad dream, but later realising that there was something different about these dreams. They were disturbing, but at the same time compelling. Each one didn't share the content of their dreams because there was an innate feeling that the images they were seeing would not be understood. Orla knew that she had chosen well. She had detected Crystal memory in each one and knew that the images she was projecting into their dreams would begin to resonate in the dark recesses of their memory.

Within a short space of time Orla made contact with them on their comms portals. They recognised her immediately from their dreams and were equally mesmerised by her beauty and energy when they saw her on the screen. There was a feeling of trust immediately, and trust was not an emotion that they experienced often under the domes. Orla was conscious that she couldn't engage with them too much whilst they were all talking on the comms. When they came to the island they would be under the protection of the Crystal Fortress and the ruby ray, and when they returned to the dome, they would be able to contact each other via a protected comms portal. Orla explained to them that they all needed to make a journey to Crystal Island, the magical place they had all experienced in their dreams. She introduced them to Finn, informing them that he would meet them and bring them to the island. To her surprise there was very little resistance from them, and under her instructions they made arrangements to spend a few days away from their offices and families, which their colleagues and wives accepted without question.

Finn arrived in the dome and waited for the six. The men had been told to walk through what appeared to be an opening in a wall at the allocated meeting place, which they did, but as they walked through the opening they were greeted by Finn and were immediately taken aback by his physique. Finn beckoned them into the group travelling machine, a vessel that had been designed years ago in the hope that leaders would want to visit Crystal Island one day.

Finn quickly ushered them through the door, instructing them to sit down, which they did with absolute obedience and partial shock. The door closed the men looked at each other in silence, too awestruck to ask questions. To prepare them to adjust to the unique atmosphere of the island, Finn gave them the usual remedies to drink. The travelling vessel landed and Finn opened the door, leading them out into the garden. As each one stepped out he squinted his eyes and moved slowly and guardedly as his feet made contact with the springy grass. They looked around and one of them said, "Pinch me, is this another dream?" Finn smiled and announced to the group that they had truly arrived on Crystal Island. Finn gave them another remedy, washed down with a large beaker of island water, which had the effect of clearing their mind and increasing the blood supply to every part of the body. They followed Finn through the garden, predictably shocked at the beauty, clarity of colours and lush gardens, and amazed at the strong lithe bodies of the gardeners. As they walked out of the garden on their way to the palace, they observed the islanders involved in their daily lives and were surprised and puzzled at the enjoyment that beamed from the faces of these people. It was as if the six were trying to understand a language they had never heard before.

They eventually arrived at the palace, slightly breathless, unaccustomed to the pure air that challenged their lungs with each inhalation. Finn advised them to take shallower breaths until they adapted to the atmosphere. When their breathing became more regular, he took them into the main reception room to meet Orla and her parents. This was yet another overwhelming experience for them all. Orla came forward first and, whilst they had been mesmerised by her on the comms screen, nothing could have prepared them for the reality of Orla. She smiled and spoke. They immediately connected with the unique tones of her voice, which soothed their underlying tension. She then introduced them to Patrick and Maeve, and their reaction was predictably like John's: *How can these two people be old enough to have parented Orla? They look so strong and healthy, with minimal signs of ageing – by dome standards anyway.*

They were invited to sit at the table and were offered some herbal tea and beautiful lemon-flavoured brioche speckled with flecks of fresh rosemary, which was light, fragrant and melted in their mouths easily.

Patrick looked at each one in turn, assessing their characters, and considered. *There is no easy way of doing this, I will just have to jump in at the deep end.* He began to address them in a serious tone because he needed them to understand the importance of their future roles. He explained how the planet had not always been the way it was and that at one time Earth had enjoyed all the benefits they had seen on the island.

They looked at each other, and Mark, who was in the Education Department, asked, "If that is the case, why hasn't any of this appeared in the history texts?"

Patrick gave them a very quick summary of Earth's history, explaining that the wisdom of nature was very intelligent and that Crystal Island was based solely on the laws of nature, while purposely excluding any reference to Crystal Wisdom. *One step at a time.* They really found this hard to believe; everything about their programming had been focused on the supremacy of man and his ability to control the planet.

"I want you to compare the environment of the island with the environment of the mainland."

They had many objections, which Patrick answered easily. He kept drawing them back to the problems that they were facing. But what really made them listen to this man was the fact that he was privy to their high-security plan to search for a planet to establish a new colony. They were each wondering who these people were and quietly questioned whether they had been drugged with the remedies and cake. The royal family observed the doubts flickering across their minds.

Patrick continued. "There is a natural order of things. Nature doesn't play dice with the universe. There is one fundamental difference between the world of nature and the world of men that had been identified by some enlightened people in the 20th century, which of course was quickly suppressed: the world of nature has a desire to receive all the gifts that creation has to offer so that it can share, whereas man has the desire to receive for self alone.

"The desire and ability to share the gifts of creation is unique to man compared with all the kingdoms that inhabit Earth, and it is that very quality that gives man the ability to understand what is best for the planet so that everyone and everything on it prosper."

"What has happened to make it change so much?" asked Phillip.

Before responding, Patrick scanned Phillip and identified that this 45-year-old-man, who looked older than his years, had undergone military training in his youth. He had lost a lot of muscle tone from having a desk-bound job for the last fifteen years, but he still held military rigidity in his posture. "At some point in man's early history, he decided to take just that bit more for himself and, when this happened, it triggered an imbalance that caused the whole framework of nature to crumble. Man became fearful that there would not be enough of everything to go around, and when that fear appears, hierarchy shifts and the society of abundance is broken." Patrick could see that the group seemed to understand the concept but were grappling to determine what was missing in their world.

"There is still time to reverse the degeneration," Patrick announced.

This shocked them all, and the glimmer of trust established by Orla's voice was beginning to be challenged by fear as they grappled with the concept of abundance.

Orla stepped in. "Once there are sufficient people who are open to change, extra help will be provided. You just have to trust in the possibilities." She omitted to explain where that help would come from.

Realising that they had a lot to comprehend, Orla suggested that they retired to their chambers to rest for a short period. Finn took them, and as each pioneer walked into his light and airy room, he was acutely conscious of the serenity and fragrance of his accommodation. The furnishings were soft and the colours calming, cleverly mirroring the natural tones of the garden. They were instructed to bathe, which, typically, they were a little reluctant to do, but were quite excited to have the luxury of so much water.

After bathing they rested and slept for a while, their dreams full of scenes they had witnessed on the island.

Finn collected them for their evening meal with the family, and when they came down it was apparent that their reprogramming had begun: they looked healthier, not markedly, but subtle changes were taking place.

They ate in silence, partly because the food was so delicious and partly because they were in awe of the whole situation. When they had finished their meal Patrick explained to them what needed to be changed, because the hierarchy of leadership that existed in the Federations did not serve the planet or its people anymore.

"You are pioneers." Fear began to creep across their faces with mention of this word. "One person has come before you, one of your peers in fact, and he was chosen for his ability to understand these new concepts." The royal family were being extremely cautious about how they introduced John. The six men became a little threatened and competitive when they were told about the other man, but Patrick insisted that they listen to everything before they made a judgement. "There is a specific plan for the transformation of the planet and it has to be followed strictly."

The group was slightly bemused, and Patrick led them to the comms room to contact John. When his face came up on the screen the six recognised him immediately. All of them respected him both as a person and as the Chief General's second-in-command.

"John will meet with you when you return to the dome and will help with all your questions."

They returned to the dining room, and Maeve delivered a bombshell. "Your wives will have to be initiated into Crystal Wisdom, otherwise it will be too dangerous not to engage them and, more importantly, they need to understand the crucial role that women will play in the future of the planet."

This was another confusing statement. *What important part could women play other than supporting their husbands?* Maeve chuckled inwardly at the naivety of their thoughts. She would enjoy working with their wives and reawakening them to their full value.

Orla took up the story. "You haven't accessed the majority of your memory, only a very primitive part. The part that you now need to access is the most intelligent and will put you above others in the dome." She knew she was pandering to their vanity and, predictably, they responded positively, enticed by the promise of being more intelligent than everyone else in their environment.

Orla was neither concerned nor surprised by their response as she knew that after they had completed their crystal transformation, they would instantly know the correct action to take; self-glory would not be part of their leadership repertoire.

Finn looked at them with sympathy and thought how simple these humans were, so susceptible to vanity that the idea of being special for the sake of itself was so appealing to them. *How easy for Shadow to manipulate such transparent vanity*, he concluded.

The group ate their meal in silence and were later taken to their chambers, where they fell into a deep sleep with an awareness of a melody playing in the deep hidden parts of their memories.

The next morning, after yet another wonderful breakfast, Orla took them to the Secret Garden to meet the grove of trees. When they arrived, Orla watched the trees' protective response to these simple humans as she instructed them to lay on the grass, close their eyes and breathe deeply. After she sprayed fragrances over their bodies, cleansing them from the dark imprint of Shadow, the trees curved their branches to create a protective canopy over the group. Orla accessed their memories and carried out the same procedure as she had done with John, going through their families' memories to identify the ancestor who possessed no fear. It was a little more difficult than John's experience. He was such a quick student. After the process was complete she instructed them to open their eyes, and they gazed up to the canopy of branches and leaves, taking in every detail, finally beginning to appreciate the gifts that nature had to offer.

Orla instructed them all to sit up. "How do you feel?" she asked, wanting them to be as open as possible.

James was the first to respond. "I feel physically stronger and," he hesitated, grappling for the right words, "more content." He shrugged his shoulders as he could find no words to adequately describe how he felt. James was an economist and dealt with nothing more than statistics from morning till night, trying to make sense of the ever-present threat of diminishing resources, so it was a challenge for him to access and interpret his feelings. He had been a first-class mathematics student but had found the rigors of pure maths boring so he had transferred his skills to economics, which had proven to be more than challenging with the current problems facing the planet. No Federation was exempt; in the 22nd century the problem was very simple – all of Earth's resources were disappearing fast.

"Good. You will now return to your homes and receive further instructions via a special comms portal that John will explain, but you will need to come to the island again and bring your wives with you," Orla announced.

They shot her looks of alarm collectively, wondering how they were going to get their wives to leave their homes for more than a day. It was normal for wives of high-ranking officials to have the odd day away from the house for relaxation as a little bonus every once in a while, but more than a day would be difficult. *Who would run the homes?* they wondered.

"We will work with your wives remotely as we have done with you, and they only need to come for a day for their initiation."

She and Finn observed their responses. They had all deduced that their wives would have a lesser role, the normal role of support, and therefore wouldn't need to receive so much information.

"*Let them enjoy their illusion for a little while longer,*" Orla projected to Finn. He smiled in agreement. They were both aware that these men were more than a little apprehensive; they had no idea of what was happening or what their lives would look like in the future, but deep down inside there was another part of them urging them to participate fully.

Orla said goodbye as Finn led them to the travelling vessel. Once inside, Finn urged them to keep all communications very secure and Phillip volunteered to create a special communication portal exclusive to their group. Finn nodded with approval, knowing that Shadow would eventually pick up on this as the group became larger, but once it was created he would protect it with the ruby ray, which would keep Shadow at bay for sufficient time.

The short journey back to the dome was silent. The doors of the vessel opened on landing and the group quietly filed out, saying goodbye to Finn. Finn looked at each one as they left and could see that there had been a shift in them. The following day Phillip contacted them all with the new secure line and made contact with John. They agreed to say nothing on the comms portal but to meet in one of the many meeting rooms in the House of Laws. There was nothing suspicious about this as back-to-back meetings were standard daily operational procedures. Meeting John was a little surprising as they recognised he had a look about him that definitely did not come from living in the dome.

As they filed into the meeting room and the doors closed, they all started speaking at once, directing a tirade of questions at John.

He raised his hand. "I know you are all confused and have many questions. But we have to conduct our meetings in a very efficient way. We do not have the luxury of time. You have obviously seen a physical difference in me, and you too will begin to change, which will be assisted by the powders that Maeve gave you. You must therefore remember to try to conceal this change as your wives and children will notice first, and then your closest colleagues." They all recognised that, as he was speaking, he had dropped his guard and was demonstrating the full impact of his initiation on the island.

When John had booked the meeting room, he had asked that the comms in the room be switched off. For someone of John's seniority this was a normal request as he had a high level of security clearance. With the observation cameras switched off, he felt confident to drop his guard and show his new self. But the most notable attribute that he was demonstrating was his ability to lead. *Where did this come from?* Phillip wondered. He had known John professionally for a number of years and had not thought he was any more remarkable than the other second-in-commands.

"Of all the things we experienced on the island, the one thing I cannot comprehend at all is the role of women," Phillip said.

"I know it is a difficult concept to understand," John explained, "and when I first came back from the island with the idea of my wife as an equal partner rather than a support, I found it very difficult to imagine what that would be like. But then I recalled how the islanders treated each other, male and female, with equal respect, and I was particularly impressed with the degree of intimacy between husbands and wives. I think I would much prefer a relationship with my wife that was more intimate, which appears to demand equality." They contemplated his words and silently nodded in agreement. They had all witnessed at close quarters the intimacy between Orla and Finn and, indeed, Patrick and Maeve.

"But how on Earth can the women be of measurable use to our work?" Mark piped up. Being the academic, he really did not understand how these relatively uneducated women could contribute anything valid.

"To be honest, I don't know how this is going to work. When I was first contacted by Orla and Finn I was as blown away as you guys, but the more time I have spent with them and, more importantly, on the island, I am beginning to trust whatever they propose," John assured them.

John could tell that they were not completely convinced, but they were open, and not putting up too much resistance.

John continued with his explanation. "The mistake I made when I got home was that I was far too animated and happy, which made my wife suspicious and my children confused. So you will have to rein in any spontaneity that you feel until your wives have come to the island. More importantly – at work – *do not question!* Remember our jobs are to take instruction from our Generals and tell them what they want to hear!"

"Wow, that's harsh!" Frederic responded. Frederic was the youngest of the group and had achieved his position as a second-in-command relatively early not just because of his brilliance with fiscal planning, but throughout his career he had demonstrated total and unswerving loyalty to his superiors. He always had a great deal of enthusiasm for whatever task he was given, which was an unusual quality for dome-dwellers. But it was this quality that attracted the royal couple to him. Enthusiasm coupled with a natural intelligence indicated that his Crystal Wisdom was relatively close to the surface.

The rest of the group had all been taken aback by John's last sentence, and after Frederic had spoken, they looked at John for further clarification.

"I know it sounds harsh, but we have no time for sentiment. Think about how we conduct our business, think about our predecessors. Did anyone ever rock the boat, can you ever remember a time when someone challenged or even questioned the Generals?"

They all scanned their memories; they found nothing and eventually had to agree with him.

"We have been sleep-walking through our lives and now we are just waking up. We cannot slip back. So getting back to the illusion that you are going to be giving to the people around you – remember the key phrase is 'no spontaneity'.

Spontaneity was a word that was not part of their everyday vocabulary, but it was there in the buried corners of their memory, an important ingredient for accessing Crystal Wisdom. John had connected with Crystal Wisdom almost immediately on the island and he realised it wouldn't be long before the other six would do the same.

They pondered over his words for a while, and the full implications of spontaneity eventually began to dawn on them.

"Tomorrow evening Orla and Finn will start to contact your wives, so be prepared. They probably won't share the contents of the dream with you but if they do, just respond with the normal bland comments that you use when talking to your wives," John warned.

They all looked slightly concerned, but because they were so used to burying their heads in the sand on a daily basis, it wouldn't be difficult to respond in a disinterested way.

Back on the island, Orla and Finn were discussing the next step for approaching the wives.

"We will only have a day to work with the women, which will be enough, but we will need to prepare ourselves for this work, as the women will need to overcome a lot of negative programming about themselves. Once they connect with the Crystal memory they will transform quickly, more so than their husbands, but the biggest obstacle that they will have to overcome is their genetic programming of being a support act rather than leaders," Orla explained.

They both made their way to the viewing chamber to prepare to contact the wives. When they arrived at the chamber, Orla carefully scanned her various crystals from the different Crystal worlds. She ran her hand over each one and decided on the golden crystal ring which she slipped carefully on her finger, running her thumb over the engraved surface of the gem.

She walked over to the centre of the room, closed her eyes and connected with the Golden Crystal beings. Finn picked up his ruby and directed the ruby ray around Orla, protecting her physical and crystal body from any interference, ensuring a direct and clear connection.

When she made contact with the Golden Crystal beings, they asked what help she needed and she asked them to give her extra memory from the early Crystal Wisdom days, before the Golden Crystalanders had joined with humans, so that she could understand women's reproductive physiology. She needed to know how their primal physiology had been improved by the introduction of the Crystalanders genetic information. Finn watched as the space above Orla's head began to radiate a golden shower that fell down around her, encasing her in golden rays. Orla focused on the rays, which began to transmit images of those early women who were treated like third-class citizens. In the pecking order of their primitive hierarchy, the husbands ranked first, then came their sons, their wives and daughters ranking equal with their animals. Orla had seen some of this when she had visited the myths of Earth on her visit to the Crystal worlds but she had not been aware that women and animals shared the same lack of freedom. Both were treated as possessions that provided a service. She saw clearly the disconnection between their reproductive organs and their voices, so that nature in all its shades of beauty had been silenced.

She knew what to do. Finn had also seen those images and felt a combination of pity and frustration. Orla thanked her mentors and the golden ray subsided. Finn released the ruby ray and they both silently replaced their crystals in the glass cabinet that housed this precious jewellery.

CHAPTER FOUR
SEVEN BECOME FOURTEEN

The men woke the following morning and viewed their wives with confusion, not knowing what their future together held.

That night Orla visited the women in their dreams. This time, as well as showing them the normal images of healthy people, lush plant life and overall abundance, she showed them images of healthy women in roles of authority being respected and acknowledged. John's wife, Sheila, woke the next morning and commented that she'd had such an interesting dream, but she did not dare relay the images she had seen of strong women. It was generally accepted not to raise the subject of women in authority.

The following night the women were visited again by Orla, and so it continued for the next two nights. On the fourth night Orla appeared in the dream and sang the melody of the universe, which roused something inside Sheila that she didn't understand. She awoke the next morning and felt disquiet deep within her – she wasn't content anymore. She had spent her whole life, like her mother and grandmother before her, accepting what life doled out, believing that the best one could expect was to be secure and safe; she had now been awoken to another experience which was causing conflict in her emotions.

John could see that there was a shift in Sheila. She had become quiet and thoughtful. The willing, pleasing smile had disappeared, replaced with a frown. John checked in with the other six and they all reported back the same story. He contacted Orla and she advised him that the women were ready to come to the island.

John and his fellow pioneers told their wives that they had been allocated a special day away from the main domes as a treat. They were all excited as it was such an experience to get away from their mundane lives and it was always good to meet up with other women.

Their husbands informed them of the structure of the day, giving very little detail other than they would be met by someone who would guide them to the venue for the day. They told them that John would be taking them to the meeting place so that they could all travel in the same vehicle, as John had clearance to access vehicles. None of the women questioned any of the instructions as nothing seemed out of place.

John was a little worried about how they would respond to Finn, this giant of a man. Would they be scared? They arrived at the normal secluded part of the dome. John led them from the vehicle to the opening of the vessel, which of course did not look like a vessel, just an opening. They went through obediently and unquestioning, and all of them stopped abruptly when they saw Finn, eyes wide and mouths open. *Predictable*, thought Finn. John realised he had to talk fast.

"Finn is from another Federation, which is why he looks so different. You are all completely safe with him and his transportation vessel is the latest technology, which is not as yet common knowledge." Like all dutiful wives of the dome hierarchy they accepted this explanation without question and deferred authority totally to this giant red-headed man. Finn guided them into the vessel and they stared at the sheer crystal walls as they sat down silently and the door closed.

Finn was amazed that they didn't utter a word or ask a question. The vessel eventually landed with a gentle thud and the door slid open slowly. The women sat still, seeing the sun streaming in, waiting for instructions from Finn, of course. He guided them out into the Secret Garden. They stood still, shading their eyes from the unfamiliar brilliance of natural sunlight that had not been dulled by the cloud of pollution that enveloped their Federation. Gazing around the garden in awe of the beauty of it all, Sheila knelt down and touched the grass. *It is real*, she thought. *Impossible, this is surely trickery.*

Orla walked up to them and greeted them each by name. They stared at her in disbelief. This was the woman who had come to them in their dreams and here she was, but so much more impressive. Her luminous skin, her healthy hair and intensely beautiful eyes fascinated them as they silently compared themselves with her overwhelming natural beauty. Yes, they were well-groomed, but they were not as healthy and were definitely lacklustre in comparison.

Orla hugged each woman in turn, which they found confusing as no one practised this form of greeting in the domes. Finally she and Finn hugged and kissed each other in greeting, which shocked and embarrassed them even more. *Such an excessive display of emotion*, Sheila observed.

When they had finished their introductions, Maeve joined them in the garden and Orla introduced her mother to the women, which gave them yet another shock. Sheila whispered to Jude, "How can this woman be Orla's mother? She is far too healthy and beautiful to be old enough to have an adult child." Jude nodded in agreement, trying to understand what she was witnessing. She was the oldest of the group and unfortunately age hadn't been kind to her. She had married late because she was regarded by most professional men in the domes as an oddity. She was an only child who had spent a lot of time with her father, an eminent astrophysicist. She had always been intrigued by his work and would ask him endless questions about space and he would always make time to answer them. Her mother frowned on this as Jude showed absolutely no interest in housewifely duties, the important skills to secure a husband. Jude had a photographic memory and sailed through school, which put her on the well trodden path of many intelligent dome women: she became a teacher. Jude met Mathew in her late twenties. It didn't seem to bother him that she was not interested in home-making, he was more interested in her mind. They eventually married but by dome standards of health she was late to start a family. She did however become pregnant, but having the baby had nearly killed her. After that she never really bounced back to full health.

The women were for the first time seeing examples of good health that they couldn't quite understand, but within their confusion another emotion was stirring.

Maeve scanned the women both physically and emotionally. Physically they were a sorry sight: quite thin and pale, all of them having the tell-tale dark circles under their eyes, indicating their kidneys were battling to remove the pollutants from their bodies. The whites of their eyes were not a healthy blue-white but slightly tinged with yellow as their livers became increasingly overwhelmed by the unnatural diet and lifestyle of a typical dome-dweller. She wondered how these women were ever able to conceive, which prompted her to scan the memory of their reproductive organs and she was taken aback by what she found. Without exception, the ovaries of these women, the little vessels of creation, were totally depleted, and with each generation the ovaries were producing fewer and fewer eggs. She focused on the memories of their ovaries and discovered what had happened to cause this depletion. Several generations before, the failing overall health of women had plummeted and infertility became increasingly common. This had prompted a knee-jerk reaction from the medical profession, which decided that the best remedy would be to harvest a girl's eggs from her ovaries as soon as she reached puberty, and freeze them until she was required to have children. When that time came, she was given a cocktail of high doses of female hormones in an attempt to provide optimum conditions for the development of an embryo. Her eggs were fertilised in a laboratory and later implanted into her uterus.

Whilst this appeared to be an efficient protocol for a dying species, the quality of the genetic memory of those eggs was unknown. Maeve searched the ovaries to see if they had any spirit guides. She saw nothing. Each egg should have had a spirit guide, but there were no eggs in the ovaries. When the eggs were removed to be frozen, the spirit guides shook their heads with distaste, turned their backs on their hosts and departed the realm of human reproduction. So these women were not only barren by the time they reached adulthood, their frozen eggs were devoid of Crystal Wisdom. The genetic memory that was present was just the experiences of a man-made world.

Added to this was their ignorance of the preparation for crystal conception, which just contributed to humans reproducing physical representations of themselves but with no higher understanding of the possibilities of the world that they inhabited. With that thought, Maeve shook her head, realising the enormity of the work Orla and Finn had in front of them.

The group of women were taken to the palace, and along the journey each one was visibly stunned by the splendour of the natural environment. They were particularly interested to see the extreme health displayed by women and children. Their generation, and many generations before them, had never experienced that degree of health. In fact they thought that they were healthy – they had no real terms of reference about health other than their own experience and that of the last two generations.

They began to feel uncomfortable. By dome standards they were confident that they did an excellent job of making their husbands and children healthy and happy – that was their role – but they were now seeing that they were failing dismally. They silently began to question why they did not know how to produce healthy children like island children. *Amazing,* Finn observed. *Orla was right, they are beginning to change very quickly. Already they are questioning.*

By the time they reached the palace they were in a state of stunned silence. Everything they were seeing was completely alien to their understanding. Orla and Maeve took them into the dining room for some refreshments, which prompted another shock to their systems. They stared at the food on the table, the colours, the textures, and more importantly, experienced the wonderful smells. They self-consciously sat down, almost too frightened to put the glorious-looking food in their mouths. Maeve urged them to start eating. They tentatively picked up their forks and began putting small amounts of food in their mouths, savouring each and every morsel.

"How do your cooks make such wonderful food?" Sheila questioned, already wondering how she could replicate this meal.

"All the food that is consumed on the island is grown here in natural conditions so the basic ingredients are full of flavour," Maeve explained.

"Is this an island?" interrupted Sheila.

"Yes, Sheila, this is. You will see later the amazing sea that surrounds our special island." Maeve left out the part about the Crystal Fortress. "The soil on the island is rich, the water full of minerals and that combination, together with the sun that shines 330 days a year, produces high-quality food."

"Why can't this be done on the mainland?" enquired Cynthia. Cynthia was another anomaly to the dome world. For the last four generations, the men in her family were physicians and Cynthia spent hours with her grandfather, who lived with them, asking him many questions about biology and the treatment of disease. He never lost patience with her endless questions but thought it was a shame that she had been born a girl and couldn't be a physician. Her grandfather had given her the title of Mrs Many Questions and her mother had warned her never to discuss with anyone what she had learned from him. She married Joshua, who loved her deeply, and to secure that love, suppressed her thirst for knowledge.

Orla explained to them very briefly how the Earth had begun its cycle of degeneration that had resulted in the dome-dwellers of today.

All the women looked shocked. They hadn't realised that the future of the planet was in jeopardy. Their husbands had never mentioned anything to them, nor had the media covered such topics.

"Can this awful downward spiral be reversed?" Cynthia asked.

Orla considered Cynthia. *Yes, this is a women who is forming many questions in her mind already; the transformation is taking place faster in her.* She knew that Sheila would learn fast, but Cynthia's response was a bonus. She knew the other women would take a while to find the confidence to question, but in time they would all have sufficient strength and authority to question and challenge.

Maeve and Orla smiled. "Yes, but it is going to take a complete change in leadership." Orla was careful with her words. What she really wanted to say was that it would need a revolution, but that word had frightening connotations for this generation of women. The keepers of the history texts had ensured that they had rewritten every act of revolution that occurred on the Earth and reframed it in a negative shroud, with the emphasis on the severe punishment meted out to revolutionaries and their families.

She added the final statement. "And the women are going to be the foundation upon which this change will take place." Orla paused, waiting for their reaction. Sheila looked both scared and puzzled, the other women just froze. Here was a language that they didn't understand: women in positions of influence.

Orla didn't push the issue, she was just sewing seeds for the time being, and the women nudged any questions away from their thoughts into parts of their memories labelled 'beyond my female intelligence'. They finished their meal and the two royal women took the group to their bedchambers where they were greeted with the luxurious baths that had just been drawn for them, enhanced by the aroma from the rich floral waters. Orla watched their faces as each one stood staring in amazement, not just at the sight of a full bath of water, but also the fragrance that was seeping from the bath, forming a cloud that enveloped them. Orla had also arranged for a specific blend of plant and mineral remedies to be added to support their hormones and circulation. She and Maeve had agreed that these women were emotionally switched off, which meant that their bodies were not working efficiently. They all lacked iron in their blood, which contributed to their lack of energy – a condition that plagued all women in and out of the domes. Iron was a key mineral that Shadow was attracted to, not just because of the strength that it gave to Shadow, but iron naturally carried the message of Crystal Wisdom around the human body, replenishing the memory in all the cells so, of course, it had to be removed.

Orla and Maeve suggested to the women that they rest after their baths to replenish their energy in preparation for the events of the day. They had all collapsed onto the soft beds and slept for a short while, their dreams peppered with scenes of healthy young children happily playing together in the warm sunshine. They all woke feeling surprisingly refreshed but with a keen desire to know more.

The women were collected from their chambers and taken to one of the viewing rooms where Orla and Maeve were waiting.

Orla, inviting the women into the room, said, "Please take a seat and make yourselves comfortable." When the group were settled, she continued. "You asked about the possibility of the reversal of the degeneration and, yes, of course, it is possible to reverse the process to restore the planet to being abundant and healthy but, as I said earlier, there has to be a change in leadership. Your husbands have been chosen because they have the ability to change: it is in their genetic makeup. You also have that ability – even more so, in fact, as you have had children."

Maeve knew that the fact that they had children indicated that they had a relatively recent small connection to Crystal Wisdom. So many women were unable to carry a child full term, even with IVF, which was a sign that their bodies were disconnected from their Crystal memory. No amount of man-science could replace that vital factor, no matter how hard they tried. The connection to Crystal Wisdom could be identified by the level of health of an individual, and when Maeve and Orla had scanned the planet seeking suitable female candidates, they had seen that the women in front of them were the best representation of female health that was available in these dark days. When the Crystalanders had given the gifts to the planet, every woman carried that special connection whether they had children or not, but when the crystal gifts receded, so did that connection. However, every time a women went through the process of creating a new life, she unconsciously reconnected with her crystal spirit guide, no matter how tenuously, which connected her to Crystal Wisdom.

Another important factor which protected women from succumbing completely to Shadow was that female hormones prevented Shadow from hooking into their memories. Shadow was mainly attracted to testosterone. Whilst women did produce a small amount of testosterone, it was obscured from Shadow by their dominant female hormones. Shadow fed on the anger that was produced when testosterone was accidently triggered by fear.

Orla was also aware of the benefit of working with the wives of the seven men as they would influence their husbands both consciously and unconsciously. As the information in the memory field around their bodies changed, projecting different terms of reference, the women would be influencing their husbands' thoughts and decisions. If she had worked just with the men she would have had to work too deeply too fast, which could have alerted Shadow. Yes, Shadow would be alerted at some point, and she knew what that would involve, but she had to make sure that there were sufficient numbers of people who had been transformed before that happened.

When they had one of their many discussions about the future, Orla had asked Finn how they were going to deal with Shadow when it started to realise that some of its hosts were slipping away. Finn had told her that when he was on the Ruby Crystal world he had received instructions to remove the motif of hatred from the memory of men, which automatically disengaged Shadow: "When this happens I will have to make sure that the ruby crystal ray is ramped up in advance to ensure that there is adequate protection. But I have no concerns."

"Ok, so what is the process for disengaging Shadow?" Orla asked.

"What we need to do initially is to go into their human genetic memory to access and bring forth memories of their ancestors who held no fear, as we did with John. By bringing them to the forefront, the fear memory recedes, although still present in the background. This allows Shadow to be tricked into believing that it is still connected. The next stage will be to overlay their memories with images that represent the perfection of Crystal Wisdom, at the same time still allowing access to the memory of the events of the planet's history. It is important that they retain the full knowledge of Earth's story so that the same mistakes are never repeated.

"When sufficient numbers have gone through this process, the information being fed into Earth's collective memory will change and influence leaders to change, but still Shadow will not know. Shadow is very two dimensional; as long as it is connected in some way to its hosts, then it is satisfied.

"Ultimately, it's my job to remove the memory of hatred and greed completely from the global and individual memory. Once this happens there will be a confrontation with Shadow, but I will be helped by the Ruby Crystalanders."

Orla looked a little puzzled.

"Once there are sufficient numbers of people, the memory field of the planet will change, which will allow me to contact the Ruby Crystalanders, who will send more ruby rays through me, my brothers and other members of my family."

Orla had been told by the Diamond Elders that one day the Golden Crystalanders would return to the planet and help with the speedy recovery of Earth, but she hadn't realised that Finn and his clan would be working directly with the Crystal worlds. She was relieved, comforted in the knowledge that Finn would be the best support available when the time came to confront Shadow.

Maeve and Orla asked the women to follow them and took them to a room covered with a thick green woollen carpet with large sumptuous cushions scattered across the floor. Maeve asked them to lie on the floor in a circle and arrange the cushions so that they could completely relax their bodies. She sprayed the flower and herb essences over them and, as the molecules absorbed quickly into their thirsty skin, opening and releasing the therapeutic information stored in the plants, the women relaxed completely and trusted enough to breathe deeply. They, like their husbands, had battled to breathe when they first arrived on the island because of the purity of the air, but the essences helped their lungs work more efficiently and the magical waters that they had been drinking since they arrived had helped remove some of the pollutants from their bodies and minds.

"Please relax and I will give you clear instructions every step of the way. All you need do is to follow my words," Orla advised.

Orla had been given the ultimate tool against Shadow and that was sound. She would teach these humans the correct words to use to each other and the correct music to assist with the healing of the planet. This was a language that Shadow just didn't comprehend.

"I want you to close your eyes and breathe deeply." Orla watched until their breathing became regular and rhythmical. She went through the process of calling up their ancestral line as far back as they could stretch their vision. Each woman diligently followed the instructions and when Orla accessed their memories, she could see queues of women bowed down by servitude and oppression for many, many generations. She gently nudged them to continue as far as was necessary to find a woman who possessed no fear.

They all hesitated as their understanding of fear had been completely whitewashed by their society and they weren't understanding what she was asking of them.

She had not really considered that these women had no terms of reference to be able to differentiate between being in a state of fear and not. Their whole reality was coloured by fear in all its punitive shades. Orla scanned their memories and saw that these women, and indeed all the women in their genetic memories, were held in a prison of poverty, chastity and obedience. And, if these three conditions were not followed, the fear was so great that they thought that the sky would fall in if they fell outside of them.

Orla needed to understand more how this trilogy of slavery had worked its way into their memories. So she delved deeper and saw how the Elite had come to manipulate man's desire to seek deity in some form throughout history to replace the gaping hole left after Crystal Wisdom had disappeared. There had been many prophets emerge from different cultures preaching a form of Crystal Wisdom, which included respect, love, acceptance and compassion. Some of them gained a huge following, speaking to that hidden and hungry part of man, awakening a desire in him that he wanted to pursue. Shadow saw this as a nuisance and directed the Elite to control this rebellion. And so the Elite harnessed the desire for deity, lassoed the emerging religions and peppered their doctrines with false truths, enshrining guilt into the framework of their philosophies. Obedience to these constraining philosophies seduced their followers into believing that they were in a state of sin from the moment of their birth, and the only pathway out of sin was to follow the guilt-ridden path of redemption, available only at the point of death.

This is pure genius, they took the desire for Crystal Wisdom and reframed it into a tableau of misery – suffering being the only path to redemption. Orla brought her attention back to the women in the room.

"I want you to go back to the image of a line of your female ancestors. Now I want you to look at the most recent ancestors, the women at the front of the line."

They all followed her instructions obediently, each one seeing more acutely how miserable the rest of the women in the line were.

"I now want you to look at the first five. Go up to each one in turn and ask them what their fears are."

They hesitated as they didn't quite understand how they were going to communicate with people in their memory.

"Just follow my instructions."

They did as they were asked and began the dialogue, each woman receiving similar answers to their question from their ancestors. They weren't answering directly, but reciting a litany of their deep-seated beliefs:

- *Don't ask questions*
- *Do as you are told*
- *We are lucky to be looked after by our husbands*
- *We don't know what is good for us, only our husbands and fathers know this*

Sheila was more courageous, and Orla saw that she was going back further with her ancestors and came upon a woman who was totally on her knees in a state of collapse. Sheila asked her what had happened to bring her to this state.

"My husband caught me learning to read. He beat me terribly and told me that women were not allowed to read, there was no reason for them to read." Sheila was horrified. She continued back and found another woman who had been repeatedly raped and was covered in disease. She was repulsed that this could have been one of her ancestors but persisted and posed the same question to this woman, who, she saw on closer inspection, was still in her early twenties.

The woman replied, "I was sold at the age of twelve by my father to a man, to be his wife and to give him sons. I could not bear children so after a year my husband sold me to a house of pleasure for men, where I serviced men day after day and received no money and no breaks. I never went outside in the sunshine. I eventually became diseased and was thrown onto the streets and became a street worker, the very worst kind, and eventually I died."

"Why didn't you try to escape?" asked Sheila.

"To where? I had no money, no family. I was a disgrace because I couldn't bear children, no man would want me. I had no choice.""

That phrase rung in Sheila's head – 'no choice'. *What did 'choice' really mean*? She knew she needed to find out more about 'choice'.

Sheila's appetite for more information was heightened by this interaction and she went further back and found a woman in abject pain in the pelvic area of her body. She was bent double, holding a lifeless baby in her arms. When Sheila looked closely she could see this was not a woman – this was a child who had been burdened by such pain it had aged her. Sheila asked her why she was in pain. Tears fell down the young girl's cheek and the words began to choke through her tears.

"When I was much younger, the elders of my village cut us in our most intimate area so that we would be able to be chosen by a man for marriage. But I had been married for a few days and the marriage bed brought me excruciating pain. I asked my mother for advice and she told me it was a woman's lot, it would get better, and I asked her why she had allowed me to be cut and sewn up so tightly as a child. My mother screamed at me, "No man would want you otherwise!" But every day became a living hell. I eventually became with child but died at the birth with my unborn child." Sheila looked at this girl with dismay. She had not really understood what she was describing initially, as female genital mutilation had been completely eradicated half a century ago and therefore removed from the history texts as it portrayed too vividly patriarchy in a brutal light. As the enormity of what the girl was describing began to dawn on Sheila, her dismay began to turn to fury.

Orla could see what she was experiencing and went into her memory and reminded her that it was for this reason that their racial memories had to stay intact, so that this abhorrence and hatred of the feminine would never occur again.

The other women had similar experiences and all came to the same conclusion as Sheila – the major issue was that these women didn't have choices.

Orla brought them back into the present and asked them what significant thing they had found. Predictably, they all agreed it was lack of choice.

"I want you to think about your lives and try to identify where you have made a choice entirely by yourselves without being influenced by your husbands." Orla watched as they scanned their memories, going from their lives at school, the jobs they did before marriage and the choices they made within their marriages. They all slowly realised that although they were given choices, the realm of choice that they inhabited had very narrow parameters.'

Helen piped up. "Well, we do have choices." Helen was a short and wiry woman with a very quick mind who was totally dedicated to the principles of dome-education. Her husband Mark was the second-in-command to the General for Education and she had been a teacher before marriage.

"What exactly? Give me an example," Orla challenged.

"When I was about to leave school I was given choices as to what I could study at college."

"Was politics on offer?" Orla asked pointedly.

There was silence. They were understanding what she was trying to get them to identify; they had choices but those choices were very restricted.

Orla brought them back to the main objective of this session.

"Ok, I would like you to go back to your ancestors and begin to walk down the line of women again."

Orla encouraged them to keep looking. "You will eventually find a woman who has no fear, you will recognise her by her body language." This took longer than it did with the men, the lines of women were going on and on for what seemed like an eternity. Orla saw the periods of history change and with each generation there was just the same old story, women being chattels of men. Eventually they were all able to access an ancestor who lived at a time in history just at the point before the Earth had turned its back on Crystal Wisdom. All the women were quite surprised to see healthy upright women taking roles of authority in the community, particularly with the upbringing and education of children and the health of the communities and, more importantly, they had the key role in understanding the bigger picture and the long-term requirements of the planet.

Orla instructed them to focus on these women for a few minutes, taking in every detail of their characters, and then to bring those women to the front of the line of ancestors. She asked them to take this image and seed it as a motif into the memories of their ovaries, thyroid and adrenal glands. They initially were confused by this as most of them were unaware of the biology of their bodies, but miraculously they followed Orla's words and found those organs, placed the motif in them as instructed and immediately sensed an awareness in these organs that had not been there before.

Their throats started to pulse, their ovaries began to burn slightly, and their adrenal glands relaxed. Orla could see that this was a very strange and disquieting feeling for them, so she sprayed more essences over them and urged them to keep in a state of relaxation whilst being aware of the subtle pulsing in their bodies. She could see that they were experiencing a warmth infusing through their bodies which, although unfamiliar, was vaguely and surprisingly reassuring. Orla kept them in this state for an hour watching their bodies change. The tissue of their wombs began to wake up and become more active. The lining of their wombs had atrophied, like all women under the domes; they had not menstruated since having their children. She brought them back into full consciousness and asked them to sit up.

They opened their eyes, blinked, and sat up slowly. Orla waited for them to feel fully present and continued with her explanation.

"Your bodies have been reprogrammed to enable your female hormones to function in the natural way they were designed. This will mean that you will start to experience your menstrual cycle again."

They all looked horrified and silently thought how awful it would be to have to go through that again. They had all been relieved when they had had their children and their cycle had ceased.

Orla could see their concerns. "Your monthly cycle will assist you in becoming more in tune with the needs of the Earth, and if you ultimately want to grow plants like those on Crystal Island, you will have to attune your bodies to be in rhythm with nature. I can understand your concerns – previously you experienced extreme discomfort during your cycles – but this will not be repeated. Your bodies have been balanced and, more importantly, your memories have been corrected. Part of the problem that women have had with their cycles is that it was viewed by patriarchy as unclean, talked about in whispers and viewed with ignorance and suspicion, blamed for various catastrophes from failing crops to diseased livestock, and even turning milk sour. There is a deep revulsion within every woman's memory of this most natural process which had been intended by nature to assist creation. This revulsion causes conflict in your bodies, and where there is conflict there is pain."

She was beginning to make them aware of the beauty and intelligence of their bodies. "The female reproductive system is not just there to produce babies, it is also a vehicle to perpetuate the wisdom of creation."

"Wow," Cynthia exclaimed. "What can that possibly mean?"

All the women looked at Cynthia, a little surprised at her spontaneity. Orla had been aware of the general reticence to contribute or ask too many questions among the women. Fortunately, she could read every thought and every emotion that crossed their minds and their bodies. More and more information was being directed towards them that they didn't quite understand on a conscious level. But Orla could see the memory of their crystal-human ancestors was working subtly in the memory of their cells, and physically, they were changing. When they changed physically, they would be stronger, which would also help them to ask questions.

"The more you are exposed to the practices you learn on the island, and continue to take the remedies, the more you will understand," Orla said. "The wisdom of creation is a multi-levelled subject which has to be approached slowly, methodically and, most importantly, without fear. As you release fear from your memory cells in your whole body, the more you will naturally access Crystal Wisdom. However, it is vital that you do not discuss any of your experiences on the island with anyone other than your husbands. People will begin to notice changes in you, but you must not give anything away at this stage. The time is coming very soon when more people will be activated, the opportunity for change will open and Crystal Wisdom will spread across the planet."

*

Orla became aware of the subtle movement in her body that brought her back from her memories from those early days many years ago to present day. She gazed out of the long window in her room, giving thanks for the beauty of the world. A day never passed that gratitude didn't pass her lips for the wonderful world that she had the privilege of inhabiting. Her thoughts drifted back again to those first women who came to the island and she reflected on their rapid change.

Yes, they had the necessary lineage, but still, after their initial hesitation and confusion, they grasped whatever she offered them with enthusiasm. Very quickly they had seen an opportunity for a brighter future for their children, which will always be the strongest motivation for most women. Orla remembered them when they first came to the island, shadows of women, programmed to serve their husbands, believing that their thoughts weren't important. After their initiations on the island and with Orla and Maeve's further guidance, these seven women had transformed to being equal partners to their husbands. They had taken a quantum leap in their development to get them to the point where they were confident of making important decisions for the future of the planet. It wasn't difficult though, she reflected, they just needed to tap into their Crystal memory and the answers would be given. They had also shared with men the true meaning of intimacy in a loving relationship and this had changed the landscape of relationships completely. But the quantum leap was not easy; she had to confront them with their memories, which were pitiful and painful, but they had not shied away from that challenge. In fact, those very memories were the spur that urged them on to make further change. Orla recalled those scenes that she had uncovered from their memories. As someone who was not emotionally connected to them, she observed the experiences of their ancestors with disbelief, but she was also deeply concerned that men could treat women so badly and think that it was acceptable. It appeared that women, such gentle, nurturing creatures, had been trampled on roughly, generation after generation until women accepted their lot without challenge. *But why am I surprised? Humans have trampled on the beautiful trees that fed the planet so well for millennia in the quest for profit. Rape of the planet, translated to the rape of women's Crystal Wisdom and, yes, there were many kinds of rape.*

During her initiation on the Crystal worlds, she had been introduced to the treatment of women and children over the millennia, but that had not really prepared her for the reality. There had been a tipping point in history where women were beginning to grasp at holding the reins of their own lives, but something had happened to stop that progression and they had unconsciously chosen a route of self-sabotage. It was as if they had knocked on the glass ceiling and asked timidly to enter. But without the emotional memory to equip them with the specific skills required to engage with the patriarchal culture of leadership, they were ignored, and when they were ignored often enough, they stopped knocking, and retreated to a safe place of obscurity.

Orla had developed a great admiration for those first women pioneers who had helped their husbands to see leadership in a different way and had successfully gone on to help others to gain connection with Crystal Wisdom.

She closed her eyes, smiling peacefully as she reflected on the early days of her relationship with them.

*

After her first visit to the island, Sheila had gone back to her husband and seen him with very different eyes, and he had also seen in her a very different woman. She now had a look in her eyes that engaged with the world around her instead of the fixed gaze with which she normally greeted the world – a lifeless gaze shared by most women. They had sat together discussing their experiences and were both confounded at the fecund and healthy environment of Crystal Island. Of course they would never have experienced that in their lifetime, but they both enthused over the happiness of the children and compared them with their own children, who were completely without spontaneity. Sheila had not even questioned the fact that their children never misbehaved; they carried out their instructions from both parents and teachers obediently, as had their parents many generations before them. It was the musical laughter of island children that truly shocked them into realising what was missing in their own childhood and had been repeated with their own children.

The evening of her return from the island, after their children had dutifully put themselves to bed, Sheila and John sat and discussed what this whole experience could mean for the future. They both had a feeling of excitement with the first inkling that they actually had personal control over their lives – what a thing to even countenance, how shocking, and something most definitely to be kept to themselves.

They sat up into the night talking of the possibilities that the future might hold, not knowing at that stage how it would ultimately look. When they were too tired to speak anymore they fell asleep in the unusual position of each other's arms. They had never spoken at length as equals and most definitely had not slept like this before. In the morning John woke first and glanced down at his sleeping wife, and felt a tenderness that was new to him – and he liked that feeling.

Orla had been quite shocked by the cold relationships that married couples endured. She had asked Finn if he had identified any specific point in history where this behaviour was established. By viewing all their memories she had seen that there had been pockets of time in history where men and women were equal in relationships and they had enjoyed each other's company and bodies, but these were few and far between. There had come a point in the 20th century when women thought they were equal to men, which they were legally, but not emotionally. Men were still calling the shots, and women, unwittingly, were falling into their trap of control.

But then something else occurred at the beginning of the 21st century that helped to polarise men and women. There was a surge of talking therapies and personal development in business that mushroomed overnight. But the goal was not personal development, the goal was development of the collective business model. Management had become no more than artificial intelligence, with the emphasis on 'artificial'. The men who enjoyed roles of leadership, or who had been identified as having the potential of leadership, had been gradually broken down and rebuilt into the corporate man, a man who didn't question. Any man who did question or make bold statements was ostracised. So the typical person who had a leadership role was ultimately controlled by a much higher authority – the Elite – which of course was controlled by Shadow. And with that programming, a deeper divide between men and women appeared.

Finn's experience on the Ruby Crystal world had enabled him to have a better understanding of this and he had explained to Orla that to be able to control people, their individuality, that part of them that is unique, has to be removed. During their many assessments and training sessions their potential was quantified into categories that had very narrow bandwidths and this definition followed them throughout their careers. They silently began to shape themselves to match that definition, which was of course limiting and ultimately suppressed the development of their true gifts.

Orla had understood completely. By being given external definition by someone in authority, it made them feel accepted, safe and secure. Society's parameters of normal were becoming worryingly narrow.

There had been a few people who initiated programmes of development which were more thorough and in keeping with accessing a pale version of Crystal Wisdom and therefore more about development of the self. However, as soon as the delegates had completed those liberating courses, they looked around at the corporate world, did not like what they saw, and, empowered by their own creativity, chose to depart the corporate world and begin their own independent organisations. This was not what Shadow wanted; too many offshoots of Crystal Wisdom could start a revolution. And so the people who ran those enlightened courses were gradually marginalised as their language of true emotional intelligence was not acknowledged by Shadow-controlled leaders.

Women had not responded in the same way to these development programmes. Because they were not completely engaged with Shadow, the blueprint of war that permeated the halls of leadership did not resonate with them. They were the nurturers of society, not the destroyers, and deep within them there was conflict when they were subjected to such debriefing.

Orla's attention went back to the women. She had recognised that they were crucial for change to take place more rapidly, and inside all these men was a desire to have a deeper connection with their wives. All the training and preparations that they had undergone were designed to make them better business or political leaders but it was also designed to alienate them from having close relationships with anyone. This was acceptable in the workplace, but it was in their intimate relationships that mankind blossomed. In the nurturing space of creative intimacy, people accessed Crystal Wisdom, and it was this very same level of creativity that was required to solve planetary problems. Without this connection a dullness began to seep across mankind like a grey smog of boredom, which became the norm, eventually removing any aspirations for more.

During one of their rare quiet moments, Orla had asked Finn to try to imagine what it would be like not to have that level of intimacy that they enjoyed with a partner. It was impossible for them to consider, and they had no desire to explore that dark possibility.

Orla had told the women that she would connect with them weekly through the comms portal, to help and support them in their discovery of their feminine side. She had kept a constant surveillance of them remotely, and the first notable development she detected was that they had started to ovulate, all at the same time. Orla was pleased it showed that the remedies she had given them, coupled with their experience of the island, had opened a portal in their distant Crystal memory. Initially, they weren't altogether pleased, because they were slightly underweight and any change in their physical bodies was felt acutely. They had also all expressed a concern over contraception. Orla knew their bodies were not ready yet to conceive, and in fact these women had finished their child-bearing years. Their reproductive creativity was meant for another task, and in the next chapter of their lives the planet would be their offspring.

Orla recognised the importance of reminding the women of the wonder of creation trapped in their wonderful bodies, and the only way to do that was to take them back in their memories to a time when women were equal to men. She contacted them and instructed them all to meet with her on the comms portal the following day and to make sure they would be undisturbed.

At the allotted time, when they had made sure that their homes were quiet, husbands at work, children in school and all the household chores done, they went to their husbands' studies and waited for Orla to connect with them through their comms portals. Orla knew that they would not like what she was about to tell them. As soon as she connected with them she began by explaining that they had all ovulated and they would menstruate in two weeks' time. They were not impressed, but she reassured them that they would be prepared so that it was both an enjoyable experience as well as being a time where they could connect more deeply to creation. She was, as always, careful with her language. She didn't want to introduce them to anything they might discount because of their lack of understanding.

She instructed them to continue with the remedies from the second envelope that she had given them. The remedies would not only help their bodies adjust, but most importantly, would remind them how to function correctly. She requested that they spray their rooms with the essences she had given them to aid relaxation.

Orla instructed them to close their eyes and to call on their female ancestral line. She saw the twitch and wrinkling of the forehead on all of them except Sheila as they attempted to recreate those images they had experienced on the island. Orla reassured them that images would come and, as promised, eventually all the women began to see their ancestors. She urged them to walk past the bowed women and to go beyond the place where they had found their women without fear. Eventually she could see that they all had long queues of women going back centuries, a grey line of bowed and submissive women. They eventually came upon a completely different image – they each found a woman who looked tall, upright, with long flowing hair, holding babies, laughing and spending time talking with other women. Each woman viewed the images of their long-distant ancestors and was impressed with not just their health and happiness, but more importantly, the robust health of the children. Orla wanted them to focus on the qualities of motherhood demonstrated by their ancestors, as this basic fundamental and beautiful gift given to women had been overwritten over the years with vulnerability, and judged as being a lesser and unimportant role.

The women looked more closely at the scene and saw that there was a whole community looking after the children and, whilst each child was particularly attached to its mother, the other women in the community were also involved. Each child was regarded as special and each woman regarded it her responsibility to ensure that every child, not just her own, had the best attention. All the women were accessing the same image, as Orla had been able to take them one step deeper with the process, which allowed them to see their shared cultural memory. They could view their ancestors, but she needed them to see the broader picture and how important women were to the development of the community.

They were equally a little shocked, finding it alarming that women were so voluptuous for one thing – they were not overweight but they had healthy tissue covering their bones, strong and firm. Their breasts were round and they could see that the new mothers were able to breastfeed their children, quite openly, which they found repugnant. These women from the past had no shame about their bodies or about breastfeeding children who were over a year old. All the dome wives were repelled at this image; they had been programmed to believe that breastfeeding was not useful. Breastfeeding was yet another aspect of motherhood that took the focus away from their husbands, in particular their husbands' sexual demands. Men wanted their women back to their pre-maternity bodies quickly; that meant no leaking of breast milk in the marital bed. Having seen this tableau of femininity, the seven began to compare their own bodies and saw for the first time their sterile frames, skeletal and without substance on so many levels.

When they had been on the island Orla immediately noticed that they were taking a cocktail of medication to control their hormones and their minds. They had all been sold a myth that their hormones caused no end of problems for them and therefore their cycle should be chemically regulated. They had been brainwashed into believing that a life without chemicals to balance their mood rendered their mental health vulnerable. Orla realised why the women looked like they were walking around in a trance and why they could not fully acknowledge or respond to the emotional needs of their children, which is the first level of understanding the needs of creation.

Orla had wished in the beginning that she could have increased the speed at which the women's transformation happened, but she had to take it very carefully, particularly for the next stage of their emotional detox. Part of their instruction on the island had been to stop taking the medication for their hormone levels, and they were horrified because they had been brainwashed to believe that without them they would be unstable. Orla promised them that this was an illusion and they would feel so much better without them. She gave them plant remedies to help rebalance their hormones. These, taken from the buds of the grove of trees in the Secret Garden, held the purest form of plant hormones, the closest to human hormones. The challenge, however, would be taking them off the mind-numbing drugs they had taken since beginning their menstrual cycle. At the very point at which their crystal intelligence was about to blossom forth, allowing them access to interpreting the needs of the planet, the needs of women and children, they were given a chemical cloche which inhibited that connection.

She brought the women back from their visions, and as they opened their eyes she asked if they had any questions. They all started to speak at once, words spilling out of their mouths in no particular order.

"So are you telling us our lives should be dedicated to having children?" Mary asked, incredulously, as they all seemed to be past that point in their lives.

Orla reassured them that producing children was just one part of a woman's role in society, but they were also responsible for providing the next generation with all the security necessary to express their natural gifts and skills to ensure the long-term success of the planet – and in fact not just success but its future existence.

"What do you mean by gifts and skills?" Sheila queried.

"Each one of you has a specific gift that has been given to you to use in service of the planet. Unfortunately, those gifts have not been identified, acknowledged or nurtured, so mankind has been unable to assist nature and that is why the planet is dying."

These two succinct but profound sentences slowly sank into the consciousness of each woman, and Orla watched their reactions closely – she could see what was causing the confusion. On the surface they still had their dome programming, but underneath, the Crystal Wisdom was beginning to percolate to the surface and was causing conflict at the point where the two opposing programmes collided. She had been particularly simplistic in explaining about the gifts as she didn't want to alarm them; once they understood more about the gifts, the more they would understand their true abilities and the influence they would have on the future of the planet.

She continued on a more mundane note. "To access these gifts we have to remove the medication that you have been taking for many years that has controlled your brain chemistry." They all became a little jittery at the mention of withdrawing from these meds. They had been fed dreadful stories of women who had stopped taking them. Everyone had heard stories of women who had ceased the chemical therapy and had gone completely off the rails, or they had never spoken a sane word again and had to be institutionalised, or in extreme cases had taken their own lives.

"As long as you take the remedies I have given you at the specific time, the transition will be painless. Obviously, you do not stop the meds all at once. I have written down a strategy of withdrawal which is matched by the strength of the island remedies."

She agreed with them to meet in two weeks for the next stage, which would coincide with their menstruation. She urged them to organise their lives so that they could take short rests in the afternoon during this time. Their bodies were going through a transition and they needed rest. This was a rather novel idea to these ladies, who busied themselves from morning till night with housewifely duties that seemed to take up every minute of the day.

"You must manage your time differently to ensure that you can take adequate rest on those days. No one needs to know what you are doing. On the days outside of this section of the month you can do more tasks; this is when your body is more energetic anyway."

The idea that they could manage their days differently was novel, as their schedule followed the same as their mothers' and grandmothers'. Orla was introducing to them the first taste of being in control and taking responsibility for their own lives. These women were the privileged in society and, as such, had lots of social events to attend as part of their duties for their husbands, but they had never thought that they could take the time to rest. Orla smiled and thought, *No wonder these women look jaundiced, they act like robots from the moment they get up till the moment they go to sleep. It is as if the alarm goes off in the morning, they got up and carry out their days without question; not dissimilar to how men function, just different.*

Orla left the women and turned her attention to the men. She had to begin preparing them to see the world differently. Yes, they had witnessed life on the island, but she needed to show them what the whole world could be like so that they really understood all possibilities.

She had also observed that their thinking processes had changed at work. This was both good and bad. Yes, they were shifting in their consciousness, but people close to them would also observe the change, and that would attract attention not just from their peers, but also from Shadow. She knew that Finn would have to monitor the situation very closely, and for that reason Finn spent most of his time being very close to them. When he walked the domes, he chose to be invisible to the masses for obvious reasons; only the seven men were aware of him. They found it reassuring because they had begun to look at their world differently. Their changing perspective began very slowly by observing people around them, and they quickly realised that their environment held a culture of total and unswerving obedience. The environment of the workplace in the House of Laws was uncannily peaceful, with no opposition. In fact, bureaucracy had replaced democracy. There were two main objectives of the domes that seemed to take up most of their time: ensuring the domed communities had all that they required, and ensuring that the communities outside of the domes stayed as far way as possible. Finn did smile at the simplicity of those objectives. *They should have spent more time making the planet work rather than putting all their energy into maintaining a two-tiered society.* And when he observed the leaders of the domes he did feel a small pang of pity. *They really are an excuse for the possibilities of men.*

He cast his mind back to the men in his family and was proud of their ability to successfully express the combined qualities of power, compassion and discernment. The men that he was seeing now carried none of these qualities. And when he recalled his experiences on the Ruby Crystal world and the immense power of the Ruby beings, there was absolutely no comparison. The qualities of crystal masculinity had disappeared, under the pressure of a diminishing world and the fear generated by the Elite. He watched them go about their business on their communication screens, generating mounds and mounds of rules and regulations. He was stunned by the complexities of the discussion and decision process in the House of Laws, before laws were committed to statute. They lacked the ability to determine the priority whilst keeping in the foreground their objective, and therefore were easily distracted from the initial objective. Equally, after such lengthy discussions, the objective often changed shape completely.

Finn was aware of the human evolution that existed immediately after the Crystalanders left Earth; there was a sharpness in man's ability to find creative solutions to any challenges that arose in those early days. But now, they appeared to go around the subject in ever-increasing circles, spending hours in discussion, achieving no concrete solutions. He couldn't believe how many hours a day they could spend roaming around in a sea of facts and figures trying to extract information in an excruciatingly convoluted effort to make a decision. One of the main problems he identified was their fear of making a mistake. These high-end executives had managed to survive by not making decisions and not putting their heads above the parapet. They avoided decision-making by discussing the issues endlessly until there was eventually a consensus of the collective, which ultimately was the road of least resistance. They had developed an awareness of the safety that resided within group approval, so they never acted, thought or spoke spontaneously; they always looked for cues from their peers and superiors before committing to any policy.

Finn pondered on the complex laws of the Federations and compared them with the laws he was given on the Ruby Crystal world.

He had been taught, very simply, that the major crime against the planet was to not respect everything on it in equal measure.

The second major crime was dominance, which comprised two parts:

- *A person who caused an 'injury' to another person, animal or plant – injury being perceived as the result of dominance;*
- *A person who failed to protect another person, animal or plant against that injury through cowardice.*

Dominance and cowardice were two qualities incompatible with Crystal Wisdom. Man had decided to dominate the planet and in so doing had suppressed all Crystal Wisdom. His arrogance deemed that wisdom was the ability to dominate but, without Crystal Wisdom, there is no planetary conscience, nothing to punctuate the selfish needs of the individual. In order to dominate the planet man had to downgrade nature, and when he downgraded nature he also downgraded women with the same stroke of the pen.

When man conveniently turned his back on any aspect of nature that cried out for help, he was a coward. After the demise of Crystal Wisdom, the cumulative Shadow conditioning that developed, which was compounded over many centuries of fear, made it too easy to fall into the hive mentality that was fearful of speaking the truth. Man became no better than reptiles and retreated to the part of his brain which held that memory.

Orla tuned in to John's comms portal at the agreed time. It had been a week since the women had returned from the island and she wanted to move the process on to the next level. As soon as they connected, the first thing she noticed was the enthusiasm that accompanied his questions.

The first thing he asked was why she had chosen him and the other six men. She hesitated, scanning his memory to see if he was ready to have some of the crystal information. He was. When she looked in to his memory she saw that some of the walls had melted away and she was able to penetrate through the quagmire of fears.

"I am able to view the qualities that people have when they are born," she said. He looked intrigued and immediately opened his mouth, eager to find out what she saw in him. She ignored his unspoken question and continued. "Quite simply, leaders of Federations need specific gifts otherwise they should not be leaders. Leadership skills can be learnt to a certain degree, and there are a lot of leadership skills that have been successfully identified. However, the most important qualities cannot be learnt, they are inherited." She didn't illuminate from where those qualities came at this stage. She proceeded to list the seven gifts of a leader.

"The first is the ability to access inspirational and unique ideas for planetary health and development.

"The second is the ability to explore an idea to its full potential without hindrance of man-made limitation.

"The third is the ability to give a unique framework upon which to develop the idea.

"The fourth is the ability to make material sense of the idea and give it form.

"The fifth is the ability to judge the emerging idea to discern its value to the planet and adapt accordingly.

"The sixth is the ability to discern all of the above processes and make the final decision based on the original objective.

"And finally, the seventh is the ability to communicate the truth of the project to all the kingdoms of the planet."

John was mesmerised by her voice and the words that were spilling from her lips.

"Each of you has been chosen because you have inherited all these qualities. However, each of you excel in one." Smiling at John, Orla continued. "We contacted you first because you hold the quality which is vitally important to the success of our venture: the ability to communicate the truth to all levels of society. You are not aware of it at the moment, but you have the ability to detect fears in people and are able to speak to them in a way that pacifies their fears and opens their minds to change."

He was quiet, taking in these words that meant absolutely nothing to him. But, as always, he trusted this special woman.

"I will share this information with the other six tomorrow and inform them of their particular strengths. Before we part, have you made any observations about the changes in yourself or how you view your environment?" Of course, she knew the answer.

He smiled. "Sheila is different. I can't really put my finger on it… but…" Orla urged him to try to explain. He thought about it and formulated an answer. "She just seems to be more connected to me and the children. She was always attentive but I realise now it was more out of duty than desire. She seems to be more receptive to the dynamics of everyday family life." Shrugging his shoulders, still slightly baffled, he said goodbye to Orla and disconnected from the screen. Orla considered the speed at which she could give them more information.

Ideally she would have liked to have shown them a film depicting Earth's history pre- and post-Crystalanders, but she knew they just would not comprehend the enormity and the ramifications of that information. It wasn't a case of their not wanting to understand, it was that they would not be able to see the Crystalanders or the first crystal-humans as their memory banks had buried those images too deeply. Their memories had no terms of reference for that degree of multi-dimensional uncontested Crystal Wisdom.

No matter, she reflected. She knew that once they shed the layers of fear that inhibited and suppressed their Crystal memory, everything would move faster, and they would have to move fast if they were to outwit Shadow.

The following day the seven logged into Orla and Finn, and Orla immediately embarked on the reasons why they were chosen to be the first seven pioneers. As with John, she highlighted the qualities of leadership and announced their individual talents. Interestingly, John had asked no questions when given his unique talent, and she was interested to see how the other six responded.

"James, you have the ability to access unique creativity." He was amazed as he was in the finance department and his working day involved immersion in disseminating vital information from the many reports that landed on his desk, which reflected every financial aspect of the world's major Federations.

Orla qualified her statement. "What you are doing now is definitely a skill, but it is a skill that any good leader can learn. What is more important is the ability to find creative solutions when faced with conflicting and challenging data."

He wondered about this and asked, "Why aren't I aware of this amazing skill?"

She smiled at him and explained that it was buried behind walls in his memory and those walls had been formed over the generations as a result of the many negative experiences of his ancestors.

This prompted a barrage of questions about these walls of experiences, how they got there and what they were. She realised they were anxious to find out as much as possible. She had opened a Pandora's box and knew there would be no return from this point.

She silenced them, promising to explain more after they had all learnt about their gifts. "Phillip, your speciality is being able to take intangible ideas and make them tangible." Phillip speculated on his suitability as his current role was in security, so he didn't really know how this quality would translate.

"Mathew, your talent is being able to take an idea and give it the first understanding of structure; you have the ability to identify importance and relevance and discard that which is not needed. Your current role in the department of environment is actually well matched."

Orla had observed that he didn't use those skills as everything in dome society had a protocol, and no one ever deviated from that dogma. She knew that his natural talents would be most important when they started looking at food production in particular, as there were so many challenges left by drought, pollution and disease which had been caused by natural degeneration and also manipulation by the Elite.

Orla moved on to Joshua. "At the moment your work is in the department of health." *Or the department of diseases*, Orla quietly reflected – "Your gift is the ability to look to the plant world and discern which plant remedies would be appropriate to the current health trends."

They had all been given the remedies from Crystal Island, and because they had a small degree of Crystal Wisdom in their memories, they responded well. But the challenge would be assessing the level of health of the general population whose genetics had no understanding of natural remedies.

"Mark, your talent is the ability to recognise and question when a solution is not following the correct priorities in relation to the needs of the planet." Mark looked bemused because in his current role in the department of education there were no questions.

"Frederic, your talent is the ability to make accurate and clear decisions for planetary healing." Frederic worked in the treasury, and Orla had recognised that he would develop his potential to approach decisions with a razor sharp mental acuity to sift through the unnecessary information quickly and fluently to reach the heart of any situation, identifying both the objective and the correct priorities.

"Finally, John has the talent for communicating, not just within his immediate environment but with all people in a language that ordinary people can understand. It is because of this ability that we have appointed him as the leader of your group. Each one of you has equally important talents, but it is the ability to communicate effectively that is vital." Orla knew that John would be successful in speaking in the House of Laws, engaging key people in the novel concept of trying to save Earth.

After announcing John's role, she could see that the six thought that he had actually drawn the short straw. They felt their talents sounded interesting, if not a little confusing, trying to marry up their individual qualities with the seven qualities of leadership. Equally they had no concept of what it could possibly lead to, but they knew that John's work in the House of Laws did give him a better understanding of the laws that had to be changed – and change they must.

Orla added, "One of the most important reasons why you have all been chosen, apart from your natural talents, is your relatively good physical health."

Before Orla and Finn had come into their lives, poor health was regarded as normal in the domes but these men had now seen the health of the islanders and realised that they were not healthy. The life expectancy of men in the domes was not good at all. It was at an all-time low. But even so, these seven had received the best that the planet could offer, and as such were in better condition than the people lower down the ranks, thanks also to their crystal genetics. Orla prepared them for their emotional change by focusing on their health.

"I don't want you to worry too much about your leadership talents at present. In time you will be prepared for these roles. What is important is that you understand the process of transformation that will happen. To do that we need to demonstrate how out of balance man is with nature. You have been used to this level of functioning for so many generations that you have accepted that you are not in control of your lives."

"Why weren't we made aware of these talents before?" Mark said. "Vast sums of money and many decades have gone into identifying the characteristics required for leadership, ranging from middle management right up to the leaders of countries."

Finn shook his head. He was thinking of the work he had done on the Ruby Crystal world to reveal the qualities of leadership, and saw from their memories that Orla was accessing that these men and their predecessors had undergone rigorous mental unraveling under the guise of trying to identify their leadership qualities, but their archetype of leadership was seriously flawed. *It's no surprise that the planet is in such a sorry condition*, he thought.

When Finn had scanned the planet looking for examples of leadership, he quickly realised that the model they were using was failing. Before the Generals were appointed, captains of industry and politicians were spiralling into an abyss of confusion. In a desperate attempt to perpetuate their brand of leadership they searched frantically and frenetically to quantify and qualify what it is to be an authentic leader. The problem was the means by which they measured these qualities was flawed, implemented by flawed people equally deficient in wisdom. Leaders and potential leaders were subjected to multi-level analyses, workshops and mentoring, but the algorithm they were using was restrictive and constraining and played into the grateful hands of Shadow. This had led to the collapse of the model of democratic leadership that had been practised for centuries, and gave birth to the totalitarian leadership of the Generals.

As the decades progressed, the creative ability of leaders became diluted and they looked to each other for terms of reference instead of looking to the wisdom of the universe inherent in all living matter. In the 20th century, man had decided that he was greater than nature. Man-science had taken the lead, ignored the signs, and at the end of the 21st century, man looked around and couldn't understand why the devastation had happened. But by that time they had lost the ability to ask "Why?"

The Elite looked down on all this and saw with glee that free will was pushed further into the recesses of man's ability to question. The women were always going to be a harder nut to crack as their hormonal network made them less attractive to Shadow. Shadow knew it had to work harder to suppress their free will. It didn't matter how much they were suppressed, history had demonstrated that women had the power to stand up for themselves and insist on having equal input to the development of the planet, but the female movement never really gathered steam. It went through cycles of erupting, followed by a flurry of activity, lots of invective promoting the equality of women and then, mysteriously, the message became diluted and was eventually buried under the myth of suspicion that men carried when confronted with assertive women.

Finn asked Orla if she had identified why this had happened.

"They cleverly put women into situations where they would find it difficult to maintain their female physiology, so they were exposed to more pressure. Eventually, Shadow wiped out all memory of strong crystal women from whom they could have learnt so much, and with no terms of reference, they responded in the workplace like men."

When Orla had gone through the history of the Earth on the Crystal worlds, she had seen many examples of women's suppression. What saddened her more was the fact that men were also being suppressed but in a different way. Their evolution and development restricted them from enjoying the complementary contribution of an equal relationship. Yes, they had dutiful support from women, but they lacked the intimate crystal connection which would have enhanced their lives as well as improving the planet's potential. They had been doing a dance of self-satisfaction for so long, believing they were progressing, but the reality was they were in a cycle of fear that was stopping them from seeing outside of their limited parameters of normal. They were constantly looking to authority to give them answers, but authority never left the realm of fear-based decisions. Shadow, the ultimate authority for man, had worked its magic of illusion on humankind perfectly.

Orla and Finn continued to observe the seven men and their wives for signs of change, and of course, the change began to surface. That change was demonstrated in the way the couples treated each other. There was a consideration and respect between them that hadn't existed before. They had begun to see themselves not as independent individuals with specific jobs and responsibilities, but as human beings who cared deeply for each other. This degree of caring was a necessary step in the development of their Crystal memory. Orla was particularly impressed with John. She could see that he was almost viewing his wife through a different lens, seeing her more as an equal than playing a supporting role. With the change in their parents, the children began to respond differently to them; as the wives began to smile more, so the children responded with a little more spontaneity, and it was when this happened that Orla and Finn, knew that they had to work fast. The genie was out of the bottle, and Shadow would begin to sit up and take notice as those tell-tale signs of spontaneity began to ripple through the community. As the spontaneity surfaced, so the Crystal Guardians would begin to move closer to individuals, waiting expectantly for Shadow to disengage, and they would be reunited with their wards.

Orla reviewed the treatment of children in the society of the dome-dwellers. A culture of child abuse had evolved where the adults had become impatient with children for being children, frustrated with their immaturity. Children had their playful childhood snatched from them, play being one of the basic ingredients necessary for the healthy development of an adult. Through the freedom of play they learned to be spontaneous and creative, but when they eventually came home from school to their families, they ate in silence and went to their separate rooms, turning on their communication screens for what was no better than indoctrination into Shadow. Orla was saddened by the miserable lives of dome children and couldn't wait for them to enjoy the many benefits awaiting them.

It had come to pass that, with the vast availability of inappropriate material available on the internet, world leaders had seen yet another opportunity to control the young with the consent of parents. At the beginning of the 21st century, some parents and educators complained about children watching aggressive behaviour on the media channels, and censorship was introduced.

With the overt conditioning of children gone, a more subtle way of controlling their moral compass evolved, and parents were unknowingly complicit. With the influence of highly sophisticated technology, subliminal images were introduced into the seemingly harmless children's programmes. The images that they were seeing consciously were depicting a view of the world that was very different from reality. These dome-dwelling children had no understanding of the plight of children outside of the domes. To them, life under the dome was normal and this illusion was reinforced from an early age by the subliminal messages that accompanied the programmes on the 'benign' children's entertainment channels. The message highlighted and engraved in their emotional memory was the perpetuation of the selfish, dominant and aggressive side of man. Because there were no conscious barriers, the images sank into their unconscious, into their memories, and became solid illusions of disconnection and fear.

Orla and Finn, having made the decision to bring both men and women to the island for the next level of initiation, contacted John and explained to him that it was not possible to conduct the next level through the comms portal. They didn't add that this level would be the most challenging so far.

It was arranged with John that the group would come to the island for the day only, as it was important they did not take too much time away from their everyday lives. Fortunately, the energy of the island allowed the royal family to bend time and cram a week of information into a day.

Finn went to the meeting place in the dome to collect the fourteen. They entered the vessel, surprised that it could accommodate so many comfortably, but they said nothing. It had become obvious that the fourteen had begun to see the couple as special, powerful and outside of their normal realm of understanding, More importantly, for the transformation process, they had silently conferred the mantle of authority onto Orla and Finn. Finn reflected on how easy it was to manipulate these people, if one was unscrupulous. They had no natural instincts to question that which was unfamiliar or challenging.

*

The group arrived in the Secret Garden and were once again enthralled by the wonders of nature. The trees looked larger and more lush than the last time they visited and the flowers were in full bloom, bursting with colour and fragrance.

Whilst in a reverie of intoxication from the many fragrances from the plants, Sheila's attention was drawn to the way that the plants were organised. From her youth, she vaguely remembered seeing pictures of farming when the plants still grew in fields, and the crops were organised in straight lines, making them easier to harvest. But in this garden the plants grew in specific formations that she couldn't quite discern as they were not at all regular. Finn noticed her puzzled look and identified immediately what the problem was.

"In nature plants have their own growing patterns. They choose the pattern from the energy of the soil that is their host and match it to the requirements of the plant. On the island all plant life is allowed to choose its own preferential pattern of growth, which ensures the yield is strong. This pattern can change from year to year depending on the weather and the needs of the community. If there is an increased need for a particular plant, the plant will change its pattern of growth the following year to increase the yield but still maintain the quality."

Sheila's eyes increased with size and also with confusion as Finn continued.

"If we put plants to grow in straight lines, they shut down as they are not able to express their own plant knowledge." Finn purposely held back the information about the plant spirits. A *step too far at this stage,* he considered wryly.

Finn took the conversation a bit further just to see her reaction. "It is the same with humans. If you constrict their natural expression, they in turn suppress their natural wisdom."

Sheila didn't look shocked; she took a deep breath in and closed her eyes, still trying to assimilate this revolutionary idea about plants, and indeed humans. The growth of any plants was a novelty to her as plant life under the domes had to be controlled because of the diminishing quality of the environment.

"I'm not sure how we are going to get all our nutritional requirements from plants," Sheila said. She was aware that decades previously, many people, unhappy with unhealthy farming practices, chose to become vegetarians, but because they had made the transition from animal protein too quickly, a lot of them had weakened themselves and their genetic line.

"To provide adequate nutrition, the plants have to contain super nutrition, and it is the precise combination of the plants that provides sufficient protein for growth and repair in humans," Finn said.

"In fact," Orla added, "the wheat is so rich on the island that flour products provide a good mix of nutrients."

"Can you expand more on the vegetarian issue?" Sheila urged.

"Over a century ago the Generals noticed that some people were trying to revert to a more natural way of living and part of that culture was adopting a diet that was plant-based. The Generals viewed this movement as a threat to their authority as it held the promise of expressing free will more fully. So, they decided to see how best they could turn the potentially threatening situation around to suit their needs – and it wasn't difficult

"At that time the vegetables offered contained a diluted quantity of nutrients. They knew that, without them lifting a finger, given time, the health of the already challenged human race would decline and that diet, together with accompanying lifestyle choices, would be deemed unhealthy and therefore not safe. As predicted, over two or three generations the health of those who had elected to follow plant-based diets suffered. The Generals took that opportunity to demonstrate the folly of following a natural lifestyle compared with the benefits of looking to their omnipotence to provide sufficient nutrients for the population."

As Orla finished her explanation, Sheila nodded her head slowly, trying to reconfigure the pieces of her life that she had believed to be normal but now appeared to be nothing but the fabrication of a few self-centred leaders.

John noticed that his wife and the other wives were fascinated with the garden, and he thought it typical of wifely interest.

"But," he asked Finn, "why are the gardeners of the Secret Garden men?" Finn smiled inwardly and explained almost as if he were talking to a child. "Whilst females on the island understand the use of plants for nutrition and health, the complete knowledge of the growing requirements for plants used for health remedies is held by a special bloodline of a family on the island." He didn't explain the important fact that the gardeners had the gift of communicating in the language of the trees and the plant spirits. *So much to teach them in such a little time*, he thought.

The group of men and women followed Finn silently. They were again transfixed by the splendour of the island. Never in their lifetimes had they experienced such a feast to their eyes, made easier by the clarity of the sun, whose sharp rays were not blocked by thick blankets of pollution.

With the warmth of the sun, they had removed their jackets. The men rolled up their sleeves and the women removed their cardigans. All of them exposed their white waxy skin to the wonderful penetrating rays of the warm sun. Orla observed that they had detected a slight moistness in the air that settled lightly on their skin. They were unaware that the moistness was their spirit guides depositing small molecules of Crystal knowledge onto their skin, which seeped through their pores and made their way into the cells of their bodies, awakening their dormant Crystal memory. The skin held the first barrier of memory that needed to be accessed before going into the deeper memory held in all the cells of their bodies. Finn could see what was happening: each person looked as if he or she was being wrapped in a cloud of mist, but on closer inspection the mist had form, which mirrored the shape of their human wards, that enveloped them in a cloak of protection.

As they walked further, Finn became aware of a quietness within them, a feeling very different, quite subtle but different. He could see that their spirit guides were beginning to influence their memories. The guides were imparting a sense of security and guidance, releasing the tension that isolation brought to a human, allowing them to release the fear that disconnection carried. One of the biggest fears that had been programmed into man was being abandoned, but for the first time in thousands of years these humans were beginning to sense what it was like to be deeply connected to something bigger and more powerful than themselves that instilled a sense of purity and light.

Eventually, the group arrived at the palace and both the men and their wives were strangely happy to be back at this comfortable old stone and crystal building. It was large but not too ornate; everything was functional, sourced from the surrounding countryside. As they entered the large foyer, rays of sunshine streamed through the window at the top of the wide sweeping staircase. The colours and complex gemoetric shapes of the window merged with the suns rays and flowed down each step to meet the group, who stood quietly, absorbing the warmth and light. As the rays of coloured light seeped through their bodies, travelling across their minds and down their spines, they felt their tense muscles begin to unravel even more. The first time they had visited the palace they hadn't noticed the coloured glass, and they asked Orla if the windows had been changed since their first visit. She shook her head, reassuring them that nothing had changed in the palace for longer than she could remember, but they were obviously seeing the island with fresh eyes. Maeve greeted them all warmly and offered them the normal island fare of welcome: herbal drinks with honey and herb cakes, which the group polished off with enthusiasm.

Orla gathered the group together, guiding them serenely to a room that had been prepared for the next level of their transformation. It was to be their special viewing room where they would discover their true history, their potential and what their role would be in the future of the planet.

The room was circular with no windows and a dome-shaped ceiling. The seats were fully reclining so that they could relax whilst watching the many chapters of the life of the planet. Orla instructed them to sit down and make themselves comfortable. Puffs of fragrances wafted around the room transporting them to a place of consciousness that was deeply relaxing but left them with the ability to observe intelligently; a place where there was least resistance to the challenging information they would receive.

The lights were dimmed and Orla spoke in a gentle voice mindful of the enormity of the challenging information that they were going to have to confront.

"You are now going to see the true history of the Earth, which is not the same that is taught in the dome schools." Aware that she did not want them to drop into any state of confusion that would limit their ability to assimilate challenging information, she gave them permission to ask questions at any time, knowing that questioning was a new skill that they were still honing. By this time they were all completely comfortable and relaxed and accepted Orla's words happily. The screen on the domed ceiling opened and the first image was that of the Earth before humans arrived on the planet. They were all surprised at the beauty of Earth before man or animals had arrived; it was a world inhabited by plant life, bursting with health and abundance.

"How could the planet have survived like that without man to help?" John asked naively.

Orla responded gently. "The Earth is a mirror of creation. Creation has an intelligence that is in all things on the planet, including man, in equal measure." John edited his stream of questions to ponder on this simple but equally immense explanation.

The scene changed, showing a landscape that had deteriorated considerably, and she knew that they would find the next piece of information very hard to accept. Orla continued with narrating Earth's story.

"Man had been created by a race of beings not from this solar system, as beasts of burden, with strong bodies but no facility in their brains to have individual thoughts or ideas, and definitely no free will. This was primitive man. They had been created to extract the minerals from the Earth's core, for their creators to transport to their own planet in another solar system. As the planet's core became more depleted, nature took a stand and rebelled at the rape of her minerals; she shut down and created an ice age which was the trigger for the plunderers to leave for easier spoils in another part of the galaxy. But they left behind those primitive humans to fend for themselves in a terrifying and unforgiving terrain. They had strength but no facility to find solutions to the ever-increasing challenges that haunted their daily lives.

"I want you to look very closely at the extreme fear etched in the bodies of these poor specimens of mankind." She paused before dropping in their laps the next piece of information.

"The fear that you are witnessing is a memory that is within each of you, in fact in all humans, and underpins your responses and actions, and ultimately your decisions."

John's legal mind could not cope with this as he expressed his disbelief at the plausibility. "I'm sorry, the very idea that our minds could be a reflection of such barbaric and primitive specimens is beyond belief."

"John, you will see how plausible it is when you understand how that primitive reactivity has adapted and translated into various aspects of man's history. You will see how the theme of fear is continually repeated through the ages," Orla reassured him, but she could tell he was not convinced.

Orla continued. "The Earth was covered in ice for many years and predictably only a handful of humans survived. The time under the ice gave the Earth the opportunity to regroup and recharge. Eventually the dampened fire in the bowels of the Earth reignited and burst forth, warming the planet's surface, and the ice began to melt slowly."

As Orla spoke, they watched the flurry of activity around the planet as the waters moved, reshaping the landscape and then, miraculously, a small island appeared surrounded by a fortress of crystal pillars, which created a dome of bright coloured light over the air space of the island. They were all watching intently, and it suddenly dawned on them that they were watching the creation of Crystal Island, the very place that they were currently enjoying.

Just as they were beginning to feel comfortable with the familiarity of the island, they saw that the island had visitors. Initially, they couldn't discern what it was: it had shape, it had colour, it was big but the detail was too difficult for them to identify. Orla increased the diffusion of fragrances into the room and, as if by magic, they began to see the detail. These were beings that had human shape in an exaggerated size and appeared to emit a golden light that came out of their core, encasing their whole bodies in an aura of sunshine, but they were not quite human. Then, suddenly, the group identified the similarity between these beings and the royal family.

"The beings that you are seeing are the Crystalanders. They are the guardians of Crystal Wisdom and it is Crystal Wisdom that keeps the whole universe in balance. Man-made knowledge will never be good enough, only Crystal Wisdom can support this important and critical role." None of the group made a sound. They had all grown up on fictional stories that described the threat of aliens invading the planet, but they had not expected that these 'aliens' would be such amazing specimens. Orla corrected their thinking.

"These are not aliens. These are pure Crystal Wisdom in a form that we can relate to, and that Crystal Wisdom is in each of us. What you see in front of you, you will eventually be able to access within your own memory."

She realised that she might as well be speaking a foreign language, but she didn't concern herself as she knew it was not their conscious mind that she was addressing, it was the deepest part of their emotional memories. The screen continued with pictures of the Crystalanders teaching early man to use Crystal Wisdom, their selection process for choosing humans to share their crystal genes, and then finally, images of the planet flourishing under their careful tutelage. But more shocking than anything else were scenes of the whole planet flourishing, the people looking healthy and happy and every aspect of society working well and integrated with each other. Orla could see that the group had sensed that something was missing from this picture, which none of them could identify. They believed that this was not an accurate picture of man because there was something missing, but they could not detect what it was. Orla knew she would have to guide them.

"Can you identify any predatory behaviour?"

"Can you see any competitive behaviour?"

"Can you see any cruelty?"

There was silence.

The truth began to dawn on the women first. Here was a society where men, women and children respected and supported one another, where the communities worked as one. There was no such thing as separate countries, Federations or principalities, just groups of smaller communities all with the same goals.

Orla decided to have a break to discuss with them how they were responding to the new history lesson. As the screen became still, Finn gradually increased the lighting in the room.

The room was quiet, each one deep in thought. Frederic was intrigued with their use of crystal for energy and expressed the desire to understand how this worked. Orla reminded them all that the temperature of the planet during the peak of Crystal Wisdom was very mild so they didn't need to have heavy-duty heating systems. There were parts of the Earth, particularly at high altitudes, that were colder, but communities were not encouraged to live in those places. However, what was valuable from the higher altitudes was the plant life that held specific valuable medicinal qualities.

Helen had particularly noticed that the women had equal authority and she rather innocently asked, "Who taught them to make such important decisions?"

"The ability to make decisions is within all mankind," Orla said. "That is the basis of free will, the ability to choose, but making choices is also a skill which has to be developed, and the more practice one has, the better one becomes. In the next screening you will see how that skill was lost in women," she warned.

"What did the communities use to defend themselves?" Phillip asked.

"Defend from what exactly?" Finn queried.

"Well, anything… from being taken over by another community, from having their valuables taken."

"There was no need to defend communities as there was a deep respect for each other, other communities and peoples from different lands; they shared a healthy interdependence. Their priority was not inward and selfish, their priority was outward, focusing on the needs of the planet. There was a group intention of care, respect and nurturing that flourished in those days, allowing people to be relaxed and spontaneous, which was necessary for nature to communicate freely with mankind. No one person owned anything; the Earth project was definitely a group project," Finn said.

"Can that ever be regained?" John asked wistfully.

"Yes, of course, that Crystal memory is still within man's memory, it has just been covered over and forgotten. It needs to be awakened."

"But how long will that take?" John queried.

"It is much closer than you think, John," Orla reassured.

What she hadn't told them, of course, was that she had visited Crystaland a year ago and asked the Diamond Elders how quickly man would respond once she and Finn started working with the pioneers. They had assured her that the timing was perfect. Humans had arrived at a point where some of them could respond but, if it were left for another five years, it would be too late and the planet would be dead as well as everyone on it.

Orla asked the group to lie back in preparation for the next viewing. The screen began to reflect the sad images of the decline of mankind after the Crystalanders left Earth. The seeds of doubt gradually took up residence in their hearts and, without the presence of those super beings, the competitive side of man began to vie for the vacant position of authority.

She only showed them the basic information, holding back from showing them everything dark that she had witnessed on Crystaland. The last thing these people needed was to reaffirm the fear myths that were already at the forefront of their memory. They just needed to see a summary of how the planet had gone from being paradise to hell in a relatively short space of time, to understand what needed to change, and more importantly to ensure that those mistakes from the past were never repeated.

Interestingly, it was the women who responded to the brutality on the screen more than the men. As they witnessed the cycles of war that blighted history and the unceasing cruelty that was unleashed by warlords, they realised how the women and children suffered more than men as a result of those actions. Whilst men were caught up in the misplaced glory of fighting to defend territories, it was the women who were left to deal with the hardship and pain of daily living that had to be endured in the presence, or indeed the aftermath, of war. The last two major world wars achieved more awareness of the brutality and futility of war, but it was still painted in a picture framed in glory. However, one thing that did attract their attention was the employment of women in factories during those wars. Whilst the men were away fighting, the women had to perform those roles and did so easily. This was yet another piece of history that had been rewritten. The dome-dwellers had been programmed to believe that women could not possibly do a job that had been carried out by a man because the capabilities of the genders had been completely polarised.

Whilst Orla watched the screen, she was reminded of women's sorry tale that she had witnessed during her awakening with Whale on the Turquoise Crystal world. Whale was the keeper of all Earth's memories and he had gently exposed her to the plight of women throughout the history of humans. Women had fallen from their natural position as elders of communities, the legacy of the Crystalanders, to being shells of their former selves. They had succumbed to the overt and covert programming that women were not as clever as men, their brains perceived as not having the capacity to work at the elevated and sophisticated levels of men, and with each generation those myths and illusions were reinforced.

Orla stopped the screening, as she could tell that the women were becoming confused and the men were becoming defensive. Finn observed the men and considered that if these were the best that the planet could offer, what did the men look like who had much deeper conditioning from Shadow? He was of course thinking of the Elite.

When the screen finally stopped and the lights turned on, Orla scanned the group and felt a little sorry for them. They had not realised that their lives had been built on fragile castles of myths, and the truth was actually horrific. Every aspect of their lives was a lie. Mark, who was responsible for education, was the first to speak.

"How do we know this is the truth and not a work of fiction? I am in charge of the curriculum of schools and none of this information has ever appeared in our history texts."

Orla asked him to remember if there was a time when there were history books, or indeed fiction books, that described events in history. He considered her question and shook his head: everyone knew that all the books had been recorded onto digital libraries so that the paper – the last remaining evidence of trees – could be used for energy. As he read Mark's thoughts, Finn shook his head, amazed yet again, by the distortion of the truth.

Yes, it was true that the trees and forests had disappeared – man had not listened at all to defenders of the environment, who had been discredited as extremists. During the early 21st century there had been a great movement of people who had tried to save the ever-depleted forests of the planet, but they lost their battle to the power leaders who were led by a philosophy that identified the need and then found the easiest way to access the resources to match that need, used it all up, and moved on. They had erroneously viewed the planet as providing everything for the comfort of mankind, completely missing the critical fact that every aspect of nature worked together in a synergy of support. Their hierarchical thinking had created a distinct pecking order based on ridiculous hedonistic priorities, and had applied this simplistic model to nature.

Orla gently asked Mark, "Do you think those texts could have been tampered with?" She knew very well what the answer was, but she needed to prompt him to begin to question.

He considered her question and realised that he had never seen a book.

"Before the domes," Orla explained, "history was committed to books, and museums also stored original written sources which supported the facts that were contained in the books. When the recording of information became more formalised in man, records were kept of every decision by every person in authority, so primary sources were verified before the facts were committed to history. Even so, those primary sources would have been written with a political bias and therefore were subjective. What I am showing you on the viewing screen, however, is the recorded history of the planet as it actually occurred, which is held in the memory of every molecule on Crystal Island."

Mark brought them back into the realm that they could understand and asked, "Could you give us more information about the books? As this is something that we have not encountered before."

John sat quietly, pondering on whether he should talk about his experiences with books. "Actually I have seen the books that Orla is referring to. When I was a boy I was shown some old books that had been archived and probably forgotten."

"Why were you shown the books?" Sheila asked, slightly shocked that this had never been spoken about before.

John considered his answer, as he did not want to appear to be different from the others.

Finn observed John's thinking process as it oscillated from being totally honest to bouncing back to the fear of rejection. Orla intervened. "John has a strong family line of writers. His love of words touched one of his teachers, who fortunately had access to those archived books and encouraged him to explore his talent for language."

Sheila stared from Orla to John, aghast. *This man that she had been married to for a number of years had a gift for words and it had never been mentioned before?* They would all eventually realise that John's gift for words combined with his natural intelligence would be qualities that would carry them all through the next stage of the Earth's evolution.

Orla and Finn brought their focus back to the viewing and realised that the group had to be exposed to more facts about their past as they were completely ignorant of the true history of the planet. Orla asked them to look back at the screen. The picture in front of them was of a building in one of the Federations that was very old, which had been destroyed in the past few decades. The scene changed to show the inside of the building, and on the wall was a plaque which stated the words 'The British Library'. She explained that every book that had ever been published had been stored there, and took them into the cold rooms where the oldest manuscripts were kept.

They could see the titles and dates of the books, and the educationalist in Mark ached to go and touch them. "In fact," Orla explained, "all these books had been destroyed before the domes were built. They had been deemed dangerous as they were a true record of man, his laws, his creative thoughts, his religions, his science." The group was intrigued by the amount of valuable information that was stored in the Library.

"Were there books about the Crystalanders?" Mark asked.

"No, Mark, the Crystalanders left an oral tradition of their existence as that is more powerful than the written word. The carriers of the Crystalander stories were originally women but they were eventually silenced."

Finn interjected. "Although Crystalanders are not mentioned, throughout the centuries reference was made to deities, and higher intelligences, from whom man obtained knowledge of the universe."

Mark's appetite was truly whetted and he was eager to see more of these books and ancient scrolls. Orla changed the view to another building in the same Federation as the British Library, and that was the British Museum.

"In this amazing building there were many artefacts from man's early history, depicting scenes which reflected an elevated level of intelligence that was inconsistent with man's natural evolution. The story that you have been told is that man was very primitive physically and intellectually, who at some point took a quantum leap in his evolution to having superior intelligence and controlled the world that he inhabited. Well, that isn't true, that is yet another myth. The ancient artefacts that were in the museum were testimony to a different story. The engraving on those artefacts depicted scenes of primitive man being visited by highly civilised beings who donated their knowledge to the Earth, which was most definitely superior to the natural intelligence of humans at that time.

"Some of the Crystaland teachings had remained on the Earth in small pockets of countries. As man became more aware, he was able to unravel some of the missing pieces of information that proved humans had received help at some time in history from beings outside of the Earth's solar system with a higher intelligence. Scientists had eventually been able to determine the exact ages of those artefacts, and were surprised to find that some had been created from a knowledge that preceded man-science by thousands of years.

"Questions began to be asked as to the authenticity of man's lineage, and towards the end of the 21st century the curators of such museums were instructed to gradually remove and destroy evidence of man's earlier intelligent helpers and only keep those pieces that were associated with war. And so, the museum was not destroyed but became a monument to the battles of men and the equipment they needed to win those wars. The same thing happened with the art galleries."

Orla changed the view on the screen, which reflected the beautiful galleries of one of the Federations that had produced gifted artists who had revolutionised art three centuries ago.

"The work of these artists gave accurate accounts of history from the level of the ordinary people, not just the people in power. Oh yes, there had been history books recording man's history, but the information gained from the primary sources was written invariably by men and most certainly by the victors of war rather than the losers.

But art was a medium that could be used to depict the real history hidden in symbolism. Recognising their power to instruct and inform, those meaningful pictures were destroyed and only those depicting the victories of war remained. Equally, paintings that reflected beautiful landscapes were destroyed as they were evidence of the possibility of a life full of natural beauty. Gradually every connection that man had with nature was overwritten by the authorship of Shadow."

Orla stopped and looked at the group, who had gone beyond questioning. They were transfixed by her every word. Finn increased the lighting in the room, and Orla continued the next part of the story without images.

"However, there was one area that they could not completely destroy and that was the music of man. The vibration of sound is key to the function of nature and is one of the gifts given to man by the Crystalanders. Music has travelled a checkered path through history, but the power leaders acknowledged its ability to uplift, heal, inspire and, more importantly, impart messages to the memory. The Crystalanders had gifted the melody of the universe into man's memory, which was available to all, and could never be erased completely, only overwritten. But the power leaders recognised that this was yet another powerful tool that they could hijack and use to influence the masses.

"In the early days of crystal music, man created instruments that reflected the sounds and vibrations of the planet. After the Crystalanders left the planet, a form of orderly and structured music evolved, which harnessed the sounds and put them into form. This was a music that had many rules and was only available to a privileged few, but, at about the same time that women had been given the authority to vote for their governments, a different sound began to emerge from those instruments which had been so strictly used for formal music. It was an unstructured form of playing that relied more on feeling and expressing the emotion of sound. This gave birth to a revolution in music that had the ability to awaken the desire to break away from the constraints and conditioning of society. The lyrics spoke about feelings and emotions, that progressed to speaking of rebellion against governments. This music influenced the young, potentially the next generation of leaders, in a big way, and they began to question. They wanted to follow a different path from the heavily conditioned life of their parents and, with the increasing degeneration of the planet, young people naturally turned to music to express their fears for their environment; the desire for mankind to express his feelings is inherent, a legacy of Crystal Wisdom. Any form of music that resonated on an emotional level, good or bad, became increasingly popular; the audience was seeking a sound that resonated and released feelings at a deeper level than was commonly expressed in society.

"Then two things happened. The leaders saw this as a form of anarchy and knew that it had to be stamped out, so they whispered into the ears of the profiteers and told them that a whole new product was emerging from which they could obtain great wealth. It was later to become known as popular music. The leaders wanted to control the music; they saw it was a very useful medium to persuade the young, to distract the young – in fact – to manipulate the young. The issue was that most naturally gifted musicians did not want to be contained, controlled or told what to write purely to make money. The new industry looked at these young anarchists and thought that they needed to be controlled, as there was big money to be made from manipulating the audiences. And so the talented musicians, who invariably were naive to the ways of business, were legally bound into contracts which fashioned them into producing music that impinged on their creative ability.

"Eventually, technology improved so much that the music industry didn't require talented musicians as any musical sound could be replicated electronically, or so they thought. The manufactured music lacked an ingredient that touched the soul of the audience, an ingredient that can only be produced by a musician. And so the sacred art of music was downgraded from being a medium for planetary healing to a middle range entertainment, until eventually popular music lost its originality and became bland, each track sounding similar to the next. The vibration of that music spoke only to the very basic levels of emotion and therefore resonated with the base side of man, which was so attractive to Shadow. The young audiences were slowly introduced to this downgraded form of music and eventually accepted this as the music of their choice but, actually, there was no real choice."

Orla finished speaking and paused. She could see they were all confused – they had no idea about the concept of music created by musicians. They had music in the domes but it was piped electronically produced music that played in the background. Music wasn't taught at school, it was produced electronically, and Orla realised that she would have to demonstrate to them the subliminal message that was coming through that music. She activated the screen and a view appeared of a music festival from just before the domes were created. Entertainers were playing music on stage at a supposedly live event, but all the music was pre-recorded.

Orla described what was happening. "Most of the audience was under the influence of mind-altering chemicals or alcohol that blew wide open the gates of their emotional memories. The gate keepers of the imaginal part of their minds had been anaesthetised." Orla instructed them to look closer, whereupon she opened up the memory of the space that engulfed the audience to reveal the phrases that were impregnated into the bland musical chords:

"The planet is a dangerous place."

"People are dangerous."

"Do not trust your family members."

"Work hard."

"Your Generals must be obeyed at all costs, otherwise you will not survive."

The screen became blank. Orla looked at them as they quietly digested the horrific information.

"How did they manage to do that with the words?" Anne asked.

"It's quite simple when you use technology, Anne. This method had been introduced into advertising in the early 20th century but had been banned because of its insidious ability to influence," Orla replied.

Orla decided to stop so that they could have a refreshment break. The women in particular were looking drained, which Orla had expected because of the concentration of information that was being crammed into just one day.

Orla shot a thought to Finn. *"How much information do you think we can expose them to?"*

"It's a difficult balance. They are here for a short while and we don't have the luxury of time to keep bringing them back to the island, but we have to show them the truths of the past otherwise they will not understand the depth of change that has to take place. We cannot afford to leave out any awful detail as they need to know the negative potential of man," Finn responded.

After their break the group silently followed Orla and Finn back to the viewing room.

Joshua had been silent throughout all of the screenings and asked, "How have the people on the island managed to maintain such robust health while the rest of the world is hanging onto life by their weakened fingernails?"

"Do you remember the quality of the plants in the Secret Garden?" Orla asked.

He nodded. "They are amazing but I still do not understand how they are involved in health."

"If you look at the screen I will show you."

Orla directed them to look at the screen. They sat back and the screen filled with images of the Crystalanders showing humans how to use the plants for medicine and nutrition.

Joshua and Cynthia looked on with keen interest and wondered what had happened to stop this. "Was it the failure of agriculture that caused those natural medicines to disappear?" Joshua asked.

Orla looked serious and replied, "Natural medicines had ceased to be used by the established health agencies and the responsibility for health was taken away from the individual by men of science funded by the large pharmaceutical companies who made vast profits from disease."

Joshua was troubled by this explanation because he believed that pharmaceutical companies were key to keeping people alive.

Orla, realising Joshua needed a simple explanation, said: "Natural medicines cannot legally be owned by any company – they belong to the planet, not to any one person or corporation. Profits in corporations can only come from owning the rights to sell a product. If profits cannot be made then there will be no investment. So, the health industry favoured profit from treating disease, real or created, with chemicals rather than using natural plants that had the power to prevent disease."

"What do you mean, 'real or created'?" Joshua asked.

"Look at the screen again," Orla instructed.

They all saw how the priority for making money became more important than improving health. Children were given increasing numbers of vaccinations, the population was pumped full of antibiotics and other chemical-based remedies until one day the whole circus came to a grinding halt. The children who had been subjected to the multitude of vaccinations over many generations grew into adults with failing immune systems. The over-use of antibiotics resulted in resistant bacterial infections, and viruses become super sophisticated, developing their own intelligence – nothing could touch them. Joshua remembered what he had been told about life before the domes: viruses had rampaged through communities and countries leaving a path of death in their wake.

Joshua was still not completely convinced. Cynthia, however, was shifting over to this understanding. She had been suspicious for a long while about vaccinations and had been concerned about her children – in fact, not just her children. Before she married she had been a teacher of primary school children and had noticed that each intake year, the children were becoming more and more introverted, very easy to deal with in fact. She also noticed that they were weaker, with very little motivation. They did as they were told, but nothing more. Her thoughts went back to her children who, before they could go to school, had to be vaccinated for a whole series of diseases, with regular boosters throughout their school life. She quickly calculated the number of people times the number of vaccinations in a child's lifetime and realised that vaccinations were a very lucrative business. She was beginning to join the dots from the information that Orla was presenting and questioned her more directly.

"What happens if you don't vaccinate for these diseases?" she asked.

"With the correct natural nutrition, natural environment and a healthy lifestyle, physically and emotionally, the immune system of mankind will be stronger and will be able to deal with any viruses that occur. The whole function of small childhood illnesses is to activate and strengthen the immune system."

The childhood illnesses that Orla was talking about were coughs and colds, relatively minor issues. However, Cynthia reminded Orla of the terrible diseases that could befall children of the 22nd century.

"Cynthia, some of them are man-made."

Cynthia looked puzzled but Orla thought this would be a good time to introduce to the group some home truths about ethnic cleansing that had been a feature of man's history for thousands of years and was still happening today.

Orla directed their attention to the screen again, where they saw a whole continent that had been devastated by a terrible disease which ripped through the immune systems of its victims. This continent had a high proportion of poverty, and the disease had left the continent depleted as the poor were the first victims. Orla showed them the laboratory that had manufactured such a disease, which was in a completely different continent. The idea had been to introduce this disease only to countries where the poor were an inconvenience. But there was a problem: this virus did not understand racial, cultural or geographical boundaries and began to infiltrate into every level of society in all the countries of the world. The Generals had failed in their attempt to only remove people who had become an inconvenience, so they asked the laboratories to release the antidote for the disease, which rendered it dormant in the recipient. But as this cost money, only the people who could afford the antidote survived, while people in poorer countries didn't. Cynthia was horrified; she had seen the women and children wiped out first, women unwittingly transmitting the disease to the next generation as it travelled like wildfire through the poorer continents. There was a moment, and only a brief moment, when the group hesitated in their belief of what they were seeing, but something deep inside their memory urged them to listen and trust Orla and Finn.

James reflected on his economics training and eventually came to the shocking realisation that the priority for all businesses and governments for the last few centuries had been solely to make a profit. The people were not important, the plant life most definitely not important, and the planet was an object of abuse. He was beginning to see patterns which began to stimulate in him the process of questioning.

Orla and Finn decided to leave them for a while to allow them some time to discuss and assimilate this new information. When the couple left the room, it was the women who started to question what had gone so wrong with the world that it had resulted in just a small percentage of people living under the safety of the domes and the rest forced to live on wastelands, waiting to die.

Anne was the first to begin questioning. "So," she started, "it is possible to live in a healthy, balanced and fulfilled way, living from the land, so what has changed to stop this?"

Phillip answered in a quiet and steady voice. His background in the military had trained him to identify patterns of behaviour in an enemy. "After seeing these viewings of Earth's history I have recognised a strategy that has been used by most great warriors of history – to instill fear into the enemy, to dominate and ultimately control. But this practice has seeped out of the offices of the warlords into every level of society. The practice of Crystal Wisdom is the complete opposite. The planet is important, not man, and if man can live in balance with nature the planet will thrive. Man has made one vital mistake with his warmongering, he has gone into battle with the planet." His razor-sharp mind had very quickly cut through the detail of what they had seen and summarised the problem.

The group got the message loud and clear and it made absolute sense to them. They needed to make friends with the planet again and learn to communicate with nature.

Orla and Finn returned to the group, and Mary asked, "There seems to be so much to change, do we have enough time to reverse the destruction? The planet looks so far down that track, a million miles away from Crystal Wisdom."

Orla, pleased with their progress, responded, "There is enough time; in fact, the planet has asked for help, knowing the time frame required for the regenerative process." They all looked astonished and she continued. "The next part of your training will be to have your Crystal memory overwrite the prominence of your fear conditioning."

Although the group was tired, they showed no lack of enthusiasm to continue. Finn gave them more plant remedies, which helped their bodies relax whilst still being able to focus mentally.

The group was then taken to a different room in the palace that was circular without windows. In preparation Finn had projected a wall of ruby ray around the room to act as a buffer from any interference from Shadow. Each of the group was still connected to Shadow, and Finn had to ensure that it was not conscious of what was happening in the room.

Orla asked them all to lay down in a circle with their heads facing inward. Finn stood in the middle of the circle, directing the ray equally amongst the group. Orla sprayed essences around the room and began to emit a sound that started very high as she walked past each one, and gradually the tone came down to a deep resonating vibration that gently activated their spines.

At that level of relaxation she asked them to once again bring to their imaginal mind their male and female ancestors and observe them more closely. She asked them first to look at the males, which they did. She then slowly removed a veil from their minds, allowing them to see the black tentacles of Shadow that were coming from the spines of each of their recent male ancestors. They were horrible, like large jagged black spider legs. The group shuddered in disgust.

"I want you to be brave and trace the tentacles back to their point of origin," Orla instructed.

To their surprise and distaste, they traced the tentacles back to the Chief Generals of the Federations, whereupon the tentacles became stronger. Finn urged them to look even further because the tentacles were still attached to another source. They went back and saw that the source was a group of twelve men, all of whom had indistinct faces. Orla explained that these men were responsible for everything that happened on Earth; they controlled absolutely everyone. The Chief Generals reported to these twelve men.

But the attachments did not finish there. "As well as your ancestors, you also have those attachments but it is not possible for you to see them." The women shuddered at the thought of these tentacles being attached to their spines. The men swallowed, trying to hide their disgust. "Finn will remove them from your spines."

Finn activated his Ruby crystal, giving him connection with the Ruby Crystal world to give him extra help for the next phase. He directed the ruby ray over John, starting at the crown of his head, then travelling down his spine. This had the desired effect of releasing the tentacles attached to his spine. With the tentacles released, a deep ruby shard of light rested above his head and went through his body. Finn projected the ray of ruby light into each of the men, starting at the top of their spine, going through each vertebra. One by one, the tentacles were released, but they did not go away – they stayed nearby, hovering and waiting. Quickly, Finn worked on each man until all seven had been disengaged. Finn turned his attention to the women and took up his place at their heads.

The women were easy to deal with as they only had one attachment, through the solar plexus. It was the main fear attachment, but although it was only one, it was much thicker as its focus was to undermine women's direct access to Crystal Wisdom. Finn directed the ray onto each woman, and Shadow reluctantly released its tentacles from them, but again stayed nearby, hovering, waiting for an opportunity to re-engage. Finn and Orla scanned the room to identify where Shadow was lurking. The men and women on the floor were oblivious to what was happening. They had slipped into a state of semi-consciousness having had the energy vampires released from their bodies and minds. Finn directed his attention to Shadow skulking in the corners of the room. It shuffled closer together to form a stronger group and Finn, cool with intention and focus, ran his hand over the Ruby crystal again, creating a stronger ray, directing it like a rapier towards the blackness of fear. Finally, he intoned the sound of courage and Shadow didn't stand a chance against the combined power of sound and crystal. The tentacles separated and shrank away with the continual onslaught, eventually disappearing through the walls. As soon as the tentacles diffused through the walls and connected with the pure atmosphere of the island, they disintegrated into a black dust. The air spirits gently moved into the space, gathered the black particles into clouds and pushed them out to the Crystal Fortress. The fortress turned its full attention on the black clouds, focusing all its energy on gathering the clouds into one ball, and with the almighty force of each and every crystal pillar, directed the dark mass above the energy field of the island where it imploded and was scattered far beyond the island, beyond the Earth and eventually beyond the solar system. Finn and Orla watched the expulsion of Shadow, knowing that those tentacles came from a dark place in the cosmos and that the black dust would eventually find its way home and reform. But that would take time.

Orla began to sing in a language none of them understood, to seal the perfection of Crystal Wisdom into the part of their memory that had previously hosted Shadow. The men experienced a feeling of stretching and lengthening down their spine and the women felt as if they could breathe much deeper.

"Why did we only have one attachment?" Sheila asked.

"You have just one attachment because Shadow does not connect to female hormones. It can only connect with your adrenal glands," Finn answered.

The wives turned to their husbands with a mixture of revulsion and fear in anticipation of seeing their husbands' attachments.

Finn smiled and explained, "I can assure you that all the tentacles of Shadow have been removed, and have been banished from our solar system, to their place of origin."

"Where is that?" Mark asked.

"They come from a place outside of the understanding of any Crystal memory, in a distant and inhospitable part of the cosmos."

Orla could see that the women were beginning to question the whole basis of their relationships with their partners. Both Orla and Finn knew that these couples would eventually need time to regroup and realign their relationships.

Orla instructed them again to close their eyes and breathe deeply as she sang to them in a different tone, bringing a sense of unity back into the room. When she stopped singing they opened their eyes and blinked, sitting up very slowly. She knew that they would be tired. The men stood up and flexed their spines with a mixture of pain and pleasure, as they were able to stretch their back like never before. Orla was surprised by the pallor of their faces. Their energy source had been released, and although that energy was not good, it was still a form of energy. Orla knew that they needed to reactivate their natural energy centres and led the group outside to have refreshments and also complexes of minerals, which would go straight into their bloodstream into their cells, fully activating the cells' energy centres that had been partially closed down for generations.

"The next part of your development will be carried out in separate groups," Orla announced.

By this time there was no questioning from the group, their trust in the royal couple was complete.

Orla took the women into a circular room at the top of the palace that formed a tower with seven crystal windows. Each window reflected a different shade of emerald, ranging from the lightest jade to a blackish green. Engraved within each window were copper geometrical designs. The women walked around the room, looking closely at each window, which reflected the height and width of each woman. Orla asked them to stand in front of the windows as she infused the room with essences, and in that instant, almost by magic, the sunshine came through each window, reflecting onto their bodies various shades of green and the geometric shapes. Orla had quietly left the room and when she came back she was wearing her emerald crystal robes that she had been given on the Emerald Crystal world. The women looked at her, taking in every detail of the cloth, which was like emerald silk with strands of copper interwoven with the same geometric shapes that were in the windows. Orla stood in the middle of the room with the women encircled around her. She closed her eyes and began to intone a high-pitched sound that activated rays from the darkest emerald window. Orla directed the rays onto each woman, immersing them in the wisdom of emerald crystal.

She instructed them to lay down on the cool floor, which they all did gladly as they were beginning to become lightheaded, and the feeble strength in their legs was being challenged by the pulsating energy travelling up and down their limbs. They lay on the floor, slightly confused by what was happening to their bodies, and Orla began to sing to them in the melody that was familiar to them, which they trusted. She stood at the foot of each one and directed different tones down their bodies. Each woman felt waves and ripples and subtle vibrations go up and down her body; it was as if each cell in their bodies was waking up for the very first time. Orla instructed them to keep their eyes closed and changed her sound to the specific song that invoked their crystal spirit guides to present themselves fully. Responding to Orla's invitation, the seven crystal guides entered the room in a human cloud-like form and descended over their hosts in an embrace that connected to each vertebra in their spine. With each connection the muscles that were connected to each vertebra began to unravel, bathing the tissue of their bodies in a crystal glow. When the guides had completely immersed themselves into their wards, Orla ceased singing and invited the women to open their eyes and sit up. They opened their eyes and gradually brought themselves up into a seated position, looking dazed and shocked. Orla waited for them to speak.

"What just happened?" asked Sheila. The others shook their heads, looking baffled.

"You have just been reintroduced to your crystal spirit guides. These guides are for you and you alone, they know you better than anyone and they know your potential. They will be with you at all times, whispering to you, reminding you of Crystal Wisdom. You can talk to them and ask them for advice," Orla said.

"How do we talk to them?" Cynthia asked

"I will give you a special essence that you spray over yourselves when you wish to communicate with your guide," Orla replied.

"Wow, and it's as simple as that?" asked Cynthia.

"Yes – Crystal Wisdom is actually quite simple," Orla said.

Maeve entered the room, greeted the women and joined them in the circle. The women looked at each other, knowing that Maeve's presence meant they would be given more information. She instructed them to be seated.

"You have to fully understand what your true role is. To do that you must understand and honour the beauty of your bodies and also the importance of correct physical union with your husbands." Orla paused and observed the women as they shuffled uncomfortably.

"There is no need to be embarrassed," Orla reassured them. "A woman's body is a wonderful creation and a reflection of the planet's creativity. Because of the nature of your hormonal system you have direct access to Crystal Wisdom, the reason why Shadow could not attach itself completely to you."

There was still no recognition from the women – they hadn't a clue what she was saying.

Orla continued, knowing that they would eventually understand. She asked them to form a circle on the floor as they had done previously, with their heads facing in towards the centre, and instructed them to close their eyes while Maeve sprayed the now familiar essences over their bodies. She guided their inner sight down to their reproductive organs and Maeve went to each woman, laying her hand over their lower abdomens, helping to connect their awareness to their bodies. Orla's voice took on a softer, more melodic tone and she asked them to travel with their inner sight into their bodies until they could see the detail of their atrophied reproductive organs. The two royal women could also see each woman's view. Maeve suspected that the island remedies and the work that Orla had done with them had given them a bit of a boost as she could see some of the tissue was beginning to look more healthy. Orla activated her diamond ring by stroking the crown of the stone, and directed its sharp ray into each of the women. Almost immediately, the tissue of the targeted organs regenerated and became pink and healthy. The healing accelerated and the ovaries became plump, the fallopian tubes cleared and the lining of the uterus activated. Instantly the women began to sense what they interpreted as painful cramps. Orla asked them to focus differently on the sensation.

"It is just your reproductive organs trying to get into sync with the planet and the moon."

They all experienced flutterings, heat and spasms. Eventually the sensations calmed, prompting a glow erupting from deep within their uteri, spilling out into the whole pelvic cavity and making its way up the body to the throat, where it penetrated a major blockage in all of them. They gasped, choked and spluttered and then finally settled, releasing a warmth that travelled from their crown to their pelvic floor. Once that connection was made, Orla activated her Sapphire crystal ring, directing its blue ray to their throats, prompting the involuntary opening and closing of the larynx, causing more coughing and spluttering. An explosion of heat followed by the sapphire ray shot out from between their eyebrows. Orla directed the ray into their throats, where it travelled down the front of their bodies, circulating up their spines and finally creating a vortex of energy encapsulating the whole body. The activity eventually subsided, leaving them with a sensation of gentle pulsing throughout their whole bodies.

Maeve asked them to open their eyes slowly and gently sit up. They obediently followed her instructions, slowly opening their eyes, looking around the room, grappling to find an explanation for what had just happened and what they were feeling. As they sat up, Orla and Maeve thought they looked as if they had been totally unravelled. Every vestige of tension had been removed from their bodies; they were completely limp. Orla gave them all some island water, and they gradually became more aware of their surroundings. When they had regained their balance fully, Maeve asked them to get up from the floor and sit on chairs that had been placed in a circle around the room.

"Do you have any questions, ladies?" Orla asked, knowing that their minds were trying to process turbulent thoughts.

"Does this mean we are going to be having periods again regularly?" asked Sheila. They had already had one cycle since coming to the island the first time and none of them were impressed.

"I need to explain to you the whole process of the menstrual cycle for you to fully understand its importance. And yes, you will now begin to menstruate again but not for long. As you have finished with your child-bearing years there is no need to continue, so your bodies will adapt." Orla knew that these women were undergoing a crash course in Crystal Wisdom and they would have to do a quantum leap of understanding before being placed into early menopause.

Orla continued with their crystal biology lesson. "The reproductive organs of human females are not just for birthing babies. There is another use for them, which is just as important. Like all of natural life there is a cycle of reproduction, and the cycles of females are no different from other plants or animals. They all reflect the cycles and rhythms of nature. Every time a woman ovulates she connects with those cycles and when she has a child it is activated yet again, and her connection to Crystal Wisdom is increased. The idea of menstruation holds much more importance than just a monthly inconvenience. With the shedding of the lining of the womb comes the shedding of the toxins experienced not just by the women, but more importantly, those experienced by the planet. As an example, the women on Crystal Island have light menstrual flows only lasting one day. There is no inconvenience to them nor do they have to rest before and during."

"So are you saying the more toxins you are trying to process, the more rest you need?" Helen queried.

"Exactly," Orla continued. "A woman is so attuned to the planet that her reproductive organs mirror the environment of the planet. If it is out of balance, as it is now, then her body will reflect that imbalance, which will reflect in her cycle. The more toxic the planet, the more a woman will suffer as it takes a lot of energy for women to process not just the physical toxins – she also reflects the hurt and anger of the planet, which is why women sometimes are more emotional or angry when premenstrual – they are just reflecting the collective emotions of the planet."

"So females would appear to be the receptors and balancers of the planet?"

"Yes, Anne, that is why women are so important in the business of finding creative solutions. It is women who interpret what is out of balance and what needs to be done to redress that balance."

This had much more impact. They were being told again that they had a very valuable role to play. Slowly, Orla, was trying to make them aware of their unique and valuable gifts.

"That sounds a huge responsibility," Mary offered timidly.

"Don't forget you have your crystal spirit guides now to help you," Orla reminded them as she realised the impact of her words. They were being told of the valuable role they had in the future of the planet, which she could see was overwhelming for them.

"What happens after the menopause?" Martha asked.

Mary and Martha were cousins and Orla reflected on their physical similarities. They were exactly the same age and looked almost like twins, which initially confused Orla but then she examined their genetic memory and saw that they were a product of IVF. Martha's mother's eggs had not survived the cryogenic storage after they had been harvested at puberty, so Mary's mother had donated her eggs to her sister and they had elected to conceive at the same time.

"During the menstrual years you are learning to listen to and interpret the needs of the planet, developing your intuition so that when your periods begin to cease you can focus all your attention on accurately interpreting the needs of the planet. During the child-bearing years the focus has to be on the needs of the children; after menopause that nurturing focus shifts to a global need. This is the time to become teachers of children, of women and men, and become the elders of the communities." At the point when they thought that they could not take on another piece of information, Orla introduced something quite radical.

Orla asked them all to close their eyes. She reminded them that they would not be expected to do this work on their own. "You have your crystal spirit guides, but also each woman has a special guardian. I want you to close your eyes now, take in a deep breath and regulate your breathing." Orla silently intoned a melody, summoning the guardians into the room. "Now, open your eyes and welcome your Crystal Guardian." They opened their eyes and gave a collective gasp, silent tears spontaneously spilling down their cheeks as they met these wonderful golden beings who stood tall above them, embodying all that was beautiful about the feminine. This prompted feelings in them that went beyond words, feelings that seemed to come from deep within their hearts, that evoked a sense of peace and gratitude that they had never experienced before.

As their guardians smiled down onto their wards, Orla explained that these beings would be invisible to everyone, even their husbands, but they would be with them at all times. Each guide extended their ethereal golden hand to their ward and indicated for them to stand. When they were all standing, each guardian embraced their ward, and each woman surrendered completely into that strong but gentle supportive embrace, feeling that they would burst with emotion as they were showered with golden particles of light over and over again like a gentle firework display.

Eventually the guardians disengaged and moved to the outer part of the room. Orla sat down as Maeve took over the final instruction.

"Only women who have undergone such an initiation can ever be Elders. Only through the correct initiation can you be connected to the Crystal Guardians of female gifts.

"When the Crystalanders left the planet, humans eventually forgot or ignored the depth of transformation that a woman has to undergo at the three main stages of her life to attain the final accolade of connecting with her own female Crystal Guardian. Although the Crystalanders left the planet, they made sure that they left behind helpers to guide the women."

Maeve could see that they all were a little relieved at this. They were becoming increasingly worried that it would appear they had the responsibility for healing the planet, but had absolutely no experience to do it. By having their Crystal Guardians, they felt supported and strong.

"There is one area that we have not covered," continued Maeve, "and that is the birthing process. Unfortunately, it has been commandeered by man-science and has been almost turned into an illness. The art of midwifery is a wonderful gift for all women to have but that is not a priority at the moment as fewer and fewer babies are being conceived."

Maeve assured them that when the time came, she would instruct the appropriate women to be midwives and those chosen would have allocated to them crystal birthing guides.

Everyone stopped talking and, after what seemed an eternity to the women, Maeve sprayed essences over each one, which refreshed their minds. The two wise women smiled at their students as they could see the beauty that was radiating from their every cell. They were beginning to feel more energetic, invigorated in mind and body, all of them sensing a difference in their bodies. It was if they had all been like a tightly sprung coil, which was being gradually released to reveal a quality that had been buried for many, many generations. Orla wondered what their husbands would think when they saw them. When they had recovered sufficiently, she led them down to meet up with the men.

*

After the women had left with Orla, the seven men followed Patrick and Finn to a special room for their next instruction. They sat on the chairs that had been placed in a circle and automatically closed their eyes. Patrick began to beat a small drum in sync with their heartbeats. Eventually, their spirit guides entered the room, slowly embracing and attaching to the spines of the men, taking up the space that Shadow had vacated. The men visibly softened as the taut muscles in their backs gradually unravelled and released. Eventually, Finn asked them to sit up and open their eyes. Patrick continued drumming lightly in the background.

"What was that?" asked John. "I felt a dampness touch my skin and a warmth enter my body, particularly down my spine."

"Your spirit guides have just attached themselves to you and they are there to help you with any problems that you might have at any point in your life," Finn replied, aware that, unlike their wives, they had no questions.

Finn instructed them again to lie down and Patrick increased the tempo of the drumming.

"I want you to use your inner sight to travel down your bodies to your adrenal glands." He could see that with each man, where two plump chestnut-shaped glands should be, there were shrivelled cones, indicating that these men were totally depleted and exhausted. *It's no wonder their brain chemistry is so depressed,* he concluded.

Finn activated his ruby crystal and directed its ray at each man's adrenal glands. They immediately responded and became plump again, prompting a surge of energy to course through their bodies to the pelvic area, where it shot up the spine to the crown. Reaching the crown, it came down the front of the body, stopping just below the naval. Each man felt a surge of strength go through him, and Patrick instructed them to breathe deeply and listen to the rhythm of the drum. The drum slowed down, slowing their heartbeat, allowing them to harness that energy so that they could use it productively. A couple of them experienced a heightened libido as the energy became stuck in the pelvic cavity, and Finn instructed them to focus on circulating the energy away from the pelvic area, back up the spine. They followed his instructions obediently and immediately felt better. The energy calmed and slipped into a general feeling of subtle pulsing throughout their bodies.

"This," Patrick instructed, "is the state where you should be at all times. This is a safe place for testosterone. Testosterone is not designed to build muscles to become fearless fighters; testosterone is a hormone to complement the female hormones. Yes, it is obviously important for reproduction, but it is also important for healing the planet."

Finn took up the story of female reproduction and instructed the men of the importance of supporting their wives so that they could interpret the needs of the planet. "With the help of testosterone, you can filter some of the destructive negative emotional programming that hangs in the molecules of space on the planet. This will help women to become more focused and not be overwhelmed by negativity. Equally, when the women need to focus deeply to determine the needs of the planet, they will need the help of their husbands. It takes tremendous strength to work through the memory of the planet and find the truth of creation. Remember, men and women are both of service to the planet, but neither is to be a servant of the other."

Finn instructed them to keep their eyes closed, and when they had become calm again, Patrick relayed to Finn that it was time to call in the Crystal Guardians. Patrick increased the volume and beat of the drum and suddenly seven ruby-iron Crystal Guardians appeared on the fringe of the room. Patrick beat the drum louder and faster and asked the men to open their eyes and stand. As they did, the guardians moved forward, which took the men by surprise. They had never experienced anything that was so otherworldly, nor had they experienced anything that embodied power and gentleness at the same time. The guardians went behind their wards and enveloped them in their energy. The men collapsed into the arms of their guardians, totally surrendering to a higher power.

Finally! Finn rejoiced. *They have lost their primal programming.*

The guardians eventually disengaged and moved to the outer part of the room. Finn explained to the group that the women had also been introduced to their Crystal Guardians. This was a relationship that was special and intimate to each individual, so the men couldn't see the women's guides and vice versa.

Finn led the men out to the garden to where the women were already having their refreshments. He held back a little to see how the men and women would greet each other. As the two groups merged, Finn stopped and observed the tableau and could not quite believe the degree of change in a group of people who were under the severe constraints of life under the domes. They were mingling, smiling and talking gently, in a very relaxed and comfortable manner but with a warmth he had not seen amongst them before. He nodded contentedly, and in that split second realised that they had to double their efforts now to speed up the process.

Orla announced to the group that they had one more experience before leaving the island that day. They all looked at her in disbelief that there could possibly be more.

She took them all back to the first room and instructed them to lay down in a circle. She sprayed the room again and promised that they would feel much better after this journey. Patrick came into the room and sat down, drumming softly in the corner. As they relaxed more she began to sing and projected into their minds the emerald crystal path. They watched as if they were taking part in a film, each one walking along the path with Orla until they came to a large crystal chamber – not the green crystal chamber that Orla had visited on the Emerald Crystal world – this was different, less complex and more in keeping with normal human design. She took them off the path into a large chamber to a pool filled with tiny jade crystals that looked more like vapour than solid crystal. She led each one to the pool, where they were immersed completely into the warm crystal vapour. The tiny droplets of crystal went through every cell of their bodies, awakening a deeper connection to Crystal Wisdom. Orla could see that they were all deeply relaxed and each cell of their bodies began to open and absorb the information coming from the emerald crystal. Whilst she had seen that the muscles of their bodies were relaxed, the cells in some of their organs were still in the habit of being held in a state of fear-based tension, so she waited until every cell in their bodies had been saturated before gathering them from the pool and taking them back along the crystal path, singing to them to bring their consciousness back into the room.

They opened their eyes and sat up, and there was a distinct difference. Gone was the pallor and weakness; in its place was a sparkle in their eyes, colour in their cheeks and an alertness in their minds. They looked at each other, as if seeing themselves for the first time, and smiled broadly. They felt so much better. The fog that had inhabited their minds for so long was gone and they felt sharper mentally than they had for many lifetimes. Orla and Finn smiled too. These special people deserved to enjoy the benefits of the planet and not be victims of its anger.

Eagerly, John asked what they should do next. Orla reassured them that their reprogramming was not completely finished, but that they needed to integrate their new state of consciousness. Shadow was gone and in its place was pure Crystal Wisdom, but that had to be assimilated. They would need a week for this to happen and would come back to the island for the further instructions.

Orla said, "All your fear myths have been removed but if Shadow realises this, gradually it will increase the fear and hatred in people around you who are still attached to Shadow, making them hyper vigilant to anyone who is different, and when that happens, punishment follows in some form. You have seen this pattern repeat itself many times throughout history. This time, I will make sure that you are thoroughly protected whilst the process of transformation takes place."

When Finn had returned from his initiation on the Ruby Crystal world he had engaged the help of his two brothers. He was told by his crystal mentors that he would need their help as they all shared the Ruby crystal genetic memory. Finn's brothers, Connor and Daniel, were exactly the same build as Finn, all three sharing similar features. Finn was the elder of the three and had always felt protective of the younger two, but the Ruby Crystalanders had told him that these boys, whilst younger, still had immense strength and were able to help Finn with the ruby crystal ray. By transmitting the ray through the two boys it increased the power of the ray to the power of ten, so more people could be deprogrammed of Shadow and brought under the protection of Crystal Wisdom.

Orla said goodbye to them all and told them that the next time they came, they would receive the final pieces of the jigsaw puzzle that was to be their future. She reminded them not to discuss any of their island experiences with anyone other than their immediate group and to be aware of their individual changes so that they could disguise them. At that point they hadn't realised how much they had changed, though Orla and Finn could both see the changes, and it was the women who reflected the most change. They were now completely immersed in their environment and engaged with their partners.

Orla spoke to the women directly. "You must be aware that you have begun to emit a radiance that humans haven't seen for decades. Thankfully they are all switched off, but their Shadow attachments will identify the change in you. Shadow is always scanning the environment for that which is different and therefore needs to be removed."

Finn addressed the group soberly. "The issue with Shadow now is that it has seen the Earth is finished, has seen the population is defeated, but knows that man's survival instinct is seeking a new planet. Unlike the original creators of man who ditched Earth when the ice age came, Shadow is desperately hanging on as it knows its survival is dependent on the survival of man. Shadow will follow man wherever he goes, it is symbiotic, and needs a constant supply of hatred that man seems to provide no matter where he resides. Shadow originated from a catabolic environment, very one-sided and primitive in its evolution, but equally very powerful. It is hanging onto the last humans desperately, in the hope that they will find another planet that could sustain human life."

"When the creators of the first humans arrived on the planet they were seeking its minerals which oozed in abundance from every waterfall and river. Once they had taken the minerals from the rivers, they resorted to taking minerals from deep in the Earth, so they created man for this purpose. Their main focus was the copper, gold and silver, because it created a high level of energy that could be used to power everything in their world. But they had not learnt to create, build or indeed regenerate."

John looked at Finn in amazement. "But isn't that exactly how the Earth has got to this point in its history?"

"Exactly," Finn continued. "The turning point for the planet was when man put aside the crystal gifts and decided he knew better, but that 'better' was the instant gratification that became prevalent in all sectors of society in all countries and Federations of the world."

The group looked at each other and were quiet. They were trying to understand the contrasting concepts of instant human gratification and planetary gratification.

Finn urged them to start their return to the dome, and Orla hugged them all as they turned to follow Finn back to the Secret Garden. She promised to talk to them every day through their secure communication portal.

They arrived at the normal entry and exit point and Finn swiftly said his goodbyes, the group separated into their vehicles and returned to their homes, all in silence.

*

When John and Sheila arrived home, the children were still with Sheila's mother, so they took the opportunity to try and make sense of what had happened.

"What is going on, John? On one hand I feel as if I

have been given the most amazing gift and on the other I feel as if I am part of some complex psychology game that is not going to end well."

"I know exactly how you feel," John replied. "Orla did mention in the early days that when we started on our journey of discovery of the Crystal Wisdom, the part of us that was controlled by Shadow would not immediately open, as it was in the habit of responding in a controlled way, which would cause conflict even though Shadow has been disengaged. I feel that we must just go along with this because, honestly, I want a life like they have on Crystal Island for our children."

Sheila listened to the actual words he was saying. 'Feel' was not normally part of his vocabulary, equally he had never voiced the opinion of wanting something for his family's future.

She agreed with him though. The degree of health that the island enjoyed was outstanding and she felt so relaxed there. Just being back in the dome made her shoulders stoop. Orla and Finn had asked them to try to keep up the appearance of being the same as before their visits to the island and Sheila had wondered how she would do that, but the oppressive environment of the domes brought a tension into her body that, this time, worked in her favour.

The children arrived back and walked into the sitting room quietly and obediently. John and Sheila looked at them and saw in that moment that they were just shells of children. Sheila's mother, Joan, looked at her daughter and thought: *Every time she goes away lately she looks different but I can't quite work out what that is.* She dismissed any further thoughts as she had to get back and tend to her husband's meal. She said her goodbyes and left.

"How was your day?" John asked the children.

"It was fine," they both responded in equal measures of respect and nonchalance.

"What did you do at grandma's?" Sheila asked.

"We worked on our school projects most of the time or watched the special children's channel on the comms portal," Christopher replied, slightly confused by the questions.

"What did you watch?" John asked.

The two children looked at each other, puzzled, as their parents had never asked that question before.

John realised that this was an unusual experience for his children, but he wanted to know. He had never before questioned what had been on the children's channel.

Rebecca responded. "We saw a film together about the olden days. It was in the days before the domes when people roamed the country and stole food, clothes and cars, and there was no medicine and children died young, and the schools were so badly run so that children did what they liked, and when they left school they couldn't get good work, so they went without food and…"

"What did you think of the film?" Sheila interjected, wanting to stop the tirade of myths.

They both chimed the answer, "Aren't we lucky to live in the dome?"

John and Sheila both nodded, quietly thinking what an effective job of brainwashing the leaders had implemented for children. Each new generation was programmed to believe that the only way to be safe was to live under the protection of the dome because the planet was an inhospitable place and dangerous, which was not a lie, but this couple now knew that this was not the complete truth.

The children went to bed happily, just wondering slightly why their parents were spending more time in dialogue with them than was normal. John and Sheila looked at each other a little wearily and decided to go to their bedroom. They both showered using the special soap that Orla had given them and dutifully took their crystal powders. When they eventually got into bed, John searched for Sheila's hand, which he held warmly, thinking that this must surely be the most intimate expression of their relationship, and that is how they both fell into a deep sleep. In the morning they went about their normal duties. John went off to work, while Sheila took the children to school and went on to meet up with the other women at Mary's house. They were pleased to see each other as, although it had been less than a day, they were already beginning to feel different and isolated. They exchanged stories with each other about their homecoming and all of them recounted similar experiences, and they all commented on the closeness that they felt with their husbands, although interestingly, their husbands had not initiated physical intimacy. They spoke openly for the first time about that side of their marriages and voiced the question, 'What is intimacy?' They had all been sold the lie that physical intercourse was the most intimate and important part of married life. They had accepted this without question, as had their mothers before them, but since being on Crystal Island and having the experience of the Emerald crystal, they had begun to realise that there was something missing from that type of relationship. They didn't know what was missing but realised that their physical relationships with their husbands were cold, almost clinical. It was just another chore for which they were responsible. At that moment the comms portal in Mary's house became active and the women huddled around the screen. Orla's familiar face appeared and they were all delighted to see her again. She asked them how their first night had been and they all commented on their increased closeness with their husbands and also the observation of their overly obedient children. Orla reassured them that on their next visit they would come to understand what it is to be truly intimate with a partner, and what their new responsibilities would be, which would also influence how children were educated. Their eyes collectively widened.

Sheila, who had quite easily stepped into the role of spokesperson for the group, asked Orla, "What do you mean by new responsibilities? Surely we would just support our husbands in their new roles."

Orla considered this response. They had been introduced to the understanding that they were important, they were equal to their husbands, but back on the mainland, when she had used the phrase *your new responsibilities*, they had fallen back into playing the dutiful supporting role.

"If you recall, on the island you were introduced to the important role that women have in the planet's healing, in particular you will become the Elders. Well, the new responsibilities are for both you and your husbands. Your roles will be different, of course, but they will be complementary." Confusion again registered across the women's faces, which reflected their unspoken thoughts.

Mary, slightly bemused, considered, *Just when I thought I was getting a handle on this whole process, Orla throws another piece of information into the cauldron which frightens me to death.*

"Please don't worry," Orla continued. "We will never put you in a situation for which you have not been fully prepared both physically and emotionally, and do not forget about your spirit guides and guardians." The group had forgotten about the guides and guardians and accepted her words as they trusted this woman more than they had every trusted anyone before.

"What will we be covering on our next visit, Orla?" Sheila asked.

"So that you understand about the true role of women and men, independently and collectively, you will learn about your new roles and the next step." There were no further questions as none of them could envision a world where both men and women were equal.

That night the men went to their comms portal, and

Finn came through to speak to them. He asked how their day had been and all of them had said that it was difficult trying to act as if they were on automatic pilot. They were beginning to formulate many questions in their minds, but dared not verbalise them as this would be the biggest sign that something in them had changed. So they hunched their shoulders, sat through the endless pointless meetings, waded through the mountains of paperwork and finally were relieved to go home. That was also a first. These men had lived and breathed their work and only really went home to be fed, watered, have a perfunctory conversation with their children and retire to the marital beds with their wives. Now they wanted to go home to talk with their wives. They were beginning to get a sense of the possibilities of their future relationships that were not there before; understanding that true intimacy offered a private space between couples where they felt safe to be spontaneous and honest with their thoughts and feelings

Finn spoke to them of their next visit to the island, and John asked what they would be covering on that visit. Finn echoed the story Orla had given the wives, and this had caused a little consternation among the men. For the women it was a process of acquiring new skills; for the men it was a little more complex. They were having to open to a very different side of themselves, a side which had very strict parameters about authority, and now those parameters were being torn down and their competitive side was not happy.

Finn knew that the human hormone testosterone, which was the main primal motivator in man, was still prominent in men in modern times and, whilst fairly under control when men were together, spiked when women came into their arena. In primitive times 'dominant males' used physical aggression to thwart 'subordinate males' from mating. Equally, women were attracted to those dominant men for their presumed superior genetic quality. This caused a problem when women began to infiltrate the male-dominated positions of authority in the workplace, prompting first conflict and then suspicion, so he wasn't surprised by Mathew's reaction:

"But surely this will not work; it has been tried before. Women are just not wired to take authority. They find it too overwhelming and they are much happier in the home."

"Clearly they are not completely happy," Finn explained, "otherwise they would not be responding so positively to their experiences on Crystal Island." Finn, a little irritated by Mathew's response, continued. "You must understand that each and every human being is special, we each have a specific job to do and a part to play in the growth and health of the planet. This is fundamental to the progress of the planet."

The men were silent. John reflected that Orla, Finn, Maeve and Patrick were a great example of this, but he did wonder if they were altogether human. Finn, reading his mind, went on to explain. "Yes, we on Crystal Island do work well together, and yes, we are as human as you, but we have not had our wisdom interrupted by Shadow, that is the only difference. You just have to relearn what is already within you."

The reassurance that the island's royal family were indeed human seemed to give them some comfort and, although the men were deeply apprehensive about the next visit, they trusted Finn sufficiently to agree.

CHAPTER FIVE
THE GIFTS

A week later the group met Finn at the usual place and quickly boarded the travel machine. They were all eager to go to the island but with more than a little trepidation. Orla met them at the Secret Garden, and to their eyes she looked even more wonderful than before.

Does this woman ever age or look tired? Cynthia pondered.

The group progressed to the palace, and it was as if they were seeing some things for the first time; the colours were definitely stronger and the smells more intense. *What was it about this environment that just kept on giving?* James considered as his senses soaked up all the offerings of nature.

As they arrived at the familiar crystalline walls of the palace and walked across the threshold, they stopped, momentarily surprised by the warm welcome they experienced by just being in the entrance hall. Maeve and Patrick greeted each one with an embrace and led them to the dining room, where refreshments were waiting. Joshua was really looking forward to this, as one of the starkly obvious differences between the domes and Crystal Island was the food. The very simple food on the island was by far superior to the manufactured mulch provided in the domes. He had noticed on the walk to the palace that there were blue-black cows in the fields and Finn had responded to his interest, explaining that the cows produced milk that was turned into various dairy products, which included a fermented drink that restored the bacterial balance of the digestive system. Cynthia's ears had pricked up at this information and she quickly caught up with the two men. Finn explained that the only animal protein they ate came from the dairy products, of cows and goats, plus the eggs from the hens, who produced a healthy supply daily.

"But that would not provide sufficient protein," Joshua interjected.

"That's true Joshua, but we obtain excellent quality protein from our plants. Acquiring sufficient protein from plants is a precise science but the quality of the plants on the island is extremely high and therefore they yield sufficient protein. If you remember, on your last journey to the palace we saw fields of grain, and you were all surprised by the strength of the crop as well as the asymmetrical growth formation. The protein in that grain alone is sufficient to provide 50 per cent of the protein needed by humans. The grain also has an abundance of vitamins and minerals which are vital for health." Finn concluded by giving them a mini lecture on the importance of crop rotation and crop formation.

"Which chemicals do you use to ensure such a good yield?" asked Mathew innocently.

"The horses, goats and cows provide a wonderful source of compost, as well as any vegetable or plant waste, plus the abundant seaweed that arrives on the beaches every day donated by the sea. In fact, we use a lot of seaweed and sea vegetables in our cooking and medicines, but everything that is a by-product of cooking or making medicines is recycled and put back into the land."

Helen, who had quite a sensitive digestive system, heaved inwardly when she thought of eating seaweed and sea vegetables, knowing how polluted the sea was that surrounded their Federation.

"The sea that embraces the island is protected by the Crystal Fortress, which keeps it separate from all of the pollution from the rest of the world," Finn reassured her, but he was not surprised by her fears. On one of the occasions that he had visited the domes, he had inspected the health of the seas and oceans and discovered that man had used the sea as a gigantic waste disposal system for both chemical and human waste. *It is like one gigantic lavatory*, he had reflected. Man had been so busy manufacturing 'things' with a limited lifespan built into them to ensure a consistently high turnover, but he hadn't thought about the disposal of the old. This high turnover meant that the old products and the packaging of the new had to go somewhere, and that place was the sea. And at the point when the population of the planet had exploded out of all proportion, the sewerage systems of cities were overwhelmed, regularly spewing sewage into the once-sacred rivers and oceans.

Orla and Finn agreed that the group had received sufficient programming to be able to reveal the gifts that the Crystalanders had bestowed on Earth, plus another layer of Earth's history. This was all preparation for the eventual unveiling of the full story of Earth's degeneration. Of course, before this, they would need to replenish their remedies.

Finn took them outside and Orla arranged for the remedies to be brought into the garden, where they were enjoying their refreshments under the shade of the protective branches of a group of trees. They were all very quiet, lost in their thoughts and partially distracted by the sensations of the remedies that were helping their cells open and absorb new information. Jude got up from sitting on the grass and walked over to where roses and lavender were growing together in a flower bed. Cynthia followed her and they both gazed down at the plants, enjoying their beauty. Orla saw Jude touch one of the petals, when suddenly she jumped back as if she had been stung. Cynthia looked concerned, and Orla walked over to them. "What happened, Jude?"

"I had the strangest feeling. I touched the petal and immediately felt like I'd had an electric shock."

She smiled at the two women, knowing exactly what had transpired. "You will fully understand what has happened after the next viewing."

They accepted her cryptic explanation without question, like the dutiful women that they still were. Jude would soon learn the importance of learning the language of nature to be able to enter into the space of a plant and communicate with its spirit guides. In the rarefied atmosphere of the plant world of Crystal Island, the plant spirits reigned supreme and protected the plants at all costs.

Orla turned her attention to the rest of the group, who were deeply immersed in the wonderful flavours of their refreshments, and walked over to join them under the trees.

"This is amazing cold soup. What are the ingredients, Orla?" Anne asked.

"Just vegetables from the vegetable garden of the palace," Orla replied.

"But which spices do you use for the flavouring?" Anne was sure that vegetables on their own could not produce this wonderful flavour.

"We use only sea salt and garden herbs to release the natural flavours from the vegetables. The plants are rich in nutrients which enhance the flavour, so it isn't necessary to add anything else."

They were all quiet as they savoured every mouthful of the soup accompanied by the herb-flavoured bread. To follow the soup Orla had organised a wonderful selection of fruit from the orchards. As Maeve laid the plates of fruit before them, the group stared in disbelief. They had never seen fresh fruit like this in their lives. Patrick joined them and he took great pleasure in seeing them enjoy what to the islanders was simple fare from the palace kitchen, but to these deprived people was a banquet. When they were finished, they all felt quite sharp, unlike their normal dome postprandial states.

The small group returned to the viewing room. Martha noticed that Orla had returned wearing more jewellery and was particularly taken by the ruby necklace she was wearing. They were a little taken aback by this ostentatious display, which seemed to be so unlike Orla. She normally wore an amazing diamond ring, which all the women had commented on privately. It was of an indescribable quality and cut quite unlike any diamonds they had seen before. She always wore her coral earrings, and they had seen her sapphires, but today she seemed to be wearing her complete collection of crystal jewellery. Orla reassured them that the jewels were part of her communication tools for the next part of the screening. Not understanding this concept at all, they chose to ignore her explanation.

As the lights dimmed, the screen filled with scenes of a planet covered with ice, populated by somewhat barbaric-looking humans. The group looked stunned as this was another aspect of history that had been rewritten by the Elite. Orla polished her golden crystal ring and the Golden Crystalanders appeared on the screen, which was depicting scenes of their arrival on the planet. The group was only now able to identify these super beings because their Shadow attachments had been disengaged.

Orla was aware that she was giving them a mere summarised version of the introduction of the crystal gifts, but time was short and they just had to be introduced to the gifts to understand them and therefore understand the possibilities for Earth.

On the screen they saw the Golden Crystalanders arriving on the planet, unwrapping their gifts and laying them at the feet of humans.

First came the crystals from Crystaland to increase the power of Earth's natural crystals so that humans could use them for energy.

Second was the gift of health. After the crystals had activated Earth's waterways, specific plants were introduced whose growth was aided by the new super waters. Humans were shown how to use the plants for food, and also the women were shown how to make remedies from different parts of plants: buds from trees, the essences from different flowers, herbs and resins, and of course all were mixed with the super waters empowering the active ingredients of the plants.

The third gift was the gift of intelligence – this was not the intelligence with which the group normally associated. They watched the super beings teaching the primitives the power of colour combined with geometric shapes; how these shapes were cleverly mirrored in nature; the ability to identify and utilise Crystal Wisdom in every aspect of the environment to be able to 'read' the terrain and communicate with the planet.

When humans had become sufficiently developed, they were instructed in the seven qualities of the intelligence of Crystal Wisdom and the importance of fully understanding and embracing those qualities to make the correct decisions for the planet:

1. The ability to connect with Crystal Wisdom in themselves and everything else on the planet. This could only be achieved when all doubt and fear were not present.

2. The ability to interpret the needs of the planet in relation to global needs rather than the needs of an individual.

3. The ability to translate those needs through crystal enquiry into a tangible concept for the material plane of Earth.

4. The ability to develop that concept using crystal architecture to develop the solution.

5. The ability to adapt and develop the solution incorporating crystal design.

6. The ability to discern objectively the merits of the solution and question whether it still fulfilled the needs of the planet.

7. The ability to embrace all previous qualities to formulate a final solution and its implementation.

Finn paused the screening to allow them to understand fully crystal intelligence. He observed the reactions of the men, and they looked as if they were being spoken to in a completely foreign language with no recognition of the grammar rules or the vocabulary. The women, however, were taking in every detail. This was the first time they had been given a formula to follow to help with solving complex challenges, and they were eager for more. They were beginning to see where they would have help in their future roles as Elders, which was giving them more confidence. The men, however, were battling with their heavily conditioned education, and although they were hearing the words and trying their hardest to give meaning to those words, nothing was connecting.

Orla also saw the difference between the two groups and paused awhile to allow the women to fully absorb the information. The men would eventually catch up.

She took over from Finn and continued with the gifts.

The fourth gift was the gift of courage and leadership. The two groups again reacted differently. Courage was a word not used in the everyday parlance of the domes and was definitely not coupled with leadership. The women viewed it again as an interesting combination and were eager to explore what this 'courage' meant. The screen filled with Ruby Crystalanders walking the planet, teaching men and women how to focus on the needs of the planet. They encouraged women to speak up and stood behind them when they spoke their truth. Often men became angry and the Crystalanders mediated, explaining that women were the natural connection to Crystal Wisdom, and encouraged them to listen and learn. This took time, but as women became more confident, men could see that they expressed the needs of the planet honestly and so birthed the first generation of men and women who worked together with the shared objective of nurturing the planet. The wives looked at those early women who possessed the courage to speak the truth and they were encouraged to do the same. The royal family knew that courage was a quality that both genders required when facing opposition from the Generals and Shadow. This courage was not that of the fighting heroes of past battles, this was a quiet inner knowing of what is right and not being persuaded otherwise.

The fifth gift was sound. The screen filled with all sorts of shapes that changed with different musical notes. They watched as the Golden Crystalanders introduced the gift of sound and the ability to understand the Melodies of Eternal Wisdom. This was a very subtle vibration that emitted a sound that radiated through all living things and connected man with the plant and animal world.

Orla requested the group close their eyes and music began drifting from the screen very quietly, increasing in volume to become a beautiful sound made from many instruments that the group couldn't identify. It had the effect of initiating a sense of calm that washed over them, blessing them with a gentle pulse of energy throughout their bodies.

The sixth gift made its presence on the screen and the Golden Crystalanders were seen activating the voice boxes of the humans, allowing them to go from basic guttural noises to shaping different sounds into words of a specific language that embodied the beauty of Crystal Wisdom. To the group, this was a language they didn't understand but they all identified with the beauty of its tone.

The seventh gift was support. The Crystalanders knew that when they eventually left Earth, man would need constant reminders of Crystal Wisdom, so they introduced crystal spirit guides for each human. These were beings from another Crystal world that were able to mirror image the human body and act as a direct reflection of an individual's thoughts, words and actions, thus being a constant reminder to their hosts when those three did not reflect the beauty of Crystal Wisdom.

The final gift was the gift of beauty. The Golden Crystalanders opened the eyes of mankind to the beauty of every single aspect of nature. Crystal Wisdom had created every part of nature and therefore reflected the perfection of that wisdom. And those early humans had been so grateful for their eyes being opened that they put all their efforts to supporting and increasing everything in their environment by using their gifts to honour in some way that natural beauty.

The screen came to a close and Finn increased the light in the room. There was absolute silence; you could hear a pin drop. Then came the expected tirade of questions.

"Where did these Crystalanders come from?"

"Where are they now?"

"What happened to the gifts?" And so the questions predictably fell confused and chaotically from their lips.

Finn raised his hands to silence them; their confusion was escalating and was beginning to challenge them. Orla silently sprayed the room with essences, which calmed and opened them to listen.

More silence, and then John asked in a calmer manner, "I noticed that when man was given the gift of words, he spoke a beautiful language, but I didn't recognise it."

Orla explained, "The language of the first crystal-humans only contained words of a positive nature. She paused to take a breath before continuing. "The most polluting aspect of any community is toxic words. Remember how important it is to tap into the natural melodies of the planet. Well, when toxic words are used, those natural melodies are put out of balance."

"What are toxic words?" Jude asked.

Orla could see they were all baffled. "Toxic words are words that denigrate a person or any aspect of nature. In the early days the humans were taught that if they couldn't say something positive, something complimentary about a person, object or situation, then they should stay silent. Toxic words are words of judgement without crystal discernment; toxic words are used to alienate and divide communities." Orla finished, knowing this would challenge them.

They were silent again, each one considering her words as she continued.

"Equally, keeping silent when you know you could impart positive and fresh energy into a negative situation is also toxic."

This last point made them think even more deeply. Before Orla and Finn had come into their lives, they hadn't realised that there had been times when they had kept quiet, times when they should have spoken out, particularly the women, but now their eyes had been opened they could see so many areas of society that were toxic.

"The fact that you have an understanding of toxicity in practice is a great step forward to change. At least now you know the difference. However, it will take practice to develop the skill of crystal language, and more importantly, you need to keep this language to the confines of this group until it is more widely accepted," Orla said.

"I would like to know more about the sound," enquired Cynthia. Orla was not surprised by Cynthia's request. She had recognised in this woman the ability to connect to the vibration of the planet, and in her role as Elder she would spearhead the use of sound for healing, not least in her role as midwife.

"But we need to continue with the story before we go on to the next stage of your education," Orla said and continued with a verbal edited story, once again not giving them the full understanding that she and other members of the royal family possessed, just sufficient for the group's understanding at this stage.

"Crystalanders were from the source of all creation and their responsibility was to rebalance planets that had been plundered and depleted, but they only focused on planets that still held the potential for transformation.

"You are right, they are definitely not human in any aspect, but they adopted a human form to make them more acceptable to mankind. They are from a different, more purified realm in the cosmos and it is for this reason that they could not stay on the planet indefinitely."

"What do you mean by 'plundered'?" asked James.

"As well as the Crystalanders, there are other travellers of the cosmos who target bountiful planets to remove their valuable minerals. Minerals are the building blocks of many planets and if they are not nurtured, eventually they become depleted. So there are space travellers with technology far advanced to that of Earth but they have not embraced crystal laws, and as we said before, one such group of travellers arrived on Earth and decided to plunder the minerals not just from the rivers but also from deep in the planet's core. But they needed strong men to do this and that's when they experimented with the primitive life that was available on Earth at that time." Orla could see that her explanation was making them bristle again.

"Do you have any real evidence to substantiate this?" Frederic demanded.

"Well yes, in fact many examples of early man had been discovered by archaeologists, and modern science had progressed sufficiently to determine fairly accurately their age. Science also identified that these early specimens of human life possessed immense strength but their intelligence was limited. Science eventually improved in the understanding of genetics, and with every step forward in science that was made, it confirmed that there was a missing step in the evolution of man that could not be identified. Remember when you saw the artefacts in the British Museum? Man could not have gone from that primitive level so quickly without some sort of interference from a higher intelligence. However, all this information had been suppressed in the last century in the quest to define mankind as the most advanced form of life in the universe, whose natural intelligence outstrips all other forms of life."

"So if the men were created to be physically strong, what were the women created for?" Helen questioned.

"There had to be a steady supply of these workers, so therefore the women provided the constant stream of the next generation of slaves. Women spent their fertile lives being in a state of impregnation or lactation. The lifespan of women was very short and the turnover of women was horrifically high. But this birthed the creation of many myths of slavery and servitude, which are etched in the memories of both men and women."

Orla urged them to continue watching the screen. She could tell they were being repulsed by this story, but they could not stop now.

The lights were lowered and the group, who were by now feeling a little traumatised, watched the Crystalanders integrate with the inhabitants of Crystal Island, blending together human and crystal DNA, which produced humans who were beautiful reflections of their environment. Scenes of the Earth flourishing under the tutelage of the Crystalanders filled the screen.

The screen changed, as it was time for them to see the stark contrast brought by Shadow. Orla didn't want to focus too much on the negative repercussions of the Crystalanders leaving, as the main objective of the group's visits to the island was to remove any programming, conscious and unconscious, of Shadow. And so, as if watching a very fast newsreel, they saw the Crystalanders leaving a planet that was in a state of perfection but, eventually, things began to change. The Crystal circles were the first to succumb, falling into neglect from disuse; man began to change, and war and slavery evolved; finally, the cumulative effects of women's subjugation and the abuse of children were mirrored by the failing condition of the planet.

The screen faded and they sat in absolute silence in the dark. The lights were turned up slowly. Orla looked at them with a little pity, as they were having all their illusions about their lives and their history totally destroyed, looking like frightened children who had been stripped naked and left outside in the cold.

"So you see," Orla continued, "this primal programming, which can resurface in man without Crystal Wisdom, has been motivating your reactions to the world around you, but it is an illusion."

Mathew had been quiet for most of the showings, but he said quietly, "I am seeing a pattern of behaviour here, particularly of the warrior leaders, that is very similar to our leaders today." The other men reflected on his words and eventually had to agree.

Yes, Orla enthused silently, *we really are progressing now.*

After a welcome break, the group returned to one of the large salons in the palace ideal for meetings, unlike the viewing room. As they all made themselves comfortable on the chairs around the large wooden carved table, Orla asked, "Having seen the possibilities of the planet, compared with its present day level of degeneration, what do you think is your first priority?"

There was silence as there were so many things that had to change. Helen was the first to speak, with her newfound confidence. "What about the Generals?"

They all looked at her with mouths open. Orla had thought that they had forgotten about this.

"Yes, what about the Generals?" Orla echoed her question.

There was silence from the group, and as she suspected, there were no suggestions.

"I will contact them in the same way that I contacted you." They looked wary. "Please do not worry. This is all in hand and it will go well."

They viewed her with a mixture of hope and suspicion.

"In the meantime, when you return to the domes you will have to begin the process of recruiting the next fifty couples. I will of course direct you, but they will not need to undergo the immersion that your group has experienced."

Orla and Finn knew that once the fourteen returned to the domes, their environment would begin to change around them; the memory in the spaces that they inhabited would change and reflect their new Crystal memory and this in turn would begin to affect the people who also shared that space. It would still be necessary for Orla to visit them in their sleep to project the images of Crystal Island into their memories and, crucially, to introduce them to the fourteen.

"After the new recruits are in place, there will be sufficient staff to be able to confront and persuade the Generals to do what is necessary for the change to be effective," Orla said.

"What will the Generals have to do?" John asked suspiciously.

"To stand aside." Finn's words prompted reactions of disbelief around the table.

"Believe me, when the time comes they will stand aside." Orla knew that in the face of such truth and Crystal Wisdom, there would be no challenge.

"And what happens when the Generals stand down?" enquired Mark.

Orla paused before responding, scanning their earnest faces. "Well, Mark, you as a group will take their place."

Their silence was heavy with fear.

Finn knew that at the point when this happened, the Elite would be alerted and would inflict a further bout of drought and disease of biblical proportions on the population. The drought and disease would be so severe that the dome-dwellers would be affected badly as well as those outside. In the past this action was designed to wear down any leanings towards individual thought. Fear was at the forefront of their minds, which always strengthened the hold of Shadow.

"You must not fall into patterns of fear at any point. If you are fearful, Shadow will get stronger; the idea is to starve out Shadow."

Orla's mind became distracted as she thought of the next group and realised that the new women were going to need more work. They would need to be initiated into their gifts and reminded of their value, which would be undertaken by the seven women in front of her. She also knew that once this Federation had shifted, it would be a case of engaging all the Federations. But that was a conversation she needed to have with Finn that would keep for another time. She also held back the information about the shifting of landmasses as the ice caps of the north and south poles finally melted. This would not be a popular conversation as there would be casualties, but, it would be necessary to sacrifice a few to save the future of not just the planet but also the solar system and ultimately the entire cosmos.

"I do think this whole process sounds very idealistic and I cannot envisage how our Generals would move over in favour of our leadership," John said.

What John hadn't factored in was the effect Orla and Finn would have on the Generals of his Federation, and indeed on all Federations. Since she had been working with this small group, Orla had become stronger. With each meeting of the group, Patrick had noticed the change in her – she was taking on Finn's ruby energy. Sheila had also noticed the change in Orla. She had been shocked when she was first introduced to Orla and quite awestruck by her almost ethereal beauty, but as she had worked with her more and more closely, she had noticed that the core of her being was becoming stronger. This encouraged Sheila, as she was worried that the Chief Generals of other Federations were more patriarchal than the Federation of the West, and would not accept her authority because of her gender. But she didn't need to worry. Orla was projecting a very different language now, never before seen by any male on the planet outside of the island. She was a powerful female warrior who was protecting her greatest prize, the planet.

CHAPTER SIX
THE RESPONSIBILITIES

The royal couple took the group to the dining room for more refreshments and remedies, as it was important to keep their physical and emotional energy levels from dipping. They observed the interaction between the two groups. Each spouse detected something different about their partner; they didn't know what it was but knew it was positive. Quite spontaneously, the male Crystal Guardians prompted their wards to embrace their wives, which startled the women initially, and then they reciprocated warmly.

Maeve and Patrick watched this little gathering and realised that from this tiny seed of mutual respect between men and women, the future of the planet would be fashioned.

With no time to waste, the group was taken to yet another room where there was a large octagonal shaped table with sixteen chairs.

Finn placed the group around the table, alternating male and female. Before Orla revealed their roles to them, she wanted to emphasise the importance of their working together.

"Before we go any further you need to understand what your responsibilities will be and also the crystal qualities that you will teach the next generation of pioneers. All of you must be aware now that you will be the pioneer group."

The men and women looked at each other, slightly startled at the enormity of the word 'pioneer' as it hung tentatively in the space around them before it slowly sank in. Orla continued. "Finn and I have discussed this with my parents and we will now announce your responsibilities." She spoke with her ever-increasing regal authority, briskly going through the responsibilities, and no one dared interrupt her.

"As you know, each one of you has a specific natural quality and you will need to use all of your skills and talents for the task ahead. The men have already learnt of their natural abilities, which are equally matched by their wives, which is the main reason why we selected you."

The men and women appeared to accept this; by now the understanding of equality between men and women was becoming increasingly apparent.

Orla began reading the list of names, matching them with their new responsibilities.

"Martha and James will manage resources from the gifts of nature. As the Earth regenerates and becomes more productive, they will need to ensure that those resources are distributed fairly and efficiently.

"Mary and Phillip, you are responsible for safeguarding the security of Crystal Wisdom." They both looked alarmed at such a daunting task. "As you have seen from the history of the Earth, the challenge to Crystal Wisdom is first doubt and then fear. It will be your job to ensure that doubt does not creep in, and to help you we shall be activating the Crystal circles again so that communities can visit them regularly to recharge their Crystal Wisdom.

"Jude and Mathew, you will be responsible for ensuring Crystal Wisdom is expressed in all the communities. This will mean that every aspect of the environment is regulated by Crystal Wisdom so that, as the planet develops, the vibration of the Earth that pulsates into the universe is purely crystal and nothing else.

"Cynthia and Joshua, you have the challenge of safeguarding the physical and emotional health of humans. This is a major task as there is so much to reverse.

"Helen and Mark, you have a very important role, and that is the education of the young so that they embrace and understand all that it means to embody Crystal Wisdom.

"Frederic and Anne will be responsible for energy." The couple looked at each other with a concerned look on their faces. "Do not worry. You will not always be faced with the limited resources you have now. When you see how we use energy on the island, it will make more sense."

Orla and Finn looked at them, watching for the familiar fears that would dart across their memories and they were still there, mainly from habit, as Shadow was gone.

"And finally we come to John and Sheila. These two people have the responsibility for ensuring that all of the above roles are followed and co-ordinated in accordance with the crystal laws and are applied in strict alignment with Crystal Wisdom. They have both been chosen for their courage and their discernment. Some difficult decisions will need to be made, and John and Sheila both share the talents that will enable them to communicate to all levels of society truthfully and effectively."

Sheila listened to these words describing her abilities and, to her dismay, didn't relate to any of them. *Is Orla hallucinating?* she wondered.

Orla, seeing her mental anguish, reassured all of them by saying, "We do not expect you to walk straight into these roles, you will be guided and supported at all times.

These are natural abilities that we have identified in you and they will soon become apparent and develop from within.

"You must all realise that you will be the nucleus of a very large network of people all over the planet."

They all nodded, reflecting quietly on the enormity of their future roles.

There was silence around the table. Finn and Orla observed the reaction of the others to the announcement of John and Sheila's role. But there was no resistance; it appeared that they had all thought that John and Sheila had drawn the short straw. Their role of overseeing all of these mammoth tasks was overwhelming to them and they were all quite happy to defer to John and Sheila. The couple looked a little shocked and were slightly apprehensive as to the response of the group, but were surprised and pleased to see there was no resistance.

Finn broke the silence. "We know this sounds daunting but the biggest obstacle you will need to face is working together with the one objective of nurturing the planet. This is a new skill for you all. But you can do it; you have received sufficient programming and you are all now accessing first level Crystal Wisdom, otherwise your Crystal Guardians would not be present."

This seemed to make them listen more closely; they had forgotten about their guardians.

"Remember," he continued, "your mantra must always be 'What is the best decision for planetary healing?' Every decision that you make must be underpinned by this."

Anne had been quietly taking in all the information, watching the other women, and then verbalised what all the women were thinking.

"I understand that we have these qualities, but we women have not had the same level of academic education as our husbands. For example, you talk about my responsibility for energy. Well, I presume I should have some understanding of science to even begin to understand what is involved. We were only taught the very basics of physics and I was terrible at it!" The other women nodded their heads in agreement.

Orla responded compassionately. "There are two issues here. The first is that you were not exposed to higher levels of science, but the rules of science that you were taught were limited and edited so, even though your husbands will have gone to a higher level in their studies, a lot of it is incorrect. Secondly, women often found studying the sciences was more challenging because of the way it was taught. It was taught in a linear and rote manner. Well, to understand the way the planet works you have to have a global view; nothing happens in isolation. Women learn by understanding concepts and their global application. Everything a woman learns has to be of use to her world. The problem is the world of women has become increasingly small over the centuries. Once you have the information in the correct format for you, you will be able to understand much more."

Anne was taken aback by Orla's explanation, as it did look as if science had deliberately written women out of its particular history book.

"Yes, you are right, Anne," interjected Finn, reading Anne's thoughts. "Man became so concerned with making the mathematical equations work that he lost the ability to look outside of the rules of man-science, to find answers. And in time, if something could not be measured, tested and proved, the men of science judged that it couldn't exist. A typical example of this is when science discovered DNA, but there were segments of the human DNA that they could not identify, so it was labelled as junk DNA. In nature there is no junk, everything has a purpose. The unidentified DNA was, in fact, the crystal memory. The planet will always give you the answers if you can speak the language of the planet."

"Are you saying that science and maths is wrong?" James spat the words out defiantly.

"Not at all, it is just limited. If the men of science had a complete understanding of the power of numbers and how those numbers are reflected over and over again in nature, they would have a better understanding of crystal science."

"So are we rewriting the science and maths texts?" Mark enquired.

"No, just adding to them. And that will all be explained to you in due course." Finn knew that they were not ready to understand the subject of the energetic value of numbers and sacred geometry just yet.

There was a silence. Orla and Finn observed the group and noticed the confusion in their thoughts. The women were still confused, stuck on their inability to comprehend why they had been given equal billing with their husbands' responsibilities.

Finn smiled at the tense look on all of the faces of the women. "As we have mentioned several times, women have an important and equal part to play in the decision-making and leadership process of the planet. The more you are exposed to Crystal Wisdom, the more you will all understand the value of shared leadership.

John was slightly embarrassed as he had never been singled out for specific leadership and had always regarded the other men as his equals.

Finn continued with the explanation. "The reason why you have been given these responsibilities is not random. We have observed your genetic line and your experience, and with the help of your Crystal Guardians we have identified your gifts and talents. We have given John and Sheila the more challenging responsibility because they both share gifts and talents that give them the ability to understand people on a much deeper level. They both have the ability to use their intuition and understand the fear motivation of humans, which is a major factor when negotiating with other leaders, and in fact anyone. The two of them can work closely with you all, assimilating and translating so that everyone on the planet can understand. Without this level of understanding and communication there will be no advancement."

They seemed a little more comfortable with this explanation. They had come from a very prescriptive and dogmatic background where men were given responsibilities based on their personality assessment, undertaken by an unknown person. All of these men had been earmarked as team players rather than principal leaders, and Finn realised that they needed to get past this myth if they were to be effective in their new roles.

Orla took up the explanation of how they had been conditioned to be limited in their aspirations. "To constrain any sort of independent thought, a person needs to be conditioned not to ask questions that are too challenging. The best way to do this is to shape and define the individual from a very early age within ever-narrowing parameters of ability. In your schools, at the age of eight, the academic ability of children is defined and streamed into specific areas of education. During their later academic lives they are gradually groomed into falling into one of six limited categories of personality applicable to the workplace."

The men all nodded, remembering that they had all been assessed at a very early age and groomed for the roles that they eventually occupied. Hierarchy had been broken down into six levels, with the Generals reporting to the Chief Generals, who took their instructions from the Elite, whose authority cascaded down the levels with no objection or challenge. When Finn had accompanied Orla on her search for the first seven, he had been struck by the lack of conflict under the domes. He wondered what had happened to secure such obedience. But when he had seen the polarisation of the living conditions of the dome-dwellers and those who lived outside, he realised that survival was paramount in this dying landscape, and they had been fed a diet of heavily edited information over the centuries that had culminated in the whole population being conditioned to be led – to be told what to do and how to do it, every minute of their waking lives.

"But now we do really have to move on to the next level of your immersion."

Jude, who had been quiet for most of these proceedings, asked tentatively, almost dreading the answer, "When will we be ready to start these new roles?"

"For the time being you need to focus on this immersion and we will guide you every step of the way, so please don't worry. You will never be put in a position where you do not know what to do. We will be instructing you in crystal strategy, which will help you make the correct decisions when the time comes."

There were visible signs of relief around the table at Orla's reassuring words. She desperately did not want to instil fear in them, as that would definitely be counterproductive.

Orla and Finn realised that these people were in a state of shock from the waves of information that they were being given and therefore needed constant reassurance.

"To help you with your new roles we are going to take you to various places on the island that reflect your new responsibilities so that you can witness Crystal Wisdom in action. You have already seen most things, but you now need to see the detail from the perspective of leaders," Finn announced.

The group went outside to breathe the crystal clear air of the island while they waited for their transportation, taking the opportunity to absorb more and more detail of the complex and beautiful landscape. The vehicles arrived and, mindful of his new responsibility, Frederic took a closer look. They were open all around, comprising just seats and wheels on a frame that produced a simple cover if it rained. V*ery basic indeed*, he thought.

"What form of energy do they use?" he asked.

"They are fitted with mini generators that are fed from an energy that is created by fusing mineral compounds with water under extreme pressure. It is very simple, but you will see we have different forms of energy all over the planet," Finn explained.

They got into the vehicles and the drivers took them on a tour of the island, where they were introduced to the farming, plant-medicines, education and energy. They also observed the day-to-day functioning of communities and were acutely aware of the co-operative and supportive spirit that was prevalent in all aspects of life.

The women were interested in looking at how the homes were run and were amazed at their simplicity and comfort, using natural ingredients for building and furnishing. Their focus and priority was the balance of the environment, and as long as they had their basic needs met, they were happy. Each family had its own crystal-and-stone-built house with crystal windows; the walls, floors and doors made from a combination of stone and wood. The shapes of the houses echoed the shapes of the landscape and were built around the natural vegetation. No trees were cut down to make way for homes, and Jude was fascinated by the sloping roofs that mimicked the rolling hills, so that, at first glance, the houses looked like just another piece of the landscape.

Mark was particularly interested in the education of the children. He could see both men and women instructing children in various situations in the open. He asked to go closer, and they all followed with equal interest. He watched the adults instructing the children to pick up a branch of a tree that was lying on the ground. He heard an adult say to a child, "Look at it, feel it and decide what that branch should become that will be useful."

Mark asked Orla how they learnt to communicate with the branches, as there didn't seem to be much instruction.

"They listen to the branch and the branch tells them how to fashion the wood," she explained. She didn't mention the spirit guides who did the actual communicating. Mark was silenced by the simplicity, quite understandably as this was a concept that had not been practised by humans for centuries.

Orla, sensing they needed to have a visual understanding of how this process worked, took them inside the large barn housing the woodwork facility where the hand machinery for making the necessary requirements for the islanders was operated by men with great strength and respect for the wood that they were fashioning. On the other side of the barn a group of children happily painted basic fashioned wood shapes, and Finn explained that this was another opportunity for the children to learn to communicate with the wood. This was woodwork 101 for them, but it was in fact the first lesson in the deep understanding of the needs of the planet.

"Everything in nature is governed by Crystal Wisdom. If everyone on the planet is in harmony with that language, then the successful future of the planet is guaranteed."

"Is it just wood that has its own language?" Anne enquired innocently.

Orla hesitated as she still didn't think they were ready to know about the spirit guides. "No, Anne, everything in nature has a way of communicating with each other: the stones, the earth, the plants, the trees, the water, they communicate constantly and humans are part of that communication network. Unfortunately, humans have lost that ability. Believing language is only conveyed orally has increasingly restricted them."

"How long will it take us to learn?"

"You will be surprised by the speed that you will pick it up."

"How do you choose the teachers?" Mark enquired.

"Interesting question, Mark. As you are becoming aware, the teachers are chosen for their natural ability to take concepts and explain them in the simplest way, in the language children understand. This is a particularly important skill and everyone chosen to be teachers undergoes rigorous tests to ensure that they can communicate with the environment fluently, as well as being able to adjust to the different learning modes of children. To be a teacher is regarded as one of the most important responsibilities in our communities and they are highly respected. Equally, parents reinforce this way of learning with their everyday interaction with the children. You will see children spend a lot of time with their parents and other adults in the community in a variety of activities so that their creative processes are constantly being stimulated. There are no bored or frustrated children on the island."

Orla had been quite appalled by the quality of the teachers in the domes, and for many centuries teachers were recruited on their academic ability alone. They were chosen on their ability to regurgitate facts but not necessarily in a format for the young. However, this was no accident; this method of teaching was designed to shut down the questioning part of young minds.

Cynthia and Joshua were particularly interested in the food production as they were beginning to understand that food was imperative for good health, as was the plant life that provided medicines.

Finn drew their attention to the different grains that they produced, each one providing different amino acids, minerals and vitamins to ensure that the fragile human body gained sufficient nutrition.

Cynthia was aware of the good quality of the cloth from which the island's clothes was manufactured, contrasting with the chemical-based fabric that formed her dress, and asked Finn how it was manufactured. He took the group to the fields that grew flax and cotton; from the fields they went to the spinning rooms where men performed the task of taking the flax and cotton, turning it into thread and then weaving it into sheaths of cloth. Women were responsible for dyeing the cloth, using natural pigment and embroidery to embellish soft furnishings for the home. Helen was intrigued as she had a latent creative streak in her that had been slapped out of her when she was young. She would often pick up a pencil when she was a child and unconsciously create wonderful shapes on random pieces of paper or card that she could find. Her parents were horrified, as to draw was regarded as a sign of low intelligence, and they were worried their child would be branded as such and selected to live in a different dome. So all pencils, pens and paper were banned from her home. Only computers were allowed. She had eventually forgotten about this until today when she was faced with the very same designs that she had drawn when she was young. Eager to find out more, she went over to get a closer look at the female embroiderer.

Orla explained that the shapes that were being embroidered represented the knowledge of creation. Having these shapes in the home ensured that Crystal Wisdom was reflected in every aspect of their lives.

Mathew had noticed that the shoes of the islanders looked like leather and suede, that he initially thought would be from animals. But he deduced there just weren't enough cows on the island to provide the skins. Orla, reading his unspoken quandary, responded, "They are made from mushrooms."

He laughed. "Mushrooms?" He knew what mushrooms were because they had mushroom farms under the domes, as they appeared to be able to grow anywhere, but the mushrooms he was used to were tiny pale button mushrooms. Finn was noticing that they were not questioning the ability that both he and Orla had of reading the unspoken questions of the group. They seemed to be taking this in their stride.

The couple took them to a dense forest, and as they walked through the damp soil they were confronted by a host of large strange-shaped growths near to the trees. "These are all mushrooms. Look how large some of them grow." Finn said. They had never seen anything like this in their entire lives and didn't know whether to be disgusted by the shapes or excited by the potential of what they were witnessing. "These mushrooms can be used for absolutely anything, from medicines, to food and weatherproof clothing," Finn added.

Frederic reminded Finn about the energy, and Finn took them to the crystal panels, the concept of which they understood as solar panels had been used for a short while in the last century but, unfortunately, the thick cloud of poisons that accumulated over communities prevented the powerful energy of the sun from activating the panels. Finn and Patrick had discussed this at length at the beginning of the project. On the Ruby Crystal world, Finn had been shown how to create special ruby crystal panels that would have the ability to attract the sun through the pollution, allowing the pure energy from the sun to play its important role in the recovery of Earth. Fortunately, that ruby crystal could be found in abundance in the soil on Crystal Island. The islanders had never needed to use it because they didn't suffer from the effects of pollution. The island also had a unique supply of energy from the Crystal Fortress, but Finn assured them that mineral-and water-based energy, coupled with the solar panels, would be sufficient for the Federations.

"Where will we get sufficient fresh water?" asked Anne.

Finn and Orla looked at each other, and Orla continued. "We will shortly show you a view of the world in the future that will demonstrate how we will have enough water. When you see this, you will realise that the water supply will not be a concern." Orla held back on the detail of how this would happen, as she knew that they would find it alarming.

Finn had one last island invention to show them. He asked them to stand on the path; around the island there were paths for walking on and for small vehicles and horses. The covering of the paths, whilst harder than the grass, was made from soil, crystal and seaweed compressed to form a hard surface. Each time someone walked or rode on the path, the vibration activated a burst of energy that built up and was stored in generators. This impressed them all. Some people had tried to introduce this technology in the last century, but it was in competition with the producers of fossil fuels who, because of their immense wealth, controlled the direction of energy. There was sufficient knowledge to have used sustainable energy forms if there had been the financial investment. But that investment would not have paid off for about 50 years and the vision of the decision makers was focussed on the immediate needs of the planet.

They completed the circuit of the island and returned to the palace. As their vehicles came to a stop Finn instructed them to follow him to the meeting room.

They trotted behind him with many thoughts trundling around their minds. Orla was not concerned. She knew that all the information they had been exposed to would eventually settle into the correct receptors of their memory and very soon all would become clear to them. They had of course asked numerous questions on the tour, which had filled Orla with confidence; it showed that they were beginning to acknowledge that there were solutions to problems that had dogged the dome-dwellers for decades, and indeed, the planet for centuries.

CHAPTER SEVEN
CRYSTAL STRATEGY

Finn announced that the next stage of their development was to learn how to make decisions using crystal strategy. He asked the men to follow him to the meeting room, and interestingly, the women didn't question their apparent exclusion. Orla and Finn did this purposely to highlight the programming of inequality that was still within them, which of course had to go.

Finn ushered the men into the meeting room. They were a little surprised to see that there were sixteen chairs placed around the table, but just as they were settling themselves into their seats, Orla entered with their wives.

None of the men uttered a word but all of them were surprised at the presence of the women as they were still getting used to the idea of the shared responsibilities. Although their trip around the island had demonstrated that the women were more than capable of forming solutions, when it came to formal decision-making the men slipped back into their dome ways.

Orla indicated for them to sit down, and the women, sensing a shift in their husbands, self-consciously took their seats, feeling very strange sitting around a table that was obviously designed to facilitate meaningful discussions and important decisions.

Orla and Finn sat down too, and Orla looked at the scene in front of her, recognising the discomfort in both groups.

"We are here to engage you into solution-based crystal strategy, which is to aid the planet's transformation. You have seen the ways of Crystal Island and have all had sufficient crystal programming to understand the qualities required to make a successful community," Finn said.

Finn knew that it would take several sessions of instruction, in tandem with their initiations, for them to fully understand and embody the strategy. They would also eventually get used to having women question them on an equal basis, an important and necessary ingredient of the strategy. Until the women stepped into that role fully, Finn and Orla would share that responsibility.

Finn continued, "Anything that is involved in creation or the creative process must follow specific evolutionary steps in order that the final result, be it tangible or intangible, is in line with planetary needs."

Finn had observed that when the dome executives came together to discuss solutions, once an idea was agreed upon, they ran full pelt towards that goal, as if they were competing in a race, without sufficient questioning. It was a feature of the warrior mentality, but equally none of the executives dared question their leaders. Orla and Finn realised that the group needed to understand the importance of questioning and the regrouping that needed to take place in any decision, and it was the women who were naturally talented to do this.

History had taken away from women their natural ability of addressing a problem from a global perspective rather than the individual's. This was a natural skill of motherhood, compounded and perfected over thousands of years. Their observations of their environment had to embrace all that was safe for the wellbeing of their children at any one time. They had to have the ability to scan a situation and, in a second, determine whether the whole environment was safe for their children. Those dangers weren't just the obvious threat from the external world, but also the everyday dangers of pots boiling over, children falling from unsecured chairs and the many potential hazards that reside in the home. Orla gave silent thanks for the multitasking abilities that came so naturally to women. She amusingly thought that maybe in one of the meetings of the Generals in the House of Laws, they should be given just one problem to resolve, but have to look after a group of three-year-olds at the same time. *Now that would be interesting.*

However, those natural leadership abilities of women had been suppressed, and their natural gifts of observation coupled with their acute ability to make lifesaving decisions ceased to be valued. Women were natural nurturers of life in the global sense, but nurturing was downgraded, and women banished to the kitchen as supportive homemakers.

So, whenever women were put in positions of power or leadership, they experienced unconscious conflict because their natural instincts led them to different priorities and objectives than they were instructed to follow; it triggered to a lesser or greater degree the memory of a time when women were the Elders of communities. This brought up two responses: one was that they understood acutely what was needed for the community, but the other memory was that they were punished for expressing that view. After the crystal laws were buried, jealousy of the Elders followed and eventually they were demoted, vilified and excluded from communities. Orla recalled those ugly scenes she had witnessed in the Halls of Experiences on the Crystal worlds, women's natural gifts of leadership being eroded bit by bit by the fears and jealousy of a few men. But that fear brought about doubt of the validity of Crystal Wisdom in the many, and where there was doubt, there lurked Shadow.

Orla cast her mind back to a memory that she had seen in Cynthia's programming, far back in history in a country that had birthed a major religious following, where a woman's opinion or testimony was viewed as unreliable because she had been judged as a lesser being and therefore was not to be taken seriously. *This programming has left an indelible mark on women, which has transcended two thousand years without any real challenges*, Orla quietly considered.

"Remember your priority and main objective is, 'what is best for the planet?' So with that in mind I would like you to re-evaluate your priorities. To help you I am going to remind you of the bounties of the Secret Garden."

She asked them to focus on the viewing screen at the end of the room. The screen quickly filled with images of the Garden, and their memories immediately connected with the smells, sounds and colours of this special place.

"Crystal Wisdom acknowledges the importance of the natural infrastructure of the planet, which incorporates equally the plant and mineral world, the quality of the air and water coupled with the warmth and light of the sun, and most importantly, the co-operation and confluence of all these components. Without these qualities, in the correct balance, life on Earth would not survive. But," Orla emphasised, "remember this is not just about survival, this is about evolution and transformation."

Sheila grasped the situation very quickly and summarised verbally just to make sure that she had interpreted the situation correctly.

"So our objective is make the rest of the planet like Crystal Island. For that to happen we have to make tremendous changes and we have to decide on the priorities. So far you have highlighted the four basic components of life on Earth from which we must draw all that we need."

Her husband and the other six men looked at her, surprised. They were amazed that a woman was able to introduce a concept and break it down into a workable formula. The other women, not surprised at all, saw the sense in her observations completely.

Finn continued. "You must understand that to be able to interpret what the planet requires, which is the main function of man on the planet, you have to use all your senses and all your gifts. Women are natural nurturers and homemakers. Translate all the decisions a woman makes in the course of a day to ensure her children are safe and healthy, and you will realise she is making a continuous chain of decisions, perfectly orchestrated, without even raising a sweat. That formula could be easily translated into any leadership decision."

Phillip and James began to open their mouths in disagreement, but when they looked at Orla, they hesitated and stopped, as here was a prime example of a woman who made decisions on a global scale with ease.

"Before you consider which priorities need to be addressed, I would ask the men to recall what decision-making was like in the House of Laws and how long it took them to find a solution," Finn asked.

John and the others thought back to the hours spent discussing; and that was the issue, they weren't really discussing at all. Finn scanned their memories and knew that they were reflecting on those tedious proceedings. Leaders would throw ideas into the arena, feeling pressured to contribute something concrete; random solutions were tossed around, each delegate throwing his opinion into the arena whether it was relevant or not. Of course, there were those who had a vested interest in the outcome of those discussions who steered the proceedings along a very cleverly manipulated route, each man ensuring that his interests were at the forefront of the solutions. Finn brought them back to the present. "You will now need to look at solutions from the planet's perspective and not from your own personal agendas, or what you think should happen based on your own relatively narrow experience."

They were all taken aback by this original concept. In the domes their departments functioned in isolation from the other departments. There was only so much money and resources to go around and they all competed for a cut of that diminishing purse.

They began to realise that their focus had been on winning rather than doing what was right for the planet.

Finn observed his students and realised that he was going to have to take them by the hand initially, walking them through crystal problem-solving until they fully understood how to identify the priorities.

"The first challenge is to address, without a doubt, the failing planet. We have demonstrated what has gone wrong with the planet and you have witnessed the possibilities of the island, so you have definite terms of reference.

"For the transformation of the planet to happen, decisions need to be made constantly, but the issue is the route that you have been trained to follow to solve problems is flawed."

The men looked defensive and the women's eyes widened.

"There are two sides to finding solutions: the creative side and the strategic side. And the key is to integrate the two. Unfortunately, history has polarised these qualities, and a person is judged to be either creative or strategic."

John considered this and knew exactly what Finn was talking about. He and all his peers had been defined early on in their careers as being strategic thinkers.

Finn, reading his mind, asked him, "What happened to all the creative people?"

"I don't know. There doesn't seem to be a category that covers creativity in defining leadership." Orla nodded. She had seen on her journey to the different Crystal worlds how man had gradually closed down his creative side. For that wonderful side of a person to function correctly, they had to be spontaneous and in touch with their Crystal Wisdom. The encroaching presence of Shadow with each generation, and their diminished contact with spirit guides, ensured that spontaneity, the precursor to creativity, was erased. With the lack of creativity, there were no original ideas, and most definitely no challenge.

Orla could see that the men were resistant to the word 'creative', as it had received an increasingly bad press over the last few centuries. Creative people were seen to be outside of society, with no control over their thinking process, therefore regarded as unpredictable and unreliable, which led to creativity being downgraded to a lesser quality. In fact, many times in history, the creative people had been the first to challenge authority, which meant they were dangerous to the world of Shadow.

Orla realised that they needed a new understanding of the word 'creative'.

"Creativity is the ability to tap into Crystal knowledge, which is available to all matter, from the stones in the fields to the animals, plants and humans. However, humans are the only living beings in the material world to be able to access the wisdom contained within all those groups and convey it to the whole planet. Mankind has been given the ability to think strategically, which embraces the seven qualities of intelligence, to be able to spread the crystal message far and wide. This is a very special gift.

"Strategy without creativity is meaningless in terms of planetary healing. Man must learn to be able to identify what the planet requires and implement a process to provide that requirement. Equally, creativity without strategy puts us at the level of plants, where we can only function at the level of our own individual parameters. We are much more than that. Can you now see what a privileged position mankind holds on this planet?"

Sheila responded first. "So, correct me if I am wrong – what you are saying is that whilst nature goes through its amazing ritual of birth, death and rebirth, depending on the weather and the seasons, we have the ability to harness all of nature's offerings to ensure that they complement each other, and the planet not only flourishes, but continues on its evolutionary pathway."

Amazing, thought Orla, *her awakening is happening rapidly. And she is using vocabulary like 'ritual' and 'amazing' in the same sentence.*

"Yes," Orla continued, "we now need to give you an insight as to what that evolution means."

Finn continued. "As you have seen from the viewings, the Earth has repeated many cycles of abundance and depletion. You have seen that it cannot go through another cycle like that again. This is the last opportunity for it to progress to the next stage of its evolution."

"But surely getting the planet back to being abundant is our main priority, and this will not happen overnight?" Frederic asked, trying to calculate how long they had before they ran out of time.

"You are quite right," said Finn, "it won't happen overnight, but it will happen faster than you think. The main purpose for restoring abundance is to allow for the next evolutionary shift to take place."

They all looked baffled and began to hurl many questions at the royal couple.

Orla lifted her hand to silence them.

"We are going to have to show you something that is going to happen, which you are only now ready to understand, and it has to take place before the next level of transformation. I have been advised by my mentors" – she deliberately did not indicate to the group that her mentors were Elders on Crystaland – "that once the Earth has been healed to a level that the plant life begins to flourish again, and Shadow has disappeared, there will be a recalibration of the vibratory levels of the planet which will allow the Crystalanders to return with their special crystal to recharge the planet."

Orla had enquired of her mentors why the Crystalanders could not return as soon as Shadow had been removed. She had been told that only when the plant life had returned, which would restore Earth's melody, could they return.

"It is only recently that I have been aware of the full extent of the planet's toxicity and I know only too well that, while the Earth remains like this, it is invisible to the Crystalanders. The universe vibrates to different tunes: some complementary, some discordant – Earth is discordant at the moment and therefore inaccessible to the purity and wisdom of the Crystalanders. But I know that once Earth's melody is restored and they return, the other planets of the solar system will also wake up from their enforced downgrade."

They were all staring at her intently, trying to grasp the words that were coming from her lips, and trying to put them into some semblance of understanding.

"When the Earth had begun to deteriorate after the Crystalanders left, the other planets in the solar system closed down because their rhythm had been interrupted, and without the melodic communication from the minerals on those planets, Earth was isolated from Crystal knowledge," Orla said.

Frederic was intrigued and interrupted. "I am not really understanding what you are saying here. What could these planets, which we have discovered are totally devoid of life, offer us in the way of knowledge?"

"Each planet is abundant in a particular mineral, and whenever there is a concentration of specific minerals there is a concentration of crystal information. Transformation can only take place if all Crystal Wisdom is accessible."

Once again there was silence in the room. The viewing continued. Finn asked them to watch closely.

The scene shifted to the ice caps of the north and south poles. The group were aware that the ice caps had reduced in size over the last century, but they watched with increasing dread as the very last piece of ice dissolved into the sea. As with everything in nature, not one blade of grass moves without repercussions being felt somewhere else. So, the seas swelled and rushed from the two extreme axes of the planet and engulfed landmasses; and where the weight of the ice had held down land below the sea level, as it melted new islands appeared to pop up from the sea in its place.

The screen was filled with dramatic scenes of continents disappearing under the swell of the oceans; continents that had lain parched and arid for decades were submerged, taking with them old buildings and even domes. Eventually the seas calmed and found their new levels and the new configuration of land appeared. Gone were the vast continents of the Americas, Africa and Europe; in their place were 24 smaller pockets of land.

The group were initially too shocked to speak, but Sheila eventually asked quietly, "When is this likely to happen?"

Orla took in a deep breath before responding. "As soon as all the Federations are in agreement, and we have sufficient active pioneers. All that is needed is the concerted effort of a few to trigger a change."

Finn was intrigued that they had not questioned how this change of leadership could trigger a planetary upheaval. The royal family knew of course that once the thought processes of a few began to change, and Shadow disengaged, the planet would go into a 'shock state', almost like a vehicle changing gear sharply.

"Does it have to be so extreme?" Helen asked with a concerned look on her face

"I'm afraid so. There had been a point in your history when man was warned about global warming, but he chose to ignore it, paying lip service mostly by implementing half-hearted measures. The window of opportunity closed and we are now faced with no alternative. But don't worry, we will be able to warn people to go to safe domes until the waters calm, which will mean opening the domes to people who live outside." Orla waited for their reaction to this, but they did not appear to see this as a problem, which was encouraging.

"I'm still not understanding what the relevance is of the melting of the ice caps and the reshaping of the continents," Phillip said.

"Your Federal world has become too vast and too complicated; it is more important to have smaller communities so that there is independent and co-operative government. When there is just one government, the qualities of Crystal Wisdom are lost through the layers of human hierarchy. Each person carries, and should implement, Crystal Wisdom. If we keep the communities smaller it allows nature to remind us of crystal laws.

"Equally, the parched land needs to go under the sea, and the mineral-rich land that has been covered by the oceans needs to come up so that we can grow healthy plants in the rich soil that has been submerged for so long."

Orla continued. "So, getting back to using creative thought and strategy in an integrated way—"

Jude interrupted. "After the shifting of the continents it looks like we will have to start afresh, but won't we have to see who is left and what their requirements are?"

Orla smiled at Jude's spontaneous interruption, and could see her mind had gone into overdrive searching for solutions.

"Yes but the important aspect of crystal strategy, which is of course using Crystal Wisdom to guide us, is to ensure that we follow the correct path that will lead us to arrive at the correct solution.

"Every idea or proposed solution to a challenge must go through a process of purification – a process of expansion, challenge and reduction, at each stage reminding yourselves of the ultimate objective: 'How will the planet benefit from this decision?' That cycle continues until the intangible becomes material.

"Creative and strategic processes of thought are both valuable and relevant qualities. One of the most important questions to be asked throughout this whole process is directed to the benefit of the planet. If at any point the benefit veers towards an individual, Crystal Wisdom is lost and the planet suffers."

Orla had seen on her journey of awakening that the quest for creative and original solutions had been regarded as the holy grail of industry and governments. But those two institutions, which controlled the world, were governed by fear under the influence of Shadow, and fear worked against the creative process.

"Man has always chased the idea of creative answers and would use anything to achieve that, and a couple of centuries ago man misused plants in their quest to access creativity in their deep memory. New age healers, striving to go back to the crystal ways, had used plants to enhance their ability to connect to a higher place of understanding in their memories. But this, unfortunately, did not give them access to Crystal memory, it just took them to a higher level of their own genetic or racial memory. Shadow was too deeply entrenched, controlling every aspect of their minds, preventing any connection to true Crystal Wisdom.

"The gatekeepers of crystal creativity are very strong and powerful and nothing is allowed to penetrate their crystal gates that carries the slightest nuance of fear. The practice of using plants to access a higher state had been used by artists and poets throughout history to enhance what they thought was their own creative ability. But, unfortunately, the extent of that creativity was limited by the fear invoked by Shadow; their creative thoughts not coming from a place of crystal creativity but from a place of man-made illusions. The thoughts that they accessed were purely projections from the vast collection of images encoded in their inherited memories.

"However, in desperation, in the middle of the 20th century, in a last attempt to bring people back to their crystal awareness, the Crystalanders spoke to the few remaining spirit guides of the plant kingdom and asked them to whisper to man of the benefits of the mind-altering plants in the hope that their use would take them to a level outside of their limiting and dense material world, reminding them, once again, that the world they inhabited was not the final story.

"This began well; man began to see possibilities, kingdoms and realms outside of the slavery myth of mankind. The issue was that Shadow judged this as an attack on its survival, so it waited till its hosts got to a place of plant-induced ecstasy and sank its tentacles, heavily laced with fear, deeper into their temporarily unprotected memories. And so, when the effects of the plant-induced bliss wore off, they were confronted with a version of fear many times amplified. With the magnification of those fears, their dependence for more of the plant increased to cease the Shadow-induced pain. And so it continued until they found a world without the support of the plants intolerable and the special plants became another form of addiction. As with alcohol, Shadow had seen the addictive qualities of the plants as a way to manipulate and control the masses. Shadow manipulated the Generals to allow the proliferation of those plants but kept them illegal to increase their glamour, which appealed to the young and the vulnerable.

"Man had failed to recognise that plants were an aid to the ancients only because the wise men and women communicated with the plant spirits. When the plant was ready for harvest, those wise people offered thanks and gratitude for their bounty and in return the plant spirits imbued the buds with special protective powers that allowed an individual to access Crystal Wisdom. The plant that the Shadow supported worked in a very different way; it gave a short glimpse of euphoria, and when that feeling wore off, it left its host depleted of their natural brain chemicals that allowed true connectivity to crystal creativity. Unfortunately, man had lost any concept of working with plant spirits to help purify the intention of the plant, so the plants they used only held the imprint that ran through the consciousness of mankind – addiction, slavery and fear.

"The Crystalanders had wanted to remind humans of their connection to nature but only succeeded in unwittingly feeding Shadow with yet another tool that kept its hosts emotionally unconscious. The desire to escape from the material world was strong and led to deeper addictions, which increased with each generation, with the result, unfortunately, that the very people who would have been suitable candidates for the pioneering groups had their minds turned to mush and were rendered useless for transformation."

There were no comments from the group. The idea of plant spirits, and indeed addictions to plants, were very much outside of their understanding. The concept of natural addictions had been taken over by chemical addictions in the domes.

As there were no questions, Orla embarked on what appeared to be a totally different and incongruent theme, particularly to the men: the importance of a woman's menstrual cycle. Whilst the group couldn't see the connection, they would in time realise the relationship between a woman's cycle and the plant world. The women had already been instructed in this critical aspect of the female body and they remained quiet and expressionless, listening to Orla's biology lesson, watching their husbands, trying to anticipate their reaction. Orla concluded the lesson with the most important fact: "Women are closely attuned to the planet, their bodies mirroring the creative process of nature, and it is they alone who can interpret what the planet needs."

Orla and Finn waited for their reactions. They both knew this was a bitter pill for the men to swallow. They had gone, in a very short space of time, from being the decision and policy makers, to what?

Finn interrupted quickly as he could see their deflated egos taking them closer to the brink of being receptive to Shadow.

"However, it is the strategy required to implement what your wives intuit that makes a solution possible. But you must listen to your wives and only work with the facts they give you. You cannot interpret those facts based on what has been done in the past. It is vital to include your wives in that strategy because they will always add the challenge necessary to keep to the creative path that provides unique solutions."

Finn observed the reactions of the men. He could see that they were confused, grappling with the idea of sharing the decisions and, in fact, erroneously interpreting that the women were leading them.

"Please don't see this as a competition," Finn said, interrupting their thoughts quickly. "Remember you must do whatever is required for the future of the planet and if that means sharing the decision-making to get the best results, then that is the only way forward.

"Do not forget, the old way has led you to this place of darkness with the prospect of no future for the human race. When you were given your responsibilities, you were told that you and your wives were both equally responsible for that role; the wives are not the support act but active participants in the decision-making."

Cynthia, having had time to think of the whole issue relating to menstruation since Orla first introduced the subject to them, asked, "If women remove toxins from their bodies through their menstrual flow, how do men remove theirs?"

"Perspiration!" Orla quickly replied. "That is why men perspire more profusely than women, and it is a contributory factor to male balding. If the perspiration is very acidic, or toxic, the hair follicles are damaged."

There was silence as the men, who were all balding, contemplated the condition of their hair follicles.

"What happens when the women stop menstruating?" Joshua asked, not quite believing he was asking questions about a woman's most intimate bodily function. "Do they go into retirement?"

"No, menstruation prepares a woman to become attuned to the needs of the planet, which she does by communicating with nature. When she eventually finishes the menopause she is connected with the planet 24/7 and moves from being the mother of her children to being one of the mothers of the planet."

The men nodded their heads. digesting the information through the conflicting emotions that were hurtling through their minds. One part of them had complete respect for and trust in Orla and Finn, but another part wrestled with all the new information. which seemed to make sense on some level but caused confusion on another.

Orla could see that there was a distinct change in the women. Gone were the timid seekers of approval waiting for their husbands' permission. They were beginning to see their husbands in a different light and were a little impatient. Another veil of fear had been removed from the many myths and illusions obscuring their natural abilities. Their new crystal experiences had given them the ability to express their own authority with confidence.

Cynthia's mind was going into overdrive with many questions running around her head. "So if women stop menstruating and they become more in tune with the planet, what happens to men at this time?"

Finn smiled and explained. "Testosterone declines in men at a similar age, which allows them to access more Crystal Wisdom directly. They can then devote their lives to the service of the planet, working in tandem with women. They lose the primal urge that runs through their veins prompting extreme reactions rather than measured responses. Their emotions are more connected to nature and are therefore in keeping with the planetary needs. Remember the gardeners in the Secret Garden – they are all strong men but possess gentle hands able to communicate freely with plants."

Orla and Finn shared the thought that the group were ready to be introduced to Crystal Union so that they could view themselves as equal partners on all levels.

Finn was also aware that when the time came to step into their roles as leaders, they would all need more assistance to help them to work together as equals and utilise the new skills effectively. But at this stage, all that was needed was to sew the first seeds of the possibility of discovering new solutions for old problems. Their worn-out decision-making process was so ingrained into their memories, and therefore their identities, that it would need to be unpicked carefully. Whilst they were now able to access Crystal Wisdom, they were still in the habit of undertaking tasks in a prescriptive manner, following strict protocols with endless and clumsy rules to anticipate every negative scenario for each situation, which was an impossible task. Creation is dynamic, the plant world is dynamic, and man is dynamic. There were not enough books or rule makers on the planet to accommodate that dynamism. It all came down to following one important but simple rule: every decision that is taken must be for the long-term benefit of the planet.

Orla looked at the sea of rules and regulations that Finn was projecting back to her from their minds and wondered how these simple humans could make situations so complex.

With her increasing confidence, Sheila asked what the next steps would be to engage others into Crystal Wisdom.

"The first step will be to engage your Generals, your immediate superiors," Orla said.

"And how will you do that?" Helen asked, knowing that they would be hard nuts to crack.

"We will engage with them in their dreams, as we did with you, but we will need to make more effort to access their imaginal minds without alerting Shadow. Once they respond to us, we will introduce the Generals to you," Finn confirmed.

"What about their wives?" Sheila asked.

"They are too far entrenched into the female Shadow programming, I am afraid. It is a great pity, but for them to have lived under the ultimate suppression of the Generals, who are totally controlled by the Elite, means that they are too far away from their Crystal memory, both physically and emotionally."

When Orla had scanned the wives of the Generals, she was horrified to see that these poor women had absolutely no visible sign of Crystal memory in any part of their body.

"Once the Generals are on side, we will explain the role of women, but we will not introduce you to them until we have engaged the Generals of all International Federations," Orla said, trying to calm their concerns.

"I don't know how that is going to work," James said, faltering.

"Don't worry, it will be possible. You are yet to understand the full capabilities and possibilities of Crystal Wisdom," Finn responded confidently.

Finn smiled; he knew that when the Generals of Federations saw Orla and, more importantly, spoke with her, there would be no problem. This group of people had become so accustomed to Orla's voice, they had forgotten how it had been in the beginning when she spoke to them in their dreams. The vibration of her voice, with its direct link to Crystal Wisdom, projected into any conversation a sensation of peace, light and intelligence. It was as if she infused the air with a special drug of sweetness.

"Ok, so we have decided how we are going to engage the other Federations, but we have to offer them a workable plan," Philip insisted.

"What do you think needs to be done?" Finn asked, trying to prompt them into formulating a strategy.

He could see they all had differing ideas jostling around their minds, darting from their responsibilities to what they thought needed to happen, to keeping the population functioning, plants for food, medicines, heat and light, oh yes, and the water for the plants – where would the water come from? And so their thoughts jostled around chaotically in their minds.

Finn quietly reminded them, "The priority is what is necessary for planetary healing, not for mankind."

There was more silence. Orla and Finn waited. Jude was the first to speak, quietly and hesitantly.

"Would it be restoring the plant life?" Orla smiled at Jude, giving her more confidence as she continued. "If that is the case, we have to learn from Crystal Island what the necessary ingredients are for healthy plant life to provide food and medicine for humans, but also to provide the correct balance for the planet."

Finn applauded her silently, as he had no wish to give her too much attention, as this could alienate the men. "Yes, that is correct, once we have sufficient successful plant life, the shift in the seas will take place."

"And then," Jude continued with more enthusiasm, "we need to know which countries will be left and how we are going to pool our resources."

"Exactly," said Finn, "but before we get caught up in the strategy for those two objectives, we need to be able to identify the gifts and talents of the next one hundred."

"How will you choose?" Mathew asked, slightly distracted by Jude's new-found confidence.

"We feel that it would be best to stay within the dome of your Federation, as you share a cultural memory that makes it easier for you all to access. What we need is for you to identify twenty people with whom you are closely connected at work. If you give us a list of names, Orla and I will scan them for their suitability and also the suitability of their wives."

The men began to write down names enthusiastically. Orla interrupted them quickly. "What criteria do you have for identifying suitable candidates?"

"I was thinking of those who had the same interests," Mathew suggested.

"Yes, a good start, but first I want you to think about how healthy they look. The most important criterion I had when searching for you was your physical health. You aren't used to observing each other, but since being on Crystal Island you have seen the health possibilities available to you. Whoever you choose must be able to physically improve quickly, otherwise there is too much of a stride for them to take."

They considered her words and began to make fresh lists. As the lists progressed, Orla directed the next question to the women. "If you know the wives of these men, could you contribute to their choice?"

The wives dutifully examined the names, recognising some of them, and after reflecting on their physical health, removed some names from the list. Eventually each couple had a list of twenty suitable couples.

"We will later evaluate the gifts, talents and available Crystal memory of the 140 and select the next 100 from that group," Orla said.

"Could you talk more about the new Federations that will be created with the movement of the seas and oceans?" Mathew was trying to take in as much information as possible with the new responsibility of environment pressing on his shoulders.

Finn repeated that the shift in the landmasses would only happen once plant life was successfully growing again. "So with this in mind, what should be the priority?" Finn again took the opportunity to bring their focus back to their main objective.

Finn knew that now was a good time to introduce them to the idea of discovering their own gifts and talents, their personal wisdom, so that he or she could make their own contribution to that objective.

"As we have told you, each one of you has a crystal gift and talent to offer the planet that will help you with your responsibilities. To reveal the wisdom of that gift, man has to undergo a series of initiations. This is not something that can be obtained from texts or video instructions; this comes from an experience. There are different initiations that are required and at the end of this session you will be introduced to the qualities of those initiations. This will ensure that you have a full understanding of each other and of creation."

Finn continued with their introduction to crystal strategy.

"As I said previously, with any process of enquiry or decision-making where you are seeking new solutions to problems, tangible as well as intangible, there are specific steps that have to be followed. If you want to claw the planet back from the jaws of the apocalypse to reflect the life on Crystal Island, you will have to follow the laws of Crystal Wisdom.

"You will need to put aside all your academic programming and begin to access your crystal intelligence, the part of you that is a reflection of the perfection of nature." They all stared at Finn, waiting for more clarification, and when there was none they began showering him with questions. Finn realised that they had no concept of the potential of nature. Trying to get them to imagine all the bounties of the island on a global scale was beyond their comprehension. Finn knew that the women would understand this concept much faster, and he was happy to leave this to Orla, but for now he had to focus on these men in front of him to make sure they began to engage with crystal strategy.

"I want you to reflect on how the domes came into existence in the first place." The men and women had to think hard, as the domes had been present for several generations and were an accepted part of their lives. "Who are the domes stopping from entering and who, indeed, are prevented from leaving?" Finn had had plenty of opportunity to roam around the domes undetected on his visits to collect the groups, and considered that the domes were just luxurious prisons.

The men and women had never thought of their lives in that way. Finn challenged them further. "You have all seen the daily lives of the islanders. Can you identify where you have access to the same level of freedom?"

They couldn't answer. Everything about daily life under the dome for any level of dome-dweller was prescriptive. They all began to feel apprehensive as they became aware that they had no idea what Finn was talking about. Freedom was always relative, they believed, but under the domes it didn't exist in any form.

Once again Finn felt compassion for them. They had been so confident in their roles, believing that they were doing a very important and responsible job, but they were only following a well-trodden path of protocols. Their parameters for decision-making were very narrow indeed. Finn was now blowing this whole idea open and they were increasingly aware that they had no understanding of true leadership.

James, gathering his thoughts quickly, contributed. "The concept of trading between countries has been nearly eradicated – there are fewer and fewer natural resources to use in manufacturing and therefore nothing to trade. Oil and gas reserves are depleted. When the Earth's resources stopped producing the metals for manufacturing, industry turned to plastics, but that polluted the environment. With the dwindling population and resources, the domes are the only thing that is conserving those resources and keeping people alive. What is going to replace the domes in the interim during the transition?"

Orla had kept quiet for the most of this discussion and, seeing that their thoughts were going into a frenzy of fear, she stepped in, her voice calming their thoughts.

"You need to think about what Finn has described, and take every aspect of your lives, examine it and see what can be changed or removed."

Finn prompted them by asking what the environment needed to allow the domes to be removed. They all concurred that it was unpolluted air.

"How does the island maintain its clean air?" Mathew asked.

"It has not been polluted by chemicals from industry but, more importantly, the trees are allowed to do their job and keep the balance of the air."

They all considered the reference to trees. It had been a long time since trees had grown healthily on the planet and none of them understood the benefit they contributed to the health of the atmosphere. Trees had been felled to make way for man and to be used in industry or had lost their inner strength over time because their environment was alien to their inner knowledge and had died.

Finn had been baffled by the arrogant attitude of conquerors over the course of history, who had attempted to replicate not just the lifestyles of their homelands in their new continents, but also the landscapes. In his arrogant attempt to control all in his domain, man had contributed to the destruction of the delicate infrastructure of the natural world.

Finn went back to prompting the group. "So if you were redesigning the planet, based on your visit to Crystal Island, what would you put in place?"

"We have to find a clean energy," Frederic said.

This prompted Joshua to suggest that the manufacturing of foods needed to be changed and the supply of natural foods be cultivated.

"Health definitely needs to be a priority," Mark added.

"Yes," Jude piped up, "to ensure that Crystal Wisdom translates to all cells of our bodies."

They were all silenced by Jude's reference to Crystal Wisdom. None of them had mentioned this phrase yet. Orla realised that Jude had been sitting quietly listening and had eventually come to the obvious conclusion that the health of the planet and everything in it was paramount.

Finn posed the next logical question. "Ok, so now I want you to think about the health of the planet and not the people."

"Why are the people being excluded?" Joshua demanded.

John interrupted before Finn could respond. "Without the health of the planet, there will be no people." Finn smiled in agreement. Yes, they are getting the very simple message: *if you look after the planet, the planet will look after you.*

Orla could see that they were grappling with this new

way of looking at problems. It was simple, and it was this simplicity that was confusing them. Solutions had become so complex because man had moved away from the natural world with each step of his fear-based strategies. Nature, whilst complex for man to harness and control, was actually very simple.

"The question we need to ask," Orla explained, "is not what can the planet do for us, but what can we do for the planet?"

John expressed his exasperation at the condition of the planet. "But look at what we are dealing with!" He was becoming increasingly aware of how far the planet had moved away from nature the more time he spent on Crystal Island.

"Remember the wonders that you experienced in the Secret Garden. Under the right circumstances there is still time for them to be reflected all over the planet," Orla reassured them.

"We therefore have to learn about the plants and their benefits," Helen said.

"We have an extreme shortage of water. How will the plants be watered?" Jude asked.

"We will show you how to turn seawater into three levels of usable water: the first level is for human drinking water, the second level for plant life, as it still retains high levels of minerals, and the third level can be used for the purpose of cleaning. Our water filtration system doesn't require the dangerous chemicals used in the domes' water systems, which has contributed to the pollution of the environment."

"How much water can your filtration system process?"

"There is no limit, Anne," replied Finn.

"Well," she continued, "we can transport water to the mainland and start by feeding the soil which is outside of the domes, but still under dome protection." She was now aware of the threat of the people outside of the domes.

"Once we can water the soil it will be able to sustain growth."

Orla and Finn were waiting for one of them to identify what other ingredient would be required.

Cynthia said quietly, "I've noticed the sun is particularly bright on the island, which I think must contribute to the healthy production of plants, but on the mainland there is too much pollution for the sun's rays to penetrate."

There was silence. Orla and Finn waited.

Mathew's eyes popped open, excited by his idea. "Would it be possible to take some of the ruby crystal panels from the island and use them to create special pods that filter and amplify the sun for growing plants?"

"Excellent idea!" Finn exclaimed.

"So we have the water and the sun, but I am sure we will need something else to stimulate production of plant life, as that would appear to be a priority and we need to be able to have rapid growth," Sheila said.

"You are correct, Sheila. Crystal Island will provide soil. In fact, you probably have not noticed yet – the soil of Crystal Island is made entirely of minute crystals which carry a specific stimulant to plant growth hormones. We will also install specific crystals in the water systems that feed the soil and the drinking water for the domes. This will ensure that both the plants and the people receive the minerals necessary for their physical growth and repair. You are probably becoming aware that the drinking water of the dome-dwellers has been chemically recycled so many times that it has become completely devitalised.

"Trees, bushes and important seeds will also be transplanted. The growth will be relatively rapid, as it initially will take place under the ruby crystal pods to protect the soil. Once the growth is established, plants can eventually come out of the pods and bees will be introduced to assist with the pollination. Gardeners from Crystal Island will be recruited to assist and teach wherever necessary.

"Until such time as the domes become self-sufficient, Crystal Island will provide a steady flow of plants for food and medicine and gradually introduce them into all people under the domes. This will have to be done slowly as their systems will need to adapt to such an onslaught of nutrients."

"When will we be able to leave the domes?" Helen asked.

"Once the oceans have finally settled. We know specifically which landmasses will be left above sea level."

"So the focus, until the poles melt, is to establish plant life again on Earth in the areas that will be left after the oceans have reconfigured the new continents."

"Yes, Phillip, we will also have to look at re-educating people and introduce new education programmes for children." Helen and Mark both sat up with a keen interest.

"You have seen our education methods on the island and that will not be an issue, but the adults will have to be educated in a different way.

"Maeve will provide Helen and Mark with texts that document the gifts that control life on the planet. Maeve, as her mother before her, has been the keeper of the texts that were created by the first Crystal Elders. The teachers will have to be selected carefully, but you will have no difficulty in choosing the correct people."

The coupled shared a worried look.

"But," Finn continued, "the most important lesson to teach adults is the dangerous effects of toxic thoughts and toxic words on the delicate balance of nature."

James reflected on the respectful way that the islanders interacted with each other and how they contributed to, and enjoyed, a spoken and unspoken culture of courtesy.

Orla asked the group if they had been taught poetry, art or music at school. Of course she knew the answer, and they shook their heads. She explained that these disciplines were a wonderful way to learn to express and maintain the beauty of creation.

Mary suggested that Orla could project on to the comms portals in homes images of the island and its way of life so that people would see the possibilities of another way of living. Sheila suggested that once they had control of the Generals, and therefore the communications of the domes, the current media broadcast would change immediately.

"Would it be possible to access the works of art we saw in the museums and broadcast them so that people can see the beauty that is possible both in people and in landscapes?" Mary enquired.

"Yes," Orla replied, "we had intended to restore as much as possible of the positive aspects of Earth's history for everyone to access and enjoy."

"I am still not seeing what we can use to provide sufficient energy to run the domes," Frederic said.

Finn explained that until the planet was in balance they could immediately start using the ruby crystal solar panels, as they would take just a little time to manufacture and they were powerful enough to provide sufficient energy, as well as rendering the atmosphere inhospitable to Shadow.

With the big question of energy answered, the team became enthusiastic.

"I am still unsure about our role of keeping the security of Crystal Wisdom," Phillip said.

"As we have explained, you and Mary will be responsible for noticing when a person begins to doubt, or withdraws in any way from the community. Not everyone will have crystal spirit guides; this will take several generations to develop. We will instruct you how to identify the first telltale signs of doubt and how to guide individuals back into living their lives according to the laws of Crystal Wisdom." Orla was yet to tell them about the importance of visiting the Crystal circles, and in fact where these circles were located.

"Remember, you are creating a blueprint for all the communities of the Earth," Finn emphasised.

Cynthia, aware of the need to learn about the plant life, asked, "When will Joshua and I start learning about the nutritional and medicinal use of plants, as it appears to be a huge subject?"

"Maeve and I will instruct you both when the time is right," Orla confirmed.

With that, all the women suggested that they could also learn about the benefits of plants, as they were becoming increasingly enthusiastic about the potential of plant life. In the short exposure they'd had to the plant remedies, they had recognised that the future health of the planet would be completely dependent on plants. Orla was delighted with their response. Yes, they had chosen the correct plan of action, but they were also enthusiastic about their future. They had shifted from their bland world of duty to the exciting world of possibilities that Crystal Wisdom had to offer.

The men sat back, a little surprised by both their wives' contributions and enthusiasm. They couldn't understand how this had happened so quickly. They were not in the habit of asking their wives advice, nor did the women offer their opinions; they had their routines, their duties, and that seemed to keep them happy. What their husbands didn't understand was that, unfettered by fear, when women were exposed to nature and the needs of natural life, they would automatically revert to their Crystal memory, no matter how small or how deeply buried it was.

It was this important fact that was taken into consideration when creating the plant remedies for the men. Before they had Shadow removed by the ruby ray, they had to start the process of physically changing the structure of their cells to make them less attractive to

Shadow, so the men had been given small doses of plants which carried natural female hormones. Not enough to change their gender, but just sufficient to reduce their testosterone levels for Shadow to gradually release it's hold – just enough to open the gates to Crystal Wisdom.

CHAPTER EIGHT
THE CRYSTAL INITIATIONS

Orla surveyed the group and could see that they were struggling to keep up with the magnitude of information they were assimilating into every level of their understanding. In normal Earth time, this process would have taken many months, but they did not have the luxury of time. Fortunately on Crystal Island, time did not equate to Earth time. Time could be bent and stretched so that days were extended to allow all their programming to be condensed.

Finn looked at Orla, and they silently agreed that the group were ready to understand the levels of initiation that completed the formation of a crystal-human.

"We are now going to explain the levels of initiation. They have a specific sequence and not one step of that sequence can be missed.

"By receiving these initiations in the correct order it ensures that communities have a common understanding of each other and of creation, thereby removing the possibility of conflict. It also ensures that there is no hierarchy of authority, only a hierarchy of responsibility, which is vital for the future of the planet."

Orla paused, allowing them to digest this information silently. The royal couple could see that they were trying their best to understand the new concept of hierarchy of responsibility.

"The first initiation is the Naming Ceremony. When a child is born the name that they are given is very important because it will carry the memory of the role that child is to play in the development of the next level of the planet." She paused and observed their responses. *Attention, yes, but no understanding*, she realised.

"The name should not be the choice of the parent based on family members or fashionable trends; the name is chosen to match the potential of the child. When a child is born it radiates a sound, a vibration, which indicates its crystal gifts. When you were introduced to the gifts you saw the importance of the relationship between words and the vibration that was attached to each word. Everything on the planet is connected by vibration, sound waves, and that is how all the kingdoms communicate. We humans also have to understand how our vibration connects and enhances the planet. At this initiation the Elders of the communities communicate with the crystal spirit guide of the child before it is born and inform the parents of the name so that the child can totally embody its potential."

The women initially felt a little sad, as they had all enjoyed the process of going through the name books when they were pregnant. But they were equally excited by the idea of spirit guides communicating the correct name for the child based on its crystal gifts.

"During the viewings of the early crystal days, you saw that dotted around the planet there were large circles of crystal pillars joined at the top with horizontal crystal platforms, which created an enclosed sacred crystal space. Those Crystal circles are where the initiations take place and we shall restore them to fulfil that purpose. When the babies are taken there for the Naming Ceremony, the Elders connect with the baby's spirit guide to be told its name. Once the name is spoken, the vibration of the name connects with each of the crystal pillars, which collectively form a geometric shape that emits a sound. That sound is absorbed into the cellular memory of the child, activating the process of developing the child's gifts.

"The next initiation happens at puberty when the child is introduced to the first understanding of its future responsibility. The child is taken to the Crystal circle, and the Elders connect to the child's crystal spirit guide again, who introduces the child to their individual song, which helps them to embody their gifts and talents."

"Who will be the Elders?" interjected Sheila.

Orla looked at the women seriously and said, "You seven women will be the first Elders of the new order."

The women looked at each other, speechless with shock. The men stared at them in both wonder and disbelief. All the female habit-insecurities surfaced and they sent forth a tirade of objections.

Orla raised her hand to silence them.

"By the time you are ready to take on this mantle of responsibility you will all be sufficiently prepared. We would never give you anything that you are not capable of undertaking, because we cannot risk failure. And, do not forget, you will have your own spirit guides and guardians as well as the islanders to help you."

This explanation seemed to alleviate their fears. Finn glanced at the men; they were all silent and a little downcast.

"The third initiation is the Binding Ceremony, when you commit to a life partner, and is usually undertaken at any age from 21 years. From the age of eighteen, crystal spirit guides and Elders assist in bringing together suitable candidates. Remember all partnerships must be for the perpetuation of the perfection of creation, so the gifts and talents of the two people must complement each other."

The men thought this was a very young age to choose a partner for life.

Finn answered their unspoken concerns. "Under the old ways it probably was, but remember the role of men and women is changing. The women aren't there to be glorified servants. They have very important roles to play, as do men. This is about choosing a partner to complement your gifts and talents, not just a biological attraction. Of course, the individuals have to be attracted and devoted to each other, but the Elders will give guidance. The union of two people is sacred and therefore has to undergo a period of questioning and qualifying. The Elders also consult with the crystal spirit guides of the couple so that the final decision is never subjective."

Finn had observed in history that there had been same-sex partnerships which worked very well, but there was a great deal of suspicion from the major religious organisation, and with the pressure of the dome life, Shadow had helped to marginalise those people and decreed that men and women be partnered for procreation only.

This prompted a memory in Finn of an aspect of dome life that he hadn't shared with Orla. There were certain domes that were solely for the pleasure and entertainment of privileged men, the leaders, and the entertainment was women. Whilst men had perfunctory relationships with their wives, they still held memories of the many depravities that man had concocted in his quest to achieve sexual pleasure. Juvenile male and females, sometimes even younger, were recruited from outside of the domes with the promise of a safe life under the protection of the domes in return for becoming no better than sex slaves. All of them came from deprived and challenging backgrounds, some were orphans, some sold by unscrupulous family members. They arrived at the pleasure domes and were gradually groomed so that by the time they were fully functioning, they didn't know any better and of course never questioned.

Every type of depravity was on offer. As life in the domes became more and more austere and sanitised, the desire for more extreme sexual practices increased. Finn could not bear to acknowledge some of the scenes he had witnessed and would avoid, for as long as possible, showing them to Orla. Fortunately, until now, he had protected her from the endless cycles of sex slavery that had occurred throughout the history of man without challenge. Those proclivities were something that Finn could not understand, and he wondered from where it had originated. Of course, the answer came quickly: Shadow. In its attempt to alienate men from women, they had planted the seed of control and domination into their relationship memory. When control and domination, combined with the human primitive programming, entered the world of sexual relationships, it brought with it primal predatory behaviour. Finn winced when he remembered some of the scenes he had witnessed as part of his induction on Ruby Crystal world. He had considered at the time that mankind could not sink any lower. He then turned his thoughts back to the wives in the domes who had no idea that their husbands went to such places; it was a heavily veiled secret, but equally their wives had no reason to suspect anything as their husbands always came home to the bosom of the family.

Finn realised that they needed to be initiated into this next level as soon as possible, and it would possibly be one of the major challenges that they had to face. He observed their reaction as Orla continued.

"Approximately five years after the Binding Ceremony they are initiated into Sacred Union. This is the energetic and physical consummation of that union used for both the benefit of the planet and also for reproduction."

They all exchanged glances of confusion. The immediate thoughts of the men were that they had to be promised for five years, which in their minds meant waiting for five years before they consummated the marriage.

"What do they do during the five years?" Mathew asked.

"Learn how to develop their gifts and talents for the planet," came the almost predictable response from Finn. "Remember, an intimate relationship between two people is sacred, and equally communication on any level between two people must be respected. This is what makes us different from other species; we have the ability to connect with Crystal Wisdom during our physical union whilst offering an intention for the benefit of the planet."

"What do you mean by 'intention'?" Anne asked.

"Well, intention is when you identify a particular need that requires support and you focus your whole being on asking for that support from creation. Of course, the intention must be for the benefit of the planet, never for selfish reasons."

"I'm sorry, I am still not understanding how sex becomes sacred and is used to heal the planet."

Orla looked into her memory and could see why Anne was putting up walls of resistance to her understanding. Whereas the other women were open to finding out more, Anne was becoming indignant. When Orla went back a few thousand years in her memory she saw that in Anne's family line there had been a woman who had been commonly referred to as a 'sacred prostitute'. This term had been reconfigured over the centuries to reflect its most base level. Some women were taken into sacred temples, forbidden to marry, and were groomed in the art of physical pleasure. Their sole purpose was to cleanse warriors from their sins of war. Sexual intimacy became a dumping ground for the horrors of war, after which the warriors were 'cleansed', allowing them to relinquish any responsibility for the barbarity that they inflicted on others in the heroic name of war.

The young princess shook her head in wonder at the ignorant behaviour of these warriors. Did they really think their blood-stained hands could ever be cleansed so easily? She was also amazed at how women's natural ability of communicating with the Crystal worlds had been translated into, once again, being another vehicle to serve men.

Just as she was about to leave Anne's memory, something caught her attention; she saw a cage, which she thought was empty, but on closer examination, could see a naked woman on the floor in a state of drugged exhaustion. Orla accessed the scene that had preceded this. The women had tremendous connection to the Crystal worlds and, although the people at the time did not understand that it was Crystal Wisdom, they just knew that this was a connection that gave incredible results. Anne's ancestor was in the hands of magicians of the 18th century. The magic of ancient alchemists had resurfaced in a very abridged form, but they had managed to understand the most powerful form of magic, and had created elaborate rituals, culminating with the head of the Order of Magicians having physical intimacy with the 'priestess', as the sometimes unwilling women were called. Unfortunately for this woman, her body, if not her mind, had always responded positively during their dark rituals. She was unique and they wanted her to be their slave, giving them a unique connection to a higher level of sorcery that most definitely was for self-gain. Any time of the day or night they would call upon her and she had to submit. She was initially told that she was special, that she was a priestess, but after a while she realised that there was nothing sacred about what was happening to her and she began to hate herself. Her body was wracked with pain from the extreme energy that passed through her body that was connected only to Shadow and not Crystal Wisdom. Her protestations fell on deaf ears – the magicians, drunk on the intoxication of power, locked her in a cage to make sure she would never escape.

No wonder she doesn't want to acknowledge the power of creative intimacy, Orla thought.

Finn saw the worried look on Orla's face and looked into Anne's memory. He was appalled that she had come across such a scene. He sent in the ruby ray and closed down Anne's memory so that Orla and Anne could leave that scene behind. Orla blinked, realising what Finn had done, and was grateful. She really didn't want to imprint that distasteful image into her memory.

"The final part of your visit will be to experience this physical union and, whilst you are feeling as if you cannot take in any more information, after that experience you will feel wonderful."

Orla continued describing the initiations. "From the age of 28 you are initiated into Crystal Parenthood. This is when you attain a level of understanding of the importance of giving children, your own or children in the community, the necessary information and knowledge to become Crystal adults.

"At the age of 58 you are initiated into Crystal Service, when you dedicate the rest of your life to ensuring that your communities follow crystal laws. Also at that time, certain women are chosen to be Elders."

"I thought you said that we would be Elders, and none of us are over 58," Martha said. So far Martha had been fairly quiet, and Orla was waiting for her to find enough confidence to ask questions.

"Ordinarily, 58 is the age of Service, but there isn't time for us to wait for you to get to that age. The people under the domes who are that age have such degeneration in their body, they would not withstand the immersion into Crystal Wisdom. In fact they would not have coped with coming to the island. So we have made an exception, but as we have repeatedly said, you will have your mentors and guides to help you."

When Orla finished, there was the usual silence, and then Jude asked why there had to be certain times marked by specific ceremonies.

"Crystal Wisdom is very fragile in the material world and it takes a lot of focus and intention to sustain this level of wisdom. Every time a person visits the Crystal circles their Crystal memory is strengthened, and each initiation that they experience ensures that they embrace every single level of Crystal Wisdom. If any stage is missed it would lead to the weakening of Crystal Wisdom in the individual. And where there is weakness, there is the possibility of doubt, and you all know where that will lead you. One of the main contributory factors to Crystal Wisdom being lost from mankind after the Crystalanders left the planet was their laziness about visiting the Crystal circles regularly and not following the crystal tradition of initiations.

"During various times in history some religious communities had tried to resurrect similar initiatory paths, which had been successful to a degree, but Shadow had cleverly drawn man away from anything that led him to that ultimate path of Crystal Wisdom by instilling doubt and fear. Equally, man had become impatient and did not want to follow a path that took time to evolve. Over the recent centuries there were sectors of communities who had sought a higher level of enlightenment, but modern man wanted to achieve that higher level in a weekend!"

All this information resonated deeply with the group. The women in particular were recognising that without these initiations to underpin an individual's life, they were more vulnerable to manipulation from anyone who represented authority.

"Orla, where are we on this initiatory ladder?" Martha asked.

Orla smiled. "You have one more to experience and that is the physical union of intimacy."

She stood up and silently indicated they follow her, leading them to the dining room where they had refreshments and relaxed for a while. Maeve had prepared the room beforehand with flower essences, which immediately lifted their mood as they walked into the room. They sat down in the pretty dining room and quietly drank their tea looking out of the various windows that were strategically placed around the room to allow in maximum sunlight.

Jude walked over to where Mathew was looking at the manicured lawns of the palace garden. She gently rested her head on his shoulder, and he responded by holding her head closer. Orla was pleased that the couple had responded to each other with such a spontaneous demonstration of affection; a definite sign that they were ready for the next stage.

When they were rested, Orla asked them to follow her to a room with no windows. They walked in, huddling in a group by the door, slightly nervous of what was to transpire. Inside the room were fourteen jade green crystal chairs arranged in pairs so that each couple was facing each other. She indicated for them to sit down. When the couples settled, the room filled with a mist of essences, which had the effect of relaxing and stimulating at the same time. The lights in the room softened and Orla asked them to close their eyes as she began to sing in a very low tone, moving around to each one in turn As she changed the tone over each person, they became aware of a sphere of green-yellow light beneath their feet. Having visited each couple, she moved into the centre of the room and changed her pitch, prompting the sphere of light to move up their legs and settle in their pelvic area, where the colour of the sphere changed to a deep orange. Orla changed her pitch and the sphere of orange moved up their bodies to the solar plexus, where it changed to a brighter orange and expanded to cover the whole of the abdomen. As she adjusted her pitch again, the sphere of colour moved up a fraction, divided into two and changed colour, one was green, which travelled to the left shoulder, and the other a deeper orange that came to rest on the right shoulder. The two shoulder orbs formed a triangle with the bright orange orb, at which point Orla changed her pitch yet again, going beyond the range of human sound, and a sapphire blue sphere appeared at the centre of each brow, connecting with all the other spheres. As soon as all the spheres connected, the orange sphere of the solar plexus reached out and connected with the solar plexus of the other partner, moving back and forth between the couple. After this connection was made, each of the spheres through their body connected to their partner's matching sphere, creating a complementary pulsing back and forth between each couple.

Orla changed her pitched and a streak of green light shot from their feet through each of the spheres, passing above their heads, hovering for a few seconds about twelve inches above the crown, then dissipated out through the ceiling of the palace, travelling up into the sky and out into the stars. The pulsing stopped and the spheres softly retreated from the couples into the room and disappeared. There was a stillness in the room that was palpable.

Orla instructed them to regulate their breathing and watched them closely, ensuring that each one was breathing correctly. She slowly increased the lighting and asked them to open their eyes. They looked at their partners, each one observing every detail of the other. There was a pause, and each person sensed that there was a connection between them that went far beyond the physical. And with perfect synchronicity, they all stood up and embraced their partners for what appeared to them to be an eternity.

When they eventually sat down, Orla raised the lights even more and asked them with a smile on her face, knowing the answer, "How do you all feel?" Phillip, who had been a little quiet for most of the day, exploded with laughter, which sent them all off into rounds of laughter and giggles. *A release of emotion often comes out in unusual ways*, Orla thought, but after they had settled down, they were again full of questions.

Orla raised her hand to calm their mood.

"You will need to do this regularly, but you will always have to agree on an intention beforehand."

By now they didn't need to ask the question about the intention – they all knew that the main intention was for planetary healing – but she would guide them further on the specifics of intention later.

"But, most importantly, if you wish to be physically intimate with your partners, it must be preceded by this ritual." The women looked a little confused and the men even more so. "Whenever you do this as a precursor to intimacy, you must always have an intention so that the crystal creative energy generated is not lost or wasted. When two people are bound in this way, the crystal energy is very powerful, so it must be used as an opportunity to broadcast, reinforce and amplify the laws of Crystal Wisdom. There will be no random loss of creative energy in the future. Any intimacy must be conducted under the protection of Crystal Wisdom to strengthen and protect the individuals. Physical intimacy can attract two different energies, that of Crystal Wisdom or that of Shadow, and I am sure I don't need to explain what the differences are. You all now need to take control of every aspect of your lives and ensure that everything, and I mean everything, follows the laws of Crystal Wisdom."

They looked from one to the other, and she could see that this was a ritual that would take time and planning. Gone were the days where physical intimacy was squeezed in at the end of a long day.

She reassured them that they would be able to recreate the spheres easily. She gave each one an emerald crystal the shape of a small egg and told them to place this in the room with the sprayed essences whenever they practised Sacred Union and it would activate the sequence of the orb connections.

The day's instructions had finally come to a close, and it was time for them to return to the dome. They looked tired but not depleted. The last exercise had invigorated them and compensated for the intensity of the day. A good night's rest would help them to recover. Finn warned them once again that they would have to protect their new demeanour from being detected by people in their environment. If they looked too healthy and too positive, they would attract unwanted attention.

As the group left the palace, quite spontaneously the women hugged Orla, which their husbands initially viewed as strange, but then accepted this new side to their personalities. They were all changing. Finn led them back through the Secret Garden, and the group realised that they were seeing things differently from their first visit. The colours and fragrances were much more intense and, as they passed a plant, they acknowledged it and expressed gratitude as they had been taught. They boarded the travelling vessel reluctantly, as the realisation dawned on them that they were going back to the grey lives of the dome that they now viewed as depressing. Finn read their thoughts and reminded them that they were pioneers; they would be the first men and women to turn the planet around to mirror Crystal Island. This gave them food for thought and they began to think more about changing the future than about the negativity of the past.

The group arrived back, quickly saying goodbye to Finn so that a large group of people appearing from nowhere did not attract attention. He assured them that he and Orla would be contacting them the next day after they had rested, with instructions for the next step. *The next step*, thought Martha. *This is enough to keep me going for a lifetime.* They went back in their cars in silence. The men shook hands and the women hugged each other when they separated, both sensing an intimacy and inclusion amongst them, which was pleasantly comforting.

*

John and Sheila walked through their front door. The house was empty as the children were returning later. They sat down in easy chairs and looked at each other, trying to make sense of the day.

"This is huge," John began.

Sheila agreed, but she had comprehended the reasons why John had been chosen as the leader – only he hadn't realised that yet. "John, did you have any idea that you would be singled out to be the leader of our group?"

"With you," he corrected. "Yes, but I thought I was always just second-in-command material. Indeed, all the tests that I have undergone identified this very quality." He had now been told a completely different story and was beginning to understand how humans could be fed myths about who they were and believe it without question.

Sheila's mother, Joan, a very well groomed woman in her 60s who looked a lot older, brought the children home. She had a rigidity in her body that Sheila hadn't noticed before, but immediately remembered that she had to reflect a similar manner. She greeted her mother in the normal air kiss way, and the children walked passed their mother with a fleeting smile. Joan glanced at her daughter and saw something in her that she couldn't quite put her finger on and asked if she was ok. Sheila told her that the travelling had made her tired and she felt out of sorts. Still, her mother thought this was not the normal look she had when she was tired. *Could she be pregnant? No, that is highly unlikely.* She dismissed the thought, becoming distracted about her next task. She said goodbye and went on her way without a backward glance.

The children had looked at their parents when they went to their rooms and noticed something different about them and mentioned it to each other. After they had put their belongings away neatly they came out of their rooms and went over to their father. John's initial reaction was to beam at them. Sheila shot him a glance of warning and he immediately returned to his normal strict bearing. The children were comforted with the familiar response and happily went off to bed.

The next day, the seven men went to work and tried to act normally, but it was very difficult. They had begun to observe the people around them with different eyes, recognising that they were all working on automatic pilot, and that was why, fortunately, they couldn't see the subtle changes taking place within the group. However, they silently began to question the policies that they had to administer. Over the next week the seven communicated freely with each other through their safe comms portal. They were eager to get things moving as they were increasingly seeing how the route of the Generals was leading them in one of two directions – planetary destruction, or moving to a new planet. The former was more likely as the latter was appearing to be impossible.

John suggested that a meeting be called of their immediate superiors as soon as possible. They didn't know how this would work and just trusted what Orla and Finn had told them, but they couldn't move forward until they had the Generals on board.

Orla and Finn kept a close eye on them from the island and could see how their spirit guides were helping them to stay on track. They also observed the wives, who had changed more. They had a lightness in their movements and a more spontaneous attitude. They did not neglect their duties, they just had more enthusiasm. When their husbands came home from work, the men shared the happenings of the day with their wives, asking advice, which the women gave freely. Often, they challenged the men, which took a little getting used to, but they realised they both had the same agenda, just different perspectives, and it was the wives who kept them on track with the larger objective.

*

After the group had gone Orla felt as if she needed to reconnect with her Crystal memory and went to her personal viewing room. She looked at her collection of jewellery and knew she should connect with the Coral Crystal world. She needed to clarify her thoughts and understood that connecting to the Coral Crystal would provide the sharpness she needed to assess the next one hundred people.

She sat in one of her comfortable easy chairs and placed an earring on each ear lobe, sat back and relaxed, inhaling flower essences, and closed her eyes. She was immediately transported to the brightness of the Coral crystal path and reunited with Unicorn. She walked for a while, familiarising herself with the many feelings of the Crystal worlds and also the deep affection she had with her equine companion. He led her off the path and they walked through the clear coral that appeared to the untrained eye to be sharp and jagged but was in reality smooth and soft. The different vibration and the tiny vortices from the crystal entered Orla's memory so that she connected directly to the mental acuity and sharpness of that world. She glided through the crystal, engaging in the geometric shapes, stopping from time to time on specific shapes, which gave more clarity. The coral beings presented themselves and greeted her with their usual sharp but warm greeting. They conveyed to Orla that they were following her work and confirmed that everything was working according to plan and on schedule.

She thanked them deeply for their continued guidance and bade them farewell. She returned to the path, walking slowly, saying goodbye to Unicorn. Becoming aware of her material surroundings, she gently opened her eyes.

"Oh, I feel so much better," she said.

Orla turned her attention to the list of men and their wives that the fourteen had selected and scanned each name. As her eyes rested on each name she was able to tap into a visual of them and their genetic line. *Hmm*, she considered, *not all of them will be a good match, but they have given me some extra people so I can choose the best of the selection.*

She went down the names again. It was no good; she would need Finn to help her. Shadow was too much in evidence in their memories and she would need the ruby rays to cut through the debris cluttering and covering their tiny Crystal memory.

She put the list to one side and went to find her parents. When she came upon Maeve and Patrick, they asked her about the last session with the group.

"It went surprisingly well. I am going to contact them to see how they are adjusting, but I don't see any problems, as I am getting very little resistance. They seem to understand the importance of healing the planet rather than concentrating on individual gains. I think I underestimated how quickly they would adjust once Shadow was removed."

"You must work fast now, Orla," Patrick urged.

"I know. When Finn returns we will contact the Generals, but for that I will need extra help from Ruby Crystaland." Orla knew that her father would not be part of this, only Finn and his brothers. This was an exercise that required the peak of physical ability and Ruby Crystal energy to stand up to such resistance. Whilst Patrick was strong, his levels of testosterone had begun to reduce with age, as was normal. Orla looked at her father fondly. He was still a bear of a man with the strength of ten men, coupled with compassion that came from having a large and pure heart. She was always impressed when the depth of Crystal Wisdom that appears with age combines with human strength and merges seamlessly and harmoniously to form a powerful representation of a truly crystal-human being.

CHAPTER NINE
THE GENERALS OF THE WEST

Finn and Orla were in their viewing room preparing to contact the Generals. They both were wearing their ruby crystals. Finn connected with the Chief General of the West in his sleep, surrounding him with the Ruby Crystal ray, allowing Orla to enter his dreams. She struggled to find the part of his memory that was imaginal, and Finn had to direct the ray into his memory to clear the clutter of darkness in his genetic experiences, being careful not to disconnect his connection to the Elite. Orla began the process of introducing herself to his dreams. But, unlike the way she had worked with the pioneers, this time it would be different. Instead of the images of their family, she used images of the Chief General himself, living outside in the domes in the future, just at the point of the Earth's destruction. The Earth was barren and the walls of the domes had been broken down, everything was in decay and the Chief was being hounded by a pack of feral humans. She observed him in his dreams as he ran and hid, desperately trying to find a safe place, but there were none to be found. The intensity of the fear was so great that the chemicals surging around his body forced him to wake up with a pounding heart and perspiration running down the sides of his temples. He regulated his breath, thankful that that experience was only a dream. He wondered if he should see the doctor. *Am I beginning to lose my grip on reality with the pressure of trying to find a new planet?* he wondered. He eventually slipped back into sleep, and in the second half of his dream Orla sang to him, appearing in his dream, talking gently. He couldn't detect the words that she was speaking but he seemed to understand her. When he woke, he had a feeling of calm pervading his whole body that he hadn't experienced possibly in his whole life – only with the help of chemicals.

Orla and Finn continued the same process with the other six Generals of the Federation, and finally after three days, knew that they were ready.

The day after the pioneers returned to the dome, Finn contacted the seven men and told them to schedule a meeting for the following week with the Generals.

"On what pretext should we call the meeting?" asked John.

"Anything that guarantees they all attend."

A meeting was called of the seven men plus their superiors, the Generals. John's superior was the leader of their Federation, the Chief General, and he sat at the head of the table. Orla knew that it had taken a lot of courage for the seven to call this meeting. The Generals had initially wanted to have a detailed agenda beforehand, but John had managed to fob them off by saying that they needed to look at the latest figures from the departments urgently, as they would impact on the future plans for the explorations into space. This was the one subject that John knew would get their undivided attention.

When all the Generals and the seven were in the meeting room, the Generals looked at the blank table and at their aides with an enquiring and impatient stare. Normally in front of them would have been a detailed agenda to direct the course of the meeting, accompanied by mountains of paper.

What is wrong with John? He is normally so efficient, but he is looking different these days, the Chief wondered.

Before they could ask any questions, John tabled the latest reports from all of the departments, which indicated that all resources were diminishing at a much faster rate than was expected, disease under the domes was increasing and the possibility of finding another planet to inhabit was becoming more and more remote. Finn saw the Generals look at John slightly puzzled: no one had ever voiced the opinion that the project to find another planet could fail. He had never challenged them before, and they, quite honestly, had not been trained to deal with challenge. Before they could contribute anything to the proceedings, John announced that he had invited someone from another Federation who had a great deal of wisdom to offer for the future living conditions of the dome-dwellers.

The Generals looked both annoyed and intrigued.

"Why were we not informed of the details of this person before? Which Federation does he come from?"

A further stream of questions rapidly fell from the Chief's lips like bullets from a repeater gun. Finn had been present from the beginning, but only visible to the seven pioneers, and he had quickly taken in the detail of the scene. His initial observation was that they were seven Generals well past their sell-by date, but he could also see Shadow lazily and securely embedded in each man's spine. When the Chief began to react defensively, Shadow was alerted and activated its tentacles, which began to twitch urgently in the Chief's spine. Finn encased John and the other six pioneers in the invisible ruby crystal energy field, which immediately connected with their Crystal memory, and they began to project an aura of authority. The combined powerful effect of the ruby ray and crystal authority pushed back Shadow, reducing its connection in all the Generals. Shadow had no consciousness as such, it just responded to negative emotions; when fear and anger were present it woke up and began to feed, but when the ruby ray cast its net around people it couldn't understand the language of pure wisdom, so it withdrew.

With Shadow relinquishing its grip, the Generals relaxed and began to listen. John continued. "What if we could return the planet to its original state?"

The Generals looked at John as if he was a bit simple, and the Chief General replied, "Don't you think, if that were a possible solution, it would have been found already? We have had the best minds of science over the last century trying to do just that, and we have made no progress. In fact, if anything, we have fallen backwards."

"What if we weren't looking in the right place for the solutions?"

"Where should we look?"

"At the planet itself. What if the planet could show us how we can revive the Earth?"

One of the Generals asked rather archly, "Why hasn't it shown us before?"

"It has. It has been clearly showing us what we have been doing wrong over the centuries by withdrawing its bounty from mankind, but we have chosen not to listen. Perhaps if we listen to someone who has more knowledge and understanding we might learn something more powerful than can be found in our science laboratories," John chided.

The Generals were struck speechless; here was one of their subordinates telling them that they, along with the leaders of the last few centuries, had been foolish and negligent. John surprised himself at his assertiveness and quietly wondered where his little speech had come from.

John continued in earnest, conscious that he had to engage Orla and Finn as quickly as possible before the Generals drifted back into Shadow consciousness. "What if we could show you somewhere on the planet where life is very different?"

"How do you know of such a place?" the Chief questioned.

John, realising that he must be particularly careful how he positioned the next statement, said: "I have always been interested in the stories about an island in the ocean that still retains the original qualities of Earth. I believed that these mythical stories had to come from somewhere and recently I was contacted by someone from such a place."

The Generals sat up in their seats, with fear and concern written all over their faces.

"Have you breached any of our security policies?" The Chief fired the question at John.

"On the contrary. These people have no need to take any information from us. In fact, they wish to share all their knowledge with us. And, from what I can see, they are far more advanced than we could ever hope to be at this stage in our development."

There was silence in the room. For centuries, the major leaders of the world had spent a great deal of time and energy hiding information from one another, fearful that if they had full disclosure a country would use it to their own advantage. So the idea of an advanced Federation wishing to share openly their knowledge for nothing in return filled them with suspicion.

The General in charge of security immediately asked, "What sort of arms do they have?"

John smiled. "They have no weaponry whatsoever."

Knowing that Finn was present, John sensed that this was a good time to introduce him to the Generals. And with that thought, Finn appeared in the centre of the room.

The seven senior men gasped when he appeared. This amazing specimen of male physical strength, who seemed to glow with authority and power, appeared before the group, and it would seem he had arrived out of thin air. Finn greeted them, and when they had recovered from the shock of his presence, they asked him what he had to offer.

Finn spoke, his voice deep and strong, filling every space in the room, commanding their undivided attention. "As John has already told you, the people of our island have the knowledge to help the planet recover fully and once again be an abundant place for humans to live."

"What do you want in return?" asked the Chief.

"Nothing," came the reply from Finn, dismissing the obvious fear-based transactional nature of the Generals' negotiations.

Finn continued. "My hope is that if we all work together for the good of the planet, we will all benefit." More shock waves rippled through the Generals. *This is definitely a language associated with anarchy,* they all thought.

Before fear prompted their complete withdrawal, Finn announced that he wanted to bring someone else into the room to help. Like Finn, Orla had been invisibly present in the room, observing the reactions of everyone. With Finn's announcement, not waiting for permission from the Generals, Orla appeared in the room, seemingly miraculously, prompting the Generals to stop and stare with utter disbelief and shock, which prompted another painful sensation deep in their spines.

The presence of Orla had prompted two responses in the Chief. It had immediately connected positively with the memory from his dream, and as that memory rose into his consciousness, it relayed a warning message to Shadow. Shadow's attention was alerted, prompting it to sink its sharp tentacles even deeper into the Chief's spine, causing him to react with hateful aggression.

"Get that woman out of this chamber!" thundered the Chief General, his face warped with rage as he jumped up, knocking over his chair behind him.

"How dare you bring a woman into this place of decisions at such a crucial time. I refuse to talk when a woman is in this room! It is a disgrace to this Federation!"

The other Generals were confused. They too were affected by Orla's presence positively – each General had recognised Orla from his dreams – but their attachment to Shadow was not as intense as the Chief's and they couldn't understand the intensity of his anger.

Orla totally ignored the Chief's ugly protestations that prompted him to slam his fist on the desk to reinforce his words. The couple glanced at each other and Finn immediately increased the intensity of ruby crystal around Orla. She continued walking towards the Generals, unaffected by the Chief's anger, and then she spoke. As the words glided from her mouth to his ears, the Chief stopped as if suspended in time as he stared at her with his mouth open, speechless. No man, let alone a woman, had ever disobeyed him before, but it was as if he was powerless to object. Orla's melodic tones seemed to magically bypass his normal fearful thought processes and address a place in his distant memory. As she spoke to them all of the wonderful possibilities of the planet, it soothed an ache that had caused them so much pain for so long that it had become the norm and far too familiar. They all visibly softened and relaxed. The Chief sat down, clumsily stumbling, looking more confused than angry. The Generals continued to connect with her voice, relaxation beginning to filter through their minds – and, more importantly, they listened.

John and his colleagues were both relieved and shocked at what had transpired. Two amazingly beautiful people had appeared magically in the room, and the Generals had appeared to accept not just their presence but also what they were proposing.

After Orla's short summary of possibilities, there came a similar litany of questions from the Generals that the pioneers had proffered. Finn and Orla responded with the same answers and extended an invitation to visit Crystal Island to experience it for themselves. They were silent and asked to have time to confer on their own.

The royal couple left the room with the seven but of course still had access to the Generals' discussion. The conversation was predictable.

"We need to check out these people. They obviously have some sort of superior knowledge, just look at their physique... have you ever seen anything like it?" the Medical General asked.

The Chief General, picking up on the health of the couple, was intrigued as he and the other Chief Generals had been charged by the Elite to find an answer to human degeneration. The Elite were in the best condition that the planet could offer, but they were still degenerating faster than they wished, and put a great deal of resources into finding an answer.

"We need to take security staff with us. This could be a ploy by some alien race to kidnap us," the security General added. Finn smiled, recognising the paranoia that had filled the world of so-called security intelligence over the last two centuries, where security staff saw danger around every corner, a symptom of the fear that was thickly layered over every aspect of life.

"Ok, we shall invite them in and ask about security," the Chief agreed.

The group came back into the room and the Security General suggested, "We cannot possibly go unless we take security staff to ensure our safety."

Orla responded, and as soon as she spoke, each of the General's features softened.

"I can assure you, you will be completely safe, and your second-in-commands have already been to our island and can vouch for our integrity."

The Security General shot a look at Mark. "You did not think to mention that you were putting the security of our domes in jeopardy by going off on what could possibly be a wild goose chase, a dangerous one at that?"

"Sir, I can understand that on the surface it might look that way, but we had been in discussion with Orla and Finn several times before we went."

John interrupted bravely. "If anyone breached security it was me. I went there first, before the others, and I helped to prepare them for their visit."

"What were you thinking? Why did you not come to me immediately? Do you realise that this is a treasonable offence?" the Chief said, rapidly firing the questions at his aide.

Finn stepped in as he could see Shadow was trying to twist this whole situation around to someone needing to be punished and, pumping out more ruby ray, he added, "When we contacted John, he asked all the correct questions about security. We reassured him sufficiently before he agreed to the visit. His intention was to find a better solution for the future of the planet, not for his own personal gain."

They were silenced by this and contemplated upon this strange concept. The Chief took a deep breath in and exhaled slowly, saying, "I don't think we have an option. We have to explore what these people have to offer."

John was transfixed, feeling as if he had walked into a parallel universe; the other aides just stared in disbelief. What he had done, under Dome Laws, which of course he knew word for word, was to potentially place the world of the domes into a state of vulnerability. But the Generals acquiesced to his explanation.

All is going perfectly! Orla thought.

The pioneers knew that once the Generals had experienced the island, they would be convinced that there was a real opportunity to save the planet. It was agreed for John to accompany the Generals, but they would only be away for a short while. The Generals wanted to go straight away, as they were eager to see what the island had to offer. Orla knew that their physiology would not be able to withstand the purity of the island, so she gave them some remedies to take, advising them that it would help with the travelling and the 'change of air', as she described it. They made their way to the travelling vessel and stopped at the entrance, which from the outside just looked like an opening into space. Finn led the way, and as they walked in, the Generals looked around in amazement, trying to make sense of what they were seeing. Finn gave them more remedies to drink and enveloped them in the ruby ray to act as a buffer against Shadow. When they arrived on the island, Finn would need his brothers to help reinforce the protective rays to keep Shadow dormant for just enough time.

They landed in the Secret Garden and the door opened. Finn and Orla went out first, just to inform the spirit guides of the plants that they were bringing low-level humans into their home. Knowing that Shadow would be attached to these humans, the spirit guides retreated swiftly under the protection of the thick low-lying bushes near the grove of trees. Finn had rendered each Shadow attachment impotent with the ruby ray but this would only last for a few hours. John led the Generals into the garden. They followed John, stumbling slightly from the change in atmosphere and the bright sunshine. They wondered around in a small circle, almost too frightened to venture far from the vessel, needing to know they could jump back in if there was a threat.

They were overwhelmed with the onslaught on their senses: sun, grass, flowers, aromas, gardeners, plants and bees. *Oh my goodness, what sort of trickery can produce this?* the Chief silently considered. And just when they thought they couldn't deal with any more, Orla walked back to the group from the grove of trees with whom she had been communicating, and stood quietly, waiting for the Generals to find a sense of balance. They sensed her calming presence and relaxed. In the setting of the garden they were dazzled by her warmth, beauty, her physical stature and health, which seemed to have increased after being with the trees.

This feeling of relaxation was unfamiliar and they thought they were sleepy. Orla could see that their minds were becoming clearer and functioning better just by being in the garden.

She needed to get them to a point of relaxation so that they could evaluate all the new information objectively. Orla reflected on how women had been branded as too emotional to be involved in leadership, but men also responded emotionally, only it was a different brand of emotion. When a woman felt under threat, she withdrew or snapped, or even cried silently. When a man felt under threat, he became defensive, territorial and selfish. Neither of these responses was at all appropriate in the decision-making world of leadership. However, because this reaction was so ingrained in their deep memory, these leaders didn't acknowledge their lack of emotional awareness.

The Generals had all received countless counselling and mentoring sessions to evaluate and increase their emotional intelligence, as it came to be known, but failed miserably. Man had once again hijacked a phrase, which they truly didn't understand, and ran with it. The ability to express emotional intelligence was determined by one's access to Crystal Wisdom and not controlled by conscious thought. The emotional responses of the world's leaders were controlled by Shadow and that was the reason why the planet was following a path of destruction.

If leaders were indeed emotionally intelligent, the planet would have been in much better shape.

Orla could see that these Generals could not be deprogrammed from Shadow completely, and therefore would never express wisdom. She and Finn had been aware of this from the beginning and it was confirmed when she met them in the flesh. They had no genetic information indicating that they had access to anything vaguely representing Crystal Wisdom, which, of course, was the very reason that qualified them to be chosen by the Elite to be Generals. All Orla and Finn could hope for was that they would eventually stand aside.

Orla's attention went back to the present and she asked the Generals to follow her through the Secret Garden. They, like the original fourteen, were amazed at the quality of the plant life but, because of their conditioning, they were unable to see the subtle activity of the garden. On the route back to the palace Finn indicated to them the different areas of activity of the island, the energy and the water purification centres, and the endless fields of active plant life. The Generals were silenced. They also observed the healthy and happy people going about their daily duties.

One of the Generals commented, "The people seem to be very simple, almost uneducated." Orla smiled, ignoring his inaccurate observations, knowing that he was being challenged and therefore needed to put the daily life of the island into a substandard level of his hierarchical thinking. If he could denigrate this lifestyle, he wouldn't have to accept it.

They eventually came into the palace and were greeted by Patrick and Maeve. The Generals stared at the powerful elder states people who took royal to a whole new level. Maeve, smiling, instructed them to follow her into the dining room, indicating for them to be seated. They all sat around the circular table, and the Generals stared at the plates of food in front of them as if they were foreign objects; one side of them wanted to dive in, but their suspicious side was questioning its safety. Maeve instructed them to eat and drink, and quite surprisingly they followed her instructions. Whilst they were eating the food and drinking the remarkable tasting water, half of their minds were conflicted with the idea of taking orders from a woman.

Orla knew that these Generals could not be shown everything that the pioneers had seen, so she worked purely from the point of view of possibility. The Chief General spoke first. "How have you managed to keep the pollution away from the island? How have you managed to keep the grass so green?" And so the obvious questions continued.

When he finished, Orla responded. "We know that you have been seeking another planet in another solar system to try to replicate life on Earth." They all looked at each other, not understanding how this woman could know information to which only a handful of people were privy. "So you have an understanding of intelligences outside of the Earth's solar system." They nodded with their eyes cast down.

"Well, many thousands of years ago, we were visited by a different species who gave the Earth gifts. They also chose this island and a handful of its human inhabitants to integrate with their genetic wisdom and they became the human Crystal Elders. The royal family of the island are direct descendants of that blood line."

The Generals looked at the four crystal-humans in front of them and did have to admit they were definitely different. They each had vibrancy, even the elder two, which was not quite like anything they had witnessed before.

"What stopped the rest of the Earth from being like the island?" asked the Chief.

"That's a very good question," Patrick responded, "but in fact, at one time the whole of the planet looked liked this."

"But how long did it last?" The Chief was pushing forward with questions, looking for a chink in the armour of their story.

"It actually lasted thousands of years after the Crystalanders left, which shows the humans are capable of running the Earth correctly," continued Patrick.

"What do you mean by 'Crystalanders'?" queried the Chief, a little perplexed at this strange language.

"The different species were from a constellation called Crystaland, the Guardians of Eternal Wisdom, and the gifts they brought were different aspects of their Crystal Wisdom."

All the Generals were confounded by this piece of information.

"So what happened to change this?"

Orla continued the story. "Before the Crystalanders came, mankind was created from a very base set of rules, and they were constructed to be a beast of burden."

All of the Generals raised their eyes, puffed out their chests and were about to protest when Orla raised her hand and indicated that they continue to listen to the story. They obediently listened. "The Crystalanders recognised that those humans had the potential to be guardians of the planet, to allow it to once again flourish."

Orla knew she was paraphrasing a lot of the information, but these were a breed of men who needed very simple facts in a short period of time, otherwise they weren't able to grasp complex concepts.

"However, they were never able to identify the original programming of those primitive humans and therefore could not completely eradicate that genetic information—"

"Meaning?" interjected the Chief brusquely.

"Well, eventually that original programming began to emerge again."

"And what exactly is that programming?"

"It is a very primitive survival programming which is ultimately selfish. The concept of Crystal Wisdom is the opposite."

Orla and Finn could see that they still did not understand.

"Crystalanders saw that humans had the basic potential, and with the help of the crystal gifts, they were able to be guardians of Earth. But to be guardians of the Earth their priority must always be the ongoing health of the planet. Their primal programming changed that to a man-focused priority dedicated to individual gain. When this happened, fear overtook beauty and Crystal Wisdom was lost."

Finn could see that this simple explanation was still completely outside of their understanding. The words that were coming from Orla's lips, even though put in very simple terms, were not being absorbed. There was nothing for it but to show them a viewing. Orla agreed with his thoughts and led the group down to the viewing room.

Finn lowered the lights and Orla instructed the Generals to watch the screen. The familiar pictures emerged showing the sad condition of humans before the Crystalanders, the arrival of the Crystalanders and their gifts, and then what happened to the planet after they left. Orla edited the screening to exclude Shadow.

When the viewing was over there was a deathly silence in the room. This was not confusion; this was arrogance that preceded anger. A few of them expressed the view that they could not be descendants of such primitive beings, and Finn urged them to focus on what the Crystalanders had brought to mankind, demonstrating that the potential of man was unlimited. But in recent centuries man's potential had become very restricted and that was now reflected in the condition of the planet.

Shadow was beginning to wake up in the Generals, and Finn called upon his brothers to help increase the ruby ray to stabilise the situation. His brothers entered the room and the Generals were once again amazed and silenced. They could not believe the power that these three men demonstrated on many levels, and in the presence of such power, conceded authority.

"If we agree with this explanation, what is it that you want us to do?" asked the Chief.

"You will need to keep in your positions for a while as you report directly to the Elite."

Shock and disbelief flashed across their faces; they thought that only they knew about the Elite. Orla continued. "The Elite are controlled by an outside parasitic influence that is hoping that you will discover another planet for their survival."

The Generals again asked to have a private conference.

The seven men sat together going over the facts that they had seen on the screen. This was challenging them on every level, but they could not argue with the physical evidence of Crystal Wisdom demonstrated in every aspect of the island's life. They were also a little concerned about their future and their connection to the Elite. The Chief had suspected for a while that they were working from a place of pure selfishness, but he dared not voice those thoughts out loud, for fear of losing his position. Equally, it would mean that he was questioning his very existence, and his memory would not allow him to go to that place of challenge for fear of painful repercussions.

Before the Generals had gone into the viewing room, Maeve had sprayed essences into the room that balanced their brain chemistry, overriding the medication that all of them were taking for one reason or another, allowing their memories to be more receptive.

The Chief uncharacteristically suggested that they look at the possibilities that this plan had to offer. Life under the domes had been so difficult, the cost of funding exploratory trips to different parts of the cosmos had proven to be expensive and, if the other Federations were to be believed, unproductive. So maybe they needed to look at the problem in a different way. Orla could see that they had come to the right conclusion but didn't have the facility to explore the possibilities. Their reasoning was totally without the creative process, so there were no new solutions to the same old questions.

Orla knocked on the door and entered the room. She had sensed that they had come to an impasse and were confused. She looked at their tired faces and felt compassion. She acknowledged they needed help and began leading them on a specific pathway of thinking that would ultimately help them all.

"I can see that you have seen merit in the Crystal way of life." They all nodded somberly. "Well, I think we may have a solution. We have identified areas that need to be changed and people who have natural abilities in those areas. We have also introduced them to the first level of Crystal Wisdom initiations." The generals looked quizzically at her. "Those people are your second-in-command." There was a collective sharp intake of breath. The Chief asked why the Generals hadn't been chosen.

Orla tried to soften the blow, acutely aware of their fragile egos and not wanting to alienate them. "Leadership should be decided on natural gifts and the ability to express the wisdom of Crystaland. These qualities can never be taught. Certain skills can be learnt, but ultimately it is the information held in genetic programming which is important."

All of the generals were dumbfounded. They had no argument for this, as there were no parameters from which to measure these qualities in their world.

The Chief asked, "Who can determine this genetic predisposition?"

"It is the royal family of Crystal Island at the moment but, eventually, the humans who become Elders will be able to do this." She purposely did not mention that the Elders would be women.

As the essences continued to work on their minds, the Chief looked at the other Generals and said, "If this is the only way forward then we will have to agree."

With that there was a schism of energy that racked through their bodies, and Orla could see that Shadow had alerted the Elite – and collectively they had sent shock waves of pain through the Generals' bodies.

"Here comes the punishment." Orla shot a thought to Finn, who had seen what was happening and immediately directed the ruby rays to cut through the attachment of Shadow. Finn and his two brothers fused their energies together, creating an almighty force field around the Generals, reducing the pain that the men were experiencing. The pain eventually left them completely and the Generals sank back in their chairs, spent. Finn announced to them that they had to return to the domes as the island was beginning to have a detrimental effect on their wellbeing.

The Generals agreed to keep up a pretence of maintaining their positions to the rest of the world. However, they agreed that they would eventually hand over the reins of leadership to their second-in-commands, the seven pioneers. Finn and Orla promised to stay in contact with them through the specially protected comms portal.

The Generals were drained, and Orla could see that these men wouldn't last very long if they kept being blasted from Shadow, their hearts and arteries being eroded with each attack. This reaction had also instilled fear in them and they were beginning to panic. Orla reassured them with her soft voice and calmed them down. *How quickly a situation can deteriorate with humans, where they can go from relaxation to chaos in the space of a few minutes*, she observed.

In the face of all the facts, the physical evidence on the island and the overwhelming sense of regal otherworldliness from the royal family, they could not object anymore. They looked deflated and resigned but Orla assured them that the future of their children and grandchildren would be happier and healthier. This seemed to give them a little comfort, but not much as these were men fashioned from the warrior leader blueprint and they only really understood the language of conflict.

*

Orla woke up from her nap, relieved that the dream about the Generals had been short, and she stretched her body, holding on to her expanding waistline. She only had eight weeks left of the pregnancy and couldn't wait to find out the gender of the twins. She looked out of the window and expressed gratitude, once again, for being a mother and for all the wonderful gifts that she had been given. Her dream had stimulated the memory of events that occurred after that meeting as she inhaled deeply, allowing the images that she hadn't reviewed for a long time to float into her consciousness.

She recalled those early discussions with the Generals of the West, and how her lovely fourteen had stepped up and taken on their new responsibilities with a passion that the Earth hadn't seen for a very long while. She laid back and quietly reflected on how that small group of people had eventually expanded.

The fourteen had gone from strength to strength; the more confident they became with their connection to Crystal Wisdom, the more they projected strength and authority. Her thoughts turned to the mammoth task of initiating the first one hundred into crystal leadership.

CHAPTER TEN
THE NEXT ONE HUNDRED

Finn entered the viewing room and sat with Orla to complete the selection of the next one hundred, and eventually whittled down the list from the 140 to 100. He prepared Orla's connection with each of the fifty men with the ruby ray as normal. Orla warned him not to destroy the tentacles of Shadow but just to act as a filter to their connection. Destroying fifty Shadow connections was most definitely going to attract the attention of the Shadow overlords. Finn nodded in agreement. Finn turned his attention to the men, as the women only had one connection and could be dealt with more easily. When he had set up a protective wall of the ruby ray, Orla stepped into their memories and presented herself in all her regal authority, wearing every single piece of crystal jewellery, and spoke to them of Crystal Island, projecting images of paradise into their memories. Not wanting to cause too much resistance at this very early and tentative stage, she projected the faces of just the male pioneers in the seats of the Generals, which eased the way to their being accepted as leaders. The introduction of women as leaders had to be done more slowly.

This is an easy job, Orla thought. *These people are easily influenced by anyone who demonstrates authority.* Orla continued this over several nights, and each morning the fifty woke feeling more positive and more refreshed. On the last night, she gave the men a message to go to their comms portals the following evening and enter specific codes to speak with John to help them understand more about the island. Their initiation would be less intense as their Crystal memory was not as strong as the pioneers, but still, they needed to be active participants in the transformation of the planet.

The following evening the fifty contacted John, as instructed, and he explained everything, taking a lot of time to answer the many questions that were presented. The fifty had already detected changes in the seven and this discussion finally confirmed what they had all suspected – the seven had changed radically. Finally, the consensus was that if the seven had dramatically improved physically, this was something worth pursuing. When they had finally agreed to that part, John introduced the idea of their wives being involved. *More resistance*, he recognised, but he went on to explain the role of women, referencing Orla as an example of a strong woman.

"Oh my goodness, this did instigate a lot of fear," John had reported to Orla, "Fortunately the comms portal is protected at all times by the ruby crystal rays, shielding Shadow from detecting fluctuations in the levels of fear."

John had eventually engaged with them all and explained the concept of the island that they had seen in their dreams.

"You will all need to experience the island and we have arranged for you to come on a day that you are not normally in the office. Your Generals are all aware of what we are proposing." This sealed any queries that they might have had. Their immersion, John had been told, would be less intense but they would have to be made aware of the importance of their wives.

Orla reflected on how these men had arrived on the island and had received their diluted crystal initiations. Their wives had been secretly brought to the island at the same time by Sheila, who had contacted them separately under the guise of organising a special surprise for their husbands.

When the wives had arrived on the island they had been informed of the true reason for their visit, and after the initial surprise from their husbands when they were reunited, Maeve and Orla helped to settle them all into a better understanding of women – and equally the women were instructed in the negative programming that had been inflicted on men. They had been instructed in the levels of initiation, but it was left to the seven pioneer women to assist in their development, gradually integrating the initiations into their daily lives.

CHAPTER ELEVEN
THE CHIEF GENERALS

The final hurdle was addressing the Chief Generals of all the Federations.

Finn and Orla sat in their viewing room, making ready to view the International Generals. They knew of them already as these were six high-profile leaders, chief decision-makers of each of the Federations. Over the decades, and indeed the last two hundred years, democracy had changed its face, and under the pretext of the planet needing to work together to pool its resources, each Federation had decided on a group of men who were responsible for the future of mankind. Democratic elections ceased to exist, and leadership was decided by the Elite, who chose men easily seduced and manipulated by wealth and power. The Elite put Chiefs in the position of controlling the ever-decreasing resources of the planet, and in return these grateful leaders would do whatever was necessary to maintain their control.

Orla sighed with disappointment. Finn acknowledged that she was constantly surprised and disappointed by the vanity and selfishness of the world leadership. The more they had looked into the planet's history, the more they had seen evidence of the manipulation by the Elite. Twelve families were responsible for the destiny of the planet. When Orla had scanned their memories, with a great deal of help from Finn and his brothers, she had seen nothing but ugliness. Each cell of their bodies carried the blueprint of pure Shadow, dating back to Shadow's first appearance on the planet.

Shadow too was an instrument of another power. The Overlords of Destruction dwelt in a dark place in the cosmos untouched by Crystal Wisdom for eons, outside of the human realm of matter and therefore unable to be detected by man-science. Their motivation for existence came from a place of destruction rather than creation and it was from this place that all the hatred in the cosmos was fashioned. The Overlords, however, had an ever-increasing requirement for minerals because of the density of their world, which pushed them further and further into the abyss. It was this constant need that motivated them to dispatch Shadow further and further from their part of the cosmos through portals in time and matter to access the abundance offered by the galaxy that Earth inhabited. Shadow was their servant, with the ability to travel between the two worlds of the Overlords and the galaxy's star systems that offered mineral abundance, undertaking any dark deed necessary to ensnare and use whatever life they found. Even though the minerals were all but depleted on Earth, Shadow was still strongly latched onto modern man. Unlike the primitive man, who was abandoned at the last ice age, man now had intelligence and technology to assist him. The Overlords knew that man's basic survival instinct, which they had perpetuated and manipulated, coupled with their understanding of science, would drive the Earthlings to search for another solar system with similar mineral combinations to replicate life on Earth.

Orla and Finn had visited each Chief in turn to inspect their memories. They, like the Chief General of the West, were heavily invaded by Shadow, and Orla shuddered as she saw those black shiny claw-like tentacles sinking into the emotional tissue of their minds. But she knew that she had to face this. Finn had called on his brothers again to help to magnify the ruby crystal ray as it would need to be sustained for a good deal of time while Orla visited each of the six Chiefs to implant very different and challenging images. The three brothers lined the viewing room with the ruby crystal ray, projecting it along Orla's viewing path, creating a buffer from the fear and hatred in the Chiefs' memories. Orla visited each one in turn, planting images of a life of health, happiness and abundance that can only be supplied by Crystal Wisdom. These men had received the best that the planet could offer and in their limited experience they thought that they did receive abundance. So, they had to be educated to understand the potential and splendour of nature's gifts.

Each Chief woke the next morning and mistakenly thought that they had experienced a premonition of a new planet that could sustain human life. The next night Orla visited them again and spoke to them in their dreams, as normal, only this time she sang to them of a life of beauty on the Earth. In fact, she was using the melody of Earth to underline the importance of re-establishing the planet's delicate ecosystem. The second morning, the Chiefs woke and were disturbed. They could not understand their dreams; more significantly, they were confused because they never had dreams. These men, chosen for their deep connection to the Elite and Shadow, had long ago given up on accessing their imaginal minds. That part of their memories had been closed down to enable them to be controlled even whilst they slept.

On the third night she visited them and spoke to them of change, of how it was possible for them as individuals to change the fortunes of the planet with a little external help. She told them that she would connect with them at a specific time the following evening and gave them the co-ordinates of her comms portal. Dutifully they had all decided independently to engage with Orla, mostly because they were intrigued by the possibility of being the main beneficiaries of an improved planet. The following evening, Orla and Finn tuned into the portal, whereupon the Chiefs realised that they all had been invited to the same meeting. Orla spoke to them, and immediately her now familiar voice made them feel more comfortable and increasingly relaxed as she spoke. She invited into the conference the Chief General of the West, with whom she had already worked, so that he could give them his interpretation of Crystal Island. They were intrigued and suspicious: this was a man who represented the largest, and at one time richest, Federation, and therefore a major stakeholder in the future of the planet.

"I know this is a lot for all of you to take on board. I also found it very difficult, but when I visited the island all became very clear." The other Chiefs asked many questions, mainly surrounding the sustainability of the abundance of the island when translated to a global level.

"Once you see how the island functions you will realise there is no limit to how far this can be applied. It is important that you experience this place to fully understand the possibilities. The scenes that I witnessed were incredible and I suggest that you visit it as soon as possible. Everything will be explained to you when you arrive, and you will realise that we are seriously running out of time to save this planet."

The Chiefs considered the invitation and, without the interference from Shadow, recognised that somewhere between the authenticity of Orla and the explanation of the Chief of the West, there was a truth that spoke to them on a deep level and they agreed to accept the invitation.

What hadn't been mentioned, of course, was that the Chiefs would lose their authority.

The Chief of the Federation of the West met the other Chiefs at the usual secluded meeting point in the dome and led them through the portal to meet Finn. They were of course stunned by the experience of walking through a portal into a travelling vehicle of crystal and, unsurprisingly, the shock of Finn's physique and demeanor stopped them in the tracks. In that moment they conceded their authority to what they believed was a superior species. From their perspective of the warrior leader, Finn represented all the qualities that were highly valued in a leader. When Finn and Orla had viewed the Chiefs collectively, they saw that their understanding of authority was based on the demonstration of power in any form, wealth or physical stature, so they knew it would be easy to subdue their authority in the presence of the crystal royal family.

The group entered the travelling vessel, trying not to lose their equilibrium, but Finn could see they were confused and perplexed, not only by Finn and the travelling vessel, but also by the temporary shielding from their Shadow attachments by the ruby ray that protected the vessel. As with all visitors, Finn had given them remedies, which they had presumed were just ordinary drinks. They arrived in the Secret Garden, and as the doors opened and Finn led them outside, they were collectively stunned by the splendour of the garden and quietly asked the Chief of the West if this could possibly be trickery. He assured them that this was completely authentic and that this was just the tip of the iceberg.

As they made their way through the garden to the palace, they began to feel a little lightheaded. They were not taking in much information as their senses were in overdrive and they were hitting a wall of resistance in their memories. The purity of air was playing havoc with their lungs and there was a lot of coughing and spluttering, so by the time they reached the palace they were feeling very queasy and uneasy. Finn looked at the Chief of the West and was pleased to see that he was adjusting much better to the island this time. *His programming is working nicely*, he thought. Finn knew that they would have the same issues as the other Generals because they were being challenged on every level of their being: physically, mentally and emotionally, which meant that they could not stay on the island for an excessive length of time, as their bodies would begin to detox too quickly, overloading their already burdened bodies. Finn knew the Chiefs would just need to meet the whole royal family for them to realise that they must stand aside to allow a new order of leadership to take over.

When they arrived at the palace, Finn arranged for them to have a tincture mixed into some tea, which had the immediate effect of calming them and unravelling their taut bodies accustomed to Shadow stimulating their muscles into a permanent state of alert. The calm of the palace had also worked its magic, layering yet another positive experience on the multi-sensory banquet that the island had to offer. Finn led the men into the main meeting room and indicated for them to sit down. Maeve and Patrick entered, joining Finn at the head of the room. There was a stunned silence. It wasn't just the magnificence and purity of these people, amplified when they stood together, it was the crystal authority that each one projected from deep within their core that infused every cell of their bodies and which, to the untrained eye, gave off a subtle glow. The Chiefs had initially judged the decor of the royal residence as somewhat simple and not really befitting a royal family. The royal family was accustomed to this reaction from humans. But what had impressed the Chiefs was what appeared to be the "glow" that came from each member of the royal family. This was in fact the rapid vibration of the constant stream of information that was transmitted to them by the Golden Crystalanders. It was the natural glamour of the royal family rather than their surroundings that impressed the Generals.

Orla entered the room, walking over to her husband and parents, and greeted the Generals warmly. They immediately reacted to her as her voice magically soothed and reassured them. They had also noticed that the glow was particularly strong between Orla and Maeve but, without the acuity of crystal vision, outsiders could not see the tiny sparks of crystal that flowed between the two women.

Orla began. "As you have seen, Crystal Island is not a fairy story, it exists and its very existence proves that life on Earth can also be like this if the planet is listened to and honoured and instructions from nature are followed."

"But how do we follow instructions of nature?" the Chief of the North enquired.

"It is quite simple, by learning to speak the language of nature you will be able to interpret what needs to be done. Gone is the importance of the language of man, and the language of nature takes precedence. "

Orla and Finn knew not to mention the Crystalanders at this stage or anything related to crystals.

After the many questions, the Chief of the Central Federation asked,"What is so special about the island that it functions so much better than the rest of the world? There must have been one fundamental thing that changed the evolution of the other Federations?"

Orla briefly explained the history of the early planet and lastly introduced the idea of Shadow. Orla paused and then continued carefully with their education. "Before Shadow took over, Earth had many helpers from another dimension. But they could not co-exist in the same environment as Shadow, so they had to leave the Earth, and it was at that point that the wisdom of nature was lost."

Interestingly they were not interested in anything to do with Crystal history – she could see this from their memory, as every vestige of their Crystal memory had been subsumed in Shadow. And so she spoke in terms of the wisdom of nature, and they were content with this language. The concept of Shadow was lost to them as its familiar presence had been a constant in their lives for so many generations. When Orla talked of its influence they did not engage with it at all. They were not interested in the past, or the present; they were completely focused on their own future.

Whilst Orla was busy explaining the basics of Crystal Wisdom in code, Finn and his brothers continued to project the ruby crystal around the room, ensuring that Shadow was oblivious to the proceedings.

Patrick addressed the Chiefs. "The first challenge that must be addressed is the reversal of the level of degeneration, and then we can focus on the regeneration. For this to happen, the leaders will have to be in total alignment with nature's wisdom so that change can happen rapidly. We will not have the luxury of time to sit around discussing possibilities for hours and days on end."

The Chiefs were a little taken aback by his directness, but indicated for him to continue.

"Therefore, we have come to the conclusion that the best people to take the first level of leadership would be the fourteen already trained from the Federation of the West."

The Chief General of the West was silent and waited for the objections.

"And why has the Federation of the West been chosen to produce the first new leaders?" the Chief of the East demanded to know.

"Because we identified that they have natural gifts and talents imperative for this new leadership, as well as the qualities to train others. This is an unusual concept for you to grasp but leadership is a gift, not a skill!" Orla said, reprimanding the Chief General. "However, in time, and it would take many generations for this to happen, everyone will have this gift to a lesser or greater degree."

He was silenced by her regal certainty.

"You must understand we have investigated and researched the best possible strategy for the regeneration of the planet and what we are offering is full proof. Crystal Island is testimony to the wisdom that we talk about and practise on a daily basis."

The room was heavy with the silence of confusion.

Orla continued confidently. "As I have mentioned, we have to move very fast. What we haven't told you yet is that the planet is about to make a shift in its oceans, and some parts of your Federations are going to disappear under water. You have experienced parts of your coastlines eroding, but whole countries will be submerged and the geography of the planet will change. This is another reason why mankind has to pool all its resources and, for the first time in a long while, work together for the common good of the planet."

Orla had found herself talking to them as if they were children. It had come to her quite easily, and although she was only 23, she outranked them in wisdom many times over.

She observed their unspoken reactions. Shock gave way to fear and fear was starting to invoke anger, but they kept silent. Ignoring their silent rejections, she continued.

"So instead of the seven federations you have now, there will be 24." By this time they were looking resigned to whatever she mentioned. Her continued strength of authority was like a physical onslaught on their fragile psyche and they were becoming exhausted by the many levels of strength that she possessed, which only served to highlight their weaknesses. "We know the positions of the 24 and we will need to put in place a strategy to reposition the population of the planet."

"All people, inside and out of the domes?" queried the General of the South.

"Yes, there can be no more exclusion. And, yes, before you ask, there will be a loss of lives but that sacrifice is worth it for the future of the planet."

"Is there a way that we can prevent the ice caps from completely melting? This seems like such an extreme way to deal with reversing the degeneration." The Chief of the North East opened the question to his colleagues as well as the royal family, trying to avoid the radical reconfiguration of the planet.

"No, there had been an opportunity to stop the ice caps melting in the last century, but the politicians and captains of industry of the day stuck their heads in the sand so that they could ignore the screams of nature."

The Chiefs looked downcast. They had no contradiction to this story and were gradually beginning to understand that leaders are born, and each one knew that they did not have the wisdom within them that was being continuously referenced. The next phase of the planet's history required knowledge that they didn't have. They were resigned and almost relieved as they had realised they had been fighting a losing battle for the last few years and it had become increasingly exhausting. Every day presented new problems that could not be solved. Everyone was looking to them to find the new planet, which was to be hailed as being humanity's salvation, but they secretly knew that such a planet did not exist within the capabilities of their science.

Orla paused, waiting for them to digest the information, and then continued.

"The fourteen have already begun their work and are busy initiating another one hundred in the Federation of the West. Once they are in place, other Federations can begin with their initiation. The domes in the West will be the places where the new plants will be trialled and, once they are successfully established, the same protocol will be introduced to all the Federations."

The Chief of the South West, who had been quiet for a long while, stared at Orla and asked a very pertinent question.

"When the Earth becomes abundant again, and the new countries reflect nature as it appears on Crystal Island, what happens then? I get a sense that this will not be the end."

Finn shot a thought at Orla. *"One of them is indeed quite a bit sharper than the others."* She smiled at the Chief, and answered. "A very good question. You are right, this is not the end. The objective is not to make the planet abundant for the sake of creating a paradise for mankind. There is another level of transformation that the planet has to go through, but that will not be known until all the key pieces on the chessboard are in place."

Finn was relieved. Orla had sidetracked the question cleverly and it had been accepted by all the Chiefs – the habit of not questioning worked in their favour this time.

Finn and Orla both knew what would happen when the Earth was once again abundant. On one of Orla's visits to the Diamond Elders, she had been told that the Earth's transformation would be the trigger to many other changes in the solar system, and in fact, the rest of the cosmos.

The Chiefs asked for some privacy while they conferred together, ignorant, of course, to the royal family's powers of insight.

"This still sounds like a fairy story, I'm afraid," the Chief of the South said.

"It is very simplistic, which makes it implausible," said the Chief of the East.

"Being born a leader sounds almost biblical, and we know how we deal with that," added the Chief of Central Federation.

And so the objections continued to fill the space in the room. After they had exhausted the possible negative outcomes, the Chief of the South West, who had been relatively positive throughout the discussions, interrupted them.

"From where I am sitting, we don't have much of a choice. None of our people have discovered another planet that we can go to; the domes are not going to last for much longer; and if these people are to be believed, most of us could end up under water. I think we have to at least meet them halfway."

Finn was waiting for the point at which all of them agreed, whereupon he and his brothers would have to send in ruby rays very quickly to counteract Shadow's rapier-like reaction to the Chiefs' relinquishing their priority of feeding Shadow and shifting their focus to the needs of the planet. Orla could see that these men were tired; the remedies she had given them had caused them to relax, and in that relaxation they had sensed a true sense of their age, recognising deep down that they were not equipped for the role of leadership in this new world.

Sensing that they had come to a conclusion, the royal family rejoined the Chiefs. The Chief of the West began. "I think we have come to a conclusion that what you propose makes sense and that we are not best suited for leadership."

Finn stood ready, waiting for the reaction from Shadow, but there was none. The Chiefs had not become angry or defensive, so Shadow was not alerted. They were reconciled to the handing over of leadership, and as Finn scanned the faces of the seven most powerful leaders on the planet, he observed their frailty and many imperfections, and gave thanks that they had decided to resign. These were a sorry example of mankind and should never have held the responsibility of the guardianship of a planet.

Orla thanked the Chiefs for their wisdom, once again pandering to their egos, and invited them to have refreshments before they returned to their domes. They sat quietly, enjoying the island's fare. Finn was eager to get them back to the domes, as they were looking weakened by the whole experience of the island. When they were sufficiently rested, Finn led them from the palace back to the Secret Garden. The Chief of the North East looked out to sea and caught sight of the Crystal Fortress.

"Look at that, what on Earth is it?" They all looked out to sea.

"They are special crystal pillars that form an energetic dome over the island. It is a source of energy as well as providing a force field of protection so that no one can ever find the island."

They looked bewildered; everything that they had believed was a truth had been dashed and now they had seen what they thought was something that only occurred in the fairy stories of a bygone time.

"I understand now why none of our agencies ever discovered the island. The more I know about this island, the more intrigued I become," the Chief of the West commented.

"What is a fairy story to one person is reality to another," Finn quipped.

They all smiled, becoming increasingly more comfortable with this strange man from this strange island whose honesty was overwhelmingly alien to their Shadow corrupted minds.

They arrived back, and as they left the vessel, Finn explained that John would make contact with them to start the ball rolling. Within a week he would have sufficient people to go to each of the Federations and start the process of initiation.

"What is the process exactly?" asked the Chief of the South East.

"We take the people with prominent natural wisdom and relieve them of all their fears." Choosing his words very carefully, he added, "When that is removed, people begin to see the world through different eyes, and our pioneers will help them to appreciate the wonderful gifts this planet will have to offer each and every person equally."

"I think I am getting too old for this. This is a language I find difficult to understand," the Chief of the Central Federation muttered to himself.

As they said goodbye to the Chiefs, Finn scanned them all for Shadow. It was there, of course, but it had not been alerted by what had transpired. Thankfully, the remedies that they had been given had led Shadow to believe that the Chiefs were sleeping. *Good*, he thought, *and that is the way it will remain.*

*

Orla woke up with a start as her father came into her chamber where she had been resting. He beamed at her.

"You know the gender of the twins?" She sat up, fully awake with anticipation.

Orla's eyes widened and she gasped with joy at his unspoken announcement. She was delighted at the news; this is what the royal family had hoped for, and a sign that confirmed all the changes were fully functioning to allow for the next step to take place. The royal family had been impatient to know the gender of the twins in these last few months, but knew that Patrick, who had the responsibility of protecting the unborn twins with his unique blend of ruby crystal and wisdom, would only be given full access to their gender at a specific time – a time in the pregnancy when the twins' Crystal memory was fully formed.

Finn came into the room and could see by the faces of Orla and Patrick what he had silently hoped for and sat down on Orla's daybed, picking up her hand and kissing it tenderly.

Patrick left the young couple alone to share that special moment. Eventually, Finn stood up, took in a deep breath, shook his head and, tipping it back, laughed loudly. Orla, quite surprised by this reaction, stared at him with a surprised look on her face.

She looked into his eyes and could see that he was reflecting on the turbulent first years of Earth's transformation and the wonderful events of the last decade which had culminated in the wonderful news about the gender of the twins. Orla also laughed and they both shared a few memories…

The fourteen pioneers had successfully initiated the first one hundred with an amazing focus. The seven couples forged a strong bond with them, and their regular rituals were making them stronger and stronger. When they had completed the initiation of the one hundred, Finn introduced them to their Crystal circle and named the seven women as the Elders of their community.

As expected, there had been resistance to women holding such important positions, interestingly more from other women, but eventually, with the help of the remedies from the island, that small group of people began to change. Maeve had taught Cynthia the crystal birthing methods, which she had embraced enthusiastically and competently. Although there were few babies being conceived, Cynthia had worked with those few mothers from the beginning of their pregnancies, guiding them and helping them to deliver healthy babies. She would eventually train many women as the need for the art of crystal birthing increased with the health of the population.

Plant life began to appear under the ruby crystal pods, as was promised, and Orla and Finn had to identify fourteen people in each of the Federations to undertake the leadership initiation. By that time it was not necessary for them to go to the island – they just needed to travel to the dome of the West for their initiation with the original pioneers.

One by one the Federations began to change; the people in the domes began to respond to the change in the drinking water and the remedies and, as suspected, just as the world began to look a little brighter, the Elite noticed that their Chiefs were quiet. Yes, it was normal to be quiet for short periods, but they had no communication with them at all. Shadow sensed this and pressurised the Elite, who in turn tried to put the Generals under pressure. The Chiefs ignored them, and when Shadow saw this, it increased the intensity of pain that projected down their tentacles into the spines of the Generals. But Maeve had given them a special remedy that protected their nervous systems from damage, which meant that they could ignore the normal painful prodding from the sharp angry tentacles of Shadow. The Elite had no lever – no pain, no fear. Shadow sent waves of fear into the Elite, and they in turn put even more pressure on the Chiefs, but to no avail. It increased the intensity of pain on the Chiefs, but still there was no response. Shadow was losing patience with the Elite, so this desperate group of puppeteers took matters further and, as they controlled the weather, which even the Chiefs knew about, they sent bitingly cold, ferocious winds across the already blistered plains of the Federations, whipping the dust from the papery soil into ferocious dust storms, filling the noses and mouths of the people outside of the domes and filling the filter systems of the airways of the domes.

Initially there was panic as very quickly the domes could become toxic and as polluted as the air outside. This onslaught prompted Finn to contact the Ruby Crystalanders, who projected a gigantic ruby force field that cut through the dust, protecting the domes, allowing the suction fans to be cleared and the bad air removed. At the same time, the Ruby Crystalanders projected the rays over a larger radius to try to protect as many people outside of the dome as possible from anything the Elite wanted to throw at them. Having failed with the weather, the next thing the Elite tried was to send a deadly virus into the world, which of course killed the people outside of the domes first. Even though the ruby rays cut through and deactivated most of the virus, people were scattered in disorganised pockets all over the planet and it was impossible to protect them all. Some survived, but most died. The virus had been introduced to products that went between domes and it quickly infiltrated those communities, affecting the old and physically fragile. Maeve sent batches of remedies to be administered to repel the virus by breaking down its cell wall and rendering it useless. The ruby ray eventually destroyed the air borne virus, molecule by molecule, the ray having the ability to destroy anything that was a poison to creation.

At the time, Orla had been a little concerned that Finn was having to devote so much energy to using the ruby ray, but each time he activated it he was also energised. Whilst she had been protective of him, he too was worried about her. Every day she went to her viewing room and contacted the women, giving them advice, scanning new recruits, and generally being the mother of the planet. In the early days the women had needed a lot of support, mainly because they lacked confidence, but with their ever-increasing access to Crystal Wisdom, their confidence increased exponentially. They had slipped into a rhythm with their husbands of combining the Crystal Wisdom with Crystal Strategy and learned how to formulate solutions without too much guidance from her or Finn. Finn had been there for the men in the early days, coaching them in Crystal Strategy and, once the fear totally receded from the people around them, as the Shadow slipped further back into the memory of mankind, they began to make serious progress.

The royal family watched the progress of each of the Federations and realised that they would need to prepare people for the shift in the landmasses, as the energy was beginning to change in the planet and the Earth was getting ready to join in with mankind to change the landscape forever. They identified 24 areas that would either be created or remain. Twelve already existed and twelve were still under water. "We shall have to arrange for everyone to go to the domes in the twelve safe areas and provide sufficient resources, " Finn informed Orla.

The leaders of the domes organised the relocation of people from both inside the domes and those remaining outside. This was a challenge because the outsiders were very different people and had to be kept separated from the dome-dwellers. They would take time to recover from the harsh life of the badlands, but they would recover. They had already responded to the kindness that people were extending to them. No more were people interested in hoarding special things for themselves. Everyone was pooling all of his or her resources. Patrick and Maeve looked on the progress of the dome-dwellers and were encouraged to see that when they worked together for a common good, there was no end to their generosity. They actually loved to help each other.

When everything was in place, Finn began scanning the planet. Shadow was beginning to shrink back. It didn't understand what was happening; it just knew that its supply of energy was diminishing. The Elite had disappeared – when they could not control the Chiefs after they relinquished their power, Shadow disengaged from them completely, leaving them like shells of beings. They and their families did not survive for very long after that as their dome did not come under the umbrella of the new Crystal Federations.

The royal family stayed on the island, as they knew that they would be safe, but Patrick had been keeping a check on the melting ice and had warned the pioneers that the last large masses of ice at both poles were about to slip into the sea.

Everything was put into place in the twelve safe areas, and the royal family watched remotely from the safety of Crystal Island as the swell from the north and south poles made its way towards the Federations. Like a great wall of water, it collided with the shores and covered the parched soil. Huge waves crashed repeatedly at fragile coastlines until they submitted and were swallowed in a swirl of foaming sea. Where once the weight of glacial islands had pinned down parcels of land, as the ice melted, new land emerged from the freezing waters, ready to take its rightful place in the new world. This process had taken several weeks, with the seas and oceans crashing when they met, receding and crashing together again until, finally, they seemed to find their own places of peace and became quiet. Then the rain came, gently at first, then in torrents. There was so much water everywhere, but it refreshed the land that had been left, filling lakes that had been empty for decades. The new pockets of land that had appeared from the sea were covered in damp soil, deeply impregnated with rich salts, offering a fertile landscape for healthy crops.

John contacted Orla and asked if it was safe for them to leave the domes.

"Yes, all is calm, you can go outside now and assess the condition of the soil and the quality of the air."

John went outside with some of the men and checked the soil, which was rich and dark from the waters that had bathed the soil surrounding the domes and had eventually receded. He took in a deep breath and realised that the air was clearer, but not completely free of pollutants. *That will take more work, and more trees*, he had reflected.

And so life began to grow and people followed the rules of Crystal Wisdom. Some of them would never contact their own Crystal Wisdom, but they could see the sense of following crystal laws, and eventually, given time, their descendants would develop their own Crystal Wisdom.

Orla and Finn's focus was brought back into the present as they looked at Orla's generous abdomen and knew that the birth of the twins would herald the imminent arrival of special visitors to the planet.

"I wonder what our fourteen will think of our crystal visitors," Orla asked, smiling.

"I can't wait to see their faces," Finn said, grinning as he gently placed his hand on Orla's abdomen and felt the active movement of the twins. "I think these two are impatient to come into the world."

Orla rolled her eyes playfully as she nodded in agreement. For one brief moment they were like any other young couple, giddy with excitement over the impending birth of new life, but they were brought sharply back into the real world with thoughts of the future beyond the birth. Yes, the planet had made a wonderful start to its transformation, but this would not be the end. The gender of the twins was an indication that in the next few decades a larger change would take place, which would not just affect Earth and its solar system, but the whole of the cosmos. The twins would play an important and pivotal role in that transformation, and the royal couple knew the challenges that lay ahead for their children – the biggest any members of the royal family had ever confronted.

Orla was naturally protective of her babies, but Finn reminded her that, in addition to the help of the royal family, the twins would be assisted by helpers from all of the Crystal worlds. Thankful for Finn's reassurance, Orla closed her eyes, preparing for sleep, knowing that her dreams would not be filled with scenes from the past. That time was gone; from now on her dreams would be filled with the possibilities for the future.